Dudley Bernard Egerton Pope was born in 1925 into an ancient Cornish seafaring family. He joined the Merchant Navy at the age of sixteen and spent much of his early life at sea. He was torpedoed during the Second World War and his resulting spinal injuries plagued him for the rest of his life. Towards the end of the war he turned to journalism becoming the Naval and Defence Correspondent for the London *Evening News*. Encouraged by Hornblower creator C S Forester, he began writing fiction using his own experiences in the Navy and his extensive historical research as a basis.

In 1965 he wrote *Ramage*, the first of his highly successful series of novels following the exploits of the heroic Lord Nicholas Ramage during the Napoleonic Wars. He continued to live aboard boats whenever possible and this was where he wrote the majority of his novels. Dudley Pope died in 1997 aged seventy-one.

BY THE SAME AUTHOR
ALL PUBLISHED BY HOUSE OF STRATUS

Fiction

Buccaneer
Convoy
Corsair
Decoy
Galleon
Ramage
Ramage and the Drumbeat
Governor Ramage RN
Ramage's Prize
Ramage and the Guillotine
Ramage's Mutiny
The Ramage Touch
Ramage's Signal
Ramage's Trial
Ramage's Challenge
Ramage at Trafalgar
Ramage and the Dido

Non-Fiction

The Biography of Sir Henry Morgan 1635–1688

ADMIRAL

DUDLEY POPE

This edition published in 2001 by House of Stratus, an imprint of House of Stratus Ltd, Thirsk Industrial Park, York Road, Thirsk, North Yorkshire, YO7 3BX, UK.
Also at: House of Stratus Inc., 2 Neptune Road, Poughkeepsie, NY 12601, USA.

www.houseofstratus.com

Typeset, printed and bound by House of Stratus.

A catalogue record for this book is available from the British Library and the Library of Congress.

ISBN 0-7551-0438-2

For the Allinghams
who remember Kingsnorth

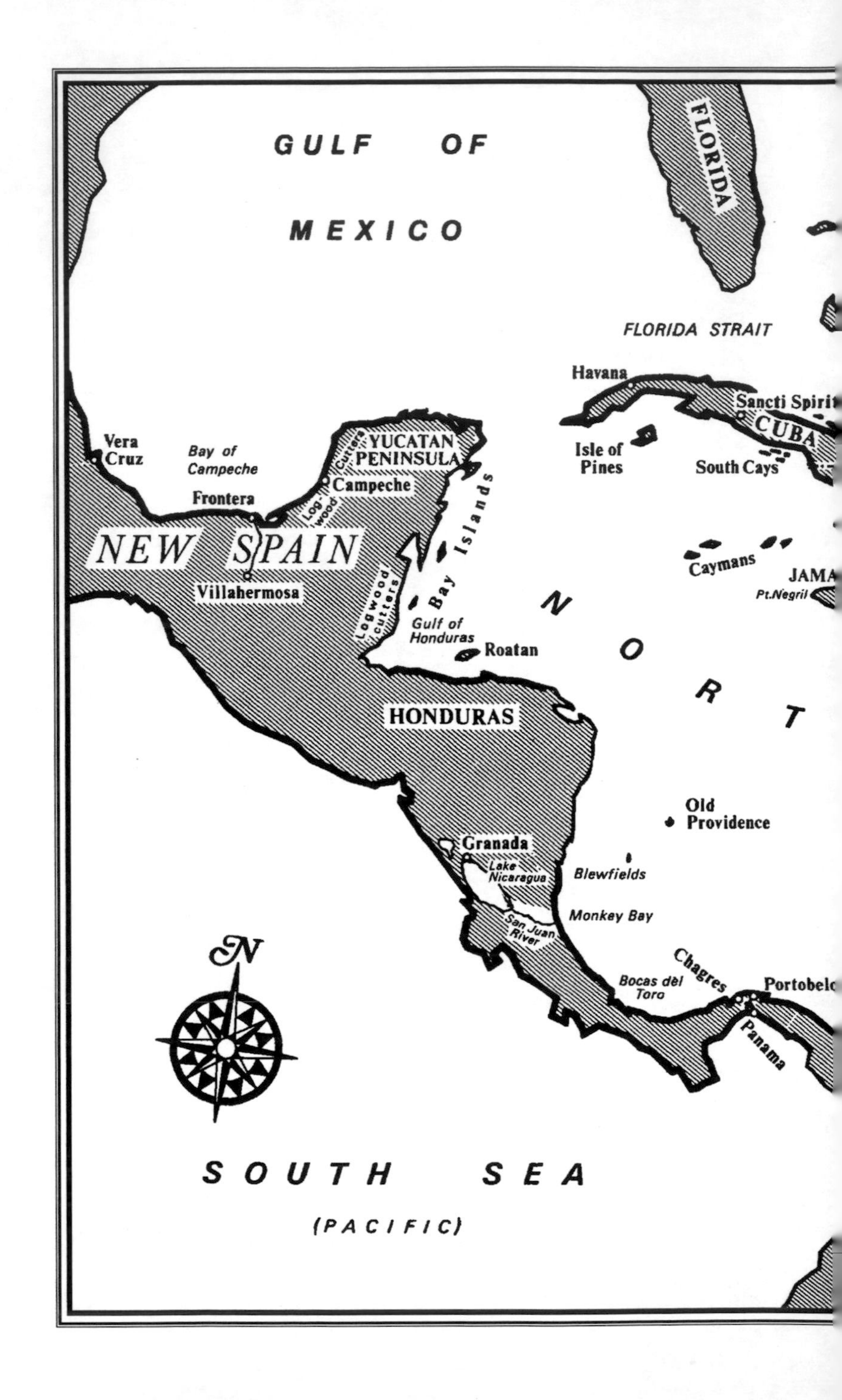

GULF OF MEXICO
FLORIDA
FLORIDA STRAIT
Havana
Sancti Spirit
CUBA
Isle of Pines
South Cays
Vera Cruz
Bay of Campeche
YUCATAN PENINSULA
Cutters
Campeche
Frontera
Log-wood
NEW SPAIN
Villahermosa
Logwood cutters
Bay Islands
Caymans
JAMA
Pt.Negril
Gulf of Honduras
Roatan
N O R T
HONDURAS
Old Providence
Granada
Lake Nicaragua
Blewfields
Monkey Bay
San Juan River
Chagres
Bocas dèl Toro
Portobelo
Panama
N
SOUTH SEA
(PACIFIC)

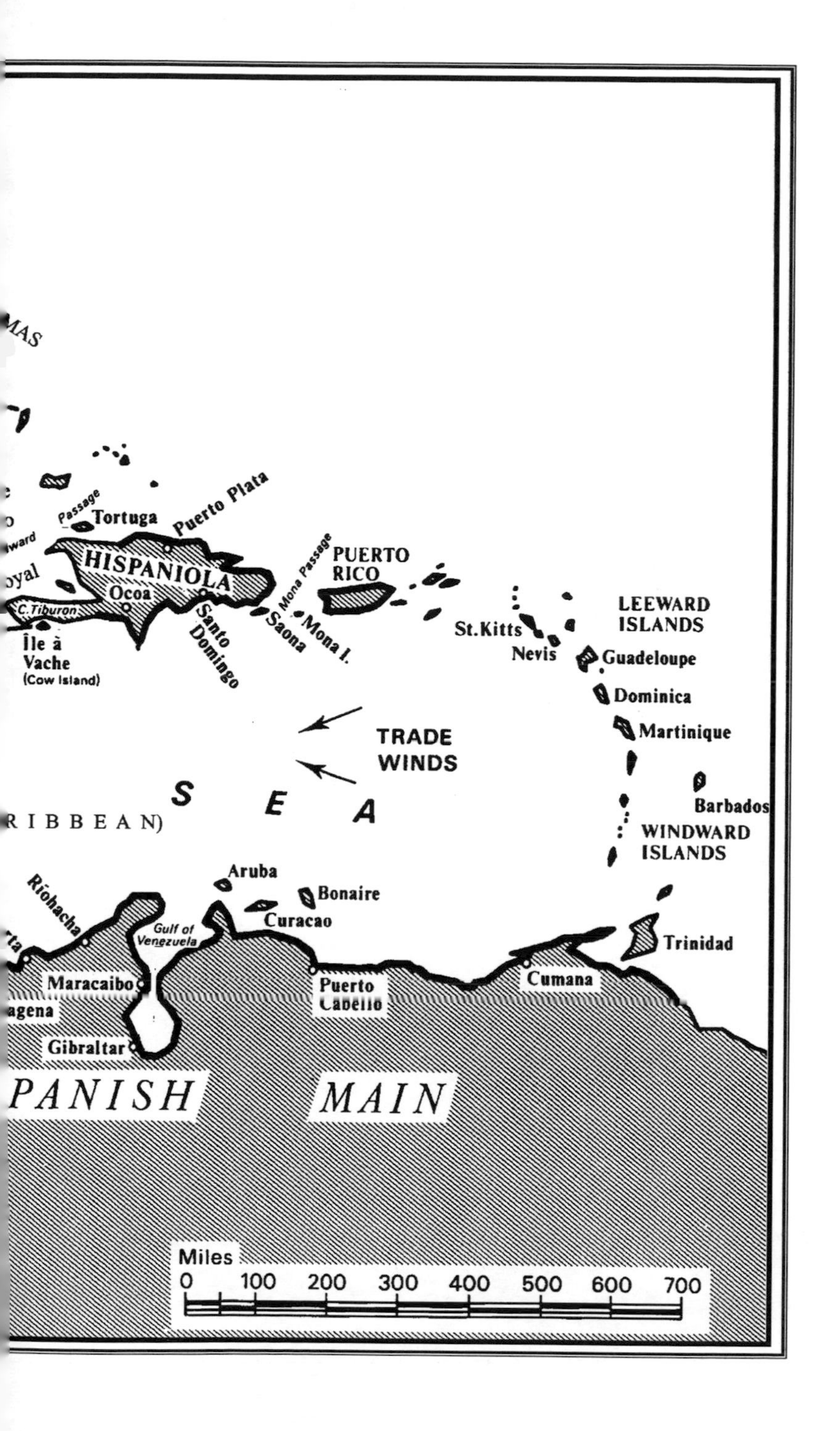
Tortuga
Puerto Plata
Passage
HISPANIOLA
Ocoa
C.Tiburon
Île à
Vache
(Cow Island)
Santo
Domingo
Saona
Mona Passage
Mona I.
PUERTO
RICO
St.Kitts
Nevis
LEEWARD
ISLANDS
Guadeloupe
Dominica
Martinique
Barbados
WINDWARD
ISLANDS
TRADE
WINDS
S E A
RIBBEAN)
Riohacha
Aruba
Bonaire
Curacao
Gulf of
Venezuela
Maracaibo
agena
Gibraltar
Puerto
Cabello
Cumana
Trinidad
PANISH
MAIN
Miles
0 100 200 300 400 500 600 700

CHAPTER **ONE**

Although Major-General Heffer unrolled the map with as much ceremony as he dared, the effect was spoiled when he realized that the parchment would curl up again the moment he let go of the ends. He snatched up the flattened pebbles he always used as paperweights and carefully placed them. Then he stood back and looked at the irregular scrawl of inks and colours that seemed like the pattern for a small Wilton rug.

"There you are," he said proudly to the two silent and unmoving men standing the other side of the table, "that's probably the first map ever made of Cagway; I'm sure the Spaniards never bothered."

The two men nodded and waited without comment.

Although the house was large, the room the general used as an office was small and uncomfortably hot, the air so humid it reminded them both so strongly of a wash house that they could almost hear the slapping and scrubbing and the pattering of water as wet cloth was wrung out. The house was stoutly built of thick stone, and most windows had heavy shutters made of bulletwood with loopholes cut in them like giant locks awaiting keys.

Heffer had apparently chosen his office with all the care of a man doing penance: it was on the west side and the single window was small so that although the direct rays of the scorching noon sun did not stream in, neither did the cooling Trade winds usually blowing from the east. Even the flies seemed listless, only briefly interested in the parchment but otherwise content to rest on the flaking whitewash of the walls. With the hurricane season beginning in Jamaica, the blazing sun and humidity drained the energy of anything that moved.

Heffer was a suspicious and bilious man who always kept a door shut; to him an open doorway was only an invitation to eavesdroppers. As one of Cromwell's generals (although as a colonel his role in the Western Design had been minor and the recent news of the Lord Protector's death had left him feeling lost like an orphan), he was ready enough to suffer for the cause: the Lord Protector had first ordered him to the West Indies to serve in the army intended to carry out the Western Design and then later honoured him with the appointment of acting governor of Jamaica. It was given to few men to serve both their God and their Leader, and Heffer was thankful he had been one of those chosen.

Though quite where he stood at this moment he was far from sure, and he was even less certain about the future of Jamaica. Somehow he had stumbled (or been manoeuvred) into a position where, for the moment at least, his fate and the island's both seemed to depend on the ideas and activities of the two buccaneers standing the other side of the table, Edward Kent and Thomas Whetheread, men who were almost strangers to him. It was in some ways fortunate that the Lord Protector was not alive to hear of it. What would his son Richard Cromwell, who now ruled in his place, think? Or supposing, as Whetheread seemed to think, Richard would by now have resigned or been overthrown by sterner officers in the army? Heffer had never met Richard, but the rumours he had heard in the last few years – that the Lord Protector's son had neither the ability nor inclination to succeed his father – had been more than confirmed by gossip. By reports, he corrected himself.

The man Heffer knew as Whetheread pointed at the map. "Did you draw this?"

Heffer nodded modestly.

"But you actually surveyed it some months ago?"

"Er, yes, before you arrived here."

"You were going to send it to the Lord Protector, eh, and when you heard that the Good Lord had suddenly withdrawn His protection from Oliver, you hurriedly redrew it without your original dedication and all the New Model Army embellishments."

Heffer, startled and unsettled by Whetheread's insight, said nothing. He was tall and painfully thin and had a remarkably long face. His head, with protruding teeth and odd tufts of hair clinging to the skull like a monk's moth-eaten tonsure, reminded the other men of a poor-quality drumskin stretched over a sheep's skull.

The heat dried the chevaux-de-frise of teeth so that as he spoke the inside of the general's lips stuck and his tongue, constantly darting round to wet them, gave the impression it was trying to stop loose ones popping out.

Heffer had long ago discovered what he considered the road to success: merely surviving. From being a lowly officer in Fairfax's army he had stayed alive, and always agreed with alacrity with his senior officers. As they were killed in battle, died of illness, or were arrested for showing Royalist tendencies, they left vacancies, steps up the ladder of promotion which the ever-pliant and ever-present Heffer had managed to climb. Having no sense of beauty, history or colour, but an abiding hatred and jealousy of tradition, honour or anything else he did not understand, he never hesitated when ordered to smash all the stained-glass windows whether in a modest church or an ancient cathedral like Ely: having his troops take axes to carved altar rails or mauls to chip away the marble of graven images gave him a thrill he never understood or admitted even to his wife: he needed only to know that he was doing the Lord's work. He recalled arresting one rector who had protested that wrecking the Lord's house could hardly be carrying out the Lord's will, and proved him to be a Royalist and probably a Papist too.

Given command of a battalion and sent out in the expedition to Hispaniola, Heffer knew that he was lucky to have so far escaped the cholera that killed thousands of men, and even luckier to escape Cromwell's wrath over the enterprise's failure. He *survived*...he had been alive and blameless and a colonel when the Lord Protector was looking for a governor of Jamaica, after the expedition's leaders, General Venables and Admiral Penn, had gone back to England (and the Tower) to face a disappointed Cromwell's anger. Promotion to major-general and the appointment as acting governor was not bad going, he told himself, for a man who had joined Cromwell only because he seemed to hate the same things.

It was unlucky that his troops – particularly the officers – loathed Jamaica (the West Indies, in fact) and plotted and schemed to be sent home from the Tropics before they were killed by yellow fever or cholera. All Heffer's attempts to have his troops plant and harvest so that they could later eat, and start doing something about capturing some of the thousands of beeves and pigs that roamed wild across the island, were a waste of time because his officers would do nothing that could lead Cromwell to decide on a permanent garrison for Jamaica. In fact, Heffer also knew that most of the officers had sent letters home by the last ship pleading with everyone they knew in London who had influence...

Yet they were fools. Heffer saw clearly enough that the threat that could stop them ever seeing their homes again came not from cholera and the black vomit but starvation and, less imminent, the Spaniards. The only other men in the island who seemed instinctively to understand all this were the buccaneers, led by Kent and Whetheread, who so far had brought in grain (at a price) to feed the garrison and recently captured enough Spanish guns from Santiago in Cuba to build batteries to defend Cagway.

Heffer grew angry and impatient at the thought of it. Everything was in a muddle. Two buccaneers were saving a

Jamaica just captured by the Roundheads while the governor himself did not know if he was still the governor, now that Cromwell was dead. Worse still, he could not rely on the loyalty of the garrison: he was half expecting some disaffected officers to mutiny and set up a council to govern the island.

That last fear he had yet to reveal to Kent and Whetheread, who had not heard the latest crop of rumours gathered (almost gleefully, he sometimes thought) by his ADC, Rowlands, who reported that the officers, regarding themselves as freed from their oath of allegiance to the Commonwealth by Cromwell's death, considered that now they were serving only God.

The man known as Kent looked carefully at the map and wished that Heffer's wits were as sharp as his quill. It was strange staring down at the long sandpit known now as Cagway, the English rendering of the original Spanish name of Caguas. Heffer had shown the outline, a long thumb of land sticking out of the wrist of the mainland and almost closing the great natural harbour, with the sea on the south side and the almost-enclosed anchorage, like a great lake, on the north.

Yes, Heffer had translated the Spanish name for the sand-spit, *Palizados*, into the Palisades, and called the tip Gallows Point – a warning, Kent decided, that Heffer intended as much for his own soldiers as for pirates. This little inked-in square represented the house in which they were standing: the next square was the military headquarters. And there was the jetty used by the fishermen and the buccaneers, with a few streets of shops and taverns in between.

The inked-in rectangle was the fish market, with the dotted line showing the lobster crawl built out into the shallow water near the jetty. The shaded section labelled "meat market" seemed a rather pretentious name for a few square yards of blood-caked sand where a bellowing beeve or a squealing pig was lashed to a post to be slaughtered and butchered for the fortunate few who had enough money to catch the eye of the Spanish butcher, a renegade who decided to stay behind when his countrymen fled before Penn and Venables' expedition.

Why had the Spaniards built the capital of the island on that flat land ten miles away, well inland and a long distance from the anchorage? To be safe from marauders? They had named it St Jago de la Vega, St Jago of the Plain, although the English now called it St Jago. Still, the effective headquarters for the island was here at Cagway, and Heffer had been lucky to be able to take over a strongly-built Spanish house and make it his home, with an almost identical building next door as the garrison headquarters.

"This battery," Whetheread said, jabbing a stubby index finger down on a point half-way along the seaward side of the Palisades, almost opposite Heffer's house, "this is going to be the most important one, don't you agree Ned?"

Kent nodded and indicated the arc over which its guns should be able to fire.

"Oh, well now, Mr Kent, I – " Heffer began nervously, and then went on as both Kent and Whetheread looked at him encouragingly, "I thought the most important one would be here, right at the tip: the guns will be able to fire at enemy ships if they try to pass through the channel between the Palisades and the mainland and enter the anchorage."

"No," Kent said, "you're looking through the wrong end of the glass. You have to prevent enemy ships getting as close as that in the first place: you need to keep up a heavy fire on them as they try to pick their way through these cays and reefs." He pointed to the scattering of obstructions in the approach from the south. "While they're trying to con their way up to the Palisades, your roundshot must be sweeping their decks – and they can only do that from a battery built here." He put his finger down where Whetheread had indicated. "You cover them whether they approach along the coast or come up from the south. Then, if any ships do get through the fire from here, they have to run the gauntlet past another battery at the end. And if they get past that, then a third battery, here, will catch them as they round up into the anchorage."

"You talk like an artilleryman," Heffer grumbled, his tongue flickering across the front of his teeth.

"No, as a seaman," Kent said cheerfully, as though to soothe Heffer. "The best way of planning the defences of a place is to picture yourself having to sail in to attack it. Which batteries could do you the most harm here? You'll find I'm right – *this* is the one that matters. What are you going to call it – Cromwell's Bastion?"

Heffer flushed but said nothing: apart from not knowing what was happening in England, he was far from sure of the buccaneers: these two, the leaders, were a whimsical pair; quite irresponsible, of course, and one could not be sure if they were serious. "Cromwell's Bastion" sounded well enough, but...

"We brought you twelve culverins and five 3-pounders back from our raid on Santiago," Ned said. "Where are you placing them?"

Heffer hurriedly changed his plans and hoped the two men could now be talked out of the proposed inspection which he had himself arranged, but which put all the emphasis (and most of the guns) on the battery out at Gallows Point. "I was proposing to put eight culverins in the battery opposite this house, to cover the approaches," Heffer said smoothly, finding it easy to change his plan, "and the remaining four culverins at Gallows Point, to cover the seaward end of the entrance. Then I thought the five 3-pounders would go well at the anchorage end of the entrance."

"Mere saluting guns," Thomas said with a contemptuous sniff. "3-pounders simply make a bang..."

"You brought them," Heffer could not resist pointing out, but hurriedly added, "and of course we are grateful."

Ned said: "Once the batteries are built, complete with magazines, sleeping quarters, water cisterns and kitchens, we can always change the guns for larger ones as we capture them from the Spanish."

Thomas slapped the table and said heartily: "Quite right, Ned, quite right: with the batteries there, we can always replace the guns. Come on then, let's look at the sites."

Outside the sun was blinding, reflecting up from the almost white sand. "Wait," Heffer said, "I'll send Rowlands for horses."

"Not for me; I want to walk," Ned said.

"Nor me," Thomas said, patting his stomach. "I need some exercise. Diana's complaining about my weight."

Heffer, who hated the heat, also hated the sensation of walking on soft sand, and had planned at most a quick canter round the sites of the batteries, relying on the buccaneers' unfamiliarity with horses to avoid a detailed inspection. Now he followed the two men, gesturing to his ADC. "We're walking, Rowlands. You, too." The youngster was getting puffy faced, and from his bloodshot eyes and lethargy in the mornings, Heffer suspected he was drinking heavily. He wished Rowlands would get rid of that sulky look while the buccaneers were here.

Ned and Thomas walked the hundred yards to the water's edge and then stopped, facing southwards towards the Spanish Main five hundred miles away. On their right the sand-spit went on to form the entrance to the anchorage; on their left the sand-spit continued until it merged with the mainland, which went on for about fifty miles to the eastern end of the island. Behind them was the great, almost enclosed anchorage, and beyond that the mountains rising higher and higher in gentle ridges to form the distant eastern spine of the island, the Blue Mountains.

The Caribbean was calm; wavelets slapped the sandy beach and occasionally a silver flash caught the eye and showed a large fish leaping out of the water to land among its prey, or a small one trying desperately to escape. Hunter or hunted came up like an arrow rising from the sea and falling amid a shoal of smaller fish which had been innocently feeding, unaware of their danger.

"Watch out for your ankles," Ned said, gesturing at the holes which pocked the beach like small coney burrows. "I've never seen so many land crab holes. Plenty of land crab for dinner, eh General?"

"Er, *land* crab? No, I haven't tried it. I thought these were rat holes."

Ned and Thomas stopped, staring at the general, hardly believing their ears.

"I thought you said your men were starving?" Thomas said.

"They are. You know we need grain, salt meat, vegetables..."

"Yet you don't bother with one of the great delicacies of the West Indies!"

"Why, are land crab different from the ones found in the sea?" Heffer asked huffily.

"I don't know – ask the crab. But the point is your men can catch land crabs at night with lanterns as easily as breaking stained-glass windows." Thomas watched Heffer and noticed the flush. "The crabs just walk about."

"Nobody told me," Heffer grumbled.

Ned shook his head impatiently, completely exasperated. "That's the epitaph of the Western Design. '*Nobody told me...nobody asked.*' Your stupid officers let their soldiers drive hundred of beeves and hogs into the mountains – and then kill the moriscos who know how to capture them. No meat to eat in a land where the cattle are numbered in thousands...

"No one has the wit to gather the fruit that grows on the trees or the vegetables which they trample on the land. You chased off all the fishermen and stole their canoes and *now* you complain you are starving. Can't your damned silly men make fishing lines? Can't they – or you – ask whether these are coney, rat or crab holes? Are buccaneers the only ones who dare go up in the hills and shoot beeves and boucan or salt the meat? How many men will a young steer feed? Your men should be living on fresh meat all the time – there's so much to be hunted that you can kill daily so you needn't salt or boucan it. Ah!" Ned broke off, angry with himself for losing his temper, exasperated with Heffer, although the beeves and hogs had been driven off before he had been made governor. "You'll be running out of fresh water next!"

"We are" admitted Heffer miserably. "That big cistern on the mainland opposite has run dry…"

"No doubt it has!" Thomas exclaimed contemptuously. "It hasn't rained for five weeks and I don't suppose you rationed water. The Spaniards didn't build that cistern for three thousand troops to use as if it was some magic Fountain of Youth! Have you rationed it now?"

"No – how was I to know it wouldn't rain?"

"Just look out of the window from time to time" Ned murmured, and then said: "It's too hot standing here – let's go over and look at the first battery."

They walked round the stunted shrubs fighting hard to grow knee-high in the sand, and insects buzzed up in clouds, whining and stinging. One or other of the men would occasionally stumble as the sand caved in round land crab holes. Ned paused for a moment to watch a pelican waddling along the water's edge a few yards away, looking like a portly and beady-eyed prelate, slightly tipsy and wearing boots much too large but well polished.

The walls of the new battery, made of rough stone and mortar, were already three feet high and banked up with sand on the seaward side so that from a ship it would look like an innocent dune.

"I've fifty men working on this battery." Heffer said crisply, striving to re-establish himself as the island commander. "I'm bringing in another fifty tomorrow or the next day to start on the magazines and sleeping quarters."

"And the cistern," Ned said.

"Oh yes, of course. Most important."

"And the sloping area of catchment for the cistern," Thomas said, "otherwise the rain will be lost in the sand."

"Of course, of course," Heffer said impatiently. "Well, now you can see our first battery."

"The cistern will hold a hundred gallons per man?" Ned asked.

"Well, I hadn't thought quite as much," Heffer said lamely.

"That's the minimum," Ned said firmly. "Eight guns, five men to each gun, a couple of corporals and a sergeant, cook and a couple of powdermen: forty-six. Four thousand, six hundred gallons."

"But that'll be enormous," Heffer protested.

"There's plenty of stone, and your men have nothing better to do," Ned pointed out. "You sit in the sun for a couple of days without water – try that and you'll insist on five hundred gallons a man."

By now the three men, followed by Rowlands, had walked up the slight slope and paused to look over the top of the stonework. Fifty bodies were scattered inside an area which had been pegged out and marked with cord in the shape of the battery and its emplacements and buildings. Several of the men had strung their coats across shovels to make some shade.

"Splendid," Ned said. "If only the Dons could see them now, sleeping peacefully like sheep. Come on, Thomas, it's too hot for all this martial excitement. By the way, I see emplacements marked out for four guns, not eight, and no sign of a cistern or catchment."

As the two of them left Heffer and walked back along the beach, they could hear the general screaming almost hysterically at the soldiers, waking them violently – kicking, judging by the yells of pain – and accusing them of everything from drunkenness to treason and threatening to hang every tenth man as a warning to the rest of the garrison.

"I don't envy him," Ned said, swerving a few steps to avoid a wave surging higher up the beach. "His men verging on mutiny, officers completely unreliable and mostly stupid, and he doesn't know if or when a ship will suddenly arrive bringing orders, let alone supplies."

"If the army has thrown out Richard, he may not get orders for years!" Thomas commented. "In the meantime we aren't getting our batteries built..."

"We will: I have a feeling that he wasn't joking back there when he threatened them with the noose."

"What a position for a Roundhead general to find himself in!"

"Just wait until he finds out who *we* are," Ned said grimly. "I want to watch when he discovers he was saved by a pair of Royalists! And let's hope it's soon; I'm getting bored with our new surnames."

Ned tapped Thomas' arm as they turned across the sand to pass Heffer's house, skirt the fish market and reach the jetty, where they could signal for a boat to take them back to their respective ships. "Don't be too harsh with the poor fellow. He's at least admitting to himself that his garrison of apparently God-fearing Roundheads are really jail sweepings. *We* knew that, but *he* couldn't accept it because he genuinely thought Cromwell, Puritanism, the New Model Army, the Western Design, being sad on Sundays, all had magically transformed this dross into pure gold"

"On the other hand," Ned said with ironic emphasis, "he has seen what he considers real scum – people like us, with our former servants, truly wicked men and women who swear, blaspheme, rarely if ever go to church, never spend an hour at prayer, live in a state of sin with our women – sail out, and bring him a cargo of grain, capture a Spanish city and give him guns, powder and shot... The poor fellow's world has been turned inside-out!"

"Well, I still think he's a psalm-singing hypocrite and I don't trust him!" Thomas said flatly.

"We don't have to, but you must admit the best way of getting this place fortified so that *we* can use it as a base is to give him guns and shot in exchange for him building the batteries."

"And you've just seen the soldiers at work!" Thomas jeered. "Wait till I tell Diana: she can't stand the man! She'll want to go off to find our own island to fortify as a base."

"You talk as if he was my hero – hey, what's happening now?"

A horse was galloping along the track from the eastward towards the general's house. The rider was an officer, his style betraying a fairly recent acquaintanceship with horsemanship.

He stopped a few moments at the general's house, where the sentry pointed to Ned and Thomas. Two or three minutes later the officer, his face soaked with perspiration and almost wide-eyed with excitement, reined up in front of the two men with a jerk as though trying to pull off the horse's head.

"The general – quickly, where's the general?"

Thomas wagged a finger at the man, pulling at his carefully trimmed black beard with the other hand. "I'm hard of hearing young man," he said querulously. "Did I understand you to say: 'Excuse me gentlemen, but can you direct me to the general?' "

"Er – well, yes sir."

"You seem in a hurry – are you going to trouble the general with some footling emergency?"

"Yes, sir, indeed! Please, *where* is the general?"

"Before you gallop off you had better tell us what the footling emergency is: we command this island's naval forces."

"That's just it sir!" the officer exclaimed. "The Spanish fleet has been sighted and – "

"Coming from which direction?" Ned asked quietly.

The man turned on his horse and pointed eastward along the coast. "There, sir, from Point Morant."

"How many ships?"

"The message doesn't say, sir; it's been passed from post to post: just that the Spanish fleet is coming!"

"You haven't actually seen it then?"

"No, sir."

Ned pointed westward towards the artificial hillock intended as the battery. "You'll find the general over there, rousing his defences."

The man thanked him and galloped off, leaving Thomas cursing and coughing in the cloud of dust. "What clodhoppers!" he exclaimed. "They pass a warning half the length of the island – God knows how many men have been galloping – which doesn't say how many ships!"

"They haven't the wits of our cane cutters," Ned agreed.

"When you think of what we achieved with that motley crowd we took to capture Santiago..."

"We'd better hurry and signal for a boat," Thomas said, "otherwise we'll have Heffer hanging round our necks bleating about a Second Armada with all the fervour of a Second Coming. And the mastheads of our ships are higher than anything else round here – our lookouts can see right across the Palisades and along the coast."

The boat put Thomas on board his ship the *Peleus* and then took Ned on to the *Griffin*, where his second-in-command, John Lobb, was waiting with Aurelia to greet him. Lobb obviously had news and Aurelia deliberately stood back while he reported.

Lobb pointed aloft and Ned saw a man perched high in the rigging. "There's a ship in sight, sir," Lobb said. "I've sent Green aloft with the perspective glass.

"*One* ship?"

"Just one, sir. Green is sure it's a frigate."

"A horseman's just arrived at General Heffer's headquarters with news from look-outs along the coast that the Spanish fleet's in sight."

"Aye, belike he has," Lobb said phlegmatically, "but no one's told them poor benighted soldiers that the Spanish 'aven't got a fleet in these waters."

"No, and it's better they don't know: they'll keep a sharper look-out if they think the Dons can come any moment. Anyway, the Spanish king might send a fleet one day and scare us all!" He looked aloft and hailed the look-out.

"Green – what do you see?"

"She's a frigate all right, sir, and just furling her courses as she comes abreast the Palisades: she'll come in under topsails."

"What flag?"

"The Union, sir, but no jack. She's English built, too, I'll take my oath on that."

Lobb coughed and pointed across to the jetty. A fisherman's canoe was just leaving with half a dozen men at the paddles and an army officer sitting in the stern.

The man whom General Heffer knew only as "Mr Kent" looked at Aurelia and grinned. "There's your friend Rowlands – coming to warn us the Spanish are coming and asking Thomas and me to go over to see the general..."

"I need a walk on the land," Aurelia said, her French accent more pronounced than usual, and, Ned noted, her voice more attractive as a result, "and I'm sure Diana does, too. Perhaps the sight of us will take the general's mind off the Spanish for a moment or two."

"You must give up tempting Puritans."

"It's the only sport you men allow us," Aurelia said demurely.

Thomas had seen Rowlands coming out by canoe and one of the *Peleus*' boats delivered him and Diana on board the *Griffin* before he arrived. Diana was wearing a dress instead of the more usual divided skirt, a fashion she had started among the women in the English ships, and Aurelia commented on it.

Diana laughed and waved towards Thomas. "He assured me that one of the general's officers has just ridden in to report the Spanish fleet is in sight, so I thought I would dress up to welcome them."

"Always surprise the enemy, Ned," Thomas rumbled. "Just when they're expecting broadsides, fire beautiful women at them."

"Or Mrs Judd," Ned said referring to his former cook, who was now living on board the *Phoenix*, a prize they had captured and put under the command of Saxby, once the *Griffin*'s mate and before that the foreman of Ned's plantation in Barbados. Mrs Judd was a very large woman; large in body, large in all her appetites and large in her generosity.

Green called down from aloft: "She's an English frigate all right, sir, twenty guns and they're run out – for saluting," he added. "She's not cleared for action."

Thomas tugged at his beard. "No Commonwealth jack, eh…" He pulled out the tube of his perspective glass and looked seaward across the low peninsula of the Palisades. "Ah, there she is. I see they've been painting her up in the last few days. Well, if she brings good news for old Heffer, it'll be bad news for us. There's one thing about this island at the moment – sauce for the goose is bound to be poison for the gander!"

Because the frigate was running close to the beach on the far side of the long sand-spit they could not see the sea. "Looks as though she's running on wheels," Thomas commented. "A Mrs Judd-size carriage."

There was a flurry of movement at the *Griffin*'s entry-port on the starboard side, and Lobb came up to Ned to report: "That soldier's arrived sir, the one who usually smells of fish."

"Let him come on board – once you've made him brush off the fish scales."

Diana gave her musical laugh. "One day poor Lieutenant Rowlands will have the sense to order a fishing canoe to be scrubbed out and reserved for his own use."

Thomas shook his head. "Perish the idea: we'd have nothing to bait him about!"

Rowlands was agitated and saluted Ned smartly. "An urgent message from the general, sir!" he said, unlacing the straps closing the leather sabretache he had been wearing slung from his belt. "The general asks that you treat it as particularly urgent," he added, handing over the paper folded four times and closed with two seals.

Because the lieutenant always annoyed him, Ned tucked the paper carelessly into a pocket, nodded a dismissal to Rowlands, and turned to Thomas. "I wish the breeze would get up, it's so damned hot. Drains all one's energy."

Thomas was always quick to join in the baiting of Rowlands. "Yes, what do you say we have dinner on deck under the awning? Too hot below, and you always give such a good meal. I've brought the wine."

"Sir," Rowlands ventured. "The general said – "

" – that it was urgent. But remember, my dear Oarlands, his messages are *always* urgent: it is the most boring thing about them."

"But sir, this really *is* urgent!"

"Of course it is!"

"But sir – "

"I know, my dear Rowman," Ned said, in yet another variation of the man's name, "the Spanish fleet is coming..."

"Yes sir, but how did you know?"

Ned looked around for his perspective glass, saw it on the binnacle box and gave it to Rowlands.

"Climb aloft and look across the Palisades and you'll see 'the Spanish fleet'." Wide-eyed, Rowlands took the glass and then saw the heavily-tarred, thick rope rigging.

"Aye, it'll spoil your shoes and stain your hose," Thomas said unsympathetically. "But by the time you're back reporting to the general, he'll have seen it anyway, providing he looks out of his window."

"Is it within gunshot?" Rowlands asked incredulously. "Yes, of the general's house and us."

"But I don't hear the gunfire."

"You will, you will," Ned assured him, and as if to punctuate his sentence a gun boomed over the anchorage from the western end and a moment later an alarmed Rowlands grasped Ned's shoulder.

"The attack has started, sir! What are you going to do? The Spanish are here!"

"I'm going to have dinner," Ned said, removing Rowlands' hand. "It helps to die on a full stomach!"

CHAPTER TWO

The *Convertine* frigate turned into the anchorage and beat her way up to the eastern end, past the *Griffin*, *Peleus* and *Phoenix* and the other four privateers, to anchor abreast the jetty on the Palisades, firing a gun in salute every five seconds so that the terns and gulls shrieked a regular protest. As soon as she had backed the foretopsail to set the anchor, a boat was hoisted out and it pulled for the shore.

Ned, watching with the glass, saw that there were two officers in it, and Lobb confirmed that from his dress one of them seemed to be the captain of the frigate.

Half an hour later Lieutenant Rowlands was out again in a canoe: the general wanted to see Ned and Thomas "as soon as would be convenient". Urgently, Rowlands added, but pulled a face as he said it, as if admitting he had made a fool of himself earlier.

"Ah," Aurelia said to Rowlands, who irritated her merely by his presence, "the general wants a favour."

Rowlands was even more ill at ease than usual, and Ned guessed that the lieutenant knew what news or orders the *Convertine* had brought but probably did not understand their significance. It must have been like that when the merchant ship had arrived several weeks ago with the first news that Cromwell was dead. But what on earth could the *Convertine* be reporting now that would be more of a blow to people like General Heffer than Oliver Cromwell's death? Even if Richard Cromwell had died, abdicated or been overthrown by the army, it could not put the general in any worse danger. It would mean that in London the Council of State had acted, which (for Heffer, anyway) would be good news rather than bad.

As the *Griffin*'s boat took him to the jetty with Thomas, both men cursing over the interrupted dinner, Ned could think of no explanation, and had merely shrugged when Thomas raised his eyebrows, unwilling to ask the question aloud. Ned had taken pity on Rowlands and brought him over, saving him yet another trip in the narrow, unstable canoe, and the lieutenant led the way into the general's office.

The general stood up as they came in, and so did two naval officers who had been sitting opposite him at the table. Heffer's face looked as if the skin had shrunk in the past hour, his eyes seemed glazed as though he was suffering from acute shock or acute fear. With a vagueness which was not intended he introduced the four men and, without sitting down again, gestured towards the naval officers and said: "These gentlemen have brought me news and orders, and a letter which I believe is for you, Mr – er, Kent. They expected to deliver it in Barbados, but you were not there, and they learned that the owner of the *Griffin*, a certain Mr *Yorke*, had left that island with most of the people from his plantation. They happened to mention it to me – would I be wrong in thinking that I had mistaken the counties, mishearing your name as Kent instead of Yorke?"

Ned smiled at Heffer's tactfulness: the name Kent had seemed suitable as a buccaneer while Cromwell was alive… "Yes, I am Edward Yorke."

The senior of the two naval officers then took a packet from a canvas pouch and gave it to Ned, who glanced at the superscription, did not recognize the writing, and pushed it inside the front of his jerkin.

The general went on, his voice dropping as though he was overawed by what he had to say: "The news these gentlemen bring is almost unbelievable. General Monck, seeing the people in England were becoming restive with the situation after the

Lord Protector's death, invited the Prince to return to the throne. He has brought him back to London from Holland. Today England is once again a monarchy; we owe allegiance to His Majesty King Charles the Second."

"God Save the King!" Thomas bellowed, making everyone jump as he leapt to his feet. "I have always owed my allegiance to him and not my damnable uncle!" He saw the naval officers' puzzled expressions. "I too should introduce myself properly, I suppose: Thomas Whetstone, Baronet, nephew of the late and, by me, unlamented Lord Protector."

"Bless my soul," Heffer exclaimed and subsided in his chair. "God bless my soul." Then, the soldier emerging once again, he asked: "You're not going to take those great guns back, are you?"

"Most certainly not!" Ned said. "They're for our own defence as much as anyone else's. I'm glad we're now helping the King's cause, of course – as no doubt you are."

"Oh, yes, my goodness me, of course. Indeed, we shall name the first battery 'Fort Charles'. That would be most appropriate, don't you think?" Heffer added cautiously, finding that thinking as a Royalist did not come naturally.

"There could be no better name," Thomas boomed. Then, a sudden fear striking him, he swung on the two naval officers. "You have no news of peace with Spain, have you?" he demanded.

"No, Sir Thomas, only that the King is restored and has proclaimed a general political amnesty in England. General Monck has thrown aside his Commonwealth allegiance and is in charge of the government. The army supports him in the restoration of the monarchy. The navy too, of course."

"And you?" Ned asked Heffer. "What happens to the army in Jamaica?"

"As you gentlemen have been acting as joint naval commanders in the defence of the island," the general said, unable to resist a dig at the *Convertine*'s captain, to emphasize the absence of the Royal Navy, I have no hesitation in telling you. I have direct orders – " and his voice took on a deeper, more reverent tone – "from General Monck himself, to remain in command of Jamaica, with the title of Acting Governor, to ensure its defences are strong and take any steps I need to protect both the island and my forces."

"Did he give you the *Convertine*?" Ned asked casually, seeing endless rows and confusions resulting in a naval captain trying to control the buccaneers.

"No, the *Convertine* has been calling at all the islands to take the news and now she sails back to England, just calling at Somers Island on the way."

"So you still have no government ships – we can call them King's ships once again – to protect you ?"

"No, but I was hoping that our arrangement, you providing the great guns and me the forts and batteries, would encourage you and Sir Thomas to stay."

"Yes, we want to use Cagway, or whatever you propose calling the harbour, as a base. Port Royal would be a good name, don't you think, in honour of the King's restoration? But we have to attack Spanish ports and towns, otherwise we shall not have the money for provisions."

"I can't think your ships will make much impression on the Dons," the captain of the *Convertine* sneered unexpectedly. "From what I saw, the ships' companies look more like gangs of poachers!"

The general said quietly: "You will apologize for that remark at once captain, and when you have done so I will tell you why I insist."

The captain flushed and, after first wondering if he dare defy the governor of Jamaica, finally apologized.

The general then said, a hint of awe still in his voice: "That 'gang of poachers' has just come back from successfully attacking Santiago de Cuba, blowing up its castle, and bringing away all of Santiago's great guns. Those cannon, carriages and shot, you saw lying on the ground at the end of the jetty, waiting for the masons to build forts and batteries, are Spanish and defended Santiago until last week. Santiago, I would remind you, is the second port of Cuba... Incidentally, the last admiral we had here, Penn, ended in the Tower because of his abilities."

Ned and Thomas returned to the *Griffin*, where Diana and Aurelia met them at the entry-port. Aurelia led the way down to the cabin. The sun was high but the crew had rigged an old sail as an awning, sheltering the afterdeck and making welcome shade so that the Trade wind blowing across the anchorage was cooled a little as it swept the after part of the ship.

Down in the cabin Diana and Aurelia sat side by side on the bunk and looked questioningly at the two men. Thomas glanced sideways at Ned. "You tell 'em; I still think I'm dreaming."

Deciding to tantalize them for a few moments, Ned said: "The *Convertine* brought new orders for the general. He keeps his job as governor, and he is to defend the island. And there has been no peace treaty signed with the Dons."

Aurelia sighed. "Now you have had your little joke, Edouard, tell us the news."

"What do you mean?" Ned asked innocently.

"I believed you up to the moment you said no peace treaty had been signed with Spain. Something unusual must have happened to make *that* of any importance. Since out here war with Spain is normal, *chéri*, peace would be unusual. Anyway, whatever happens in Europe does not affect us out here – remember, 'No peace beyond the Line'."

"The King is back on the throne in London," Ned said.

The two women stared at him wide-eyed and then at Thomas, wary of a joke yet wanting to believe it.

"It's true," Thomas said. "General Monck fetched him back from Holland. And he's proclaimed a general amnesty for political affairs. The King isn't going to put the leading Roundheads on the block."

"That's wise," Diana said unexpectedly. "God knows they deserve it, but recriminations are pointless. What's done is done and that's that."

Thomas growled: "Except that I lost my land, and Ned's father lost two estates – three including Ilex, as well as the plantation in Barbados." He grinned at Aurelia and added: "Even though he'll have the plantation back by the most devious circumstances, once he's married."

"The King will make it all right," Aurelia said. "You must give him time."

"The King has been out of England too long," Thomas said cautiously. "He doesn't know who are his friends. Who knows what gossip was poured into his ear while he was in France, and then Spain? Think of him spending years in Catholic countries, living on the bounty of Catholic kings, and surrounded by court lackeys…"

"You don't sound very happy at the Restoration, darling,"Diana said.

"It's just that I wish I was in England. There's bound to be a long period of confusion and that's when an innocent man's enemies can strike."

"Oh stop grumbling," Diana said sharply, adding unsympathetically: "You have more to fear from debtors than anyone else. Ned, fetch out a bottle of something special and let's drink out of glasses for once!"

Aurelia jumped up and opened a locker which held glasses fitting into circular holes cut in a shelf. "What shall we drink?"

"Anything but rumbullion," Diana said firmly.

"Cognac. Here, hold the glasses while I pour."

As soon as the four of them were holding their glasses, Thomas said: "I give you a toast, one I don't think any of us expected to drink to with a king on the throne: Here's health unto His Majesty!"

As soon as they had emptied their glasses, Ned said: "We must tell the ship's company, and give them the rest of the day off to celebrate. And pass the word to the *Peleus* and the *Phoenix*."

Aurelia suddenly said: "*Chéri*, you are a most peculiar shape in front. What have you in your jerkin?"

Ned pulled out the packet. "A letter from England. Sent out to Barbados with the *Convertine*'s captain. Luckily they told him there that I had fled in the *Griffin*."

"Open it, open it!" Aurelia said impatiently. "How can you walk round for hours with an unopened letter!"

"It's of no consequence, of that I'm sure," Ned said. "I don't recognize the writing." He broke the seal and unfolded the paper. There were three sheets, the last two being lists.

"Sir," he read:

> It is with the deepest regret that I have to inform you of the death of your father, the sixth Earl of Ilex. This occurred near Toledo in Spain on the fifth day of May last, when he was out hunting and his horse fell heavily. He was riding in a group accompanying His Majesty, who commands me to convey to you His Majesty's sympathy in your grievous loss.
>
> Your father died intestate, and of course your elder brother George succeeds to his titles, estates and possessions, and as your late father's steward, who was with him at the time of the fatal accident but who returned to England with His Majesty, I am enclosing a copy of the accounting of the estates which I sent to your brother. This account is of necessity cursory in its nature, but His Majesty commands me to inform you both that as your father refused to compound with Cromwell and instead went into exile, joining His Majesty, the title and estates pass to your brother without any stop, let or hindrance.
>
> In the meantime I assure you that all is well with the estates at Godmersham, Saltwood and Ilex, and that the family gold and silver plate has been recovered from the

hiding place where your late father and I put it, and is in safe custody. Your brother will be writing to you as soon as he returns to England.

The letter was signed by Henry Grey, who must by now be seventy years old, and who had begun serving the Yorke family when he was about eight years old.

Ned suddenly realized that there was complete silence in the cabin, apart from the lapping of the waves against the hull, and a white-faced and distraught-looking Aurelia was waiting for him to say something. Diana too seemed close to tears, sensing that his concentration on the letter meant that it was both important and probably bad news. Thomas was running his fingers through his beard in the nearest approach to agitation that Ned had seen.

"I'm sorry, but this is rather a shock. My father – he's been killed in a hunting accident in Spain – the King's sympathy – the steward is writing…"

Thomas was the first to react. "So your brother George is the new Earl. Diana and I can only extend our sympathies at your loss. Do you get the estates back? Your father didn't compound, did he?"

"We get the estates back, so the steward says."

A moment later Aurelia was holding him, sobbing. He held her tight and then, when she had stopped, whispered: "Don't grieve; he was my father but we were not really close. We went our own ways. That was why I came out to Barbados."

Ned folded the letter and put it in a drawer. The steward's lists could be read later. "I'd better assemble the ship's company and tell them about the King's restoration."

Thomas stood up, looking embarrassed. "Ned…" he paused a few moments, "…you remember the Brethren of the Coast, and their new leader?"

Ned nodded: "That's all forgotten now, I suppose?"

"Why should it be?" Thomas seemed startled.

"Well, I assume Sir Thomas Whetstone and the Lady Diana Gilbert-Manners will now return to England and resume a life of remarkable respectability?"

"No!" Diana said violently. "At least, I shan't. Thomas might, but I doubt it. Tell us, Thomas, you're not getting too old for buccaneering?"

"Not while the Dons say 'No peace beyond the Line'!" Ned laughed and looked at Aurelia. "I think the Yorkes, after their wedding, might have to return to Barbados to put their affairs in order, and by that time perhaps the forts and batteries will be built here, and those guns mounted."

Just before noon next day Lobb reported to Ned that the *Peleus*' boat was bringing over Sir Thomas Whetstone "and his lady". There was no doubt about how the Griffins viewed the Restoration: they had asked for a boat and, with the exception of the Bullocks, the couple who had left Barbados with Aurelia and acted as her servants, had all gone over to the *Phoenix*. There they celebrated the final overthrow of their real enemy, Cromwell, with Saxby and the rest of the men and women who had fled from the Kingsnorth estate.

Ned had sent for Saxby to give him the news, and the foreman from the Kingsnorth plantation (and now master of the first prize captured by Ned and his men) had at first just grinned happily, without saying anything, as though he had not understood Ned's words.

Then he said: "Means we could all go back to Kingsnorth and start planting again. Except – " he broke off, doubtful.

"Except what?" Ned prompted.

"Except that I don't reckon many of them will want to."

At that moment Ned realized that he had been so excited by the news of the Restoration that he had not really considered how it affected him. Affected not just him, but every man and woman now on board the *Griffin* and the *Phoenix* – and affected the future of Kingsnorth. There was plenty of excitement – at the

Restoration, at his forthcoming marriage to Aurelia, at the fact that neither he nor Thomas needed to use false names any longer.

Now Saxby, the stolid and reliable Lincolnshire man who long ago deserted from the Royal Navy and proved himself a very competent plantation manager, was doing the thinking for him.

"Except" – that was the key. Except that the men and women on board the two ships might not think the same way as Mr Yorke.

"No," Saxby said quietly, "I can't see 'em wanting to go back to plantation life. You see, sir, they came out here in the first place because of Cromwell: transported because he'd captured them in battle – the Irish after Drogheda and Wexford, the Scots after Dunbar – or was emptying the jails. Some just decided they couldn't go on living in the funeral atmosphere the Puritans spread everywhere. Not everyone reckons it's a crime to laugh; not everyone measures a man's honesty and generosity by the length of his face and the frequency of his prayers and psalm singing. So thanks to Cromwell, we all go out to the West Indies; thanks to Cromwell we all then had to make a bolt for it from Barbados to escape from those Roundheads."

Saxby, now launched into one of the longest speeches Ned had ever heard him make – six or a dozen words were his normal limit – took a deep breath.

"The fact is, sir, we like this life. I know most of the men and women are indentured to you, sir, and they've got more time to serve, but I reckon if you gave us the choice of continuing to go privateering with you or going back to Kingsnorth with you, we'd all choose privateering."

"You've talked this over with them?"

"In a manner o' speaking, sir: after we heard Cromwell was dead, most of us agreed we really owed our new life at sea to him, an' preferred it to plantin'."

"What did Mrs Judd think?"

"She likes privateering, sir. Says the excitement – well..." Saxby's normally red face reddened with embarrassment "...gives her more zest for things."

The dark rings under Saxby's eyes told the rest of the story, and he had returned to the *Phoenix* leaving Ned with questions but no answers. He realized he had not really thought about what would happen to Kingsnorth – presumably the weeds had already spread across the land, and no doubt the termites were busy eating the woodwork of the house. Planting or privateering? He had, without much thought, assumed that Saxby and the men would want to go back to Kingsnorth. But what about Aurelia and, for that matter, Thomas and Diana? All he knew was the brief reference they had made yesterday, but had Thomas really thought about his own people in the *Peleus*? If they could return to England –the Restoration presumably cancelled all the transportations ordered by the Commonwealth – surely most of them would? Diana alone had said that she had no wish to return to England: out here she was completely free: one week in battle, the next returning from it in the *Peleus*, the third looking for more excitement. No, a woman with such a zest for life and action was not likely to return to an English drawing-room life where watching the men play backgammon, surely the dullest of games, would be the highlight of a week, and deciding the day's menus and drawing up a guest list for next Thursday, the usual run of events. Diana, who had sailed the *Peleus* into Santiago while he and Thomas attacked it overland... She would have little to talk about with the vapid wives of Royalists, even though for a few months they would be telling stories of living as refugees in France. No, come to think of it, the King has been back on the throne for several weeks, and by the time anyone reached England from the West Indies, the refugees' stories would be forgotten... Further discussion about the future had been stopped yesterday by the determined way that they celebrated the Restoration: at one point, mug in one hand and linstock in the other, the four of them fired the *Griffin*'s guns in a salute, loaded them all again, and fired a second. The *Peleus* and *Phoenix* had followed suit and then the *Convertine* had fired more salutes with the four privateers (after they had sent over to the *Griffin* to find out what was happening) firing their great guns sporadically through most of the night, glad of something to celebrate and beating drums and singing wild songs in several languages. Now, it was very much the morning after, with only Aurelia looking fresh because she rarely drank anything intoxicating, and his own head throbbing because he normally drank little but had made an exception for the Restoration. Lobb, too, kept his voice low when he reported the *Peleus'* boat, as though fearing that loud noises would split his head open.

Diana came through the entry-port like the sun suddenly rising but Thomas was walking with care, as if knowing that jarring his heels would make his head ring like a chime of cathedral bells. Diana again wore one of her divided skirts, a white dress the skirt of which had been cut up the length of her legs and resewn into two tubes, like men's trousers. The top of her dress was cut low and the shoulders were bare, keeping her cool and revealing and increasing the sun tan. She kissed Aurelia and grimaced at Ned. "Sir is a trifle brittle this morning. He growls like a bear but if anyone stamps their feet he will fall to pieces."

"She has a Puritanical streak," Thomas muttered, his eyes red-rimmed and his beard uncombed. "Or perhaps she's become a Jesuit, all piety and reforming zeal."

Ned looked at the generous body, the half exposed and heavily tanned bosoms, the warm and full-lipped mouth, and the laughing eyes. "Yes, you're probably right. But what else put you into such an ill humour?"

"I confess to you, Ned and Aurelia, that I drank far too much yesterday, during the night and well into today, and now I am paying the price. But I did not expect to face a deputation from the privateers as soon as I dared open an eye this morning."

"A deputation?"

"Yes. All but pounding on my door, they were."

"But they were drinking most of the night, too!"

"They're used to it," Thomas said, not attempting to conceal the awe in his voice. "They drink raw rumbullion as you and I might take the juice of a lime."

"What did they come to see you about?"

"Several things. You, the Restoration, the election of a new leader of the buccaneers, the future of this place – Cagway, or whatever it's called – and a raid."

"Let's go below," Aurelia said. "The sun is scorching. The deck is so hot it makes my feet swell."

"Feet!" Thomas grumbled. "It's boiling my brains!"

Down in the *Griffin*'s cabin, Aurelia looked questioningly at Diana.

"Shall I offer Thomas a drink?"

"No," Diana said firmly. "We celebrated the King's restoration yesterday; today we must concentrate on restoring Thomas."

Thomas laughed and then winced. "If only one was rewarded for celebrating the Restoration, I'd get a peerage."

"Your name should have been Touchstone, or Drystone; anything but 'Whet'," Diana said.

"No, the lady has made up my mind," Thomas said. "Anyway, we have a lot to decide before Ned and I go to see the privateersmen."

Ned looked puzzled. "They're not grumbling about their share of the Santiago purchase, are they?"

"On the contrary! Their only complaint is that here there aren't enough taverns and wenches to spend it!"

"What is – "

"Ned, I have a list of questions more or less committed to memory. In my present state you could easily jolt them into the wrong order, so listen carefully. Now, I'm here as a representative of the privateers: they came to me simply because they've known me for some years."

"And trust you," Diana added.

"I suppose they do," Thomas said, "though I don't always trust them. Anyway, their first question, Ned, is whether or not you're going to continue buccaneering now that the King is back."

Ned looked at Aurelia, puzzled by the question. She shrugged her shoulders, as if indicating she could not account for the doubt either, and he said: "Of course, providing we stay at war with Spain, so that we're privateers, not pirates. But what about you? Have you made up your mind whether or not you are going back to England?"

Diana gave a disdainful wave, as if to indicate that Thomas' answer was of no consequence. "He only talks of going back when he's in his cups. He can't afford London; neither can London afford him."

Thomas grunted. "I was thinking of living on your money, m'dear."

"I know," Diana retorted, "but we shall continue living out here, with the king of Spain paying our expenses."

Aurelia coughed and the three of them looked at her. "That answers your first question, Thomas. What is the second?"

"Ah yes. Barbados. They want to know if it is necessary for you to go to Barbados at once. They say you'd be away for at least six months, if you were planning to start up Kingsnorth again, quite apart from doing up the plantation Aurelia inherited on her husband's death."

Ned shook his head. "I don't understand the question. Or, rather, I don't see how it affects the privateersmen."

Aurelia said promptly: "*Mon chéri*, if you are away in Barbados putting two plantations in order, you can't be here privateering!"

Thomas nodded and again winced as the movement made his headache worse. "That's about it, Ned; they say they can send an island sloop to Barbados with a letter, but they'd rather not lose you and the *Griffin* for so long."

"Six months is not very long."

"It's also very optimistic," Thomas said. "More likely to be a year."

"That's true," Aurelia said, and turned to Ned. "Remember, *chéri*, that Barbados has only just heard of the Restoration. It will take months to get the island running properly again. My late husband – " she refused to mention his name " – died intestate, so the lawyers will squabble about the probate. We may not be allowed to start work on either plantation until the legal papers are cleared up. It will probably have to be referred to London. That alone could take a year, probably two…"

"What do you suggest, then? They're your plantations at the moment."

Aurelia held out her hands, palm uppermost. She looked directly at Ned and said in a low voice: "My late husband used to beat me every day. I never want to see that plantation again. The one he stole from you and which I want to give back to you as soon as the probate is done, I value only because it's yours. I don't want to see it again. I will, of course, because I will be with you."

"Sell 'em," Thomas growled. "Sell Kingsnorth. I suppose you'll have to give the money to your brother, because it was a family plantation until that man Wilson stole it, and it could be argued it still belongs to the family. Use the money raised by *your* plantation, Aurelia, as a reserve when the Dons are parsimonious with prizes."

Diana said: "Or rent yours, Aurelia. I agree with Thomas about Kingsnorth: Ned was managing it for his family. But if you rent out both of them, it means you have an income until you feel like retiring from the sea in your old age. By then everyone will have forgotten the words Cromwell, Roundhead and Commonwealth."

Ned said: "I am more concerned that Aurelia and I get married. But I didn't realize she was reluctant to go back to Barbados. You said nothing, *chérie*."

The Frenchwoman shook her head. "I thought you wanted to go back," she said simply. "Where you go, I go."

Ned gestured to Thomas. "Well, the answer for the moment, then, is that we shall not hasten back to Barbados. I might write to John Alston, my only friend while I lived in the island, and if he's survived I'll see what he thinks about renting or selling. So let's have the next question."

Thomas waved them aside. "There were only more questions if you'd given different answers to the first ones. Now we need to talk to the privateers again."

"What about?" Ned demanded.

Thomas ran his fingers through his beard. "Why don't you wait and see? I know what it is, but they swore me to secrecy. It is nothing unpleasant, I can assure you."

CHAPTER THREE

The French privateer *Perdrix* was, as Thomas quickly pointed out, a ship with a strange name. The most powerfully armed of the four other privateers and so bereft of paint that she seemed made of bare wood, her decks were filthy with scraps of food lying in the scuppers, her side stained where rubbish was thrown or poured over the side, and her French colours looked like a torn blouse left pegged out for the wind and rain to clean and now bleached by the sun.

"Partridge!" Thomas exclaimed as he helped Aurelia on board from the *Griffin*'s boat. " 'Vulture' would be a better name!"

"Look at the rigging – and the sails," Ned said quietly. "Freshly tarred rope, and that hemp looks almost new." He looked round, saw a sharp-eyed, fat-bellied man he recognized as the owner, and waved a salute.

The man bustled over. "Forgive me," he said in a cultured voice that belied his appearance – he looked, Ned thought, like the foreman in a slaughterhouse – "but I did not hear you arrive and these *canaille* did not bother to tell me." He turned and bowed to Aurelia, welcoming her on board in French, but changing back to his excellent English as he kissed Diana's hand. Obviously Diana knew both ship and owner well, because she immediately began teasing him.

"If you won't give the order to swab the decks, why don't you drive this old bird to windward for an hour or two and ship a few seas to start the job?"

The man shrugged and patted his stomach. "We look after the important things, milady Diana. You will find no fault in the *Perdrix*'s rigging, sails or guns, so as a privateer she is *formidable*. You have many times in the past praised our *cuisine*. What else is of importance?"

Diana laughed and turned to Aurelia. "It's true about the *cuisine*. That is why these four privateers make him their leader – it gives them an excuse to dine on board the *Perdrix*!"

The privateersman shook hands with Thomas and Ned realized that this man, Leclerc, was the one with the questions – and, he hoped, some answers.

"If you will follow me," Leclerc said, leading the way aft and disappearing down a companion-way. The cabin was large, the full width of the ship, with standing headroom, and Ned turned as he reached the bottom of the ladder to find three more men, obviously the other captains, already greeting Diana and being introduced by her to Aurelia.

The cabin was a startling change from the rest of the ship: it was panelled in rich polished mahogany; the handrails for the companion-way were covered in fine ropework; the hammock, now pushed to one side out of the way, was edged with lacework and a large cot, or box, was fitted into it – big enough, Ned noted, for two people, even allowing for Leclerc's paunch. A rack pierced with circular holes held several onion-shaped bottles inserted neck downwards, so that the tropical heat should not dry the corks and spoil the wine. The rack must contain Leclerc's favourite wines: most privateersmen seemed to prefer tapping a barrel.

Leclerc, now seating Aurelia and Diana with all the courtesy of a host with highly regarded guests, was a complete contradiction, and Ned wondered if Thomas and Diana had deliberately not warned him, to avoid influencing his opinion. The man's ship was outwardly filthy yet, as he had said, the masts, spars, rigging and guns could not be faulted. But the rotted scraps of food in various corners of the deck, the smell of rotting food fighting with the reek of garlic, the man himself gross, unshaven yet not bearded, his face greasy and obviously unwashed for days, his clothes giving the appearance of having been slept in for several weeks – and yet this cabin, spotlessly clean, the panelling and furniture highly polished (could he detect the smell of the beeswax polish?) and lockers and table fitted with well-polished brass hinges. And that swinging cot – it was too elaborate to be called a hammock. A woman's touch? That could explain the cabin, and obviously Leclerc kept her hidden away.

"Now, M'sieur Yorke, you have met these gentlemen only briefly before the Santiago raid," Leclerc said, "so I will introduce you again. First, your fellow countrymen, Charles Coles, who owns the *Argonauta* and Edward Brace, who commands the *Mercury*."

One *owned* a ship with a Spanish name; the other *commanded* one with an English. Ned wondered at the significance and decided there was none. He immediately recognized Coles, who was stocky, blond-haired and blue-eyed, had a hearty manner and a vigorous handshake. "My lads want to thank you for the biggest purchase they've ever shared – and, when you blew up the castle at Santiago, the biggest bang they've ever heard!"

"The same goes for the *Mercury*," Brace said. Red-headed and thin, the bones of his face angular, he was the taller of the two men. "Cursing the lack of taverns and whores though: they don't have any use for money they can't spend!" Brace was the only man present, apart from Thomas, who had a beard. But while Thomas' beard was a thick black growth, the bottom of which Diana occasionally squared off with a carefully sharpened pair of scissors, Brace's was pointed, neatly trimmed and combed several times daily. He had a special comb made from turtle shell and edged with silver, and which he kept in the top left-hand pocket of his jerkin. The point of the beard curled forward; Brace had a habit of twirling it between the first two fingers of his left hand. Pale of skin and his eyes deep-set and in the poor light seeming black, Brace was a man who smiled frequently and would sooner joke than give a serious answer – that was clear within a couple of minutes of him being introduced.

Both Coles and Brace came from northern England. Yorkshire or Lancashire? Ned could not distinguish, and did not have time to ask before yet another blue-eyed, blond man was standing in front of him, hand outstretched, and repeating: "Gottlieb, Gottlieb, Gottlieb."

"You remember our Dutch friend," Leclerc said. "Mr Gottlieb who owns the *Dolphyn*."

"Very good, very good," Gottlieb said, and Ned realized that he was agreeing with what Cole and Brace had just said. The Dutchman had a flat face and his widely-spaced eyes and blond eyebrows gave him a perpetually startled appearance, as though dazzled by a bright light. Small but well built, Gottlieb gave the impression of quiet competence.

Aurelia sat back in her chair and looked round at the six men in the cabin, marvelling at the circumstances that brought such different characters together. Leclerc, she suspected, was a French version of Thomas: a well-bred man who for reasons of his own had deliberately quit France. Was it religion? He could be a Protestant, and out here, among some of the islands, religion was of little consequence – or, rather, the Catholic priests had much less power and influence.

The Dutchman was a typical refugee from the Spanish occupation of the Netherlands; he probably hated the Spanish for much more than "No peace beyond the Line". He was a quiet man who said little: a blond version of Ned and, she suspected, as deceptive. Ned gave the impression of a calmness bordering on remoteness. She knew that to other people he often seemed a thousand miles away, yet once there was anything to be done he had a power of concentration which was frightening in its intensity. She guessed Thomas knew all this because over the past months he had seen Ned slowly change from the uncertain and harried young plantation owner to the man using his ship for smuggling in order to feed his people and finally becoming a buccaneer because – well, because there was no peace beyond the Line, and his enemies had been the Roundheads (until Cromwell died) and the Spanish. She also guessed that Diana knew all this instinctively, in the way that many women can look at a man and assess him as a lover.

Yet what was this meeting now on board *Perdrix* all about? Why were they all gathered in this cabin? Thomas was so mysterious that Aurelia doubted if Diana had been able to do more than guess. Were the two of them eventually going to sail back to England, now the King was back on the throne? Aurelia was far from sure. Thomas seemed to want to go but Diana appeared determined to stay in the West Indies. Thomas commanded the *Peleus* – but she had been bought with Diana's money.

There seemed to be no particular reason for Thomas to go back: as Diana had pointed out to him with her usual candour, only his debtors would welcome him! There was no family estate; simply, she thought, that Thomas could imagine the fascination of court life with a new King and wanted to be part of it, overlooking that it would need money... It was indeed a Restoration: as Ned had commented, people could openly laugh and sing now, and wear bright clothes.

For the next few months no doubt England would be an exciting place, with the people throwing off all the greyness brought down on them by the Puritans. Yes, life in Restoration England would be joyful and expensive, and Thomas had only his share of the Santiago purchase, while if Diana had any money left in England she would be wise to keep it out of Thomas' hands.

She looked across at Ned, who was laughing at something Leclerc had just said to Thomas. What was Ned finally going to do? He had the choice of either going back to Barbados and putting the plantation in order or continue buccaneering, making this new island of Jamaica a base. To her surprise (and disappointment) he had seemed rather cool towards Thomas' notion of going on buccaneering, although admitting that Spain was still the enemy. Yet would Spain remain the enemy? Both Ned and Thomas were worried about these rumours, said to have originated from the *Convertine*'s captain, that the King's long exile, much of it spent in Spain, meant that there would be a peace treaty as a return for Spain's hospitality.

Where, Aurelia asked herself bitterly, would that leave Jamaica, so recently captured from Spain? Would the Spanish king demand its return – even before Heffer had a chance to anglicise all the place names? Certainly it was a tiny island in the middle of Spanish territory...like a fly on the back of a bullock. But in time it could become a horsefly with a vicious sting. The Spanish king already knew that, though whether or not he would do anything was anyone's guess.

Anyway, she cared little for what the king of Spain decided. What concerned her in the next hour or so, sitting in this stuffy cabin listening to these droll fellows make proposals, was what *Ned* would decide: what would be their future? Had she persuaded him that she *really* had no interest in Barbados? That she *hated* Antigua? That she (like Diana) *preferred* this present almost gypsy existence afloat? Ned seemed unable to believe it; he gave an impatient shrug and assumed that she and Diana were merely being loyal to their men: "Whither thou goest..."

Diana was nervous: Aurelia suddenly realized that with a shock. The Englishwoman was always so calm, whether with the enemy coming over the horizon or Thomas in one of his tantrums. It was an inner calm that came from complete confidence in herself. Like Ned's calm in a way and, for a moment, she realized they were probably in some ways very much alike – outwardly calm and inwardly capable of almost frightening passion. She could not be certain about Diana, of course, but judging from Thomas' infatuation with her and their obvious joy in each other's company, it must be so. Was this outward calm a particularly English trait? Her late husband was just the opposite, but she chased the thought of him away; he had been a greedy, brutal schoolboy and now he was dead. And Leclerc was coughing, to get everyone's attention.

"Gentlemen," he said, "only M. Yorke (and Mme. Wilson and Mlle. Diana, of course)," he added with a bow, "do not know why we are here today, but as it is important that M. Yorke understands our proposals and plans, I intend to start right at the beginning. First, M. Yorke and Sir Thomas, we thank you for inviting us to accompany you on the Santiago raid and the very satisfactory purchase it yielded. The important thing that expedition showed us, M. Yorke, is what we buccaneers can achieve if we act together and if we are properly led. You know what has been happening until now – "

" I don't," Ned interrupted. "Apart from Sir Thomas, you are the first buccaneers I've ever met!"

Leclerc looked startled and then laughed. "The irony of that escapes you for the moment, but I will point it out later. Well, we buccaneers are a mixture, but in the case of those of us here, we have fallen foul of the governments in our own countries – for religious or political reasons. And our attempts to trade in the West Indies have, as you know only too well, brought us up against Spain, which always says 'No peace beyond the Line' and refuses to allow us to trade. Legally, you understand!"

Thomas chuckled. "The Spanish authorities' actions keep the prices up for those of us who care to smuggle! If they allowed merchant ships to trade freely, it would bring in dozens of our countrymen, and prices would tumble rapidly!"

"Aye, I'd have to go back to England and carry sea coal down to London," Brace said lugubriously.

"*Alors,*" Leclerc said, "We must not forget we are by no means the only buccaneers afloat. To resume my narration, M. Yorke, we happened to hear that some of Cromwell's soldiers had captured Jamaica, so we sailed over to investigate and met Sir Thomas, whom we already knew."

Ned held up his hand to interrupt Leclerc. "Where are the other buccaneers, then?"

"Their base? At La Tortue – Tortuga, you call it, the turtle, a small island off the northwestern corner of Hispaniola. Not far from here – just across the Windward Passage. It's sheltered, and because that end of Hispaniola is thick jungle and mountains, the Spanish cannot attack us by land, and they certainly don't have the ships."

"Yet," said Thomas, "the good King Carlos may spend some money on new ships."

"We should get a warning in good time," Leclerc said. "That is the least of our worries."

"What is the biggest of them?" Ned asked, curious.

"Leave that for a moment," Leclerc said. "Let me finish describing the buccaneers. There are about twenty-one other ships, mostly English or French, but some Dutch, two Portuguese and one Spanish, with crews varying between twenty and a hundred."

"I've heard the name 'The Brethren of the Coast' mentioned," Ned said.

Leclerc smiled. "That's the name given us originally by our enemies and which we have adopted – with pride! And that brings me to your question. Our biggest worry at the moment is finding a leader."

Aurelia did a quick sum in her head. They had twenty-five ships altogether – the twenty-one in Tortuga and the four here – with between twenty and a hundred men on board each of them… Say an average of fifty. That meant about 1,250 "Brethren of the Coast". She knew now why Thomas had given no details and why they were sitting here in *Perdrix*'s cabin.

"No leader among more than a thousand men?" Ned sounded incredulous.

"No. The four captains here – myself, Gottlieb, Coles and Brace – have all been asked to become the admiral of the Brethren."

"Why did you all refuse?"

"Speaking for myself – but I know it is the same for my fellow captains – we do not have the necessary courage to make decisions which affect the lives (and possible deaths) of more than a thousand of our fellow buccaneers. We will gladly follow; we are reluctant to lead. To decide, rather."

Ned pointed to Thomas, who promptly shook his head. "I've been asked and refused," he said. "Leclerc was speaking for me too."

"One of you is going to have to take the job or else the buccaneers will fall apart like a leaderless flock of – " Ned broke off.

"Sheep," Leclerc said. "You are quite correct. That is why only four ships left Tortuga to see what was happening at Jamaica: the rest could not make up their minds. I'm happy to say that now there are fewer to share the purchase!"

Aurelia saw that Ned was considering the question in the same way he had considered the attack on Santiago: that it was a puzzle which must have a solution, if only one thought hard enough.

Leclerc coughed and Ned looked up as the Frenchman said: "Whoever we recomend to the Brethren would of course be elected. Would *you* become our admiral, M. Yorke?"

Back on board the *Griffin* Ned was angry, although far from sure why. He told Thomas, for the fifth or sixth time: "You might have warned me that they intended to propose this straight away!"

"What difference does it make?" said an exasperated Thomas. "You don't have to give an answer until tomorrow."

"I know but – "

"But what?" Aurelia asked innocently. "You just have to say 'yes' or 'no'."

"Just 'yes' or 'no' – it isn't as easy as that!"

Diana said sympathetically: "Why not just think aloud, Ned? It always seems to help Thomas reach a decision."

Ned stood up abruptly and began pacing the length of the cabin. "It's not just a question of saying 'yes' or 'no' to being the leader of the Brethren. It's deciding whether to go back to Barbados as a planter or stay here to be a pirate."

"I say, 'pirate' is a strong word, Ned," protested Thomas. "We're fighting the Spaniards. Don't forget you might settle down in Barbados and then have your estate burned down by the Dons and no one could do anything about it. What the Brethren do is buccaneering, Ned. And as far as I can see, the buccaneers are going to have to defend Jamaica and the rest of the islands for the next few years. The King won't be able to send out any frigates for a long time: his Treasury is empty and anyway the navy doesn't have many seaworthy ships left – that much I discovered from the *Convertine*'s captain."

"You sound as though you've made up your mind to stay out here buccaneering," Ned said.

"Buccaneering or buying land in Jamaica," Diana said, answering for Thomas, and Aurelia felt he was being told. "We are not going back to England, whatever grand ideas Thomas might parade in his cups."

Aurelia nodded because Diana had already explained to her while they changed their clothes after returning from the *Perdrix*. The Trade winds were kicking up a lop in the anchorage which had soaked them in spray, and Aurelia had lent her a dress which, since the Frenchwoman was much slimmer, emphasized Diana's more voluptuous figure.

Although Thomas would never admit it, Diana had said, he could never settle down in England, no matter what he thought now. He needed an active life and plenty of challenges, and would be forced to seek the excitement on horseback, hunting, and in the gaming rooms. Here Diana had commented: "I persuaded him that chasing a stag or rolling dice hardly compares with blowing up castles or fighting the Dons, and furthermore it costs money, while buccaneering gives us a good income."

Aurelia realized that Thomas was lucky to have a woman who not only understood him, but loved the life he needed to live. Who had really made the final decision, Diana or Thomas? One thing was sure: Diana was not going to let Thomas get near enough to the gaming tables to lose the *Peleus* in a rash bet! Lose the ship and perhaps their lives in a raid on the Spaniards, yes; lose a penny at the gaming tables to some pallid youngster whose bets were backed by an inherited fortune, no!

Aurelia also realized that Diana, like her, had guessed what London must be like during this first year or so of the Restoration: a sudden surge of gaiety to make up for the years of enforced Puritan dreariness; a false and brittle brilliance because most of the aristocracy had spent years in exile and were now almost strangers in their own country: Englishmen and women with a veneer of French or Spanish manners and attitudes, impatient with those who had stayed in England and must now be stunned at the swift change from gloom to gaiety.

So the decision was made for Diana and Thomas, but Ned was still wrestling with it, and he was wrestling alone because since they had all returned from the *Perdrix*, he and Aurelia had not been able to talk. Aurelia could have made an opportunity – and Diana and Thomas were sensitive people who would need only the gentlest of hints. Yet Aurelia had deliberately not made the opportunity; she wanted Ned to reach his decision alone.

Barbados or the Brethren…

Leclerc, she recalled, had said that if Ned chose to be their leader, they would be preparing almost at once for an expedition against the Spanish the like of which the Caribbean had never seen…

At first, Aurelia had been surprised at Leclerc mentioning it (whatever it was) at this stage, when Ned was still undecided, but she realized, during the row back to the *Griffin*, that the Frenchman and his companions only wanted Ned as their leader if he knew he could lead: the attack on Santiago had been his first and perhaps, from the buccaneers' point of view, there *might* have been an element of chance; he *might* have been carried along by events.

Ned suddenly stopped his pacing and, glaring down at Thomas, exclaimed: "There's not just one plantation at Barbados, you know! There are two, Aurelia's and Kingsnorth."

"I know, I know," said Thomas calmly, "and every day the land is getting more overgrown and the termites are eating up the houses. But tell me, all those Roundhead gentlemen who were after your blood and your land while Uncle Oliver was alive – have they miraculously turned Royalist now the King is back and decided to welcome you back with roisterous parties and offers of help?"

"How do *I* know?" Ned snapped.

"You can guess, Ned," Diana said quietly, and Thomas said: "It doesn't seem to have changed people here. Changed their official allegiances, yes; Heffer's a good example of that. But Heffer and his ilk are still Puritans and Republicans at heart. Once a psalm-singing hypocrite, then always a psalm-singing hypocrite. Here in Jamaica," he pointed out, slapping his knee for emphasis, "you and I have power because this island needs ships for its defence, and we've got 'em. Or at least Heffer thinks he needs 'em, which is the same thing, so what we say matters. But what sort of a mess is there in Barbados, which has a House of Assembly and political parties to complicate matters? It will take a year or two to settle down.

"You can be sure that the *Convertine*'s captain calling in and giving a hail that the King is restored to the throne has not yet made the island safe for Royalists. Why, if you go back within the next year – before more Royalists have come out from England, and that's going to take time – I wouldn't put down a bet that they won't arrest you the moment you land on the island, Restoration or no."

"What the devil for?"

"Come *on*, Ned," Thomas growled. "You and Saxby fought your way out with the *Griffin*. Were no Roundhead soldiers killed? They could charge you with the murder of each and every one of them, wounding Aurelia's late husband, treason...the charges are limited only by an attorney-general's imagination... Don't let's fall into the trap of trusting politicians, whether Republican or Royalist."

Diana said quietly, "Remember, Ned, the Commonwealth still has the power among the islands. Yes, the Roundheads now know the King is back. They also know they have plenty of time to settle a few old scores before they have to give up power. If Heffer wasn't frightened of a Spanish attack, you don't think he would be so friendly, do you?"

Aurelia said a silent prayer of thanks to Diana and Thomas. They had explained flatly and firmly what was frightening her; that for many months the Roundheads would still have the actual power, if not the legal authority, in Barbados: Ned could be charged, tried, sentenced to death, strung up on a gibbet and buried in an unmarked grave within twelve hours of setting foot in Bridgetown, and who but Roundheads would know? No Royalist remained in Barbados after all these years to be able to take over effective command of the island in the King's name. And even if it was revealed afterwards that Edward Yorke had been executed, who in the excitement of the Restoration in England would care what happened in a remote island in the West Indies?

Suddenly Ned turned to her. "What do you think?"

"I think Thomas and Diana are right. Barbados is not safe yet."

"What about your plantation? What about Kingsnorth?"

"Both were overgrown with forests at the beginning. A year's neglect won't do much harm! Or two or three years."

"So what do *you* want me to do?"

It was a naked plea; the tone of Ned's voice made it clear that, in front of Thomas and Diana, he was asking her what he should do – or, rather,asking her to confirm what she wanted to do – and telling her he would abide by her decision. She paused a moment, thinking of his natural pride and sensitivity. For the past two hours the four of them had been so serious, like churchmen plotting politics. They needed to laugh, and then they could sit down to dinner with a good appetite.

She fluffed out her hair and ran a finger along her eyebrows, and then looked down demurely. "I think I would make an excellent wife for an admiral," she said. "We can marry here just as well as in Barbados."

In the *Perdrix*'s cabin next morning Diana noticed that everyone had taken the same place as yesterday, but there was a definite tension. Leclerc's occasional laughs as he ushered everyone down the companion-way tended to end as nervous giggles; even more than ever Gottlieb looked as though he had been dazzled by a bright light. Edward Brace quickly took out his comb and ran it through his beard, and then resumed twirling the tip in his fingers. Only Coles sat still and silent, avoiding staring at Ned. But occasionally glancing at Thomas, as though hoping his expression might reveal Ned's decision.

Diana guessed that Thomas knew no more about it than the other buccaneers and, she suspected, Aurelia. In fact, Diana was far from sure that Ned had even yet reached a decision, and she was basing this on Aurelia's behaviour: the Frenchwoman was being remarkably patient with Ned; the kind of patience, Diana recognized, that was the result of complete exasperation.

Diana could understand the exasperation. She had managed to persuade Thomas to do what she wanted – not, she admitted, that he had much choice. She held the purse strings and knew his weaknesses: few men played a worse game of backgammon; no man, she was certain, could so consistently roll dice and get the wrong number; yet no man loved gambling more. She had two weapons, her money and her body, and Thomas needed both. She had no hesitation in withholding either. But was Aurelia so well armed? A gorgeous body, yes, but Ned had his own money.

There was a considerable difference between the two men. Thomas was hale and hearty, a drinker and trencherman, a lusty man who never brooded, never said more or less than he thought, who was quite incapable of sulking or being tactful or behaving deceitfully. Thomas would argue with her, bellow, lose his temper, and, occasionally, hit her in sheer exasperation. But he was always so amorously repentant afterwards that she enjoyed his lapses.

Ned, however, was different. He was almost the opposite of Thomas in every way: she had never seen Ned slap a man on the back, lift a tankard of rumbullion with the relish of Thomas, or attack a meal with Thomas' gusto. But it was clear, from Aurelia's radiant expression, that Ned's feelings were no less strong for being controlled; that Aurelia could release those feelings, though Diana was not so sure that the French girl could control them as well as she could Thomas'.

It was much more important that the two men worked well together, and almost a miracle that together they were an extraordinarily powerful combination. Aurelia had once said that one of them was the pistol while the other was the powder and ball; that together they were lethal but apart they were comparatively useless. A shrewd assessment, Diana realized.

Now Leclerc was looking at Ned with raised eyebrows. "Has M'sieur Yorke…?"

Ned stood up and looked round at the four buccaneers. "I have a question to ask, before finally deciding."

"Then ask it," Coles said bluntly.

"We don't beat around the bush, y'know."

Ned nodded, as if to make clear he was not implying any evasiveness. "You mentioned yesterday that if I became your leader, you had plans for an expedition against the Spanish 'the like of which the West Indies had never seen before'."

"That is correct," Leclerc said. "We have."

"Will you tell me what it is?"

"If you are going to be our admiral, yes; if not, no," Leclerc said without hesitation or a glance at his fellow buccaneers. "It is not that we do not trust you," he added quickly, "but if you knew and then fell into Spanish hands, they have means of making you reveal secrets…"

Ned nodded and glanced across at Aurelia who, dressed in white cotton, her hair hanging in spiral ringlets, looked more like an aristocrat's demure bride than the young woman who had stood on the *Griffin*'s deck as she sailed into Santiago.

"You see," Ned said, "I am expected to be their leader and at once lead them on such an expedition…"

If he was expecting sympathy from Aurelia he was unlucky. "They'd be mad to tell you if you then decide not to lead them," she said. "Why should they? Why do you want to know?"

"I would like some idea of the first job that I'm expected to undertake." Ned said mildly.

"This next expedition might be one 'the like of which the West Indies has never seen before'," Aurelia said, equally mildly, though Diana was not deceived, "but with respect to Captain Leclerc, I trust the one after that will be bigger, and the third greater than that. Otherwise, if each successive expedition is smaller, then eventually the buccaneers will starve."

"She's right, yer naw," Coles said in his deep North Country accent. "Bigger'n better, that's what we want. A *thinking* man is what we need – beggin' yer pardon ma'am, it's as clear as fresh brewed ale that you're a thinking lady."

Gottlieb slapped his knee in agreement. "Coles and Mrs Wilson are right. Planning, that's the secret; we don't need someone to cheer us on and wave a sword as he leads us through the breach in a castle wall; we want someone who *plots*: who says: 'No, we do not raid *this* place because it will alert the Spanish and spoil our chances for a much more important expedition against *that* place'."

There was a sudden silence and everyone's eyes were on Ned. Diana realized that his whole decision, on which depended their future as well as that of all the buccaneers, was at that moment balanced on a knife edge. The wrong word, the wrong gesture, would make him refuse.

"Come on, Ned," Thomas said gruffly, "we need you."

And then suddenly Ned was nodding his head, and saying: "Yes, all right then," and the buccaneers were crowding round him to shake his hand and Aurelia had stood up and moved towards him.

The men stood back the moment they realized she was there. Leclerc bowed to her. "Kiss him," he said, "because we cannot, and then we kiss the hand of the admiral's wife."

Finally, with the congratulations completed, Ned turned to Leclerc, "So far, four of you have elected me the admiral. What about the rest of the Brethren?"

"It will be unanimous," Leclerc said. "You will see. Our old admiral died some weeks before we left Tortuga, and we all knew there was no one else suitable."

"What about this great expedition, then?"

"We all decided we could not start it without a proper leader. As Coles says, a *thinking* man. This great expedition needs much thought."

"When do I hear about it?"

"You are our leader, and Sir Thomas is joining us?"

"I've already joined," Thomas growled. "As from yesterday, so I have twenty-four hours' seniority over Ned."

"And the ladies…"

Ned eyed Leclerc. "It is a question of the ladies trusting the buccaneers, not the other way around. Don't forget, you came with us to Santiago; we didn't go with you!"

Coles gave a great bellow of laughter, in which Gottlieb and Brace joined. "Tell 'im about it, Jean-Pierre, because 'e's right, yer naw," Coles said, "they took us on trust, and look what a purchase we got – and not a buccaneer's life lost nor a ship damaged."

Leclerc looked at the other buccaneers, who nodded in agreement. "*Alors,*" Leclerc said, "for you, M. Yorke, I hope this is the beginning of a long voyage."

CHAPTER FOUR

Ned was surprised to hear how many buccaneers, taken prisoner by the Spaniards along the Main, managed over the years to escape and eventually get back to Tortuga. It seemed that once the priests had finished with the heretics among them, the prisoners were handed over to the army to work at quarrying stone for repairing or building fortifications. If the particular fortifications were finally completed or brought into good condition, the army simply locked the prisoners in cells. However, the army was not as zealous as the Inquisition, and unless the prisoners were chained to the walls (as was often the case), many managed to escape.

The main problem in escaping from an inland prison, Thomas said, speaking from experience, was getting to the sea through tangled jungle or waterless desert: thirst or sickness frequently struck down a man before he reached the coast. The more fortunate found a fisherman's dugout canoe in some creek well inland, and simply paddled to freedom, staying hidden on the coast until he saw a smuggling ship hovering, waiting for darkness to fall.

Several buccaneers had escaped in the past three months from places as widely spaced as Riohacha and Chagres, and reported two things. The first was that the government in Spain – the king, in other words – was in such financial straits that there was no money to fit out in Spain the annual two plate fleets (already much reduced in size in the last decade). For the second year running there would be no galleons arriving at Cartagena or

Portobelo, and no *flota* visiting Vera Cruz in Mexico. This in turn meant that once again the Spanish merchants along the Main would not receive goods from Spain (their main complaint was the shortage of wine and olive oil, cloth and mundane things like cooking pots, needles and thread) and could not ship out goods for sale in Spain, mainly leather and dyewoods.

The second report by the escaped buccaneers, obvious when you thought about it but hard to confirm, was that the bullion and gems were piling up, waiting for shipment to Spain – ingots of silver, ingots of gold, all stamped with the royal arms of Spain and numbered, all recorded in the great assay registers, all desperately needed by the Spanish king, who was being pressed by the bankers of Italy, Austria and France, who wanted either the interest due on their loans, or the capital repaid… And the Spanish king was going bankrupt in Spain because he could not afford to equip a fleet to sail across the Atlantic to collect his bullion…

Thomas chortled as Leclerc outlined the story. "It's like a rich man starving because he's lost the key to his treasure chest!" he exclaimed.

Diana and Aurelia had both watched Ned as the Frenchman gave the facts he knew. Ned's expression did not change, but both women sensed that he was no longer in the cabin: he was darting along the coast, looking into Riohacha, spotting an escaping buccaneer paddling his canoe among the tortured mangrove roots almost blocking a creek like rheumatic fingers; watching the Spanish king trying to avoid seeing the representatives of the Fuggers or the Welsers or the Strozzi, the bankers, and making desperate promises like any of his bankrupt subjects, that he would cut back expenditure – but all the time the Spanish army in the Netherlands was eating up money…

Aurelia wondered whether the Spanish kings ever used the enormous wealth they were digging from the ground over here to build in Europe great cathedrals or galleries or found universities, commission artists, sculptors or musicians, encourage writers and poets; or if they used all the money to harass the Protestants...

"Where is the bullion being stored?" Ned asked.

Leclerc's face lit up. "Ah, now we approach the heart of the matter. This is like an artichoke; one peels off a leaf at a time, savouring each piece but knowing that as one approaches the centre the next piece will be even tastier."

Ned sat motionless, his eyes on Leclerc although Aurelia knew he was not seeing him.

"I must paint in some of the background," Leclerc said. "First, whence comes the bullion with which we are concerned. The Spaniards long ago took all the gold, silver and gems from the natives here in the big islands of Hispaniola and Cuba: now they have to mine. Most of the silver is coming from a place called Potosi, up in the mountains along the west coast. They carry the ingots down to the port of Arica and then ship it about two thousand miles north to Panama.

"It is cast into cones – like sugar loaves – each weighing about seventy pounds; or into wedges of usually about ten pounds; or cakes or discs, of a pound or two. All these castings are of the purest silver, stamped with the royal arms.

"Coins are minted usually at Potosi or Lima, most of them as pieces of eight, or dollars, but some are doubloons. And of course there are 'cobs' as you English call them, from the Spanish *cabo de barra*, 'cut from the bar'. They look crude coins – some have only half the royal arms stamped on them – because they're made by a hammer and die. Still, the silver is the right quality and weight, which is what matters."

Ned held up a hand to interrupt Leclerc. "Have we any idea how much silver is usually shipped to Spain each year?"

"Silver – yes, but not gold, which goes out by way of Mexico. The only figures I have are for 1640, when they shipped out a registered consignment worth 256,114,000 pesos."

"Pesos, pieces of eight, ducats, escudos, reals," Diana grumbled, "we have enough sorts of money in the West Indies, and I don't understand any of them!"

Coles laughed and pointed to Leclerc. "You've picked the right man: cross between a banker and a counting house clerk he is. Come on, Jean-Pierre!"

Leclerc gestured modestly, dismissing Coles' description, but Thomas said: "Come on, tell the ladies!"

"Well, let's begin with one English pound. That is roughly equal to one Spanish doubloon or one French pistole. Now, take an English crown, four to the pound or five shillings. That is worth a French crown or a little more than a Spanish piece of eight, whether minted in Potosi, Mexico or Seville."

Diana said, "You were talking of pesos..."

"Ah, yes, with the Spanish one might be talking in Spanish or Portuguese terms. The smallest coin is usually the maravedi. Three hundred and fifty of them are worth an escudo and three hundred and seventy-five will get you a ducat.

"But let's think in terms of reals, pesos and pieces of eight. The real is worth – well, between sixpence and sevenpence in English money. If you have eight reals, you have a 'piece of eight', which is worth – well, four or five shillings in English money. A 'piece of eight' is also a dollar and also a peso!"

Aurelia was frowning. "The amount registered – what does 'registered' mean?"

" 'Registered' is the amount shipped by private individuals – don't forget the king does not own the mines; he simply levies a royalty, 'the royal fifth'. That year there was a total of 256,114,000 pesos registered – which, with a peso valued at five shillings, comes to about sixty-four million pounds..."

Ned nodded as the Frenchman worked out the figures. "I can hardly visualise even a sum like the royalties. The registered amount is quite beyond me – sixty-four million pounds... Are there that many people in the world?"

"Aye," Coles said slowly, "now you see why we wanted to choose an admiral with a brain in 'is 'ead."

"Is there any indication that last year's consignment is anywhere as large as 1640's? That's a quarter of a century ago."

"It's less," Leclerc said. "We hear the consignment gets less each year. Apart from anything else, the mines need quicksilver to extract the silver from the ore – don't ask me why, or how it is used, but they do. The quicksilver comes from Spain in jars. Or it should do."

Ned sighed so deeply that everyone looked at him and Aurelia said questioningly: "*Chéri*?"

"I was thinking that His Most Catholic Majesty really is in a mess. Unless he can find the money to fit out a fleet, he can't send the galleons to Portobelo and the *flota* to Vera Cruz to collect the bullion to pay his debts. But soon unless he can send out quicksilver there will be no silver mined for him to collect when he gets enough money to fit out a fleet…and so on!"

"Thomas knows the feeling," Diana said.

"Ah, my creditors were muttering harsh words like 'Marshalsea' – the debtor's prison," he explained to Leclerc and Gottlieb, "when her ladyship sailed to my rescue."

"His Most Catholic Majesty must be praying for a Lady Diana." Leclerc said, adding with a bow: "I'm thankful we have her!"

"Potosi… Potosi…" Thomas said the name, rolling the word on his tongue. "Two thousand miles from Panama, you say. Pity we can't get at the silver before it arrives at Panama. Two thousand miles, and with no enemy ships in the South Sea I doubt if the Dons bother to escort it."

"Not since Sir Francis Drake," Ned said.

"About one hundred and fifty years ago! Yet even here in the North Sea they still talk of *El Draco*."

Leclerc gave a mirthless laugh. "*El Draco*'s ghost is a good friend of the buccaneers: he has conjured the Spanish into believing that they can *never* win at sea and rarely on land."

"They shouldn't have needed much persuasion," Thomas said.

"Well," Leclerc said, "let us continue to follow the voyage of the bullion. Panama is a poor port, very shallow, but a large and wealthy city. The Viceroy and all the rich merchants live there. The silver is landed and put in the treasury to await the most difficult part of the journey, and I'll leave it there for a moment to outline the story from this side, from the North Sea.

"Those two names tell the story: on our side, our sea is called the North Sea because it is on the north side of the Isthmus; the South Sea is so called because it is on the south side of it. And the Isthmus is one hundred miles wide, and where there aren't swamps and dozens of rivers, like the veins on the back of an old man's hand, there are mountains. Their galleons from Spain arrive in the North Sea, and – as I'm sure you know M. Yorke – they go to Cartagena."

"Why not Portobelo?"

"Ah, because Portobelo suffers from the same problem as Panama: it is very shallow. The galleons draw too much water, and Portobelo has been silting up for years. Now the problem for the Spanish is that they have the bullion in Panama and the ships in Cartagena, but the journey from Panama by land to Cartagena is, as far as bullion is concerned, impossible."

Leclerc finished on a note of triumph, as though he personally had made it impossible, but Ned merely glanced up and said: "So what happens?"

"Well," Leclerc said lamely, "when the galleons are due the bullion is carried from Panama to Portobelo – a tedious journey of a hundred miles over the mountains by donkey and mule – and stored there in one of the forts (Portobelo is well guarded by forts) until the galleons actually arrive."

"In Cartagena," Ned said.

"Yes, in Cartagena. But the word is passed in good time to Portobelo and smaller, shallow-draught ships begin to carry the bullion round to Cartagena, and take back to Portobelo the trade goods brought out by the galleons."

"From where they are carried over the mountains to Panama?"

"Yes, once the galleons arrive and goods are shipped round, the Panama merchants hold a fair in Portobelo, buy and sell the trade goods, and take their purchases back to Panama by donkey and mule. Then I suppose they ship them down the coast to all the other places, like Arica and Potosi."

"I understand that well enough," Ned said. "So the bullion (from our point of view) is vulnerable while being carried by sea from Portobelo to Cartagena."

Leclerc shook his head sadly. "I'm afraid not. The galleons bring with them enough smaller ships to provide strong escorts."

Ned was puzzled. He had been told how the bullion reached Portobelo and was shipped on to the great port of Cartagena; he understood that the galleons went to Cartagena and the bullion was brought to them; and Leclerc said there was little or no chance of getting at the bullion while it was on its way from Portobelo to Cartagena. Quite apart from all that, the king of Spain was not in any case sending galleons to Cartagena or the *flota* to Vera Cruz this year.

"Forgive me," he said politely but firmly. "but I can't see where any of this concerns the buccaneers. The bullion is stored in Panama, on the other side of the Isthmus..."

Leclerc shook his head. "Not all of it. One of our brothers escaping from a prison on the Main and reaching Tortuga found out that all of last year's silver production was brought to Portobelo ready for the galleons which never came."

Ned glanced up and Thomas looked at him quickly to judge his reaction.

"And the Spaniards never carried it back to the Treasury in Panama for safekeeping?"

"No," Leclerc said. "Our brother reported that he had spoken to several witnesses who said the Spaniards have it stored in the dungeon at 'the main castle', which almost certainly is San Gerónimo."

"Witnesses? How reliable is he?"

"He is dead now – he died of consumption contracted in prison. But he was a shrewd man we all knew, loved and trusted. He knew exactly how many cones, wedges and cakes of silver, canvas bags and barrels of coin the witnesses were forced to carry down the steps to the dungeon. The Spaniards didn't trust their Negro slaves..."

"And now you want us to carry it all back up the steps again, eh?"

Leclerc grinned happily. "Forty-seven steps," he said. "Our brother even told us that, too." Suddenly, appalled at Leclerc's ideas, Ned hoped that when they reached Tortuga and all the buccaneers met to vote on his election as their admiral, they would take an instant dislike to him and vote for someone who could plan but had no imagination. For the moment, although he had never seen San Gerónimo Castle at Portobelo, he could picture the smoke of cannon and the unreal popping of musket, the hollow boom of mortar shells and stinkpots exploding, the chilling twang of arrows launched by crossbows... A few thousand Dons defending the year's bullion shipment from the Main.

Back on board the *Griffin*, even Thomas was quiet, as though he had at last realized the enormity of Leclerc's proposal. Diana and Aurelia retired to the tiny cabin that Aurelia called her "dressing-room" and changed their dresses and tidied their hair, and had a hurried whispered discussion about how to cheer up the two men. Because Thomas had told Diana nothing of the buccaneers' Portobelo plan, Leclerc's announcement had been as big a surprise to her as to Aurelia, and she had as many misgivings.

"Thomas is doubtful – I could tell," Diana whispered. "We've always stayed well away from Portobelo because of the fortresses, and Thomas guessed the Spanish had ships there. Even if they're only *petachas* – they're small, fast vessels, used for carrying dispatches – " she explained, "three or four of them could probably take the *Peleus*. Anyway, Thomas would never risk it. Still, there are two dozen buccaneer ships..."

They went back to the main cabin to hear Thomas asking Ned: "What do you think of it?"

"Can we assume the information they have about the bullion is reliable?"

"Yes, because it's from an escaped prisoner they all knew and trusted – even though he has since died."

Ned considered Thomas' answer. There was a certain harsh logic about it, but what allowance did one make for greed? An escaped prisoner's memory of ingots of silver piled in a dungeon might well lead to him lessening the height and thickness of a castle's wall and reduce the size of the garrison.

"Greed creates optimism," Ned said.

"Brings sudden death, too," Thomas agreed. "More lethal than a wheel-lock pistol on a dry day with no wind."

"We've got to get a good chart of Portobelo. And drawings of the forts. Do we need to make scaling ladders? How do we carry the ingots? How big is the garrison – ?"

"Red or white?" Aurelia asked.

"What?" Ned asked, coming back from San Gerónimo.

"Wine."

"Have we fresh limes? I'd prefer juice."

Thomas looked mournful. "The future admiral of the Brethren of the Coast choosing lime juice when offered wine... The last admiral was chosen for the amount of rumbullion he could drink at one sitting."

"And all that brought him was an early death in his hammock and an elaborate funeral at sea," said Diana. "The sharks stayed drunk for a month."

"He was a good man, though," Thomas said defensively.

"Good man! Thomas, you know perfectly well he lost his manhood the day after he was elected. He was frightened of every shadow. He drank so much because only hot liquors drove the shadows away! Towards the end the Brethren wouldn't follow him; they just stayed in port or skulked out on nice little coastal raids."

Ned looked up at Diana with interest. "Go on, my dear. What else do you know about my predecessor?"

"That you should forget all about him; he was disastrous. The Brethren made the mistake of thinking that a man with a great thirst, a very loud voice and a heavy hand to slap backs must be a good leader. They should have talked to his woman."

"What would she have told them?" Thomas demanded.

"That like all thirsty, loud-mouthed back-slappers, he was impotent most of the time and drank, shouted and slapped backs to hide the fact."

"Oh, what saves me then?"

"Your voice is not so loud," Diana said with mock sweetness.

Ned grinned at the two of them. "Then you think that once – " he broke off to listen to the voices on deck, and almost at once Lobb was knocking on the door and calling apologetically: "Sir, there's a canoe from the shore with that Rowlands fellow. Says he has a message from the general."

Ned made a face at Thomas. "I suppose we have to be nice to him now we're officially on the same side." To Lobb he called: "Very well, I'm coming."

He found the young lieutenant perspiring as he waited in the shade of the awning and the moment he saw Ned he stood stiffly to attention. When Ned was five paces away, Rowlands saluted and received a nodded acknowledgement.

"The general, sir," he said, opening his sabretache. "A letter from him." He handed over what was becoming a familiar sight, a piece of folded paper, only this time the blobs of red wax bore no seal. As Ned noticed that, he realized that Heffer's only official seal had borne the impression of the Commonwealth arms. Having no crest of his own, he now had to leave the wax as it dripped on to the letter, instead of applying the usual square of paper and impressing it into the wax. The ramifications of the Restoration, Ned reflected, are widespread...

"Are you expected to take back a reply?"

Ned usually refused to write any replies to Heffer, although he had no particular reason beyond the fact that Heffer always seemed the kind of man with whom one did not commit anything to writing. Rowlands nodded emphatically. "Yes, sir!"

"Wait here then," Ned said and went back to the cabin. He passed the letter to Thomas. "Your turn to read the general's next epistle to the heathen buccaneers."

"Hmm, no seal, eh?" Thomas noted as he broke the wax and unfolded the paper. He finished reading it and passed it to Ned. "You had better read this one: it has a slight odour of possibility about it."

Ned read:

> Gentlemen. In the past there have been false alarms about the activities of the Spanish in Cuba, but I have just received news from an agent in Cartagena which is sufficiently alarming for me to trouble you to come to my headquarters so that you too may question my informant and satisfy yourselves, or otherwise, of his veracity.

Thomas grinned. "You know what makes me think there might be something in this report?"

"He says 'satisfy yourselves or *otherwise*'."

Thomas looked disappointed. "I thought I was being clever..."

"What is all this about?" Diana demanded. "Dinner will be served in an hour; now you talk of going over to see that man."

Ned passed her the letter, which she read and handed to Aurelia. The Frenchwoman read it and said: "Whatever it is, it will certainly delay dinner, and probably our wedding and the visit to Tortuga. So we'll come with you to see the general."

Aurelia noted that the general was in an uncomfortable state of nervousness. It always ruffled him when she and Diana came with the two men. He was obviously far from comfortable with women at the best of times, but having to deal with two women whom clearly he regarded as coming from the upper reaches of the aristocracy reduced a man whose Puritanism was based on jealousy to almost tongue-tied incoherence. That the two women were also buccaneers only clinched Heffer's fervent prayer that they would stay on board their ships.

Ned and Thomas settled the women in their chairs while Heffer blundered about the hot room, hoping almost incoherently that they were comfortable and apologizing for the crudeness of the seats. Ned noticed that four chairs faced the general's desk but a fifth one was placed to one side, on the general's right.

As soon as his guests were seated, Heffer sat down, mopped his long face with a cloth and ran his tongue over his protruding teeth.

"My letter – you will see how unfortunate it is that the *Convertine* has just sailed for England. She would have been able to help us – "

" Nonsense!" Thomas said conversationally. "Her captain was under orders to deliver dispatches to you and return at once for England. He had no choice."

"Well, yes, I suppose so," Heffer admitted. "We seem to be forgotten in London in all the excitement of the King's restoration – "

" More nonsense," Thomas said firmly. "Capturing this island was the idea of Cromwell's two nincompoops, Penn and Venables; you can't even blame my late and unlamented uncle, since he expected 'em to give him Hispaniola, which is ten times as big – though fifty times more useless. Why should the King worry about Jamaica? I'm sure that as far as he's concerned it was stolen from His Most Catholic Majesty just when our King was expressing his gratitude for being allowed to spend part of his exile in Spain..."

"Well, yes, I suppose so," Heffer said yet again, "but if I should let the island fall to a Spanish attack, I should be culpable, never fear: I should be court-martialled and – "

"Oh no, I trust you would have died leading your troops in a desperate defence of Cagway – or have you already renamed it Port Royal?" Ned said innocently. "In fact, if you think there is any chance of losing the island, I should announce the change of name at once: the King will be more impressed that you perished in the siege of Port Royal than the siege of Cagway. 'Cagway' is a dreary name, while 'Port Royal' has a certain grandeur..."

"Yes, yes, I'll do that. Very well gentlemen – ladies and gentlemen," he corrected himself, "I know that I was badly informed in the matter of Santiago de Cuba, but I have now received very bad news from an unimpeachable source."

"The only unimpeachable source," Thomas muttered, "is the Almighty Himself, and I doubt if He confides in you yet."

"Well, yes, but this information comes from one of my own officers who was captured in our unfortunate attack on Hispaniola – "

"Supposing you give us the information first, then the source," Thomas said impatiently.

"Ah yes, let me do that. Well, five Spanish ships are at present in Providencia – that's a small island half-way between here and the Isthmus –with troops from the Portobelo and other towns and orders to embark all the Spanish garrison at Providencia as well, and then land them on the north coast of Jamaica. The ships will then go on to Cuba for supplies and many more troops."

Thomas roared with laughter and when he had wiped his eyes he said to Ned: "I'm sorry, I can just imagine that. The Spanish commander of the squadron lands the troops without trouble – there's nothing to stop him, although certainly the troops have a few mountain ranges to climb – and then goes off to Cuba for the supplies and extra troops. When he arrives he's met with '*What* troops? *What* supplies? *Caramba*, we know nothing about it! Orders from the Viceroy of Panama? He has no jurisdiction here!"

"And that's why the Spanish troops already landed in Jamaica would have to be re-embarked and taken back to the Main: they could not find the enemy, they couldn't cross the mountains, they had nothing to eat or drink, the rain in the hills soaked their powder...oh dear me!"

Heffer looked appealingly at Ned, hoping he would contradict Sir Thomas Whetstone, but Mr Yorke just nodded in agreement.

"What had you in mind for us to do?" Ned asked.

"Well, I was hoping you could sink or capture these ships before they land the Spanish troops on the north coast..."

Ned stared at him and then said coldly: "You have three thousand men doing nothing, apart from the hundred or so building the batteries here on the Palisades. Why don't you move them to the north coast so they can kill or capture the Dons? Good training for them."

Heffer suddenly looked like a man whose adored wife had just walked out of the house saying she really despised him. Ned had expected him to answer that the northern coastline, 165 miles or so from Morant Point in the east to Point Negril in the west, was all cliffs, jungle and mountains and too long and inaccessible for him to be able to cover it and still have enough men to defend Cagway. But Heffer made no such excuse.

"The obvious place to capture them is at sea, surely Mr Yorke?" he said, licking his teeth nervously.

"Perhaps," Ned said, and Aurelia saw at once that he was gently luring Heffer into a position where they could take their leave and sail for Tortuga. "You have some idea how many soldiers the Dons will be carrying in those five ships?"

"My informant says there will be a total of about two thousand soldiers."

"Plus the crews of the ships."

"Of course."

"Say two thousand, five hundred men altogether, at the most."

"About that," Heffer agreed.

"Hmm...two thousand, five hundred in five ships...all heavily armed..." Ned seemed to be murmuring to himself, but now Thomas waited: he too could see what was coming, and Diana turned her face away to hide a smile.

"Against them we have seven ships..."

"Ah indeed," Heffer said cheerfully, "you have a majority."

"...but the Spanish ships are very much bigger, and in men they would outnumber us more than five to one: two thousand, five hundred men against five hundred or so buccaneers."

Heffer looked startled. "But you won't be fighting them hand to hand, surely? Won't you keep your distance and sink the ships so the Spaniards drown?"

"Unfortunately the buccaneer squadron here" (he was pleased with the way the word 'squadron' came out so easily) "is made up of seven merchant ships, all small. Even if we concentrated all our guns on one Spanish ship – an obvious impossibility – we'd never sink her."

"But...but I thought you buccaneers existed by attacking other ships!"

"How did you get that idea?" Ned asked. "We stole the grain you needed for your starving garrison by raiding Riohacha; we dealt with your fears of a Spanish fleet by raiding Santiago. We are sea soldiers, General Heffer, not sailors."

"Bless my soul!" Heffer exclaimed. "I hadn't realized that! Sea soldiers, eh? Yes, a good name."

Ned shrugged. "It is quite obvious when you think about it. Our ships are not built for fighting. As former merchant ships they can carry a certain number of men and a quantity of purchase, but they are not built to carry a number of guns. Apart from that, the buccaneers have no Spanish targets at sea. The plate fleet never appears; the coasting trade along the Main is tiny – most of the vessesl are foreign smugglers.

"So obviously our targets are *places*. We look for gold and silver and jewellery belonging to the inhabitants; we hold the richest to ransom; we rob the churches and the town treasuries. We are not very nice people. We raid from the sea, like the Vikings a few centuries ago. Like *El Draco* more recently."

Heffer wetted his teeth again and said: "Now I understand, but what about these Spanish troops? It's a whole army!"

"Is it *really* a threat? Suppose it does land on the north coast. It'll probably come ashore at Runaway Bay, where the last of the original Spaniards fled to Cuba. Do you think they can threaten Cagway? The harbour? The Palisades? Will they *really* get across the mountains without losing half their men from sickness? It's the rainy season now and humidity makes even a healthy man lethargic."

"You are not going to help me, then," Heffer said flatly.

" 'Are not'? Those aren't the right words! 'Cannot' would describe it exactly. In any case we have much to do."

"What can be more important than saving Jamaica?" Heffer asked, almost wailing.

"It depends on your point of view," Thomas said unexpectedly. "Ned here is going to get married, and that's the most important step in a man's life, for better or worse, as I know to my cost. Then we all have to go to Tortuga, to meet the rest of the buccaneers..."

" '*The rest*'?" Heffer echoed. "Why, how many are there at Tortuga?"

"About twenty ships," Thomas said.

"Bless my soul!" Heffer exclaimed. "Can you not persuade them to come here?" Twenty buccaneer ships, he realized, would be a big reinforcement with the ones already here; twenty-seven or more ships to act as transports for his own troops, if he suddenly wanted to shift them round to the north coast – or indeed, to any of the island's coasts, since there were no roads to speak of.

Ned decided to take over. He looked carefully at Heffer, like a tailor preparing to give an estimate for an elaborate jerkin. "Shall I speak honestly and frankly? Shall I answer your question and risk shocking you? Do you, as a Godfearing former church and cathedral despoiler committed never to laugh on Sundays feel strong enough to hear my words?"

Heffer, already shocked at Ned's emphatic little speech, ran his tongue over his teeth as the muscles of his face worked hard to pull it into a reassuring smile. The smile failed; the best Heffer could manage was a nervous smirk.

"I am a man of the world, Mr Yorke," he said nervously.

"Indeed you are not, or else you would never have been mixed up with Cromwell. You have broken the stained-glass windows in beautiful churches; you have destroyed the stone and wood carvings on tombs, pews reredos and choir stalls. No, don't bother to deny it, because that's all past now, although I loved the beauty. What I want to know, General, is have you ever been inside a brothel and dragged your choice into a back room? Have you ever lurched from one tavern to another too drunk to know where the devil you are? Have you ever cursed and sworn at a potman or innkeeper for being tardy with fresh tankards of ale?"

A distressed Heffer looked first at Diana and then at Aurelia, then back at Diana, to whom he made an appeal. "Miss Diana, it distresses me that there should be such talk in front of ladies. Can you – er, persuade Mr Yorke..."

"Indeed not," Diana retorted. "I'm more interested in hearing your answer!"

"Yes," Aurelia added, "please do not be shy!"

"But what does it matter – I mean, how can it affect the buccaneers if I have never – well, I am a married man!"

"I'll tell you, then," Ned rasped. "You've shut down the only brothel in Cagway, and put a curfew on the taverns. This may suit your soldiers, who were, officially anyway, Roundheads until very recently. The New Model Army may be the New Model Eunuchs who do not want the company of women or the relief of hot liquors. But buccaneers do, *mon général*, buccaneers do! Each arm round a half-naked woman and four tankards of rum in front of him – that's a buccaneer's idea of an evening on shore. And he'll pay for it!"

Heffer looked like a prelate who had just heard five drunken bishops gathered round the pulpit singing blasphemous and obscene songs.

"Are you suggesting that I permit brothels here in Cagway? Permit more taverns to open? Let loose women roam the street? Allow Cagway to become a town of sin, a sanctuary for the devil, a sink of iniquity?"

"Yes," Thomas said promptly, "you'll have to if you expect the buccaneers to use this as a base."

Ned tapped the table. "You'll also have to rename it Port Royal, to honour the King and flatter Thomas and me; you'll have to get those batteries finished by the end of the month; you'll have to allow the brothels and the taverns...then we have something to offer the buccaneers at Tortuga. It may not be enough to tempt them, but you can always increase the offer by not charging customs and excise duty on their liquors and tobacco, and issuing each buccaneer vessel a letter of marque without charge. You might even call it a commission."

"But you are suggesting I do the Devil's work!"

"The Devil doesn't need your help; he would regard it as puny," Ned said. "But *you* need help. You need a squadron of ships based here in Port Royal. Do you expect the buccaneers to live like monks? Because in my limited experience men who live like monks usually fight like monks. To defend Port Royal, Jamaica, and all these other islands against the Spanish, you need men with normal appetites who fight like demons when necessary. And women too."

Aurelia blushed and Diana laughed, and Heffer's face turned crimson, surprising Ned that the man had enough blood in his body.

"Supposing I refuse any brothels or more taverns?" Heffer demanded.

Again Ned shrugged his shoulders. "Five minutes ago I told you that we were going to Tortuga. You suggested that those buccaneers join us here, and we told you the terms. It's of little concern to us whether or not you accept them, because if you don't then we simply forget this conversation, bid you farewell and sail for Tortuga."

"You don't give me much choice," Heffer said, his voice taking on a whining note.

"You have all the choice you need," Ned said unsympathetically. "When you go into a shop and inquire the price of an object, you don't have to buy. There's no obligation. Is Jamaica worth a brothel or two, that's what you have to decide."

Thomas gestured at Heffer, a gesture which could only be interpreted as contemptuous. "Teffler, my dear fellow," he said, reverting to his habit of deliberately getting men's names wrong, "*your* answer to *our* question is really based on *your* answer to *your own* question."

"I don't understand!" the general said nervously.

"It is simple. Ask yourself just one question: Am I defending Jamaica for myself, Cromwell and Puritan principles, or am I defending it for the King and red-blooded Englishmen?"

"Well, it's obvious what I'm trying to do!" Heffer said lamely.

"Indeed, it is," Thomas said harshly. "You are trying to defend it with Puritan principles. The trouble is you don't have Puritan ships to go with 'em. The King doesn't want to be defended with Puritan principles, especially if they drive away Royalists. In fact he may ask awkward questions like 'Why is Teffler still working in Jamaica for Cromwell's ghost?' And if he gets an answer which displeases him, he might decide Teffler is a traitor to the country, and since Teffler is being a naughty boy he'd better be brought home because he don't qualify for General Monck's amnesty, because he committed his offences *after* the Restoration."

"They can never accuse me of that!"

"They most certainly can, and I'd give evidence. For the want of a brothel, the island was lost – oh yes, the King would see the humour of that, and the crowds watching your execution would roar with laughter; not often they get a bawdy hanging."

Ned stood up and gestured to the women. "We must be going; we're wasting the general's time with all this gossip. Sometimes we forget he has command of 3,000 soldiers and the whole island: a heavy responsibility!"

Both women stood and walked towards the door, smiling a farewell over their shoulders. Thomas barked a gruff and friendly goodbye and Ned made his half apologetic. By now Heffer was standing at his desk, his face frozen by the suddenness of their move.

"Please, give me time to consider!" he gabbled, but Ned waved airily as he went through the door and closed it behind him.

They had gone back to the *Peleus* for a change, Aurelia declaring that the dinner being prepared on board the *Griffin* must be ruined by now. The four of them sat in the small cabin which Diana had hung with tapestries she had bought, or Thomas had looted, from the Spaniards. They were bright, the designs influenced by local Indian patterns, and lightened the dark polished mahogany of the panelling. The cot was enormous; the richly woven hammock in which it fitted had been pulled to one side, allowing more room in the cabin, and the heavy table, held to the deck by a chain from the centre of the underside, was just comfortably large enough to seat four.

Diana joined them from the galley with the news that "a dinner worth eating" would be ready in half an hour, and Thomas put carafes and bottles on the table.

"Rumbullion or wine, Ned? Aurelia m'dear, I recommend this white wine. One of my last few dozen of French, but today seems a pleasantly sinful occasion for you and Ned to ignore your quaint prohibition on drinking before the sun has sunk to the horizon."

He poured for both of them and glanced at Diana, who said: "Wine, please; rumbullion is making my skin leathery. Look at Aurelia's wonderful complexion, and she drinks only wine."

"Perhaps it will do something for mine," Thomas said, rasping the side of his beard with his hand. "Now, Leclerc and his friends want to leave for Tortuga tomorrow. We have the question of your wedding. Do we leave for Tortuga before or after the wedding?"

Aurelia said, without even glancing at Ned: "Don't worry about that, Thomas; we will have the ceremony at a suitable time and at a suitable church. Ned is being silly. The church here is a depressing affair built by Heffer from old planks and bits of jetsam. It looks as squalid as the watchman's shelter in the meat market. I refuse to be married there."

"I agree with you," Diana said, looking at Ned. "A wedding is the most special day in a woman's life. We must find you a good church. The Catholic one in St Jago de Vega is no good, although I must admit it's impressive. Heffer's little monstrosity ought to be destroyed, but the site is splendid, overlooking the Palisades north and south. When we have a really big purchase and Heffer's gone, we might be able to afford to build a proper church there in stone. We need bells, gentlemen. Remember that when we raid a town."

"Very well," Thomas said briskly, after raising his glass in a silent toast, "if the bride is not impatient to rush to the altar because of the lack of a church, let's consider the problem raised by the guardian of our morals, General Teffler."

Diana groaned."Why spoil good wine and a good dinner by thinking about that sheep's carcass?"

"My dear, that man is making a problem for us."

"I don't see why," Diana said acidly. "For his wife, perhaps; but he is not bothering me."

"Think, woman," Thomas said impatiently. "The buccaneers have elected Ned their admiral – we just have to visit Tortuga to confirm it. We have enough information to plan a most fantastic attack on Portobelo that will make us rich beyond the dreams of even a king of Spain. Now all we want is a good base. We've found this place, but if that fool Teffler insists on running it like a monastery, we'll never get the Brethren here and we'll have to find another. Use Tortuga, perhaps."

"Forget Portobelo for the moment," Diana said."What about all those Spanish troops arriving at the island of Providencia, and collecting the garrison for an attack on Jamaica?"

Thomas drained his glass and reached for the onion-shaped bottle of rumbullion. The dark-green glass made the liquid inside seem black, and Thomas pulled out the cork with care. "We're getting short of cork," he told Diana. "We must find a sheet of it and have the men cut out some more bungs."

"What about those Spanish troops attacking Jamaica," Diana repeated, ignoring talk of corks.

Thomas shook his head. "They're no concern of ours. If we can't use Port Royal as a base, then it's none of our affair. We have Tortuga, or we can make a rendezvous where we want: the Isle of Pines, the Queen's Gardens, Ile de Vache..." He named the island at the southwestern corner of Cuba, the scattering of cays on the south side of central Cuba, and an island off the southwestern side of Hispaniola. "Or wherever you will: just name a place!"

"Don't bother to drink any more," Diana said. "Already you talk and think like a drunken man. Tortuga is a bad anchorage and depresses me. Ned, say something!"

Ned grinned at Diana's exasperation with Thomas and then glanced across at Aurelia, to see if she was still irritated with him. She smiled and the cloud over his head slid away. "What do you think about it all?" she asked.

"Yes, come on, Ned," Diana said, "tell us before dinner is served, because you'll eat and drink so much you'll want to doze afterwards."

"'Well', as General Teffler would say, I'm prepared to lead the Brethren, if they'll have me, but we have to move fast. Very fast. Not just the seven ships here, but all the buccaneer fleet."

"What's the hurry, Ned?" Thomas twiddled his beard and went cross-eyed looking down at it."There won't be a plate fleet out here until next year at the earliest. The Dons aren't going to carry all those ingots back to Panama; obviously they think it's safe enough where it is."

"We need to hurry for two reasons, perhaps more. Let me jump ahead for a moment. We'll have Port Royal as our base eventually – as soon as Heffer gets really frightened, he'll agree to make Port Royal less of a monastery.

"But the main reasons we need to hurry are that first, as soon as the buccaneers have a real success under my leadership, they'll do whatever I tell 'em, which means that the Brethren are united and strong. (Although they won't realize it they'll then be in a much more powerful position to bargain with people like Heffer, and infinitely stronger when they demand ransom from the Spanish.)"

Aurelia said proudly: "*Chéri*, you sound like Machiavelli! Do you think you can mould those scoundrels? Because they are scoundrels, you know: brave scoundrels and good-natured ones, but how do you say, feckless, and with no loyalty except to the man who finds them the biggest purchase!"

Ned shrugged his shoulders and grinned. "Do you seek loyalty in a shopkeeper? He's trying to sell you the least quantity of the lowest quality for the most money. You're loyal to him only as long as you can't find a shopkeeper who sells cheaper!"

Aurelia laughed and agreed. "Now let's hear your second reason."

"The second is very obvious. We've more chance of attacking Portobelo successfully if we do it while most of its garrison is away. It's unlucky for Heffer that they'll be attempting to recapture Jamaica, but I don't think he has much to fear. Anyway at Portobelo we shall give the Dons a terrible fright. We could perhaps seize the island of Providencia, if its garrison has been taken away: who knows, Providencia – I prefer the proper name, Old Providence – might make us better base than Port Royal. I haven't seen it, but the chart shows it's half the distance from Jamaica to the Main and Isthmus."

"Aye, it is," Thomas said. "You know, Ned, it's a long time since I heard anyone talking such sense. How about that dinner, girl? Can't you hustle them in the galley?"

CHAPTER **FIVE**

Thomas and Diana stood with Ned and Aurelia on the quarterdeck of the *Griffin* as she made the last tack up the Chenal de Tortuga which would bring them into Cayona, which was no more than a hamlet on the edge of the bay forming one of the two anchorages of the island.

"You can see how it got its Spanish name, *Tortuga de mar,*" Thomas said.

Aurelia laughed excitedly. "Yes, when we first saw the island it looked in the distance just like a turtle sleeping on the water. I half expected it to dive and swim away!"

The mainland of Haiti, forming the south side of the channel, was covered in thick jungle, a green mat right down to the coast where occasional strips of sand, dazzling now in the sunlight, showed the beaches between outcrops of rock.

Tortuga, oval-shaped and lying five miles away along the coast like a large marrow, stretched between West Point, which they had just passed to larboard, and East Point. The southwestern corner had a remarkable red cliff, like a scar, and Ned and Aurelia could see that the south side of the island justified the name given to the anchorage off Cayona, *Rada de Tierra Baja,* because the land was low but like a vast wedge it sloped up rocky and heavily forested to the north coast facing the Atlantic, which Thomas said was a mass of cliffs and rocks. There were only two main peaks. The island was like so many others in the Greater and Lesser Antilles: a layer of soil spread thinly on rocky hills and just supporting knee-high, dark-green bushes and occasional banks of trees.

Even from this distance Ned could see dozens of the small trees which the French called *chandelle anglaise,* the branches of which burned like a candle and because of their steady flame were used by the fisherman when trying their luck at night. Its dark-grey bark helped treat fevers, though not as well as cinchona. He could see plenty of aloes growing, too, the West Indies' most popular herb. According to many, if the aloe leaf, used as a dressing or boiled or soaked to prepare an infusion, would not cure the ill, then the sick person was doomed. Another tree which grew freely here, twenty or thirty feet high with a dense but drooping crown, was *lignum sanctum*. Almost alone the blue-flowered tree could account for Tortuga's popularity among the buccaneers; an extract from it was used by physicians and witch doctors alike for treating venereal diseases, as well as ordinary fevers – it was famous for bringing on the sweat.

"The buccaneers," Thomas said, gesturing to many masts looking like rushes on the far side of a pond and now coming into sight. "Looks as though most of the ships are here."

"And no doubt hurriedly getting ready for action," Diana commented. "They won't have recognized the *Griffin,* although –" she looked astern " – by now they might be able to see the *Perdrix* and the other three, which they know well enough."

"There's the fort," Thomas said, pointing above the anchorage. "Built by a mad genius!"

It was perched high on a hill and surrounded by almost perpendicular rocks, as though a giant had put a completed fort down on top of a steep hill beyond the ability of even a wild boar to climb. The fort had only two guns, but they covered the anchorage, which was simply a dent in the coast almost completely closed off by a reef running alongside it, a low and wide brown wall of coral over which waves broke like waving sheets as the wind swept them westward through the channel.

"There's a strong current," Thomas explained. "One entrance through the reef is at this end" – he pointed over the *Griffin*'s bow as she thrashed northeastward – "but the deepest channel is at the other end. Anyway, you can't get trapped here: if an enemy appears at one end of the anchorage, you simply bolt out the other!"

Four or five boats were already leaving some of the anchored vessels and pulling towards the reef. "The welcoming party," Diana said. "Once they hear how much purchase Leclerc and his friends brought back from Santiago, they'll settle down to a few days' drinking: Leclerc bought up all the rumbullion he could in Jamaica!"

Ned nodded but said: "Before they start drinking we need them to vote for me leading them. I want to be making plans for our next expedition once we know how many men we have and while they are sleeping off their celebration..."

Thomas shrugged his shoulders, unwilling to commit himself to their sobriety. "Shall I help Lobb with the pilotage? I've been in here a couple of times, and with your draught you'll have to use the eastern entrance and anchor as soon as maybe once you get inside."

By now the *Griffin* was the leader of a long snake of ships: this last tack up to the entrance to Cayona had now been copied by the rest of the little flotilla as the entrances to the reef opened up. The *Perdrix* was now immediately astern of the *Griffin*; then came the *Peleus*, the Dutchman Gottlieb's *Dolphyn*, Charles Coles' *Argonauta*, Edward Brace's *Mercury* and finally Saxby with the *Phoenix*.

Ned watched as Lobb gave orders to drop the big and baggy jib, using only the mainsail to get the *Griffin* through the eastern entrance, which was simply a gap in the line of the coral reef which grew up within a few inches of the surface like staghorns, flat-topped and brown under the water.

The buccaneers' vessels anchored behind the reef were small: he was surprised to see that none was as big as Leclerc's *Perdrix*, The *Griffin* was by far the largest vessel present, followed by the *Peleus* and then the *Phoenix*. He recognized three or four of the hulls as Spanish: like Coles' *Argonauta* they must be prizes. Like Ned Yorke's *Phoenix*, he reminded himself, which until recently was the *Nuestra Señora del Carmen*... There were two Dutchmen, apple-cheeked bows and beamy, probably shallow-draughted and built for the shoal waters of the Netherlands coast.

Then the *Griffin* was inside the reef, the water calm, although there was nothing to shelter Cayona or the anchored ships from the wind, and a sudden popping and booming startled Ned until he realized that the men in the boats were firing muskets and several of the ships were letting off cannon to greet the *Perdrix* as she came through the reef. Soon he heard the honking of men blowing horns made from conch shells.

"They waste a lot of powder and breath, but they mean well!" Thomas grinned, watching the *Griffin*'s seamen let go the anchor as the ship turned head to wind and lost her way. "It's good to be back among these scoundrels!"

Diana wagged a warning finger. "Whetstone – watch the rumbillian and mobbie. Especially the mobbie!"

Aurelia turned to her. "How do they *keep* mobbie?"

"They don't; it doesn't get a chance of being kept, even if it could be, if you know what I mean! No, they boil their potatoes into a mash early in morning, strain through a bag with a little water and drink it before nightfall, so it doesn't have time to ferment. It's ruined by midnight."

Ned sat on the barrel of the *Perdrix*'s windlass and looked at the men round him. All the captains of buccaneer ships, including Saxby, were sitting or standing on the French vessel's fo'c'sle, while Thomas perched beside him. Even without Thomas it would be hard to find twenty-six more contrasting men. Each was tanned; few looked as though they had seen, let alone been attended by, a barber for several years. Even the two English captains he already knew could not be more unalike: Brace of the *Mercury* was thin and angular, his red beard and red hair carefully combed; Cole of the *Argonauta* was stocky with blond hair, cheerful blue eyes and a hearty manner. He looked around him with the air of a man trying to find an excuse for a celebration. The single Spanish captain, Secco, although black-haired and with a sallow, almost swarthy skin, was as neat as Brace: his beard was trimmed to a point, his hair held back by a band of red cloth.

Several of the Frenchmen had the small, slightly flat faces with hard black eyes that Ned regarded as typical of the nation. Brace could only be an Englishman, Gottlieb a Dutchman with his fair hair, moon face and widely spaced eyes, Secco – well, Spanish, Portuguese or Italian. Leclerc could only be a Frenchman. Thomas – yes, typical of a kind of Englishman.

Their dress was bizarre. If twenty-six men had undressed and thrown their clothes into a basket, mixed everything up and then donned what first came to hand, Ned decided the result would look something like this group of buccaneers. Secco wore black breeches and no stockings, but instead of a jerkin he wore a tattered blouse of white cotton which had an ominous stain on the left shoulder, like a rust mark. The blood of the original Spanish owner which had marked the material and defied laundering? Brace could pass for a country parson with stern principles, Coles would be the host at an expensive tavern. Leclerc? A well-educated glutton fallen on hard times and now tutor to a rich man's son? And Thomas? Well, in mustard-coloured breeches, purple jerkin, and a wide-brimmed hat with a large red plume round its crown, he looked very much what he was.

Diana and Aurelia stood over on the larboard side, deliberately keeping apart from all the men to emphasize that they were merely onlookers. This resulted from a warning by Leclerc: many of the captains, he said would not at this stage regard women as worthy of joining any conversation, let alone taking any part in planning.

Leclerc had grinned when he said: "It would be better to let the captains remain like Mr Yorke and Sir Thomas – under the impression that where the ladies were concerned they make the decisions!"

Leclerc had surprised both Ned and Thomas with the news that none of the Tortuga captains knew of the Portobelo proposal: the information about the bullion was known only to the four privateers on the Santiago raid, because they had picked up the man escaping from the Main. Ned had at once asked Leclerc to keep the business secret for the time being and the Frenchman agreed, saying that there was no need even to ask Gottlieb, Coles or Brace to keep silent.

The first hour on board the *Perdrix* had been a time for meeting each of the other captains. There was none of the drawing-room and very little of the tavern about it. They had heard from Leclerc and the others about the Santiago purchase and were obviously anxious to size up this man Yorke, who came as a stranger. He had two recommendations – one was from Leclerc and the other three, who had seen him in action, planning and leading the Santiago raid, and the second was his being a friend of Sir Thomas.

Not more than eight or nine of them actually knew Sir Thomas, but what they had heard was good: he was a bonny fighter. The only thing that puzzled some of them was that up to now Sir Thomas had always preferred to sail alone, except for his woman, who, Leclerc had been quick to report, was such a one as to dream about. Sir Thomas could have joined the Brethren a long time ago, but he went his own way with the *Pearl*, now renamed the *Peleus*. Leclerc was also the source for information about Mr Yorke's woman, whose reputation for beauty, bravery and intelligence lost nothing from the fact that she too was French and a Protestant like Leclerc.

Ned had kept a careful count as he met the captains. There were twenty-five buccaneer ships altogether, so that the *Griffin*, *Phoenix* and *Peleus* made a total of twenty-eight. Nine of the captains were French, eight British, five Dutch, two Portuguese and one, unlikely as it seemed, but obviously completely trusted by the others, was Spanish, the bearded Secco, who spoke good English of the kind that came from an education, not just usage.

With no awning rigged, the *Perdrix*'s deck was hot, and from the smell of rotting food it was clear that the seas in the Windward Passage had not been rough enough on the way up from Jamaica to give the decks a good wash down.

The six other English captains (Ned was irritated to find he was adopting the habit of using "English" when the person might be Scots, Welsh or Irish) had gathered round Coles and Brace, but obviously their questions were quickly answered because they soon mingled with Thomas and Ned. Similarly the four other Dutchmen questioned Gottlieb, leaving only the two Portuguese and the Spaniard with no countrymen of their own to reassure them.

Both Portuguese spoke English and soon cornered Ned with the Spaniard, who commented on Ned drinking wine instead of rumbullion.

"The influence of the French lady, eh?" he said, gesturing at Aurelia.

"It's Spanish wine," Ned said "from Santiago!"

"Ah," Secco said wistfully, "I should have been there."

"Just for the wine," one of the Portuguese said. "For the wine alone it would have been good. Rumbullion sits heavily, drunk month after month. Well, Mr Yorke, you enjoyed Santiago?"

Ned shrugged his shoulders and said casually: "There was no real fighting. We made a good choice for purchase, but we sharpened our cutlasses for nothing."

The second Portuguese sniffed. "I go on a raid for the purchase, not the glory, Mr Yorke," he said heavily. "I don't like my men being killed or wounded."

Ned nodded and smiled. The Portuguese, in reacting as he expected, enabled him to make a point without being suspected of cowardice. "I agree with you; better a bag of doubloons than a sack of glory, but the Spanish aren't frightened enough yet."

"Frightened?" echoed the Portuguese.

"Yes – but I'll explain that when I talk to you all."

"Very well," said the Portuguese. "But tell me, Mr Yorke, how do you go on a raid with the women? I hear all three of your English ships carried women to Santiago."

The man was curious, not critical; and the other two nodded, to establish a friendly interest. Ned decided in a moment that genuine interest deserved a genuine answer, and there might come a time when all the women might be in some danger and benefit from the buccaneer captains knowing they were not just kept whores.

"Do you know how I became a buccaneer?" he asked the men, and noticed two Frenchmen joining the group.

Secco shook his head on behalf of the rest. "Tell us, please," he asked courteously.

"I was a planter in Barbados, a Royalist. The lady over there" – he nodded – towards Aurelia " – was the wife of a neighbour. A bad and cruel man. He's since been killed – not by me," he added hastily, but then realized that these men would have regarded "bad and cruel" as being reason enough.

"Well, the Roundheads drove me out: I escaped with my ship, the lady and all my plantation workers that wanted to come. They included Saxby, who now commands the *Phoenix*.

"At the time we left, the lady's husband was still alive; in fact he took over my estate. And while we sailed away, trying to make up our minds what to do, we met Sir Thomas Whetstone."

"And that decided you," the Spaniard said with a grin.

"It certainly helped. But the lady really persuaded me. Anyway, it led to Santiago, and when we returned to Jamaica she and I heard that her husband had been killed, which meant we could get married."

"So she is your wife, then." Secco said.

"No, not yet."

"You are a cautious man, eh?"

"No," Ned said, "our wedding was delayed."

"That is bad. With such a lovely woman it is not good to delay."

Ned touched the Spaniard's shoulder reassuringly. "You gentleman have caused the delay: in Jamaica, Leclerc wanted us to leave for Tortuga at once, so..."

"Ah, we'll have to build you a special church! But what about Sir Thomas? He is not married, surely?"

"He has a wife in England – an unpleasant woman, I believe, so he cannot marry the present lady. They are very much in love, as you can see. They have been together for a long time: they left England in the *Peleus*."

"That used to be the *Pearl*," Secco said as if pedantically wanting the record to be correct while also establishing that he had known Sir Thomas for a long time.

"Yes, she was the *Pearl*. Anyway, they are happy just being together."

"Yes, a priest can't make a couple happy," the Spaniard said gravely, "he can only make it legal. But tell us about the woman of the *Phoenix*: we hear she is an enormous woman of enormous appetites."

Ned smiled at this description of Mrs Judd. "She worked for me in Barbados. Her friend was the foreman of the plantation – that man over there." He nodded towards Saxby. "The foreman acted as the master of my ship, the *Griffin*, when we needed to use her, so the pair of them came – with most of my other people – when we left. Then we captured a Spanish prize and Saxby took command of her. I now command the *Griffin*."

"Why did you not command the *Griffin* at the beginning?" the Spaniard asked shrewdly.

Ned thought for a moment, then decided to be frank. "When we left Barbados, I knew very little about seamanship. I have learned quickly because I had good teachers."

"Enough to lead the Brethren?"

Again Ned hesitated. "Are you sure you need a *seaman* to lead you?" he asked, speaking clearly so that the three men, and the others who were now gathering around, should hear him distinctly.

"Why, of course!" the Spaniard said. "We are all seamen; we use our ships for our raids!"

Ned knew that a wrong emphasis now or a misunderstood phrase could make just one of these men angry, and then the whole point of his visit to Tortuga would be lost.

"I've been thinking about all that," Ned said, working a judicial tone into his voice. "Certainly one needs fine seamanship to sail back and forth in these seas; to navigate from here to the Main and find exactly the town you intend to attack. But what happens when you arrive at the town and anchor?"

"What happens? Well," said Secco, "we get into our boats and land and capture it!"

"Supposing it has forts, and needs a few days' siege?"

The Spaniard held his hands out, palms uppermost. "So we besiege it!"

"What about capturing Spanish ships, then?"

"We don't, *señor*, because there haven't been any Spanish ships in these waters worth attacking. There's no point in trying to seize a *guardacosta* because he has no purchase on board, and the plate fleets are too strongly defended for our little ships. And anyway there has been no plate fleet for two years."

Ned turned so that he faced the majority of men. The meeting that was to have taken place on the fo'c'sle and ended with them voting was taking place now, and he saw no reason to postpone it.

"I come as a stranger," he said, "but since Leclerc spoke to me in Jamaica, I have been considering the position of the Brethren.

I saw how four of your ships behaved at Santiago, and I liked what I saw.

"But I will be completely honest with you. I think your whole approach to buccaneering is wrong. Very wrong."

Thomas, Aurelia and Diana were watching the group of men. Close by the ship a pair of terns quarrelled noisily over a small fish; a pelican splashed into the water. A halyard slatted against the mast, rattling in the wind with the insistent noise of a woodpecker. All these isolated noises suddenly seemed very loud.

The Spaniard glanced round at the other buccaneers, as if seeking approval to act as their spokesman.

"Wrong *señor*? Why, we are still alive!"

"Alive, yes, thanks to your own bravery and probably luck – "

"Who are you to say we are wrong?" Leclerc suddenly interrupted, having realized that he might be held responsible if his protégé caused a fight.

Thomas Whetstone strode into the centre of the group of men, his beard seeming to bristle and his eyes glinting.

"I'll tell you who he is to say you're wrong: he's the man who thought of the raid on Santiago, planned it and led it. I have not heard of the Brethren ever attempting, let alone successfully carrying out, such a raid. So, brothers, you should listen to him. You don't have to agree, you don't have to act, but listen!"

"Very well, M. Yorke," Leclerc said warily, "we will listen."

Ned looked around at the couple of dozen faces. Yes, indeed they belonged to a motley collection of men; he could see a half-drunken Falstaff at the head of an army press gang leading them fettered out of a sleepy and unsuspecting town. But he had their attention! Yet did he want it? The picture of Kingsnorth was suddenly bright in his mind: he longed to be back, but he knew Aurelia did not want to see Barbados for a long time. He had been turned into a sea gypsy by the Roundheads; it remained to be seen whether he would (or could?) ever return to the old life. But, now he looked at them, did he really want to lead this rabble? Did he want to be a sober Falstaff? Why not just the *Griffin* and the *Phoenix*, and the *Peleus* if Thomas wanted to come along? Surely better to plan raids on small towns, with no need to share the purchase among this crowd. No chance of treachery, everyone understanding all aspects of the particular raid… No, he wanted no part of this crowd. The decision was sudden, but he could see no alternative. He was not going to lead a rabble, of that he was sure.

"Gentlemen, I would like you to come over to the *Griffin*, where there will be plenty to eat and drink, because at dawn the *Griffin* returns to Jamaica."

"Dawn… Jamaica?" Leclerc was dumbfounded. "But you have only just arrived in Tortuga, M'sieur. We have not even voted…"

"I have no wish to lead you," Ned said amiably. "I thought I had, but now I've met you all, I have changed my mind. Not," he added quickly, "that I think any the less of you: simply that I now realize that you are quite content with the scale of what you are doing, and do not wish to change anything."

A flustered Leclerc took over the role of spokesman. "You made a statement and we simply asked for details. If you think we are going about our work the wrong way, then please tell us the right way!"

"Very well, I'll give you my views, but that doesn't change my attitude towards leading you. The person you eventually choose as the leader may disagree with me.

"I asked our Spanish friend here about your work. He said you sail to a town and raid it, but there were no Spanish ships at sea – or very few, anyway – for you to attack.

"Now, just consider a raid on a Spanish coastal town. You sail in, anchor, land on the beach from your boats, and attack the town." He paused for several long moments, to be sure of their attention. "Tell me, what are you when you attack the town, sailors or soldiers? Which skill is the most useful, furling a sail or knowing how to outflank a crowd of Spaniards making a defence in the *plaza*?"

Again he paused. He knew each man was now imaging a raid, reliving the wild rush from the boats to the town, taking care to keep the slow-match alight for the muskets, the hurried search through pockets for the spanning keys to prepare the wheel-lock pistols. Soldier or sailor? *Soldat ou matelot? Soldado o marinero*? And whatever they were in Portuguese.

Suddenly Leclerc nodded violently. "Yes, we need both skills, and I admit the soldier is the most important!"

Several men murmured in disagreement and Ned said: "Surely the point is that each ship needs enough seamen to sail her, but the extra men should have particular training in the art of soldiering on land."

"Who will train the soldiers – if one agreed that they needed it?" the Spaniard asked cautiously.

"We have a garrison of three thousand soldiers at Jamaica. If you agreed to make Jamaica your base, I am sure the general commanding the garrison would be only too glad to supply instructors. Perhaps even extra muskets, pistols, pikes and powder for particular raids."

Rideau, one of the French captains, said pleasantly but indicating the point was important: "That English general has turned Cagway into a convent. Only a few taverns and no 'houses'. One feels he expects us to use our purchase to buy English hymnbooks."

"But where else can you find such a good natural and friendly harbour?" Thomas asked.

"Agreed, agreed. Here, if we get a storm, let alone a hurricane, we all end up on the beach. Cagway has that great advantage." Rideau grinned. "But if we went there, and you were our leader, you could persuade the general about the 'houses, eh?"

Ned said: "Why don't you persuade him yourselves? Tell him you'll help defend Cagway – I think he is going to rename it Port Royal – and things might change. Slowly, but they'll change. Remember, he was one of Cromwell's generals and he's forgotten how to laugh."

"So you will lead us?" Leclerc said.

"No," Ned said. "I will speak to the general for you, but you must find another leader."

After giving a deep cough, Thomas said: "The ladies want to talk to Mr Yorke, so please excuse us for a few minutes. Anyway, I expect you will all want to discuss among yourselves what's just been said."

Ned followed Thomas to where Aurelia and Diana were sitting with, he noted, all the demureness of well brought up young ladies likely to have the vapours at the sound of a cuss word – until one realized that they were sitting gracefully not on a silk-covered settee but the breech of a gun.

Thomas grinned at Ned. "You've got them eating out of your hand," he said. "That was a clever idea, telling them that you didn't want to lead them after all!"

"I don't," Ned said.

Diana and Aurelia turned and stared at him. The Frenchwoman was the first to speak.

"What's the matter *chéri*? Why did you suddenly change your mind? Half an hour ago you were proud at being asked!"

"I suddenly realized I'd have to give these dolts the reason for every move we make on a raid. That's not leading; that's being chairman of a committee," he said stubbornly. "And I thought of Kingsnorth. I want to go back there one day."

"If you go back to Kingsnorth," Aurelia said quietly, "you will have to go alone." None of them had any doubt about how much it cost her to speak those dozen words. No one doubted she meant every one of them.

Diana said quickly: "Ned, none of us is ready for life on land again. And supposing the Restoration doesn't last? Supposing General Monck is overthrown and the Roundheads rally and force the King to escape to France again? The King hasn't had time to prove himself. It seems his only chance rests on the people's boredom with the Puritans. Not a very strong foundation. He needs time – a year or two."

"And what about Jamaica?" Thomas added bluntly. "Unless we get the buccaneers to move there, I reckon the Dons will find out just how vulnerable it is. With Heffer as stupid as he is, if they keep landing troops along that north coast... Don't forget, the one thing the Dons can muster is plenty of troops. Not many ships to carry 'em admittedly, but landing a thousand a month at Runaway Bay could see Heffer thrown out in six months."

Ned found the fate of Jamaica, General Heffer and the entire garrison was of little interest, because he had seen in Aurelia's eyes the answer he had to give. She had been saying for a long time that the *Griffin* was her home; that she did not want to return to plantation life in Barbados. He had not really believed her; women did not lead this sort of life – or rather, Diana was an exception. But the hurt look in Aurelia's eyes a few moments ago had finally convinced him. She had thought he had let himself be persuaded to become the leader of the buccaneers so that he would stay at sea and she with him. Then suddenly, without any warning, she had heard him tell this polyglot crowd that he did not want to lead them. She thought he had betrayed her. She thought – the Devil take it – he had! But there was still time to make amends.

"Go tell 'em, Ned," Thomas said. "Sea soldiers, that's what we've got to be. Tell 'em Ned, they're on the brink of accepting it. Sea soldiers."

CHAPTER **SIX**

Standing up on the barrel of the windlass and looking down at the buccaneers, Ned found that he was having to take important decisions with conflicting ideas bouncing round his head like peppercorns in a mill. Item, lead the Brethren – and be condemned to roam the seas, never to walk the boundaries of his own property and watch seed sprouting and giving fruit. Item, return to Barbados – and lose Aurelia, because she had just said she would not go back. Item, carry on buccaneering with just the *Griffin, Phoenix,* and *Peleus* (assuming Thomas would come with them). Item, buy a plantation in Jamaica (or, rather, get a grant of land and clear it and start a plantation) knowing the new King might give the islands back to the Spaniards, or the Spaniards might send out a fleet to recapture it (a fleet which could collect the waiting bullion and at the same time retrieve Jamaica).

The buccaneers were patiently watching him, and then Leclerc called out: "Tell us, M. Yorke, if we vote unanimously for you, will you lead us?"

Just say what you think, he told himself, and then realized that even now he was far from sure what he thought. At least, he knew what he was thinking – half a dozen contradictory ideas – but had no idea, despite Aurelia, what he had decided.

"Well, even though it's not Sunday, you're going to hear a sermon," he said, keeping his voice crisp and carefully avoiding any emotion. "First, as I've just told you – at least, I think you all heard, but I'll repeat it – you are soldiers, not sailors. Buccaneering means attacking Spanish towns and large villages, and ransoming the leading citizens, relieving the wealthy of their gold and silver plate, and such like. A few sailors are needed to sail your ships to the new target. But the true buccaneer, the man who gets the purchase and brings it on board, must be a well-trained soldier.

"You are *not* well-trained soldiers," he told them flatly. "You are a noisy rabble. Brave but so untrained that you forget to light your slow-match and are incapable of carrying out orders. Anything distracts you. Men ordered to seize the town hall forget about it if they see a tavern on the way: they'll stop and get drunk.

"Do you want to be buccaneers, collecting a good purchase and bringing it on board your ships, or are you simply satisfied to be drunken looters? Four of your ships had a good purchase from Santiago, but that was because every man had orders and most – most, but not all – carried them out.

"You should regard yourselves as sea soldiers. You should drill with musket, pistol, sword, halberd, pike and cannon. Each of you should know how to lay a train of powder to blow up a building; you must learn how to make petards and secure them to the doors of fortresses. Building scaling ladders and using them must be second nature. You must know how to light and throw grenades so you blow up the enemy, not yourself because of your fumbling."

He paused and looked round at the men. To his surprise they were not looking resentful; instead they seemed sheepish, like boys just caught by a farmer with their pockets full of his apples. They were listening; they were *accepting* his criticisms. Were they accepting his suggestions, though?

Leclerc said: "Who can train us, then? Obviously we don't know about all this soldiering. We need instructors."

"They're available in Jamaica, as I've told you. The general commanding the garrison will provide them."

"But that means going to Jamaica," Leclerc exclaimed.

"Of course it does! And it gives you as a base one of the finest, most protected anchorages in the West Indies. Do you want to stay in this rathole, sheltered by a narrow reef? One hurricane, perhaps even a storm will see every one of your ships cast up on that beach over there. In Jamaica, the general is bulding forts to defend the entrance to Cagway, or Port Royal, as it is to be called. We've given him the Spanish guns, shot and powder we took from Santiago. Or perhaps you prefer to rely on that crazy fortress up there with its two guns? You don't keep men on watch so it'd take you an hour to fire a single shot – assuming the shot haven't rusted and swollen so they jam in the bore, or that the powder isn't damp, or that the wood of the carriages hasn't rotted."

"Tortuga's served us well up to now," protested Coles.

"Yes, indeed, Tortuga has served you – but you've had no hurricanes and the Spanish have never attacked. By the same token your present methods of buccaneering serve you. They've never brought you a decent purchase, but they serve!"

"What do you propose then?" Coles asked.

Ned noted the word "propose". Not "suggest", which could mean an idea from someone who might not stay to carry it out, but "propose". To him, that implied a plan that he was expected to stay and carry out.

"Move to Port Royal and train, and don't embark on any raid until the training is complete."

"But there aren't enough women and wine in Port Royal," Brace protested. "We're not monks!"

Ned turned to the north and looked carefully at the village of Cayona and then he stared across the so-called "Low Lands" on either side of it. Then he turned to inspect the mainland shore.

"They must be well concealed among the rocks and bushes," he said. "At first glance a stranger cannot see any streets lined with taverns and brothels. One cannot even see a street. Nor even a single trollop waiting in the shade of a tree."

"Aye, true enough," Brace admitted, "but Port Royal's no better."

"Oh yes, it is. The streets are there and so are the taverns and the brothels. Wait – " he told Brace " – let me finish. They are there but closed at present. Although in the future the general may not officially permit brothels, if they happen by chance to reopen I think I can guarantee he won't close them again."

"*Mon Dieu,* how can you guarantee that?" Leclerc exclaimed.

"If I was the leader of the Brethren, I should call on the general and make a bargain. I should say that if my ships were there at a time of danger to Jamaica, the buccaneers would help defend it. In return, Port Royal must be allowed to grow like any other port. I would also need some guarantees about customs duties and excise tax on the liquor and tobacco we need, and instructors for the training of my sea soldiers…"

"Do you now mean, then, you will in fact consider being our leader?" Leclerc asked quickly.

"Yes, – providing you accept my terms."

Leclerc leapt up onto the barrel of the windlass, showing a remarkable agility for such a plump man. "Brothers, you have heard M. Yorke's ideas. Have you any more questions to ask him?"

No one spoke as Leclerc pointed at each man in turn.

"Then let us vote. I propose M. Yorke as our new admiral, and the man to whom we give our allegiance. First, hands up those *against* him."

The men stood still, waiting.

"Hands up those in his favour."

Every man raised an arm and a few laughingly lifted both.

"I declare M. Edward Yorke unanimously elected admiral of the Brethren of the Coast," Leclerc said, speaking slowly and clearly. He repeated it in French and Spanish, and apologized to the Dutchmen and the two Portuguese, who assured him they understood.

Leclerc turned to Ned and held out his hand. As the two men shook, Leclerc said, "You should appoint your own second-in-command. Because he must work closely with you, it's better he's a friend than someone forced on you by popular vote."

Ned looked round at the buccaneers, who began cheering him. He held up his hand for silence. "Thank you. I hope you've made a good choice. As far as my second-in-command is concerned, most of you know Sir Thomas..." Ned said. "In the meantime, I give my first order: tomorrow at one hour after dawn we sail for Port Royal."

As the *Griffin* came head to wind off the governor's jetty at Port Royal, with twenty-seven other buccaneer ships following her like the tail of a kite, Aurelia waited until she heard the anchor splash down and then said: "You know, I feel as though I'm coming home again!" She waved towards the Blue Mountains to the north, now a pearl grey in the early light, and then across to the flat sand-spit. "Do you realize that the second and third times you came in here were triumphs?"

Ned, thinking of his forthcoming visit to General Heffer, looked blankly at her, and she explained: "The second time you brought back the maize from Riohacha and the prize which Saxby now commands, and the third you were returning from Santiago. Now, for the fourth, you're a species of admiral!"

Ned grinned and gestured astern. "And I've brought along a crowd of scoundrels whom Heffer will consider as having only one aim, to turn Port Royal into a vast bordello!"

"I haven't inspected the town," Aurelia said, "but isn't there a shortage of women?"

Ned shook his head. "On the contrary. Cromwell sent out a thousand young women – orphans, trollops, dependants of prisoners of war, and some who had been jailed for picking pockets, robbing their mistresses... They weren't very welcome in the eastern islands, and several hundred (I'm not sure exactly how many) were sent on to Jamaica, to be indentured as servants."

"Servants? But surely there are no plantations working here, and few private inhabitants?"

"No, and that's why the brothels opened, to be closed later by Heffer. It was the only way the women had of making a living."

"How do they live now, then?"

"I can't think Heffer's garrison entirely share his views," Ned said. "Three thousand soldiers..."

"But the soldiers aren't being paid!"

"No, so I presume they barter food. The buccaneers with cash will be a blessing for the women, and tavern keepers are going to make fortunes!"

Aurelia sighed. "The poor buccaneers..."

A startled Ned turned back to her. "Why 'poor buccaneers'?"

Aurelia blushed. "I was thinking that in our three ships we seem to have a fair and happy arrangement!"

"Floating bordellos, eh?"

General Heffer was delighted to see Ned and Thomas again, but obviously nervous: he too could count twenty-eight ships at anchor, and even if he had not seen it himself, Rowlands would have reported that the *Griffin* had led in a small fleet.

Ned watched Heffer as he sat down again behind his table, and was reminded of a dishonest servant whose master had returned unexpectedly. Heffer was puzzled and worried; if he had been a butler, Ned would have assumed he had been secretly drinking in the pantry, yet the more Ned observed him the more he suspected that although the man was puzzled and worried, it was Heffer's normal state. He trusted no man, living his life in constant fear of eavesdroppers. And one thing Ned had long ago learned was never to trust a man who trusted no one else: distrust soon became a disease.

Being puzzled was, for Heffer, undoubtedly the result of being one of Cromwell's followers – after the civil war he must have received many orders which were nearly inexplicable. Now, of course, Heffer's normal indecisive state was augmented by the Restoration. He had no orders at all; he had heard from London only that the King was granting an amnesty...

"Mr Yorke... Sir Thomas... I am glad to see you both back."

Was there, Ned wondered, just a slight emphasis on "both", indicating a reservation about the rest of the buccaneers. It was worth just being sure.

"Water," Ned said. "We just want to fill some butts, then we'll be on our way."

"Can one inquire where...?"

"One can," Thomas said with an exaggerated guffaw, "as long as one doesn't expect an answer!"

"Of course, of course," Heffer said hastily. "But please don't misunderstand me: you are all very welcome to stay as long as you wish."

Heffer's welcoming smile, Ned thought, must be similar to a ram's grimace at the moment of castration. "Oh, they'd stay readily enough," Ned said casually, apparently making polite conversation, "if there was something to entertain them in the evening. But they want taverns and bordellos, which" – he decided on a white lie – "means Tortuga – or Barbados."

Heffer's eyebrows slid up his forehead in surprise. "Oh, I hadn't realized there was much to offer in Tortuga."

"Ah," Thomas gave a lecherous bellow, "remarkable place, Cayona – that's the capital of Tortuga. Quite remarkable, don't you agree, Ned? Why, we – "

The door flung open and slammed back against the wall. Four men burst into the room as a startled Ned and Thomas leapt to their feet. Two of the men held wheel-lock pistols, two waved swords. All four wore the breast plates and helmets which had become the hallmark of Cromwell's New Model Army.

Ned just had time to realize that the four men wore the uniform of officers, to recognize one as Slinger, Heffer's deputy, and glimpse a grinning Rowlands through the doorway, before an excited Slinger yelled at Heffer in a shrill voice: "You are under arrest. The Seventh Regiment has taken over government of the island!"

Heffer, by now on his feet but careful to make no sudden movement, as both pistols pointed at him, bellowed: "Mutiny, by God! This is mutiny. No, it's treason, Colonel Slinger; you are threatening the governor, who represents the King!"

Slinger, almost gibbering with excitement, waved his pistol at Heffer. "Sit down, put your hands flat on the table. Treason!" he screamed, "you accuse *me* of treason? You damnable traitor, talking of the King: *you* have betrayed the Commonwealth!"

Ned noted that Slinger had been promoted since he last saw him. He glanced at Thomas. One of the officers stood close to them, a pistol at the ready, and the other two looked excited enough to use their swords before their brains. Conversation, not action, was needed for a while.

So not only the Dons were worrying Heffer, Ned thought, remembering that the general had been having trouble with his officers from the beginning. Long before Cromwell died, as soon as they realized that the Lord Protector might keep them out here to garrison Jamaica, the majority of them had been conspiring to get back to England, scared that yellow fever would kill them. Letters had been sent to England describing the uselessness of the island, accusing Heffer of every military and spiritual offence possible, and accusing any officers who wanted to stay of being secret Royalists.

All this Ned had heard even before the Santiago raid: it was obvious that at least half the officers were completely incompetent, half were surly and unreliable, and all disloyal to Heffer. But Ned realized he had been wrong in assuming that Cromwell's death had changed anything. The restoration of the King merely added an extra complication – an extra complication for Heffer, and an extra grudge for the dissident officers. Not only could they not get home, but their general was changing sides!

Slinger and Heffer glared at each other across the table, one man sitting with his hands flat on the top as though holding it down, the other leaning across the waving the pistol as if it was a bunch of flowers whose perfume he wanted Heffer to smell.

Suddenly he turned on Ned and Thomas. "Who are you?"

"The son of the ghost of Hamlet's father," Ned said, "and allow me to introduce Yorick, His Grace the Bishop of Woolwich. Recently defrocked, alas, but still a good man: I know him well."

Slinger looked suspiciously from one man to another. Clearly Shakespeare had never crossed his path; he and his friends never discussed anything so frivolous as theatricals. Finely-wrought phrases were dangerous, hinting at luxury or, much worse, blasphemous thoughts.

"You look and talk like Royalists," he said. "Ah! I recognize you! You are buccaneers!"

Ned looked him up and down. Boots not polished and never had been; they were greased, model boots in the New Model Army – but quite unsuitable for the August heat of Jamaica. The man's feet must be swollen and throbbing, and the Palisades being a sand-spit meant that Slinger's boots looked almost tan coloured: sand stuck to the grease was mixed with dried salt so that the boots also had a fringe of white crystals. His wrinkled hose must have once been white, but the cotton had become a bedraggled brown. The breeches had been tailored using the minimum of material so that his shanks looked as though they had been wedged into them. The sleeves of his jerkin were darned, but so inexpertly that each mend was like a shrivelled scar. The front of his breastplate was rusty, as though dusted with a pepperpot: obviously it had last seen service at the Santo Domingo fiasco, and no one had bothered to grease it since. More absurdly, one of the leather straps under the arms, joining front to back, had cracked and parted altogether in the tropical heat, so that the front and back parts of the armour moved against each other like an anxious innkeeper rubbing his hands together.

The helmet fitted well, the chin strap had been greased, and over each ear the metal was worn: clearly Slinger wore his helmet daily, a bent and dented halo. But Ned found the face beneath the helmet intriguing: if Heffer's face was large and long and sheeplike, then Slinger's belonged to a mangy fox lurking round the flock waiting to snap up a newly-born lamb. It was narrow, pointed, the eyes close together, the teeth small and yellowed. The moustache was usually trained back and down, but the heat of excitement had melted the wax so it drooped, thin and straggly. Slinger, Ned considered, looked more like an impoverished but enraged apothecary than a colonel of infantry.

"Royalist, Colonel Slinger? How does a Royalist talk? Anyway, you haven't heard us talk yet."

"You know what I mean! Come," he brandished the pistol like an acolyte waving a censer, "are you Royalist traitors, too?"

"Stop waving that pistol," Ned snapped. "It's General Teffler's affair if he lets inexperienced soldiers enter his office without knocking, but I'm sure he doesn't expect his visitors to put up with those soldiers waving pistols."

Slinger's jaw dropped, making him look like a breathless fox. "How dare you call me an inexperienced soldier – "

"Your only experience of soldiering was at Santo Domingo when you ran away, and no one with experience would wave a pistol like that," Ned said, reaching out and taking it from the man's hand as Slinger watched unbelievingly.

Ned flicked back the pan cover, tilted the pistol to shake out the priming powder and then tossed the pistol on to the floor, making sure that it fell on to the flint, which would almost certainly be dislodged.

The other three officers were more in control of themselves than Slinger: already the remaining pistol was aimed at Ned and two swords were lifted.

"Tell this other fellow to stop waggling his pistol, Teffler," Thomas growled, "otherwise I'll take down his breeches and smack his bottom..."

But Heffer said nothing, and Slinger, who had gone white when Ned removed his pistol, now recovered himself enough to start blustering again. "I am in command here, not this man Heffer, who is under an arrest," Slinger said crossly.

"And who the devil are *you*, then?" Thomas demanded. "Some dam' soldier I remember seeing once, now dressed up in rusty armour and who has lost his gun. Colonel Falstaff looking for yokels to press, eh? Oh, what's the good: you're too much of a yokel to know who Falstaff was," he said disgustedly.

Slinger flushed: he did not understand exactly what the black-bearded scoundrel was saying, but he knew he was being insulted.

"You two are under arrest, along with Heffer!"

"On what charges?" Ned inquired mildly.

"Plotting with a known traitor!" Slinger exclaimed, as though it was absurd even to ask the question.

"And who is making the charges?"

"I am," Slinger said.

"And apart from being called Slinger," Ned said politely, "who or what do you claim to be?"

"I am not *claiming* to be anyone. I *am* Colonel Ezekiel Slinger, the most senior colonel serving in this island, and I have removed General Heffer from his command and assumed it myself."

Slinger unexpectedly stood to attention and gave a slight bow.

"Thank you," Ned said politely, "but the bishop and I are strangers to the island. What exactly was General Teffler before you removed him?"

"Heffer, Heffer," Slinger corrected impatiently. "General Heffer was the commanding officer of all Commonwealth land forces on the island of Jamaica."

"Are you *sure* it isn't Teffler?" Ned asked. " 'Heffer' sounds so bovine. It *is* Heffer? Well, if you say so. So now you have arrested him, you say?"

"Yes, he is under an arrest and removed from his post."

"And you have taken – would you mind saying it again? I'm afraid everything was happening so quickly I became muddled."

"I have assumed the position of governor of the island and commander of the land forces on behalf of the Commonwealth. Now, who are you?"

Ned smiled and said apologetically. "Someone of no importance, I am afraid; my friend the bishop and I are passengers in one of those little ships which arrived this morning. We were just looking round and General Teffler – I beg your pardon, General Heffer – was kind enough to invite us in. I thought to offer us a drink, but I was disappointed."

At that moment Ned saw Rowlands stepping through the doorway, and knew that at last the wretched young man was going to attempt to get his revenge for scores of fish scales and a dozen or so uncomfortable trips out to the *Griffin* in fishing canoes, his sabretache clutched to his scrawny chest.

"Colonel!" he cried triumphantly, "these two men are Royalists and the leaders of the buccaneers. That one's father – he pointed at Ned " – is the Earl of Ilex; the other, with the beard is Sir Thomas Whetstone, the Lord Protector's traitorous nephew!"

"Good for you, laddie," Thomas said amiably, "you'll make your mark at Billingsgate fishmarket, as long as the yellow fever doesn't keep you here permanently."

"That's enough of that; you are both under an arrest!" Slinger suddenly screamed. "I am in command here!"

"Of the land forces, not the buccaneers," Ned said, still speaking quietly.

"I have no interest in that rabble," Slinger sneered. "I want to get my hands on all the Royalists and their lackeys!"

"Treason, no less, since the King is back on the throne," Ned said conversationally. Thomas breathed out noisily. "He'll be brave enough until the Dons attack the island. As soon as he hears they're on their way, he'll be pleading with the buccaneers to drive them off!"

"We'll meet *that* emergency when it arises," Slinger said contemptuously.

Ned stared questioningly at Heffer, who, although careful to keep his hands on the table, shrugged his shoulders and said apologetically. "He doesn't know. There were only half a dozen of them I could trust and he wasn't one of them."

"What don't I know? Tell me at once!" Slinger demanded in his shrill voice.

Ned said quickly, before Heffer could speak: "If the general didn't trust you before, obviously he doesn't trust you now, so he'd be silly – and so would we –" he added icily, "to tell you."

"We'll see about that!" Slinger exclaimed, and gestured to Rowlands. "Come with me. You – " he pointed to one of the officers " – go and inform the other colonels that I have assumed all powers. You other two will guard these men. I shall lock the door from outside and within the hour three companies of my men will be guarding this house."

"Only *three* companies?" Thomas protested. "You insult all three of us!"

Slinger looked uncertain and then suddenly left the room, followed by Rowlands, who pulled the door closed after him. There was some whispering, and then they heard the key being turned.

Ned looked at Heffer. "You are a fool, you know," he said conversationally. "You ought to enter politics, because you can't distinguish your friends from your enemies; by trying to be popular you end up trusting the wrong people."

"Yes," Heffer said miserably, "I know. My mother and my wife say the same thing."

Thomas looked round at the guards and found himself staring into the bore of a pistol. "That flint is chipped," he commented. "It'll give a poor spark."

The officer grinned and nudged the other soldier. "Yes, if Lieutenant Foot will pick up the other pistol and replace the priming powder, we shall have a reliable gun."

While the other officer picked up the pistol and began shaking out powder from a small horn powder flask, Ned sighed: "I'm tired, Thomas. I presume these gentlemen have no objection to us sitting down." Without waiting for a reply he sat at the table opposite Heffer, who seemed to have aged ten years in ten minutes. There was no chance of talking to him confidentially, so Ned said lightly: "Can we expect dozens of loyal battalions to come thundering across the Palisades to rescue us, or are they likely to listen to this jumped-up apothecary, Slinger?"

"Apothecary?" Heffer said. "He's not an – "

"No, he just looks like one. I was insulting him," Ned explained patiently, noting how difficult it was to make jokes when talking to a humourless man. "Be patient with me and answer my question."

"Well no, I don't think so," Heffer said miserably.

"Please, General Heffer, 'yes' or 'no' does not answer the question…"

Heffer shook his head as though starting a clock ticking. "I am not relying on being rescued by loyal battalions," he said. "The loyal battalions are the ones furthest from here – I decided I could risk only certain commanding officers at places like Runaway Bay. The doubtful ones I kept close to Cagway."

Thomas sniffed disparagingly. "Now you know better than nursing vipers to your bosom. You should have had the loyal battalions close round you; then it doesn't matter what the devil the distant ones do."

"Yes, I see that now," Heffer said ruefully. "I'm afraid all the battalions within fifty miles will obey Slinger. Can we expect any help from the buccaneers?"

Ned looked at Heffer disbelievingly. The man really was a fool. In front of two mutinous officers who were guarding him, he could ask questions about rescue…

"To start with, we didn't come on shore until about five o'clock, which means that no one will expect us back until at least midnight. No," Ned shook his head regretfully, noting that the officers were listening carefully while pretending to be doing other things, like adjusting a sword belt, "probably not until morning because the women won't wait up for us. It'll be dark in half an hour...they'll be going to bed soon."

"What about the crew of your boat?"

"They'll be in some tavern and drunk by now. They won't start worrying until they wake up in the morning, when the mosquitoes and sandflies start to eat them."

Thomas was quick to realize what Ned was trying to do. "By the time we're missed it'll be noon tomorrow. The buccaneers will question the boat's crew, who'll know nothing, and then they'll come here, looking for us in this office. By then, I suppose, Slinger will have taken us away somewhere..."

One of the officers laughed, delighted at the idea that such a famous Royalist could be so miserable. "Yes, you'll be a long way away by then, "he said. "Up in the mountains among the clouds. Cold and wet." He gave a brutal laugh. "Yellow fever up there; you'll see the graves. Spanish, some of them; they soon learned that this is an island for dying."

Within half an hour it was almost dark, and one of the officers went to fetch candles. It took him ten minutes with his tinder box, cursing and gently blowing the tinder, to produce enough flame to light the crude rush candles, and then he set them down on the table, jamming them into three empty bottles he had found outside.

The dim light did not encourage talking, and Ned tried to remember which six men had rowed the *Griffin*'s boat. Yes, they were sensible men. What would they do when their captain and Sir Thomas did not arrive back at the jetty?

Probably one of them would walk over to this house, quietly, and ask the sentry, what was delaying his master. Either there would be no sentry, or he would get an unsatisfactory answer. Or he would be made a prisoner. Certainly within fifteen minutes the rest of the boat's crew would be suspicious: they would come over to the house – and one glance through the window would be enough to warn them.

Ned suddenly felt a twinge of doubt. Supposing the boat's crew had already been made prisoner? He then decided it was unlikely that Slinger would think of it: he was in a whirling fury of rage, excitement and righteousness when he left the house and, being a soldier, he would not associate buccaneers on land with boats – any more, Ned admitted, than buccaneers would necessarily associate a band of soldiers with horses.

Well, without risking a pistol ball in the gizzard or a slash from one of the heavy swords, there was nothing to do but wait for an opportunity. These two officers were conscientious: there was no chance of them dozing off or getting drunk...though a chance remark told him that they were getting hungry.

One of them had a watch which he opened and held the face towards the nearest candle. "Nearly nine o'clock. If the colonel remembered, they should be along with some supper in a few minutes."

Ned caught Thomas' eye and casually looked round the room. Heffer had the table in the centre so that the door was on his right, and thus on the left of Ned and Thomas sitting opposite him. The guards were behind, between the table and the window, the two of them making do with one chair and taking it in turns to sit down. The only light came from the three candles stuck in bottles on the table. He had been listening ever since Slinger and Rowlands left, and there was no hint of anyone in the ante-room, which opened on to a large hall and led to the front door.

He attracted Thomas' attention again and with his eyes tried to indicate his plan. Finally Thomas rubbed his nose and gave an uncharacteristic belch.

When it happened it took Ned unawares: he had not realized how thick was the door and what a good fit the Spanish carpenters had made so many years ago. The key grated in the lock and first Rowlands, carrying a lantern, and then Slinger came into the room. Rowlands, obviously put out that both Ned and Thomas completely ignored him, almost flounced, making the heels of his boots thud on the stone floor and, Ned noted, passing right across the room. Slinger stopped a couple of paces inside the door and looked questioningly at one of the guards.

"Everything in order, sir; the prisoners have been quiet."

"Very well. A couple of men are coming with your supper. Nothing elaborate." Ned saw a faint glow of light through the door. He could picture a soldier carrying a saucepan or bucket in one hand and a lantern in the other. The second man – bearing in mind that only two soldiers were carrying food for six people – must be laden with pots and pans.

Slinger said to Ned: "I hope you have been having second thoughts. You must have realized you are a long way from London. By now the Commonwealth will be re-established and the King either executed or forced to flee back to France."

"The Netherlands, I believe."

"The Netherlands?"

"Yes, General Monck brought him back from the Netherlands, I'm told."

"Oh, the Netherlands, eh?" Slinger muttered, completely confused by Ned's remark. "Well, I expect they'll have him back."

Ned then heard footsteps which were slowing up as they neared the door, then he saw the glow of a lantern, and pictured a nervous soldier slowing down, perhaps intending to poke his head round the door jamb and ask where to place the food.

He leapt up and flung over the table in the same moment, sending the candles flying, and ran the few steps to the door. In the same motion he thrust Slinger in front of him so that the little colonel bounced off the startled soldier, who dropped the lantern and saucepan with a loud clatter.

With only Rowlands' lantern left alight, the ante-room was in almost total darkness, and Ned tried to guess where the front door was, somewhere on the far side of the hall. He heard an oath, a crash and a whimper of pain and the single lantern went out: Thomas had obviously flung Rowlands to one side and with a triumphant bellow of "Make way for Whetstone, you mumbling yokels!" crashed through the ante-room and hall after Ned, hurling aside furniture and somehow staying on his feet.

"Gallows Point! Make for Gallows Point," Ned hissed as they flung open the front door and plunged down the three wide steps.

"What about the boat?"

"If they haven't seized it yet, it'll be the first thing they'll make for now!"

As the two men ran along the track over the dunes towards the battery which Heffer had shown them only a few days earlier, Thomas said: "What's the attraction of Gallows Point?"

"Last place they'll look for us!"

"They'll find us – blast, nearly broke my ankle in a land crab hole – at daylight!"

"We'll see," Ned said. "Save your breath for running."

Behind them they heard the crack of a pistol, followed by a second shot.

"Aimed away from us," Thomas said. "Firing towards the jetty. You were right, they think we're making for the boat."

The sea on their left reflected the stars, but the moon, in its last quarter, would not rise for several hours. They reached the battery, and once past it the track narrowed down to an almost indistinguishable path as it went on towards the end of the sand-spit.

"We can walk now," Ned said, slowing down. "Less risk of twisting an ankle."

"We're just about abreast the *Griffin* and *Peleus*. Want to risk swimming out to them?"

"No," said Ned firmly. "I doubt if you're good for half a mile. I know I'm not."

"Sheer bravado," Thomas admitted cheerfully. "With this paunch twenty yards would scuttle me."

Now they were standing among knee-high shrubs, and Ned said: "I'm hoping we'll find a fisherman's canoe on the beach up here."

Thomas held his arm so that the two men stopped.

"We're safe enough now, Ned. Let's sit here and think for a while. What about Teffler? Do you think this fellow Slinger will hold on as governor?"

"Heffer has three thousand men. Your guess is as good as mine about who picks Slinger and who picks Heffer. It boils down to a handful of colonels and two handsful of majors: the subalterns and the rest follow their commanding officers."

"But what happens when the news reaches London?"

Ned shrugged his shoulders. "Slinger is clearly mad, and can't accept that the King is restored permanently – "

"We don't know that for sure, Ned!"

"We can make a good guess, though. Because General Monck and the army decided to bring the King back, and the navy sent a ship to fetch him, then the army and the navy are so involved that the Restoration must be a success. It *has* to work. The old monarchy was overthrown but the Commonwealth replacing it was obviously failing even before its leader, your benighted uncle, had died."

"And the first real news the King will get from Jamaica is that a group of fanatical Roundheads have turned the island into a republic."

"Exactly, and I suspect that Heffer has only just worked that out!"

"So what can we do?"

"Do with 1,250 buccaneers against perhaps three thousand soldiers? I don't know. I can't see the Brethren wanting to do anything: after all, the Restoration in England is no concern of theirs. They're interested in Port Royal only as a base. I'm sure most of the French, Dutch, Portuguese and Spanish Brethren barely know the name of their own king!"

"Let's be selfish, Ned. The Brethren have no brains and precious little organization. The Portobelo business will be a farce, unless we organize it for them and you lead. If we're going to put purchase in their pockets, then in return they can give us a hand when need be."

Ned was silent for a minute or two. "Better if they gave us a hand without realizing it."

"How so, Ned?"

"Well, they'd cut throats by the dozen to rescue you and me – they'll start as soon as they discover we are missing. But if we warned Slinger that we'd turn the Brethren loose on him...he doesn't know how many men we have, and it looks an impressive fleet at anchor...and..." His voice tailed off and Thomas left him with his thoughts for three or four minutes.

"And..." Thomas prompted.

"I was thinking; Heffer warned Slinger that the Spaniards were coming, and Slinger brushed it aside. I suspect that by now Slinger has had second thoughts. I believe Slinger was one of the first to run away in that farcical attack on Santo Domingo, so he has a healthy respect for the Spanish soldiery!"

"How does all that help us ? If the buccaneers won't budge to support us Royalists, and Slinger controls Jamaica for the Commonwealth – which no longer exists, except here in the person of Slinger – and Slinger chooses to ignore the Spanish threat, then I'm going to suggest the Brethren return to Tortuga."

"Keep talking in this tone of voice. Thomas, I don't know what's going on but we are surrounded by men crawling through the bushes. That damned man – "

A bush rose and struck him across the head and the whine of mosquitoes and rattling of tree frogs suddenly stopped.

CHAPTER SEVEN

Above the throbbing which threatened to burst his skull he heard Leclerc giving instructions in an agitated voice. "Break off more branches and build up that bonfire – we must have light!"

"Supposing the soldiers see it?" another voice protested.

"They'll think it is fishermen boiling conch. Look, Sir Thomas is moving – and there, M. Yorke opens his eyes: M'sieur, how are you? *Mon Dieu,* what a mistake!"

The little bonfire spurted more flame as branches caught fire; Ned felt he was inside a black tent. Then he remembered the bush that moved, and tried to sit up.

A man crouching beside him – was it the Englishman Coles? – said gently: "No rush, Mr Yorke, wait until you feel steady again."

"What the devil happened?"

Leclerc heard the mumbled question and said to Coles: "You tell him!"

"Well, Mr Yorke, your boatmen came back and reported what they'd seen through the window of the general's house; all three o' you held prisoner by soldiers. So Leclerc landed at the point with a hundred men while Rideau collected the rest of them and landed at the jetty. We reckoned that'd be enough to get you all out – and occupy the Palisades, if need be."

"Yes, but who hit me and Sir Thomas?"

"Well, we're sorry about that Mr Yorke, but we saw two men just sitting and we reckoned they were soldiers acting as sentries, guarding the house against anyone coming from the point. It was too dark to recognize you, sir – anyway, we thought you was still prisoners in the house. So..."

"Leclerc," Ned said, reassured to hear Thomas beginning to curse and sit up, "now we are here, we'll go down to the house and free the general. He's an old fool but Sir Thomas and I were just making arrangements with him for our base here when those traitors arrived."

"Yes – but what is going on?"

"It's an army quarrel: a few colonels want to take over. A simple mutiny. They haven't enough to occupy their time so they plot."

"Let me help you," Leclerc said, "I understand perfectly. We can free the general, hang a few colonels and be back on board in time for breakfast. Ah, Sir Thomas, my apologies!"

"Our fault for not spotting you crawling through the bush. Trouble was we were busy talking."

"Yes, we thought you were gossiping sentries."

Thomas lurched over to Ned. "You are all right? Good, shall we go back and rescue old Teffler? I feel sorry for him. And I want to get my hands round young Rowlands' throat!"

Within three minutes the bonfire had been put out and the glowing embers stamped into the sand, and Ned and Thomas were leading the buccaneers back along the path to the battery, and then along the wide track to the house.

"Do you want swords and pistols?" Leclerc asked. "Most of us have two of each."

"Not for me," Ned said. "My head throbs so much I couldn't aim a pistol!"

They were well past the battery when Leclerc stopped them. "There's a light ahead. A window?"

"The general's office faces this way. They've still got him there."

Thomas said: "I wonder if they've given up looking for us?"

"I should think so. We're of no importance to Slinger. He thinks only of the army – quite rightly. He's worried about the other colonels, not us."

Ned told Leclerc: "There's a back door on the north side and the front door is on the east. The window we see is on the west. The road leads up to the front door but goes on round to the back. Now, listen carefully. We want to rescue General Heffer alive. He is a tall man with white hair and a long face like a sheep and protruding teeth. The traitor, Slinger, is small with a face like a fox. Black hair, cut short, Roundhead style. He moves quickly like a fox or a burglar."

"We want him alive?"

"Don't kill him unnecessarily. There'll be other officers with him but I doubt if any private soldiers. So – I shall go through the front door and into the office with Sir Thomas. You and Coles and Brace will follow but at first stay outside the office. You'll see when you need to come in."

"At the same time I want five men crouching below that window with pistols ready to cover us – or shoot any of these soldiers if they don't behave. Another five men to guard the back door and stop anyone entering or leaving the building. The rest stay a few yards from the front door: our *corps de réserve*."

Leclerc walked back, picked his men and then returned.

"We are ready," he said. "Here are Coles and Brace and Rideau."

Ned quickly described the route to the office through the front door and across the hall and ante-room. "We'll go barefoot," he added. "Don't let the rude soldiery stamp on your toes, Thomas!"

A few yards from the house they stopped and removed their shoes and boots, putting them in a pile beside a small bush. Coles crept up to the door from one side to make absolutely sure there was no sentry, and then Ned led the way through the entrance.

Suddenly they could hear voices from inside the office: Ned could distinguish the querulous tone of Slinger and the deeper reply of Heffer. Slinger was angry and excited – it seemed a permanent state for him – but Heffer was frightened.

There was a third voice and it spoke with some authority. Another mutinous colonel, Ned thought. And a fourth. Now a fifth interrupted, and was in turn interrupted by Slinger.

He moved across the hall to the ante-room door. Here he could distinguish words, not just voices and it took him three or four incredulous minutes to be certain what was going on. He pictured the buccaneers getting into position, especially the five crouching below the sill of the window.

The office was well lit now, and the candles and lanterns threw dancing shadows on the whitewashed walls of the ante-room. There was no doubt about it: Slinger had set up a court in the office: Heffer was being tried by court-martial. He was protesting that he was not being allowed to call witnesses.

One of the other colonels was jeering at him, saying that his only witnesses, the two Royalists, had run away to rejoin the buccaneers. Then Slinger declared that the evidence against him spoke for itself: Heffer had accepted the orders sent out from London in the name of the King.

"And General Monck: he signed them!" Heffer exclaimed angrily.

"It is obvious that Monck has turned traitor to the Commonwealth," Slinger said contemptuously.

"How can you be sure? The Lord Protector is dead; we all know that Richard Cromwell has no taste for succeeding him. The army in England may – "

"So now you slander the whole army," Slinger almost screamed. "Your own words, and the written orders bearing his signature that you have put in as evidence, prove both you and Monck are traitors. He gives you orders and you obey them. That alone makes you a traitor. A traitor!" Slinger spat out the word. "Worse, far worse, than those libertine Royalists. They live sinful lives in their ships, all drunkenness and lechery, but at least they are true to the man they call their king. We'll hang them for it, of course, but at least they betrayed no one!"

"Let the court vote." The voice was insistent. "We've heard the charge, we've heard the evidence, and we've heard the defence, so we can vote: is he guilty as charged or not?"

"But you *haven't* heard my defence," Heffer protested. "I cannot call witnesses!"

"The very documents you put in as your defence, Monck's orders, proved your guilt; Rowlands has given detailed evidence proving how you collaborated with those Royalists, Yorke and Whetstone."

"Vote...vote..." the other two voices formed a chorus, and Slinger agreed.

"Very well, starting with the most junior of us – do you find General Heffer guilty as charged or not guilty?"

"Guilty..."

"Guilty..."

"Guilty..."

The three colonels were emphatic, and Slinger added his verdict, then tapped the table with something intended to be a judge's gavel. "General Heffer, this court, formally constituted here at Cagway on the island of Jamaica to consider various charges against you of mutiny and high treason, hereby finds you guilty on all counts. You will stand to attention while the court passes its sentence."

A chair scraped, and Slinger continued, his voice trembling with satisfaction: "The sentence of this court is that first you shall be shot, and then your body be hanged in chains at the gateway to the Palisades as a dreadful warning to other traitors. Sergeant of the Guard – take him away and guard him well!"

Ned tapped Thomas' arm and walked into the room.

The three colonels were seated at the table with their backs to the window and a hunched Heffer was standing in front of his usual chair. Slinger sat at the head of the table at the far end facing the door.

A soldier – presumably the sergeant – stood behind Heffer, while Rowlands and the three original subaltern guards stood against the far wall, their backs to the window. Every man stared at Ned and Thomas, and Slinger was the first to react, leaping up and exclaiming: "You!"

Ned gave a slight bow and said sharply: "All of you get back from the table!" and at the same time seized the nearest lantern. Chairs crashed over as the sergeant and four colonels, three of them having no idea what was happening, hurried to obey orders given by someone who sounded in authority.

"Now," said Ned evenly, "all you gentlemen are in danger of your lives, so keep absolutely still." I've about a minute, he told himself, before the reaction sets in and they all start yapping at once, like hungry puppies when the bitch comes back.

"General Heffer, please collect General Monck's orders and then go outside and wait in the hall."

Thomas slapped the dazed man on the back as he went out. "Wake up, Teffler; we hadn't deserted you – just went for a glass of wine!"

Ned looked at Slinger. "Introduce these three men, please."

Slinger glanced nervously at the other colonels and Ned suddenly realized that Slinger was in fact the cat's-paw: these three men had planned the coup, letting Slinger take the credit at first – just as he would take the blame if it all failed.

"Keep your mouth shut!" one of the colonels ordered, and Ned recognized the voice of the man who had first called for the vote. "These men aren't armed. We – "

"Wait!" Ned snapped. "Turn round and look at the window!"

Five pistols with five unshaven faces, all sporting wicked grins looked through the window out of the darkness, and each muzzle pointed at a colonel with the fifth angled round to cover Rowlands, the guards and the sergeant.

"Now look at the door!"

Leclerc stepped into the room, followed by Coles, Rideau and Brace, each holding a pistol in one hand and a sword in the other. Ned gave a lantern to Coles, who put his sword in its scabbard and held the light higher.

"I have no more authority to arrest you all than you had to arrest General Heffer – except that every loyal citizen has a right and duty to prevent treason. What you men are doing *is* treason and you know it: you have seen General Monck's orders and you know the King has been – "

Slinger tipped the table over and as the two remaining lanterns crashed to the floor there was a drumroll of gunfire. In the light of Coles' lantern Ned saw Slinger look startled and then collapse; two of the colonels crumpled and Rowlands gave a scream. There was a moment's silence and Ned saw Leclerc still poised, aiming his pistol. Before Ned could shout the Frenchman fired and the fourth colonel collapsed.

"No more problems now," Leclerc said briskly, "unless these four – " he gestured at the former guards and the sergeant, " – want to fight."

As Ned stood stock-still in the room, suddenly conscious in the silence of the sharp tang of the candle smoke and gunpowder, his ears ringing from the explosions, he realized that Leclerc had thought faster than him. The revolt was over because the four ringleaders – there was little doubt that these four had led the whole business – were dead or wounded: no courts-martial would be needed to restore General Heffer's authority.

Thomas said: "I think we'll put up some gibbets on Gallows Point and hang the bodies in chains. It was a good idea they had."

Ned said: "Yes, like the carrion crow hung up outside the gamekeeper's lodge. Still, we'd better make sure they're all dead. And get half a dozen of our men from the front door to secure our former guards."

Leclerc and Brace inspected the bodies as Coles held the lantern over them, and Ned called to Heffer through the door. He was surprised at the general's appearance – it was as if the pistol shots had reminded the man that he was a soldier.

Ned put the table back on its legs and Thomas picked up the extinguished lanterns. He flicked open the doors, removed the candles and took them over to Coles' lantern to light them.

With the chairs back in place, Ned waved Heffer to be seated, and sat down opposite him.

"Tell me, General, were these four the only traitors?"

"There are two more who stayed with their battalions. A couple of hours' ride from here."

"Will the soldiers stay loyal if those two colonels are arrested?"

"The major of one battalion would have to be taken as well."

"Very well, do you have a few men you can trust to bring them in? Some of my buccaneers might enjoy a few hours on horseback, if you need reliable men. You'd better put the orders to the battalion in writing, though, along with the warrants for the arrest of the three men."

"*Can* I arrest them?" Heffer asked uncertainly, betraying the effect the last hour had had on him.

"You're the governor," Ned said. "If you can shut the bordellos, you can certainly arrest traitors," he added sarcastically.

Leclerc bent over to whisper in Ned's ear: "The one in the end chair, the foxy-faced one who pushed over the table, he is dead. The one I shot is dead. The third is dead and the fourth bleeding badly. We are doing what we can to save him," he said, "but I don't hold out much hope. The youngest subaltern – "

"That would be Rowlands, I suppose," the general said. "A grave disappointment to me..."

" – will be ready for the grave in ten minutes or so. The ranges were too short to offer a long life to the targets," Leclerc said. "How do you like that for a joke in a foreign language?"

"It's not foreign to me," Thomas said with a straight face. "So we have three live and unwounded subalterns and a sergeant left, eh?"

"At the moment," Leclerc said unambiguously. "We will walk them down to the jetty."

Ned looked at Heffer, considered for a moment that but for the buccaneers the general would have been hanged within the hour by these same three subalterns, turned back to Leclerc and nodded.

Heffer coughed apologetically. "First I must thank you, then I must apologize that you were submitted to all this." He waved a hand round the room to indicate the bodies and the prisoners. "Might I ask what you are now going to do with your – er, your little fleet?"

"Return to Tortuga," Ned said, shortly, knowing that he had won the battle for his buccaneers. "Once my captains have bought more stocks of rumbullion, they'll be anxious to get back."

"*Your* captains?" Heffer said, with a heavy-handed attempt at humour. "You sound like an admiral!"

"I am. At least the buccaneers have just elected me their admiral, so I have a little fleet of twenty-eight ships. Four times the size of the one that took Santiago."

Heffer tugged at his jerkin to straighten it up. A night without sleep was being unkind to him, and the long face sagged as though the muscles holding the flesh were gradually surrendering. "I must congratulate you. What do they call themselves, 'The Brethren of the Coast'?"

"Yes, and I trust that when you write your dispatch to General Monck describing tonight's affair, you will mention the help you received from them."

Heffer looked embarrassed. He shifted the position of the lantern a few inches and turned it so that his face was in shadow.

"I was hoping...somehow...the confidential nature..."

Ned stared at him. "How will you account for the loss of four colonels and three subalterns?"

"With your agreement," Heffer said, "it can be done."

"I'm not signing any false declarations," Ned said firmly.

"No, no, nor would I ask. No, it is only a question of you and your people maintaining a discreet silence. The seven of them are dead or dying. My next dispatch has to report the death already of nine officers and twenty-three private soldiers from yellow fever, various fluxes and malaria. The extra seven – " he waved a hand around the room " – it matters little how their deaths are described in my dispatch."

Ned gave a dry laugh. "Well, they can't have died of yellow fever if you are going to hang their bodies in chains at Gallows Point."

"My goodness!" Heffer said, and Ned realized that he must be the only man who could make that expression sound like an oath. "I'd forgotten all about that. What a decision to have to make. If I conceal the mutiny from London, I can't hang the men in chains. But I want to string them up, as a dreadful example to the rest of the garrison of the perils of mutiny. What *shall* I do?"

"Are you really asking me?" Ned said, trying to sound friendly.

"Well, yes, you've always spoken freely and honestly – haven't you?"

"Yes, but you rarely like what I say."

"But these are unusual times," Heffer said. "What do you think I should do?"

"I don't think," Ned said quietly. "I know, and I know Sir Thomas agrees. The fact that four colonels still supported Cromwell and the Commonwealth, despite the Restoration is not your fault. Why not tell them in London? It gives them a good idea of the problems you face. Point out that you have to defend yourself against the Spanish with officers you cannot fully trust. But at the same time describe the batteries you're building with the guns the buccaneers brought from Santiago.

"Who knows? The army or the government might send you some more guns, powder and shot. Emphasize that while the main threat is from the sea, you have no ships. You can say you have to rely on the buccaneers.

"Meanwhile, string up these colonels and subalterns in chains. Get the gibbets built first thing in the morning – put a couple on that stretch of beach at the end of the spit but on the landward side, so everyone can see them as they're rowed over to the landing stage to go to St Jago, and the rest beside the road where the Palisades begin."

Thomas rapped the table with his knuckles. "That's the best advice you've had for years, Teffler; worth a guinea a word. You can't keep the mutiny secret, and since you've quashed it and shot the mutineers, why the devil should you try? Bodies wrapped in chains will stop anyone with similar ideas dead in his tracks. And let me add my penn'orth: here in the island give the buccaneers all the credit you can for helping you stop the mutiny: let your garrison think the buccaneers are on your side and will support you."

"But aren't they? Won't they?"

"No, they're not, and I doubt it," said Ned brutally. "Why should they? They're not English – or, rather, those that are have been ill-treated by Cromwell's England. No, Teffler my friend, the buccaneers came on shore tonight to rescue their admiral and Sir Thomas, and they punished the men who had kidnapped us. The fact this led to your rescue was – for you –a lucky coincidence."

"Perhaps I ought to give them a reward? What should it be?"

"Ah, you're a lucky man," Thomas said. "Just think of it, Ned, our friend Teffler can give a reward that not only costs him nothing but brings him even more advantages!"

Ned simply laughed and nodded.

"I don't understand," Heffer said. "What must I do?"

Ned leaned forward and lowered his voice, to provide more emphasis.

"The scuffle this evening with those wretched colonels has made you forget what the main threat is – to this island, not to you personally."

"You mean the Spanish troops from Portobelo and Providencia landing on the north coast?"

"Yes. *Is* there a greater threat?"

"No, indeed not. I was telling you before you went to Tortuga, I don't know what I am going to do!"

"You ask for our advice, so I'll give it. For yourself, get those batteries completed here on the Palisades – I noticed that first one, where we found the men asleep, is still not finished. Concentrate your troops – if the Spanish are going to land and march, there's no point in you exhausting your men by marching them over the mountains and through the jungle. Place them in positions you want to hold. After all, that's how the Spanish beat you in Santo Domingo, wasn't it? They just massed their men between you and the city and you bolted as soon as you smelled powder – no, not you personally, but just about everyone else."

"Why can't your ships stop the Spaniards landing?" Heffer asked plaintively. "That would be the best defence!"

"We have just told you: the buccaneers have absolutely no interest in defending Jamaica for you: they've no allegiance to England."

"Sir Thomas mentioned a reward," Heffer said, finally accepting that he could expect no more help from the buccaneers.

"Yes, I'm coming to that: I wanted first to remind you about the Dons. You can reward these buccaneers and at the same time give yourself a considerable insurance by offering them Port Royal as a base."

"But you've already said they won't come!"

"I said they won't come while you shut down most of the taverns and make the place like the inside of a Puritan church!"

"What must I do then?"

"There's no need for you to do anything – except not *forbid* everything. First, invite the buccaneers to use Port Royal – that means making the offer to me. Second, assure them that you will leave the town to develop normally. Third, issue every ship with a commission, or letter of marque to operate as a privateer – "

"But you have already said the Spaniards ignore commissions," Heffer interrupted.

"Yes, but I'm not concerned with the Spanish; I'm concerned with you, or the government of Jamaica. If you set up an Admiralty Court and have it administered fairly, we'll bring in our prizes and have them condemned in court, so that the King gets his share and so does the Lord High Admiral, if one has been appointed. The prizes are then legally condemned, and local men can buy the hulls or use them for trading – or buccaneering. In that way Jamaica gets defended and also prospers."

"But you said the buccaneers won't fight for England!"

"They won't, as such," Ned said patiently. "They'll fight for purchase and they'll fight for a base which lets them turn their purchase into money and their money into liquor and women: it's as simple as that!"

Thomas roared with laughter. "Don't look so shocked, Teffler. Instead of paying out cash for a navy, you are getting one free. Listen, if a buccaneer takes a prize ship into Tortuga, he has trouble selling the cargo and the hull. But here he'll be able to sell the ship and the cargo – you are short of everything, and the merchants are going out of business – so your people, merchants and gamblers, can trade, or even start buccaneering."

"Yes, but...well..."

"Yes, all your psalm-singing hypocrites will be shocked o' nights, hearing the roisterers sing raucous songs as they stagger out of the taverns and bordellos, but remember – drink, food, women and trinkets and fine dresses to put on them: it all costs money. The buccaneers will be *spending* the money, and your merchants and the tavern keepers will be *pocketing* it. And no doubt you'll be charging customs and excise soon, and landing charges once the trading ships start bringing cargoes. The buccaneers will make the place prosperous, Teffler, and in the meantime they'll make it safe!"

Heffer turned to Ned. "If I do all this, will you as admiral guarantee to keep the ships here while the Spaniards from Portobelo and Providencia threaten us?"

"No," Ned said promptly. "If you invite the buccaneers to make Port Royal their base, they'll defend their base, but as their leader I warn you that the best way of defending Port Royal is by attacking the Spanish elsewhere!"

"I don't understand what you mean," Heffer grumbled.

"Well, the best way of preventing the Spaniards landing in Jamaica," Ned explained patiently, "or making them withdraw if they're already here, is to threaten one of their own towns. One which suddenly needs the Dons in Jamaica to defend or retake it."

"Yes, I can see that, but where can you attack so that the Spanish take fright and leave us alone? And will the buccaneers agree to such an attack if they think it is simply to defend Jamaica?"

Ned and Thomas both laughed together and Ned said: "Buccaneers will only fight to get purchase, but you need purchase, too, General, so that your merchants and tavern keepers prosper. Why don't you issue the invitation and the commissions, all signed and drawn up in legal form, and with no charge, and then leave the rest to Sir Thomas and me? But while we are away, tell the tavern keepers and bordello owners and merchants what you've done, so they're ready for our return…"

CHAPTER EIGHT

"It is beyond belief that we are becalmed in sight of the island after three days of being flung about in that dreadful weather," Diana grumbled crossly. "And where are the rest of them?"

"Ask Ned," Thomas said wearily. "He's to blame for all bad weather and straying ships. I'm responsible only for your moral downfall."

"Immoral," Ned corrected. "And give me credit for having four ships still with the three of us, rather than twenty-one missing!"

"When it blows a storm for three days and seven ships out of twenty-eight manage to stay together, that's chance, not good seamanship," Thomas said amiably. "But you're the admiral..."

"My lord bishop," Ned said, "you are too generous. I am sure it was divine intervention."

"What is this 'bishop' joke?" Diana asked.

Ned explained: "When the mutinous colonel broke into the general's office he wanted to know who we were. I introduced Thomas as the unfrocked bishop of Woolwich, because he had that sanctimonious but well-fed look..."

"I know it," Diana said. "It usually means I've caught him out doing something wrong, like taking an extra glass of rumbullion."

"Extra?" Aurelia asked. "Do you ration him?"

"I have in the last few months. A bottle of wine with dinner and only two glasses of rumbullion."

"Those hills," Thomas said conversationally to Ned, pointing to the pearl-grey blob on the southern horizon, indistinct and seeming to shimmer because the sun reflected from every wavelet on the almost flat sea. "You can always identify Old Providence, or Providencia, as the Dons call it, by the three peaks in the middle, each about the same height. And remember the main danger is Low Cay, lying about nine miles north of the northern end of the island. You can't distinguish the small island at this distance. Let's look at the chart."

Carefully he unrolled the sheet of parchment. It was small, about a foot square, with round-cheeked cherubs blowing from each corner. Beneath an ornate scroll were drawn two islands, Isla Providencia and the tiny Isla Catalina, and beneath the title was the name of the Spaniard who had drawn it. A cartographer? Master of a ship? There was no indication of its origin – or, Thomas noted, its accuracy.

As soon as Thomas had unrolled it on the deck and weighted down the ends, the four of them knelt and examined it once again. In a different handwriting – by comparison a scribble – was noted a latitude, 13° 25′ North and a longitude, 81° 25′ West.

"Coincidence that the minutes of the latitude and longitude are the same," Ned commented.

"Well, judging by our noon sight, the charted latitude seems fairly accurate," Thomas said. "It put us thirty miles north of this latitude, and I reckon we're about thirty miles from those peaks."

"Those peaks" were now astern as the *Griffin*, her sails hanging like limp laundry, slowly turned as she lay becalmed, twisted by currents which they could see only as thin and curling lines of grass-like brown weed all round them, as though the sea was veined.

The *Peleus* was heading east and the *Phoenix* south. The other privateers had their bows pointing in different directions: like bird feathers floating down a Kentish stream, Ned thought, a sudden spasm of nostalgia reminding him of the sharp, clean smell of stinging nettles lining the banks. The low clouds, which earlier seemed to stretch down to the wavetops, bringing howling winds and steep waves leaping along the backs of the long swells, had broken into patches and then vanished altogether, taking the wind with them and leaving a great dome of clear blue sky. In the distance, over to the east and low on the horizon, were tiny, insubstantial balls like cotton growing on a plant, giving a hint that the Trade winds would return in a few hours. Meanwhile the sun was scorching and the sea had turned a vivid purplish blue, as though for centuries it had been stealing colour from the sky.

Aurelia looked down at the gaudy colours painted on the chart: compared with the natural tints and shades of the sea and the sky, the hanging sails and coarse grain of the deck planking, they were vulgar, exaggerated. She ran her finger round the outline of the oval-shaped larger island. "I shall call it Old Providence, not the Spanish name. But why 'Old'?"

"I think there's a 'New' Providence somewhere north of the Bahamas," Thomas said. "One of those dozens of islands."

"This design, like a broken wreath, inked in almost all the way round the island – that is a coral reef?"

"Coral reefs, small cays, rocks," Ned said. "You can see here, this is Low Cay. Now, measure off on the scale – " he opened his fingers to span the distance with his outstretched thumb and little finger and putting them on the scale " – and you see it is about nine miles north of the island. The coral starts there and goes on round the entire eastern side, down to the southwestern end."

"Like a clock face, with Low Cay at midnight, and this reef ends at seven o'clock!" Diana said. "Then it goes on in fits and starts round to midnight. The bishop had a clock like that once, didn't you Thomas?"

Thomas grunted as he examined the chart. "Look Ned, there's a cut through the reef here, at five o'clock, called 'Tinkham'. Must be English, surely; there's no Spanish word or name remotely like that."

"Look at the northern end of the island. The writing isn't very clear but that's 'Jones Point'. And look, at one o'clock out on the reef, 'Crab Cayo'. And – " Ned laughed delightedly " – this must have been copied from an original English chart: the eastern point on the island is Kalaloo Point!"

"Kalaloo?" Diana exclaimed. "Who was he?"

"What is it, you mean," Thomas said. "Sort of vegetable, isn't it Ned, rather like spinach."

"Yes, makes a good soup. And look, just south of Jones Point, there's 'Split Hill'."

"I remember Leclerc telling me something about that," Thomas said, scratching his head. "Yes, there's a great chasm in a mountain about one hundred feet deep and fifty wide, and you can only see it – look along it, rather – from northwest or south east: useful for establishing your bearing."

Ned nodded and said: "You know, these must be the original names given when the early Puritans came and settled here."

"*English* puritans?" Aurelia was obviously startled. "*Here* – thousands of miles from anywhere?"

Ned smiled and felt a contradictory pride. "Yes – this is probably where it all began – what gave Cromwell the original idea for his Western Design, and which eventually led to the capture of Jamaica."

Aurelia shook her head. "That is too long a jump for me!"

"It all happened thirty years ago or more. From what I've been told, Robert Rich – he was the Earl of Warwick – was one of the leaders of the Virginia Company, colonizing America. He tried to colonize the Bermudas, also known as Somers Island: he and his friends started plantations there but they failed.

"About that time some Puritans, led by John Pym, were looking for a place to start a colony. Not so much to plant for profit but to settle and start a new political and religious community. Pym and his friends chose these two islands, the larger of which they called Providence and this little one," he tapped the top left-hand corner of the chart, "Henrietta. They moved in with a number of Warwick's discontented colonists from the Bermudas.

"As far as I can see, while Warwick's friends regarded Providence as a base for privateering against the Spanish, stirring up the old spirit of Drake, the Puritans wanted only to plant and pray..."

"A fine mixture," Thomas commented, "and here the islands are right on the main route for the Spanish galleons coming laden from Cartagena bound for Havana to meet the *flota* from Mexico..."

"How long did the Puritan colony last?" Diana asked.

"I think it started in about 1630; then five or six years later the Spanish managed to launch a big attack, but the reefs and mountains beat them. For the next six years or so, privateering was more practical for the colonists than praying and planting.

"Rich and his brother, the Earl of Holland, with Pym's help – he was back in England, of course – planned great colonies out here in the West Indies, but the Scottish wars began."

"Ah," Thomas interrupted, "I know Uncle Oliver, as a young man, was very influenced by John Pym, and at one time was thinking about emigrating to Providence."

"A pity he didn't," Diana said bitterly. "Yellow fever might have got him!"

"Anyway," Ned continued, "when the civil war came a few years ago Pym was close to Cromwell, so we can only suppose that Cromwell's idea for an 'English West India Association', although like the Dutch West India Company, was based on the Providence Company."

Diana bent and looked more closely at the chart. "Is there anywhere named after Pym? If so I'm not going there! But what happened in the end?"

"The place became a privateering and pirate base: they used to raid the Isthmus, particularly the Nicaragua coast. They hated anything Catholic, so there was plenty of opportunity for profit, too, helped by the Dutch. Then, in '40, the Spanish launched an attack from Cartagena, which failed, but they came back the next year with more soldiers and seized the place. They've held it ever since – for the last seventeen years or so."

Aurelia, pointing at the chart, said: "While you've been telling that story, Ned, I've found 'Alligator Point', here on the west side. Then, on this other island – " she pointed to the tiny one nestling in a curving bay on the northwest corner of Providence " – which I suppose was called 'Henrietta' in Pym's time, but which the Dons call 'Santa Catalina', there is 'Black Point', 'Cat Rock', 'Boat Rock'... Still, the town, probably just a large village, is here on the Old Providence side of the channel between the two islands, and is called Isabella. After the queen, I suppose. The port near it is called 'Puerto Catalina', but perhaps the English call it 'Port Henrietta'."

"*We* called it Henrietta," Ned corrected her with a grin. "You are not only English by marriage to your late husband, but you'll be English by marriage to your next one, and I'm sure commanding an English buccaneer makes you English yet again."

Diana said: "Have you seen how many forts and castles there are on Santa Catalina? Just look – nine! What a mixture of names – I wonder which were originally English and the map-maker translated..." She read some of them. "Fort St Jerome – that obviously just covers this bridge connecting Santa Catalina to the mainland. Santa Teresa seems to be the biggest – it's called a castle. St Matthew, St Joseph, St Augustine, Santa Cruz, San Salvador – and, just to make a change, 'La Plataforma de la Concepción', and 'La Plataforma de los Artilleros'."

"Two batteries," Thomas said. "But from the way they describe things out here, a 'battery' means guns on a flat space, 'fort' can mean it has walls or rocks, or tubs filled with sand or pebbles or even small rocks or earth. 'Castle' – well, that's a regular castle, like the one at Santiago. Still, this one must be a good deal smaller. Probably where the governor lives."

"Nine forts and batteries and castle...that must add up to quite a number of guns," Ned said, wondering what the total could be. Two to a battery meant four, the fort covering the bridge would have ten, which made fourteen; five forts with four each brought the total to thirty-four. And how many in the castle of Santa Teresa? Twenty (five facing each way seemed a reasonable assumption), making a grand total of fifty-four guns.

"Will you attack as soon as we arrive or wait for the rest?" Thomas asked.

"Surprise – without it we don't stand a chance," Ned said, and thought they had precious little chance even with it. He wished he had not told the story of the Earl of Warwick and Pym: it reminded him, much too late, of a fact he had long ago forgotten – that the Spaniards finally had to use a large number of trained soldiers to capture the island...

It was a lapse of memory that could cost them dear. When Thomas had first mentioned leadership of the Brethren and then Leclerc had subsequently described the bullion at Portobelo and the stripping of the garrison at Providencia to reinforce the Spanish troops to land on Jamaica, he had been thinking only of the name they had used, 'Providencia'.

Admittedly he had known at once where it was when they mentioned it. He had noted it and thought no more about it as an island, except to remember that they must find a chart of the place, preferably Spanish. And one of the buccaneers had produced the one he was looking at now, found on board a small Spanish prize.

Yet until Aurelia asked about its early history, and why so many places on the chart had English names, he had completely forgotten about Pym and the Earl of Warwick and the English occupation for so many years of an island only 250 miles from Portobelo and more than 1,250 miles to leeward of Barbados. From Old Providence it was 1,250 miles to windward – which could mean having to cover twice or three times that distance to get there, tacking against the Trade winds. More than half the distance across the Atlantic... But, most important, only 250 miles from Portobelo, the centre for the bullion: the place to which donkeys and mules carried the silver in panniers in the last stage of the journey that began half-way down the South American coast at Arica, the port for the Potosi mines...

Here in Providencia – Old Providence rather – English religious fanatics had lived cheek by jowl with privateers, pirates and early buccaneers, and they all shared one thing in common (about the only thing, he thought to himself) a hatred of the papacy. Perhaps papacy in the case of the Puritans; Spaniards in general as far as the pirates and privateersmen were concerned.

For years Spain was too weak at sea to do anything about getting rid of this hornet's nest – because Old Providence was just that, with its hornets flying out to sting more or less at will. Then came an unsuccessful Spanish attack in 1635... His memory was working well now: five years later they attacked again with one thousand soldiers in six frigates and failed...finally they succeeded in 1641 with nine ships carrying more than two thousand trained soldiers. Oh yes, the more he thought the more he remembered, and it was time he stopped before his misgivings were spotted by Thomas and the two women. He was glad that Saxby remained on board the *Phoenix*; that man had an uncanny way of guessing one's thoughts. Two thousand troops and nine ships... He felt a cold shiver despite the scorching sun which was making the parchment of the chart kink and bump, drying out old dampness.

Old Providence and Henrietta, now Providencia and Santa Catalina. He could only hope the change of name would bring a change of fortune.

Ned stood up and called to the look-out at the *Griffin*'s masthead, a man almost enveloped in the tent-like awning he had rigged to protect himself from the burning sun. "Anything else in sight, Blackett?"

"Nothin' sorr, just the six ships round us."

"No sign of any wind shadows?"

"I saw one whiffle of wind to the north, sir, but it died."

Ned turned to Thomas, who had just stood up beside him as the two women, tanned a deep golden brown, remained kneeling and looking at the chart.

"Y'know, Ned, I've been thinking about the bad weather…" He scratched his beard and then twiddled the end between two fingers to make it curl. "What with the swell for the days before it, and the swell it left behind, I think it was really a small hurricane, not just a storm."

Ned grinned. "Well, my lord bishop, you've been at sea so long I was shy about mentioning it, but the wind did seem rather strong and the waves rather high…"

"I was going to mention it earlier, but – " Thomas glanced down at Diana and Aurelia " – I didn't want to alarm the ladies."

"You didn't, eh?" Diana said, looking up and winking at Ned. "Well, bishop, I was certain of *that* that after twelve hours. I didn't say anything," she added mischievously, "for fear of alarming *you*."

Aurelia held out a hand for Ned to help her to her feet. "Being of a nervous disposition anyway," she said, "I knew it was a hurricane before any of you. The way those swell waves grew higher and higher, even though at first we had a clear sky and a gentle breeze… I remember one of the men on the plantation telling me the swells – ground seas he called them – usually give the first warning, often several days before the hurricane arrives."

"So we all knew and we all said nothing," Ned commented. "Now we can speculate without embarrassment – are we the only survivors of the Brethren?"

"That's what's bothering me," Thomas admitted.

If losing the rest of the ships was his only bother, Ned thought to himself, he'd count himself lucky, but the figures of two thousand Spanish soldiers and nine frigates kept coming to mind like the persistent drumming of thunder. He said: "There's a chance they've been blown a long way to leeward and then the wind dropped so that they're becalmed like us, but spread over a hundred miles of sea."

"Seven, instead of twenty-eight," Thomas grumbled miserably, too absorbed to listen to Ned. "Good men lost."

"Whoa, bishop," Ned exclaimed. "You sink twenty-one ships with a wave of the hand? Or should I say a wave of your crozier."

Thomas turned to face Ned, his fingers now clasping his beard and his brows lowered. "We've lost two thirds of our men. Or we might have. Let's say that, with Old Providence in sight, we can't see two thirds of our ships. Don't you think *that*'s disastrous?"

Ned looked round quickly. None of the *Griffin*'s men was within earshot. With the ship becalmed most of those on watch were in the shade and Lobb had tactfully moved up to the fo'c'sle, from where he could keep an eye on the rest of the deck.

Ned shook his head and assumed a nonchalance he was far from feeling. "We have here – " he waved round the horizon at the seven ships " – 250 in our own three ships, and probably an average of fifty in each of the other four. That's 250 plus 200. So we have at least 450 men, all of them better trained than they were before, thanks to the three weeks with Heffer's instructors.

"So, leaving some men in the ships, we have to do with 400 (and complete surprise) what the Spanish could only do with thousands. But we can be fairly sure that most of Providence's Spanish garrison has gone to Jamaica with the Portobelo people."

Thomas wagged a warning finger. "You can't be *sure* of that!"

"No," Ned admitted, "but I believe the reports that Heffer received the day before we sailed, that Spanish troops had landed at Runaway Bay. They could only be the men from Portobelo and Providence. The Dons are leaving us open doors, my lord bishop. We need not bother to knock."

The breeze began at five o'clock in the evening with a series of light puffs making dancing shadows on the water, and by six o'clock it had settled in steadily from the northeast, sending Thomas and Diana back to the *Peleus* and allowing the seven ships to stretch down towards Old Providence. The conditions were perfect for being sure of keeping just far enough to the west to avoid running up on Low Cay but close enough to Santa Catalina to need only a few tacks to arrive off the little port.

A clear sky meant a starlit night, and with the darkness they could see Old Providence clearly as they approached, a black hump on a bluish-black horizon. By dawn the *Griffin*, leading the little squadron, was about three miles from the northwestern corner of Santa Catalina, and as soon as it was light Lobb spotted the particular cliff which looked like an enormous profile of a man's face. After that it became something of a competition between Lobb, Ned and Aurelia to identify objects marked on the chart.

From the northwest, Santa Catalina at first looked like a part of the main island, although a sharp eye could pick out the castle of Santa Teresa sitting four-square in the middle of the smaller island.

Finally they had worked out the approach through the rocks, coral reefs and cays: from northwest of Santa Catalina they had to steer for "The Face" as they christened the profile on the cliff, keeping it southeast by east, which also held a hill on the mainland – which they dubbed Fairway Hill – in line with it.

Once the two cays off the north coast lined up, the *Griffin* turned a couple of points to the east to avoid Cat Rock and then, as soon as they could see Split Hill with its great chasm over the southern end of Santa Catalina, they steered southeast.

Both Ned and Lobb were perspiring. It was a warm morning, although the sun was still below the horizon, but the seas breaking over isolated rocks and swirling over long stretches of coral reef warned that one mistake in identifying a hill, cay or rock (or a slight inaccuracy in the chart) would sink the *Griffin* and, because they were following close in their anxiety to steer precisely in the *Griffin*'s wake, the rest of the ships.

Lobb pointed to a position about five hundred yards to the southwest of "The Face". "That's about where you wanted us to anchor, wasn't it sir?"

It was the place Ned had chosen from the chart, but before answering he looked closely at the forts, which he could now distinguish as shadowy geometric shapes compared with the humps and bumps of Puerto Catalina on Old Providence, and they would be able to see along the narrow channel between the two islands. He turned to Lobb. "Yes, anchor there, and hoist out the boat and canoes as quickly as possible: the place seems asleep."

Lobb gave a series of orders and the *Griffin* turned into the wind and, as her headsails came sliding down, the big mainsail slatted. A shout and a wave of the hand set several men to work lowering the anchor and letting it go with a splash. The cable snaked out and as the *Griffin* dropped back the *Peleus*, with sails flapping, came in to anchor on one side and the *Phoenix* on the other, while the remaining buccaneers anchored close to leeward.

Within twenty minutes, the *Griffin*'s boats and canoes were leading nearly a score of other boats crowded with heavily-armed men and being rowed and paddled for the town. Ned had managed to persuade Aurelia to stay on board by convincing her that someone responsible had to remain with the five boatkeepers, and that she had the authority (and by implication the knowledge) to shift the *Griffin*'s berth in an emergency. He had anchored the buccaneer ships out of range of any Spanish guns – and by the same token the forts were out of range of the buccaneer guns.

The oar blades spattered him with drops of spray and the outline of the roofs of the houses forming the little port were becoming sharper as the sun, still beyond the horizon, reflected in the dawn haze behind them. It was too early for colours; Puerto Catalina was heavy with shadow, a jumbled mosaic of black and various greys. No doubt when it came the sun would show that the colours daubed on the houses were gaudy, and peeling or crumbling. Ned reflected that one rarely noticed a French or Spanish house newly painted, yet they must have been at some time or another to reach the faded state in which one always saw them.

The wind was light – too weak to carry out to sea the stench of the town, which was strong enough to make Ned wish he smoked a pipe. A year's rotting vegetables, a decade's sewage, and straw befouled and rejected long since by donkeys and horses – all must be heaped in the *plaza* and left to mull under the scorching sun. Spasmodically it would be spread by the torrential typical thunderstorms that frequently came of an afternoon and delivered in an hour as much water as a couple of days' steady rain in England.

As Ned's eyes searched the beach, cobbled streets, wide balconies and flat roofs he wondered that the smell was not visible, like a fog, or cloud of smoke spreading of its own accord from a giant bonfire. The idea of a visible smell amused him for two or three minutes, until he was roused by the grunts and curses of the men at the oars, and the hurried warning that one of the *Peleus'* boats was catching up and likely to reach the beach first.

As his boat's keel scraped on the sand and he leapt over the gunwale, careful to protect his pistol from the splashing, Ned realized what was strange about Puerto Catalina: there was not a man, woman or child in sight. No fisherman was preparing his rowing boat before the heat of the sun made it hard work, no woman stared curiously from a balcony as she hung bedding over the rail to air, there were no black-haired, dark-eyed children peering round a corner, curiosity overcoming fear, no old women were sitting on the ground mending nets ready for their men to start the day's fishing.

A cockerel crowed and fluttered its feathers to remind its brood who was master; a pack of five mongrel dogs ran yapping down a side-street on to the track between the beach and the buildings. The leader saw the boats, suddenly stopped and turned snarling on its four pursuers, who turned and slunk away, fearful of the strangers.

No shouted challenge, no scraping of a sword pulled from its scabbard, no musket shot, no flash and blast of a cannon, no sign of an ambush. Puerto Catalina was deserted: everyone must have fled inland or rushed over the bridge to Catalina Island. Gesturing to Lobb and several seamen to follow, and waving to Thomas, who was just about to jump down from his beached boat, Ned walked across the dusty track to the nearest house, which was built of wood on stone foundations. The front door was locked and so was the back, but a row of cabbages growing in the garden were missing the first three in the row and the gardener's footprints had not been washed away by the rain.

All the houses by the track obviously belonged to poor people: higher up the hillside above the port the homes were larger and more imposing, and no doubt there lived the port captain, the garrison commander, the mayor, and the town treasurer. The island governor, though, would probably live in remote splendour in Santa Teresa castle, across on Santa Catalina.

Thomas walked up to him, followed by a worried-looking Leclerc.

"Have the birds flown?" Thomas asked.

"Only walked across the bridge, I suspect," Ned gestured to Santa Catalina. "They must have spotted us last night..."

Thomas nodded and grimaced. "They could have seen us with a good perspective glass, I suppose. I thought we were too far away and didn't expect them to be keeping much of a look-out."

Leclerc held out his hands, palms uppermost. "There was nothing we could do about it – we were becalmed where Nature left us. Shall we look at the houses here before we call on the Spaniards over at the island?"

"Looking at the houses" was a polite way of asking if the buccaneers could search them for purchase, and forcing himself to remember that if the positions were reversed, the Spaniards would not only loot but then probably set fire to the town, Ned nodded. After passing the word to Lobb, he walked with Thomas along the track beside the channel between the two islands, away from the town.

Thomas stopped and pointed to a trail of horse droppings. They were still damp, an indication that a horse had passed within the last hour. Then Ned noticed that the bridge, a crude affair of planks, had been pulled back on to Santa Catalina island.

A bucket full of earth seemed suddenly to hit Ned in the face, and while falling he heard the noise of tearing calico and then the thump of a cannon firing. As he hit the ground he remembered noticing the ditch on the seaward side of the track and rolled a couple of times and then fell into it with a thump that knocked the breath out of him. A moment later the whole side of the hill seemed to collapse on him. He still had his eyes tight shut when the hill started to wriggle and curse, and although for the moment Ned could not clear the dust from his eyes, it became quite obvious that the landslide was called Thomas Whetstone, who had chosen the same ditch for shelter.

"You alright, Ned?"

"Will be, when I clear my eyes. Get your knee out of my stomach. What about you?"

"M'dignity suffered, but that's all."

"I saw that damn'd fort just as we stopped: until then it was hidden by a hill. We walked right into their – "

Ned stopped talking a moment as two more cannon balls thudded into the bank below them and whined as they ricocheted up from rocks.

" – field of fire and, to make it easier for them to aim, stopped and stood there gossiping."

"They're dropping the balls about ten yards short," Thomas said. "That first one was well down the bank. You were unlucky it heaved up a shovelful of earth."

"Better be hit by that than a ricocheting ball… Ah I can see again… I hope Leclerc doesn't try to rescue us."

"I shan't dissuade anyone from trying," Thomas said, "otherwise we'll be here until nightfall – that is, unless they start firing langrage."

"My lord bishop," Ned said, "forget about your dignity and start counting."

"Counting what?"

"Cannons. I'm sure that fort – " He broke off as two more roundshot fell short, but one of them sprayed stones and earth into the ditch.

" – has only two guns. It takes time to load 'em and we're out of the effective range of muskets. So we'll just wait for the next two rounds, then climb out of this ditch and rejoin our friends with all speed, and wait for them to finish looting."

"I noticed you walked away after giving them permission. Doesn't sit well with you, eh?"

"No. If they were warehouses or the treasury, I'd join in. But people's homes..."

Thomas rumbled his agreement. "Yes, it's the part I don't like either. Dam' poor gunners at that fort – they take so long to load."

"You're ready to leave here the moment after they next fire?"

Thomas was just answering when the ripping of calico and two thumps, then the sound of the guns firing, warned that the Spanish gunners had increased the elevation so that both shot hit the hillside ten yards above them, and rocks were still tumbling down on to the track as the two men scrambled out of the ditch and stood for moment looking across at the fort.

"No muskets," Ned said. "Let's walk back, though I feel like running."

"Yes, walk," Thomas agreed. "Looks better, and anyway my knees are a little shaky. That first ball ricocheted between us, you know!"

"Did it?" exclaimed a startled Ned. "How do you know?"

"Didn't you see it? A greyish blur, like an owl swooping over you at night."

They met Leclerc half-way back to the port, and once the Frenchman had assured himself they were unwounded he waved and scrambled back up the slope among the houses, passing some of the buccaneers carrying their spoils down to the boats.

Thomas sat down on the worn stone step of a house overlooking the beach, his back against the front door. "Buccaneers! They look more like wives coming back from the market," he exclaimed. "Sacks of rice and baskets of fruit and vegetables instead of gold and silver!"

"The people must have had good warning and carried their valuables into Santa Catalina," Ned said. "I wonder what they've done with their livestock – driven it into the mountains?"

Thomas looked across at Santa Catalina, sitting squarely in front of him like the top of a large hill sliced off and set down in the sea.

"There's only one way into that place," he said, "and that's across the bridge they've inconveniently removed. We'd never get up those cliffs – it'd be hard work for goats."

When Ned did not reply, Thomas said diffidently: "There's no reason why we should bother with it, I suppose; Portobelo is our target."

Thomas was quite right; Ned knew that if he was honest with himself his sole idea in attacking the two islands was to stir up the Spanish, frightening the Viceroy in Panama into withdrawing his soldiers from Jamaica. Yet the Providence garrison could only be recalled once the Spanish Viceroy knew that Providence and Portobelo were in danger or lost – and that could only be after the Portobelo raid. It would take days, perhaps two or three weeks, for the word to cross the Isthmus...

"You could say we've captured Providence without firing a shot," Ned said dryly. "With the Spanish shut up in that island across the way, there's not much they can do. Nor us, I suppose, although we can use the anchorage and hunt down their beeves..."

As if the Spanish had been listening to him, the crash of a cannon echoed between the two islands.

Both men, realizing this new gun was on the south side of Santa Catalina, looked across at the ships. A tall column of water leapt up two hundred yards or more short of the nearest privateer.

"Extreme range," Thomas commented. "No need to worry."

"What makes you say that?"

"The ball didn't bounce. When you throw a flat stone low on to the surface of a pond, it skates because of the low elevation. Throw a rounded pebble into the middle and it sinks where it hits because it is landing almost vertically. Obvious, Ned."

"Yes, your grace; it was a silly question."

"More to the point, though, one can see it is the extreme range for any guns they are likely to have over there."

At that moment Leclerc and several other captains appeared, breathless, after running down some of the side-streets. Ned pointed out where the shot had landed, but two of the captains were not convinced about the range, wanting to go back on board their ships and anchor further out.

"You can't get much further out because there's a reef to seaward of us," Ned said. "You can come closer in towards here, or back the way we came."

At that moment the gun fired again and there was another spurt of water in the same place.

"That's his ship," Leclerc said, pointing to one of the captains.

"Don't expect any sympathy from us," Thomas said sourly. "This earth on our clothes comes from the ditch up the hill there, where we were the sole targets of two guns, as you saw. *Well* within range, I assure you."

Leclerc spoke in rapid French to the captain, Rideau, who shrugged and started off up the hill to rejoin his men.

"What do we do now?" Leclerc asked.

"Capture Santa Catalina and then get under way for Portobelo," Ned said, and was surprised to hear his own voice speaking so matter-of-factly about a decision he was unaware he had made.

"This afternoon?" Leclerc asked, with more than a hint of sarcasm in his voice.

"No, tomorrow morning. It'll take the rest of the day for the men to get what they want from Puerto Catalina."

Back on board the *Griffin*, with Thomas having collected Diana from the *Peleus* on the way, Ned heard Aurelia's description of the cannon which had fired at the anchorage.

"Five shots, as you heard," she said. "And all the balls landed in more or less the same place, two or three hundred yards short of the nearest ship, *La Meduse*. When they fired no more I decided that was as far as they could reach, so I told the men we should not move the *Griffin*. They wanted to fire back, but with the perspective glass I could see the Spanish have the gun almost hidden among the rocks. And if they couldn't reach us I guessed we could not reach them..."

Ned looked at Diana, who was sitting on the settee in the cabin next to Aurelia, her hair hanging down in well-brushed ringlets and looking, but for her divided skirt, as though she was paying a social call on a country neighbour. "And what did the bishop's lady think?"

"The bishop's lady was rather cross. She had decided to make use of the bishop's absence by trimming her hair and washing it, we having plenty of water after that bad weather. So with wet hair wrapped up in a towel I came up on deck after the first bang, watched the fall of shot, used the perspective glass to see exactly where the gun was, reached the same decision as Aurelia, and went below to finish my hair."

"And very nice it looks." Ned said.

"Have the men finished looting Puerto Catalina yet?" Aurelia asked.

"No, they won't be done until nightfall. Don't sound so disapproving – this is their pay!" Ned said.

"I'm not disapproving," Aurelia said. "It's just that they're going into people's *homes*..."

"I agree," Diana said. "Rob the treasury, the governor's residence, the bishop's house, the arsenal, warehouses and shops – but I have the same feeling about homes."

"Ned's as soft as you are, " Thomas growled. "The Spanish landing in Jamaica would *burn* the homes after looting them..."

Ned put tankards on the table and reached for a bottle. "Thomas, would you open the door and pass the word for Lobb?"

The *Griffin*'s mate came down to the cabin.

Ned said: "I want you to pick a couple of men – ask for volunteers – to take a perspective glass and go over to Providence. They must climb up to the top of the easiest of these two closest peaks and watch for sail on the horizon. They should get back to the beach again an hour before sunset, and report to me."

Lobb grinned as he said: "I've just the right men, sir: a couple of Highlanders who've been telling me how these peaks and valleys remind them of home. Can they take muskets in case they see something worth shooting for fresh meat?"

"As long as they get to the top of a peak and then report to me an hour before sunset. They must be on board here by that time, or earlier if they sight more than four ships."

Lobb left the cabin and Thomas pointed to the glasses. "You're getting absent-minded: they're still empty." As soon as he had taken a sip or two of rum, he said: "The captains are due on board an hour before sunset, too."

"Yes," said Ned casually, "it's beginning to get cool by then."

"What are you hatching?"

Ned gave a mock frown. "The admiral of the Brethren doesn't 'hatch' anything. He makes well considered plans – like diving into a ditch – and gives well considered orders – like 'Get your knee out of my stomach!' "

The two women looked puzzled, and Thomas described the gun firing at them as they walked up the hill, and their leap into the ditch. He then looked at Ned. "You're not talking about the captains' meeting then?" Ned shook his head. "I'm not being mysterious, but it all depends on those Highlanders."

CHAPTER **NINE**

The captains arrived punctually in one boat, the rest of the craft still drawn up on the beach and being loaded with their purchase from the port, and Ned had just finished greeting them when Lobb reported that the two Highlanders were returning in a canoe.

Ned hurriedly handed the captains over to Thomas and took the Highlanders down to the cabin to hear their report in private. He had first to listen to one of them grumble bitterly at the amount of game to shoot, and after the second man had carefully returned the perspective glass, he heard what they had seen.

Then, after being assured in a dialect so broad he could barely understand it that Providence and Jamaica, with their mountains and valleys, crags and rocky spines, had so much more to offer than an island as flat as Barbados or as parched as Antigua, Ned thanked the men and went on deck to join the captains. They were gathered round Aurelia and Diana, both of whom were now wearing dresses with normal skirts and, Ned saw with pleasure, looked as though they were standing on their own lawns being agreeable at some function involving the estate's male employees.

There was not much time to waste: the sun seemed to drop faster and faster in its plunge to the western horizon, and Ned quickly told the captains what he intended to do. They listened and then grinned as they agreed to it. The only disagreement came from Nicolo Secco, the Spanish captain.

"They will trick you," he said flatly. "I know my countrymen. I must come as well. Do not introduce me – I will pretend to be your coxswain and bodyguard – I shall be able to hear any whispering and warn you in English without them realizing I speak Spanish."

Ned did not have to think twice: Secco was a shrewd man and according to Leclerc a good seaman and completely trustworthy.

"Come on then, Thomas, it's time we left." Ned looked round and saw Lobb standing beside the entry-port holding a boarding pike. He waved when he saw Ned glance towards him, indicating that the canoe was alongside.

Ned kissed Aurelia and whispered a promise for the night; Thomas gave Diana a bear-like hug. Secco gave the women a courtly bow and followed the two men.

Five minutes later, squatting in the canoe being paddled round the southern end of Santa Catalina and into the channel separating it from the main island, the three men discussed the plan as Thomas took the boarding pike and twirled it to unwind the large white flag which had been secured to the upper half.

"Paddle faster," he growled at the six seamen, "this cloth isn't streaming out enough!"

Would the Spaniards honour a flag of truce? Ned thought they had nothing to lose and perhaps much to gain. If they had any sense they would meet the boat on the narrow beach just below where the bridge had been pulled back on to Santa Catalina.

There were no signals from the stark cliffs on their left, no sign from this angle that a human being had ever set foot on the hills behind. Puerto Catalina on the big island, now well over on their right, looked completely deserted at this distance, apart from the buccaneer boats on the beach.

He called to the men at the paddles and pointed to the small beach now coming into view on Santa Catalina. Thomas jerked a thumb upwards towards the top of the cliffs. "That dam' fortress will be in sight in a moment – it's just round this square-topped cliff."

"We'll rename it Fort Whetstone!"

"You'll do no such thing! Leave it with its sainted name!"

The canoe had gone another three hundred yards, nearing the beach which was scooped out of the cliffs, when Ned noticed that steps had been carved out of the rock from the top of the cliffs down to sea level, and that five men were now standing on the sand. A movement at the top of the cliff soon turned into four more men coming down the steps, one of them carrying a white flag.

"The reception committee is arriving," he commented to Thomas and Secco.

"Thank goodness," Thomas muttered. "I was waiting for the fort to start target practice again."

Secco said: "Don't forget that my name is 'Brown'. If they suspected I was Spanish they might demand that I'm handed over as part of some agreement."

Thomas laughed and slapped Secco on the back. "Don't worry, we don't sell our friends and no one would take you for a Spaniard, my dear Brown. You might almost pass for an Englishman. A Welshman, anyway."

Two of the men paddling laughed delightedly, and Thomas added: "Sounds as though you have two countrymen there."

"Come round a little to larboard," Ned ordered. "We'll run the boat's stem up on the sand, but gently. A couple of you can stand in the water and hold her in case we have to leave in a hurry."

They were now a hundred yards from the sand and could see wavelets lapping on it. Twenty yards back ("Careful not to get their feet wet!" Thomas observed) stood two Spanish officers with three soldiers who were holding swords.

"They should be unarmed," Thomas grumbled, standing up with his white flag.

"Stop paddling," Ned ordered, and murmured to Thomas: "We'll wait until the Spaniard with their white flag has joined these chaps, just in case..."

As the boat drifted thirty yards from the water's edge, one of the Spanish officers made an impatient gesture, waving it in to the beach. Ned called in the careful Spanish which Aurelia had been teaching him: "We wait until your flag of truce has arrived and your men have removed their swords."

"You could be armed," came the uncompromising answer.

"We are not, but one man standing up in a canoe is enough; more might capsize it. Only three of us will land."

The officer turned to the soldiers, who thrust their swords into scabbards and walked over to the cliff, ostentatiously unbuckling their belts and leaving the swords and then returning.

By now the four men with the flag of truce had arrived at the far end of the beach. Ned saw that only the man carrying the flag and one other wore uniform; the other two were in ordinary clothes.

"Beach the boat," Ned said to the men with the paddles, and warned Thomas to sit down, in case the impact unbalanced him.

Within two minutes Ned, Thomas and "Brown" were standing on the beach, three seamen were holding the canoe so that it would not drift broadside-on, and the remaining three seamen stayed on board, paddling to help keep it in position.

Ned walked up to the two officers. "You see we are not armed," Ned said, "and we land under the flag of truce. My name is Yorke."

"Hernández," the older of the two officers said, bowing stiffly. "Commander of the garrison. And you are...?"

"An admiral. You see some of my ships." Ned gestured seaward.

"Pah, they are pirates. You are a pirate leader!"

Ned shrugged his shoulders and smiled pleasantly. He continued in slow, careful Spanish: "Do not let us quarrel over words. Pirates, privateers, buccaneers – you can see only a few of my ships. Their men are pleased to call me their admiral. You," and Ned's smile became even friendlier, "are less fortunate: you call yourself the garrison commander, but you have no garrison!"

The man went white. He had been lulled by Ned's quiet voice and smiling manner, little realizing that he was being led into a trap by a Ned who still was not sure that the garrison had been taken off and shipped to Jamaica.

"What's wrong with the fellow?" Thomas asked anxiously. "Looks as though he's going to faint."

"He said he was the garrison commander, but now he's just accidentally told me, without using words, that he has no garrison!"

At that moment the Spanish flag of truce and the two civilians arrived. One was obviously in command; he brusquely inquired of Hernández what was happening and was told, in fast nervous Spanish, that the pirates knew the garrison was gone.

The civilian swore at Hernández for saying it, since obviously one of the English spoke Spanish, but the soldier said angrily: "He speaks it very slowly, that was why I spoke quickly!"

Ned said to Hernández, deliberately thickening his accent and using wrong tenses: "You should introduce us."

Hernández asked the other man's permission, but before Hernández could speak the man snapped: "Vásquez, the Governor of Providencia. Why have you come here under a flag of truce? You raided our port first, now you want a truce!"

Ned shook his head politely and still spoke softly in bad Spanish. "No, you must give me an opportunity to explain. Your Excellency, *you* want the truce."

The governor, a portly, sallow-faced man in a large plumed hat and with drooping moustaches and clearly very short-sighted, obviously could hardly believe his ears. "*I* want a truce? Why, that is absurd! We sighted your ships – your *seven* ships," he said with sarcastic emphasis, "last night. We evacuated Providencia, manned our *nine* castles, fortresses, and batteries, and removed the bridge. So tell me please, why should *I* want a truce?" Hernández and the other officers and the civilian laughed dutifully.

"You had good look-outs on duty yesterday evening," Ned said, "and this morning at first light you saw the seven ships come in and anchor. Yes?"

"Yes," Vásquez said, his voice patronizing. "Seven ships. Seven small ships. And their boats took less than 400 men on shore, leaving four or five on board each ship."

"Your men have sharp eyes," Ned said admiringly, and both Vásquez and Hernández nodded their heads, as if accepting the praise. "But the look-outs on duty yesterday evening – what happened to them?"

Vásquez turned to Hernández. "Tell him. No, tell me first."

"They were sent to the guns. They fired at the ships this morning," he said very quickly.

"Did you understand that?" Vásquez asked, and when Ned shook his head, repeated it slowly.

Ned managed to look both sad and disappointed. "Oh," he said, like a man who had just found the answer to a puzzle. "So that is why you do not realize that *you* need the truce – "

"Explain yourself!" Vásquez interrupted angrily. "I did not ask for a truce, I do not *want* a truce, and I've granted *you* one against my better judgement."

Again Ned shook his head, hard put to avoid bursting out laughing as he adopted the more-in-sorrow-than-in-anger role, and thankful Thomas could not understand.

"I suggest, Your Excellency," he said politely, "that you send those look-outs up the hill again with a good – " he broke off, using his hands to imitate a perspective glass. "I do not know the word in Spanish."

Both Vásquez and Hernández stared at him. "What would they see?" the governor asked suspiciously.

"At this moment they would see in the last of the sunlight twenty-one ships – the rest of my fleet – on the horizon, approaching Santa Catalina. They will come in and anchor at daylight, so you see, I have twenty-eight ships, not seven."

Vásquez and Hernández began a violent argument with each other. The governor wanted to know why the look-outs had been sent to the guns instead of keeping a watch, and the garrison commander, forgetting Ned in his anger, said they were two of only eleven men who knew how to aim and fire a gun.

Secco's eyes caught Ned's for a moment, and Ned was thankful he had not misheard the commander. Nine forts, castles and batteries, with an estimated fifty guns, and only eleven men on Santa Catalina who could aim and fire them. The Spaniards had vastly underestimated the English: obviously when taking the garrisons of Portobelo and Providence they knew there were no English ships of war at Jamaica, simply the garrison of three thousand men to defend the island. Equally obviously, the Spanish authorities on the Main (the Viceroy of Panama? Ned was not sure) thought there was no danger in taking Providence's garrison – the island had never been attacked since the English were driven out seventeen years ago, and the English had run away after attempting Santo Domingo, losing thousands...

After telling Hernández to hold his tongue – using a vulgar phrase which he obviously assumed Ned would not know – Vásquez stood stiffly, pushing out his chest and bracing up his stomach, and told Ned: "The truce is over. You cannot possibly capture Santa Catalina, there is nothing to discuss."

Ned decided to play all his aces. This was a game that could be won in the next five minutes or otherwise last a couple of months – and certainly no buccaneer would wait that long.

"Nothing to *discuss,*" he said agreeably. "However, you should listen to my terms. They are generous – very generous."

"A pirate's terms *generous*?" Vásquez sneered.

"Yes. You see, I know that you have nine forts and half a hundred guns, and probably about three hundred quintals of powder in your magazines – enough to defend Santa Catalina for months, because of course you have a well of sweet water and no doubt plenty of grain. But, Your Excellency, who will aim and fire all those guns?

"You have only eleven trained men... And yes, you have drawn back the bridge, but I have three thousand men, agile as mountain goats – more so, because climbing rigging in a storm is much more difficult than scrambling up rocks... And of course, we would put the port to the torch before doing anything else. That would mean none of the refugees in your little fortress island will have a house when it is all over. Not a house, not a shop, not a tavern; just charred wood and blackened stone."

"You mentioned 'generous'..." Vásquez said, his voice strangled, his hands now shaking as he loosened the collar of his jerkin and took off his hat with its large white plume, " 'generous terms'?"

"Yes. We take or destroy all your cannon, shot, musket, pistols, and powder, pikes and swords and armour. We destroy any of the forts on Santa Catalina that I choose. That is all."

"All? What about the women and children?" Vásquez asked, unaware that he was revealing that he would accept the terms. "You promise to send all the prisoners to Portobelo or Cartagena? You give me a safe-conduct? No hostages – you must guarantee that – "

"You have heard my terms," Ned said, deliberately speaking in a harsh tone. "I want all your weapons. No prisoners, no hostages, no ransoms and no safe-conducts."

Vásquez slid down on to the sand in a faint, and Thomas said triumphantly: "I knew he would, he was swaying like a drunken curate. Dead faint. What on earth did you say?"

As Hernández and the other Spaniards knelt down round the governor, Secco muttered in English: "He misunderstood you – your grammar was bad. He thought you meant you were taking no prisoners or hostages, that you were going to kill everyone."

Thomas roared with laughter. "No wonder he fainted. Still, just shows you, Ned, he reckons you can do it. He can't have any defences up there!"

"They haven't," Ned said quickly. "Or at least, they have plenty of guns but no men to fire them."

Hernández stood up and coughed. "The governor will be himself in a minute – ah!" He bent and helped the man to his feet. Vásquez brushed the sand from his sleeves, breathing deeply, and then turned on Ned.

"I protest!" he said angrily. "I have four hundred women and children up there, and five hundred old people, and – "

"Your Excellency, be silent. Let me say my terms again; my grammar was bad. I want all guns, powder, muskets, other weapons and armour. I shall destroy any forts, castles or batteries I please. I shall *not* touch any man, woman or child you now have in Santa Catalina. When we sail you will all be left here as you are now. Puerto Catalina will not be burned."

He looked at Vásquez, who looked down at the sand.

"And if I do not agree to these terms?"

Ned turned and waved dramatically to where the sun had just dropped below the horizon, leaving a crimson haze. "Then you and every man, woman and child on Santa Catalina have seen their last sunset!"

Vásquez dropped to his knees and began praying, and Ned tried to compose his face into a ruthless mask for the sake of Hernández, although fearful that Thomas would wink and destroy the effect. "I have no need to tell you *what* it means because you are a soldier. The smoke of the guns, the screams of the wounded, the earth shaking as magazines explode..."

"Madre de Dios," Hernández muttered. "I am a retired soldier, of the quartermaster branch. I allocated supplies in the Netherlands, not fired guns... This morning was the nearest I have ever been to guns when they are fired."

Ned shook his head sadly and pointed down to Vásquez. "You had better interrupt his prayers to see what the Good Lord has advised him, because I am going back to my ship and unless he agrees to my terms the next time I see him will be when my sailors bury him."

As Hernández knelt beside the praying governor, Ned cursed that Thomas did not speak Spanish: he was pleased with the way the most bloodcurdling of threats came easily to his tongue. On the other hand, Thomas better than anyone else knew that he could never carry them out, and was likely to laugh – or at least tease him for weeks.

Then the governor and the garrison commander were standing to attention in front of him, hose and breeches covered in sand.

"I accept your terms," Vásquez said hurriedly. "But they must be in writing. Properly signed."

"Yes, yes, yes," Ned said, guessing the man would go on qualifying it for hours. "You can come out to the ship now and we will draw up the document – two copies, one for you and one for me," he added hurriedly, "and we can all sleep soundly, and tomorrow we can start carrying out the terms."

"I come out to your ship?" Vásquez asked fearfully. "But I have no security! You must leave a hostage!"

"You cannot dictate terms. However, I shall also want the garrison commander's signature on the documents, and there is not room for both of you in the canoe unless I leave one of my people behind. I shall leave this gentleman – " he pointed to Thomas " – he is my second in command."

Vásquez nodded but eyed the narrow canoe fearfully. "That is safe?"

"Safe enough," Ned said. "Now, you can remove your shoes or get them wet!"

He explained to the boatmen that they had two passengers, and told Thomas he would have to stay behind for half an hour. Because neither Vásquez nor Hernández had explained anything to the other men on the beach, none knew that Thomas was supposed to be a hostage. Ned explained: "You're supposed to be a hostage, your grace, but I'll send a canoe for you as soon as I get back on board. You'll have half an hour of mosquitoes, then you can join us and watch the signing, and listen to the governor call me a cheat for not leaving you here."

"By the way, Ned, why have they agreed to surrender?"

"They know there are twenty-one more of our ships in sight. At least, because they've taken away their look-outs, they've taken my word for it."

"*Are* there twenty-one?"

"Yes. My Highlanders climbed to the top of that hill and saw them in the distance. A bit strung out, but obviously they can see Providence."

Vásquez climbed up the rope ladder behind Ned, stepped warily on to the *Griffin*'s deck and, without looking round the ship, waited for Hernández to follow. He did not see who greeted Ned until, with the garrison commander beside him, he turned to find two beautiful women smiling at him, one with ash-coloured hair and the other black hair in long ringlets.

Ned, whose quick wink had warned the women what to do, watched Vásquez for a few moments and there was little doubt that the man was going pale again. However, he knew enough of the Spanish pride to know that it was important to stop the governor making a fool of himself in front of women. Then he realized that, although the two women had given Vásquez a shock, what had made him go pale was the sight of the buccaneer captains, who were still on board, standing in a group close by the entry-port. Each had a tankard of rum in his hands, all wore swords of different patterns, all were unshaven and had that desperate look that went with independent men. It was not, of course, desperate: that was simply how it was interpreted by other men living a more routine life, and Governor Vásquez's life was obviously bounded on all sides by routine and the narrow confines of Providence and Santa Catalina.

Vásquez, Ned reflected, had seen first the Sirens to lure him and then, beyond them, the bearded rocks that could be his doom.

He stepped forward. "Your Excellency…permit me to introduce you to Mrs Yorke – " he thought the exaggeration was only one of time, and permissible " – and Miss Diana Gilbert-Manners. His Excellency the Governor of Providence."

Ned had deliberately spoken in a leisurely voice, giving the man time to recover. Vásquez bowed deeply but as Aurelia and Diana were both deliberately standing with their hands behind their backs to avoid it, he made no attempt to kiss them. He turned and gestured to Hernández, introducing him as the garrison commander, but managing to imply that he was of little consequence. After gesturing to Secco and Lobb to take the two Spaniards down to the cabin, Ned took the women by the arm and moved aft. "Thomas will be along in a few minutes: the canoe has gone back to fetch him."

"I was beginning to wonder," Diana admitted. "Are we permitted to ask what is happening?"

"Yes, of course you are," Ned said with the vagueness he knew irritated Aurelia.

"Very well, we *are* asking," Aurelia said. "Why do we now have the governor of Providencia and the commander of the garrison on board?"

"We have some documents to sign."

"Documents?" Diana exclaimed. "Is he selling you beeves, or vegetables?"

"Oh no, he's given us both islands..."

"Given?"

"Well, surrendered is the correct word."

Diana turned and put her arms round him and kissed him full on the lips. "I don't know how you did it," she said, "but that's your reward from me."

He turned to Aurelia with a grin, but she shook her head. "You'll get mine later," she said and then blushed.

Ned led the way down to the cabin, where Lobb and Secco were lighting lanterns and the two Spaniards were trying to look at ease. The two women followed, and in excellent Spanish Aurelia asked the men what refreshment they would like. Both Spaniards refused with an elaborate politeness that made Ned think they were secretly congratulating themselves on avoiding poisoned wine.

Ned put paper, quill and ink on the table, waited while Secco and Lobb trimmed the wicks of the lanterns, and then said: "Your Excellency, let us prepare an inventory of Santa Catalina's defences."

He pulled the wooden plug from the ink bottle. "Now, the castle, Santa Teresa, I believe you call it."

Vásquez told Hernández: "You know all the figures. Tell him."

The garrison commander wrinkled his brow. "Twenty guns in four different sizes, all English – 18-, 12-, 8- and 6-pounders. Ten pipes of Spanish muskets with ten muskets to each pipe. Spanish-made swords, pikes, breast and back plates of armour..."

"Continue with the various forts," Ned instructed, dipping the quill into the bottle again and taking a fresh sheet of paper.

"The next biggest is Fort St Jerome, by the bridge. Eight guns, all English, 12-, 8- and 6- pounders. Two pipes of muskets, I think, but I don't know about swords and armour."

"What about powder?" Ned asked.

"Altogether there are three hundred quintals of coarse, and fifty quintals of priming powder, Spanish of course, but it is distributed among the forts and batteries according to the number of guns they have."

Ned finished writing and said: "Carry on with the forts – names and numbers of guns."

"Well, St Joseph's fort has six guns, 12- and 8-pounders. Like the rest of them it has muskets, armour, swords, but I do not know the figures. St Matthew's Fort has three 8-pounders; St Augustine's has three guns, 8- and 6-pounders; Santa Cruz has three guns but I cannot remember the weights, except that they were cast in Spain. San Salvador's Fort, and the two batteries, each have two guns, Spanish, but I do not recall the sizes. And twelve falcons with carriages – they are in the courtyard of Santa Teresa."

"And roundshot?" Ned asked.

"I cannot remember exactly, but not too many for the English guns because the shot are old and they rust and get smaller when they are scaled. You saw this morning that the shot would not reach your ships – they were such a poor fit in the bore of the guns that they rolled about like an orange in a bucket."

"Give me a rough figure."

"About two hundred shot for each English gun, and three hundred for the Spanish."

"And totals of armour?"

"I think there are one hundred breast plates, one hundred back plates, and fifty helmets."

"What else?"

"Eighteen barrels of balls for the muskets – they are all in the magazine of Santa Teresa, because we were just about to issue them. Let me see...four hundred empty grenade cases, in good condition and newly painted...fourteen barrels of brimstone, but the barrels are not in good condition..."

"Slow-match, pistols, pistol balls, flints?"

"Ah yes, a total of three hundred bundles of slow-match in Santa Teresa, and two bundles in each of the other positions. Four skips of pistols – about five hundred altogether, all fine Spanish wheel-locks. Fifteen barrels of balls for them. Flints – about five thousand: a ship brought us several barrels recently. We get them from the Netherlands," he said vaguely.

"That is the whole inventory?"

"All that's left. You see, the garrison – " he broke off when he realized the significance of what he had been about to say.

Ned gave a dry laugh. "The garrison was taken to Jamaica. Yes, I was aware of that."

Vásquez said: "Do you know what has happened to them?"

Ned shrugged his shoulders expressively. "The English were expecting them and they have a large garrison..." Both facts, Ned thought, were quite true; Vásquez, judging from his long face, was drawing the wrong conclusion.

A bellow of laughter told Ned that Thomas had arrived on board, and Vásquez looked up, startled. "My second-in-command has returned," Ned said, forestalling any protest. "There was no point leaving him standing on the beach to be eaten by your mosquitoes, which probably welcome a change to Protestant blood."

He collected the sheets of paper listing Santa Catalina's inventory and handed them to Aurelia. "I shall need four copies of that for tomorrow, when we start collecting it."

He turned back to Vásquez but paused as Thomas came down the companionway scratching himself and cursing.

"Those sandflies and mosquitoes," he growled. "They have bites like sword thrusts!"

"You're just in time to help draw up the surrender terms."

"Keep it short and simple, Ned. Then we can't argue afterwards about the wording."

Ned nodded. "You're quite right. Let's draft it in English on one side of a sheet of paper, and then translate it. Two copies and all four of us to sign."

For the next fifteen minutes Ned and Thomas wrote, crossed out, altered and rewrote a draft while the two women, Lobb and Secco made criticisms and suggestions, and Vásquez and Hernández sat in the lantern light looking like subjects waiting to model for a painting by one of the sadder Dutch masters.

Finally Ned sighed and put down his quill. "I think that will do. Let me read it aloud in English from beginning to end without anyone interrupting."

When he had finished and Thomas, Secco and Lobb agreed it was adequate, Aurelia suddenly said: "I have just been looking through the inventory. Your surrender terms really mean that the Spaniards hand over all the arms on Santa Catalina, true?"

Ned nodded warily: he knew only too well that when Aurelia used this tone of voice she felt very strongly about something.

"You are not making them provide grain, cattle, hogs; you are not even making them provide labour to restore the bridge and carry this stuff across so that you can load it from the port."

"No, well," Ned began lamely, and Thomas offered a tentative: "Well, you see – "

"I do *not* see," Aurelia said firmly. "You men have made an agreement with these two – these two poltroons – where you allow them to give you back English guns, a few paltry Spanish pistols, and a few quintals of Spanish powder which is probably damp and you know is always unreliable. This," she said with a contemptuous gesture which threw the pages of the inventory across the table and made one of the lanterns flicker, "you call a great victory. It is – for the Spanish. They give you back your guns and get rid of you!"

There was a full minute of complete silence in the cabin, broken eventually by Diana. "And take that silly grin off your face, Thomas. At least Ned bluffed them into surrendering the place – "

"He didn't bluff them!" Thomas protested. "The rest of the ships are in sight!"

Diana waved away the protest, but Ned said: "You're right, *ma chérie*, and I've handled it all very stupidly – "

"But," Thomas interrupted, "Don Poltroon here will agree to our terms, so that's like a contract. It's as though we've given our word."

"One does not give one's word to a scoundrel, nor accept his," Diana said haughtily. "Anyway, he hasn't heard the terms yet."

"Yes, dear," Thomas said, a plaintive note in his voice. "But Ned and I, slow-witted coxcombs that we are, have given our word, so there's nothing we can do about it."

Vásquez said nervously in Spanish: "You quarrel: There are difficulties? Do we not sign the papers?"

"It is nothing," Ned said, "my wife is complaining that she cannot read my writing – she is to make copies of the inventory."

Vásquez smiled understandingly. "The words used by artillerymen are hard to understand, and you had to write quickly."

Ned did not bother to translate for the others: he was becoming angry, the more so because he knew Aurelia was right. He and Thomas had behaved like two excited schoolboys raiding a neighbour's orchard.

Yet...yet...the fact was he never wanted to capture and keep Old Providence; never even considered the idea. He wanted to seize it long enough to scare the Spanish authorities into recalling the Jamaica expedition, and while he held it he wanted to pull its teeth by taking or destroying its guns, so that when the garrison returned their only weapons would be the muskets, swords and pikes they carried with them.

The idea of holding on to Providence was nonsense, despite the arguments of Leclerc and the other buccaneers. Why burden buccaneers with guarding and garrisoning Providence as a base when Heffer and three thousand soldiers were going to do it all for nothing at Jamaica? Certainly Providence was only a couple of hundred miles from the Main and near the Isthmus, but it was further from Cuba and Hispaniola by as much as it was nearer the Main.

If the English government (providing ships) wanted to control the West Indies, then having Barbados to windward of everything and Jamaica to leeward and covering it from the north and acting as a main base, was sound strategy, with Providence a hornet's nest close to Portobelo and Cartagena. But let the King provide troops, guns, powder and ships; the buccaneers were being generous enough already, taking on the seaward defence of Jamaica.

"Well?" Aurelia demanded. "You are just daydreaming."

Ned picked up the sheet of paper on which they had drafted the terms of surrender and sat down. He read them through and then said in English to Secco: "As it can't complicate anything now, would you like to read this to the governor in Spanish? I don't want any misunderstandings."

Secco grinned wickedly. "It will be an honour. And from now on each of them will fear a knife in the back!"

Ned looked puzzled and Secco explained: "I am his enemy but I am also Spanish, so they trust you but won't trust me. They know I would be happy to use a knife; they know you never would."

Ned shrugged his shoulders. "Don't be too sure about that. Now, read it aloud and then write a copy in Spanish."

The remaining twenty-one buccaneer ships arrived off the island just after dawn to find an open boat – a local fishing boat confiscated by Ned – tacking back and forth under a tattered sail a couple of miles offshore, ready to pilot them in, round rocks and coral reefs that would not be visible under the water until the sun was higher in the sky.

With their ships anchored, the twenty-one captains had themselves rowed over to the *Griffin* to get the latest news and describe how, after being scattered by the hurricane, they collected themselves together, waited out the subsequent calm and then, led by Brace, made for the rendezvous at Old Providence.

Because they had noted that the seven ships were all anchored out of the arcs of fire of Santa Catalina's forts, and probably out of range anyway, they did not think to ask what had been happening; instead they wanted to hear Ned's plans for attacking both the large and small islands.

Two or three of them had noticed that Puerto Catalina was deserted, and guessed that the inhabitants had fled across to the little island. Most of them at first thought Ned was joking when he said that the governor had surrendered both islands the previous evening, and the seven ships had the purchase from Puerto Catalina waiting for the share-out, but in the meantime all the weapons, powder and armour on Santa Catalina were waiting for them to collect or destroy.

After the captains were convinced and left hurriedly with their orders, Ned had himself rowed to Santa Catalina, collecting Thomas from the *Peleus* on the way and joining Leclerc on the beach, where he was waiting with the captains and crews.

As soon as all the captains were standing about waiting on the strip of sand, he climbed on to a flat-topped rock at the eastern end so that all could hear him and read out the inventory provided by Hernández.

"Our first task is to get the bridge hauled across again. Then we need to confiscate all carts – and horses, donkeys and mules. We need to bring everything across the bridge and take it down to the port so that we can carry it out to the ships. Now, who needs more cannon? They are mostly iron guns. I need a couple of light bronze, but the twelve falcons on field carriages we'll take with us to Portobelo."

Several of the captains spoke up for guns, but all agreed that using Santa Catalina's falcons to attack Portobelo would be a fine joke to play on the Dons.

The breast and back plates of armour, and the helmets, one of the captains pointed out, would be useful at Portobelo. "No man using it should put it on until he's landed," Brace warned. "Anyone who falls into the sea wearing a breast plate and back won't come up again, and anyway that's the way armour goes rusty!"

The five Dutch captains did not laugh, Ned noticed, and wondered if it was the lack of a sense of humour or if anything significant had happened to them concerning armour.

All the captains wanted a few muskets, pistols, swords and pikes, and it was agreed to share them out once they were brought down to the port. Everyone was suspicious of Spanish powder until Ned pointed out it could be used for blasting, something they might well be doing against the forts in Portobelo.

One of the captains pointed out that if they all scattered and began work at different forts, some unsuitable guns might be moved to the bridge, causing unnecessary work when men could be used more usefully elsewhere. This led to Ned and Thomas deciding to go first to each position and inspect the guns, marking with a piece of chalk which should be taken and which spiked or destroyed. Leclerc was told to pick a hundred men to start moving armour, muskets, pistols, swords and pikes.

CHAPTER TEN

It took an hour to slide the heavy planks of the bridge back in place, with both Hernández and Vásquez watching, the former giving the heaving and cursing buccaneers advice how it should be done. Both Ned and Thomas had agreed not to accept Spanish help; that was a certain way, Ned had warned, for the Spaniards to let it drop "accidentally" into the sea below.

While Leclerc supervised the bridge, Ned and Thomas began inspecting Santa Teresa, a move which brought Vásquez along, dogging their heels like a spaniel and apparently anxious to steer the two Englishmen away from his living quarters. His efforts were so clumsy that Ned and Thomas, thoroughly suspicious, suddenly smashed down the door, crossed the hall and went into the nearest room to see an enormous near-naked woman rushing through the opposite door, scattering combs and lingerie, screaming that the English were coming, *Madre de Dios,* and appealing to several saints for help.

"My wife," Vásquez said in some agitation.

"I am sorry, you have my sympathy," Ned said politely, but the governor missed the irony.

In the armoury they inspected the breast and back plates of armour and helmets hanging on hooks, the metal rubbed over with goose grease.

"Several of the leather straps need renewing," Thomas observed, pointing at the straps and buckles fastening the front and back at each side.

"Your helmet," Ned said, nodding to the only one with a plume. The helmets were well made and carefully designed, looking like an elaborate version of a Roman centurion's, but with a lower crest and more pronounced peak, as well as a wide lip at the back, angled out to protect the nape of the neck.

The halberds reminded Ned of a past age. They were as long as the pikes in racks beside them, and each had a sharp pike head for stabbing, while on one side there was a blade shaped like the head of an executioner's axe, and on the other a short claw, curved and sharp.

Also hanging down from hooks were powder flasks. Ned noted that, decorated in bright enamels and without the straps, they would look well on my lady's dressing table. The flasks were triangular brass boxes with spouts at the apex. A lever on the side worked a measure, so when the nozzle of the flask pointed downwards into the bore of a musket, only a certain quantity of gunpowder came out. There were two sizes of flask, the larger for ordinary powder and the smaller for priming, which was always finer and supposedly of better quality.

Swords were also hung up on hooks. Ned drew one from its scabbard. Double-edged with guillons but no knuckle guard or pommel, it was a simple military broadsword but well made. Between each was a short sword, a wide-bladed dirk with a heavy guard and guillons which stuck out and down like horns. "Used as a *main-gauche,* I should think." Thomas commented. "You use your broadsword to deflect your opponent's sword to one side, and with his body then unprotected, you give him a jab with this overgrown dagger which you are holding in your other hand."

"So every man with a broadsword also has one of these," commented Ned. "Helmet, breast and back plates, broadsword and *main-gauche* – or a pike and halberd. Or, of course, a musket, sword and *main-gauche.*"

"Where are the muskets and pistols?" he asked Vásquez in Spanish. The governor led the way into the next room and pointed to several long wooden cylinders and to two tubs.

"Ten muskets to a pipe," Ned murmured to Thomas. "There should be a hundred here." He saw a pipe with its end levered off and pulled out one of the muskets. It was thickly coated with goose grease but, Ned was irritated to note, was a matchlock, not a wheel-lock. He pointed it out to Thomas, who shrugged his shoulders.

"Wheel-locks are all right, but look at that trusty serpentine there." He pointed to an S-shaped fitting on the right-hand side, a screw through the bottom allowing the claw at the top to swing over. "A nice glowing piece of slow-match stuck in the claw of the serpentine, and a pan cover that flicks aside easily..."

"Yes, all very nice, especially in pouring rain and a high wind, so you end up with a sodden slow-match and an empty pan!"

"The enemy would have the same problem," Thomas said, "so you toss the musket aside and set to with swords. But with a wheel-lock, a weak spring won't spark the wheel against the pyrites fast enough to make sparks, or the pyrites are faulty. So your pistol doesn't fire, but your enemy, with a strong spring or better pyrites, deposits a pistol ball in your gizzard with a bang you won't hear."

Ned grunted and walked over to the tubs of pistols and saw they too were matchlocks.

"Mind you, a good Italian wheel-lock pistol," Thomas said, "which I had owned since it was made – ah, that would be worth having. But a pistol that has been tossed about, fitted with pyrites that no one has selected, spanned by clumsy oafs paying no heed to the tension spring – suicide!"

It took two hours to inspect all the guns and discover that Hernández had been correct in saying that many of the guns had been cast in England, but he had not mentioned that most of them bore the rose and crown and initials of Queen Elizabeth. Nor had he said they were made of bronze, not iron.

"I expect Pym's expedition visited the Tower of London before leaving England," Ned said, "and found these carriage pieces and took them before they could be melted down again. Fine guns," he added, peering into the muzzle of one of them, "just as long as we have enough shot of the English size. We must find some shot gauges, too; otherwise in the excitement of action someone might use Spanish shot and blow up a gun."

"Just think of it, Ned, *El Draco* could have used these guns," Thomas mused. "Drake was a hero of my boyhood. We'll be using the falcons at Portobelo within a few leagues of where they buried him at sea."

Ned was inspecting the touch-hole of one culverin at that moment and said: "This gun looks as though it hasn't fired a dozen rounds since Gloriana died more than half a century ago!"

There were iron guns at St Jerome, St Joseph, and La Plataforma de los Artilleros which had rusted to the point where they were more danger to their users than the target: rust had been hammered off and the guns painted so many times that it was difficult to read any gunfounder's marks.

Ned noted them on his list. "These get turned so their breeches are seaward. Double-shot them with a double-charge, then run a slow-match to the pan. Get everyone out of the way and then as each gun fires, its own recoil will hurl it over the cliff and into the sea."

"Where did you learn that trick?"

"I've just thought of it."

"You have a pleasantly devious mind." Thomas said.

Aurelia and Diana walked along the street forming the front of Puerto Catalina, both commenting that because they had been at sea so long they seemed to be walking uphill. Nor could they walk an absolutely straight line. "We shall end up like drunken sailors rolling down the high street," Diana grumbled, standing to one side as a dozen seamen came running down the hill from the bridge with a small brass cannon on a carriage.

They were followed by several French sailors steering a four-wheel cart which was almost running away with them and clattering as though scores of pots and pans were being kicked round a stone-floored kitchen. Aurelia's question about their load so startled the sailors, who expected neither to see a beautiful woman standing beside the road nor to hear her speak French, that three of them let go of the shafts, anxious to hear her, until their shipmates yelled at them in alarm.

"Armour," Aurelia told Diana. "We might have guessed that from the noise."

"I'd have expected kettles, with a dozen drunken tinkers mending them."

Diana then asked the men hauling the next cart what was in the barrels, and received the cryptic answer: "Powder, ma'am."

She turned to Aurelia and, pointing across to the island of Santa Catalina, crowned by its castle, said: "You were rather hard on Ned last night, you know. He captured Puerto Catalina and that island entirely by bluff, with not a life lost."

Aurelia nodded in partial agreement. "Yes," she admitted, "but why bluff like that and accept a small prize when you could have a large one?"

Diana said soberly: "I don't think Ned really wants these islands. He thinks that extra guns and powder might be helpful in the attack on Portobelo. Extra so that he can leave them there when he's finished."

"I suppose I was angry at a Spaniard getting the better of him," Aurelia admitted. "Giving him guns that originally belonged to Queen Elizabeth... Still, the powder is Spanish!"

"The cannons matter less, I think, than the muskets, pistols, swords and pikes. The Spanish make the best swords, so Thomas says, and the buccaneers were short of hand-guns. Now I think they're well satisfied."

"Will they argue with Ned about leaving Santa Catalina?"

"No, I don't think so," Diana assured her. "They respect his judgement. They'll follow – and obey – him just as long as he is successful. He was successful at Santiago and he has been successful here."

"Supposing he fails at Portobelo?"

"It depends why. If it was his fault, they'd probably elect a new leader. Portobelo is the greatest raid they've ever undertaken, so one can only guess."

"But they would never have been able to plan it themselves," Aurelia protested.

Diana laughed and patted Aurelia's arm to take the sting out of what she was going to say. "Let's bear in mind that we also don't know for sure that Ned and Thomas can do it. Snatching a year's bullion won't be easy. The Dons are poor sailors, but no one's faulted them as builders and defenders of castles."

"Ned never wanted to be elected admiral," Aurelia said quietly, as though talking to herself. "I suspect he was happier with just Thomas and Saxby."

"I know Thomas and Saxby were but, as Thomas says, the only way to get rich enough to be able to settle down is by leading all the buccaneers on a few big raids."

"Settle down!" Aurelia exclaimed. "I don't think I could go back to that life again, either in Barbados or London. All that making lace and needlepoint and conversation limited to the colours of the thread and the patterns and some dreary woman saying she is expecting her fifth child and looking for a good wet-nurse – yes, and unfaithful husbands and sordid *affaires* and what is happening at court: not the politics but who was seen flirting with whom... Who *cares*? Life does not bore me, but people can – and do!"

Diana sighed. "That's exactly why I left England with Thomas: I didn't care. I love Thomas, life with him is exciting, we're never reduced to talking about the harvest or the cattle not giving so much milk."

She stopped and looked calmly at Aurelia. "My dear, in a way we've already ruined our lives, or committed ourselves. If we lived near each other in England, we would, as you say, be reduced to discussing lace bobbins and other people's *affaires*. But out here, we discuss the capture of Santiago. In England as a dutiful wife you might chide your husband for selling one of your favourite horses, but out here you've just been chiding him for the terms he laid down for the Spaniards to surrender two islands."

"I wonder if, even in old age, we could ever go back again to bobbins and *affaires*. Supposing Ned and Thomas each made a fortune from buccaneering, and hung us with jewels and gave us fine clothes and splendid homes with dozens of servants...could you bear it?"

"For a year, perhaps," Aurelia said. "For six months I could look at the jewellery, finger the fine cloth, train the servants, plan a beautiful garden, furnish the house as I would want it, and for another six months live on the memories of Santiago, Santa Catalina, Portobelo and a dozen other raids.

"Then would begin *le grand ennui*: an immense boredom. An immense boredom because I *have* the finest jewels, I *have* the finest clothes, I *have* a house everyone envies, I *have* three splendid coaches, drawn by black, white, grey and brown – bay, do you call them? – horses. The excitement is in *getting*; the boredom is *having*. Ned would grow as dull as a cabbage. I should grow as fat as a turnip. We should bore each other."

"My dear," Diana said, "you think too much. What was it that Shakespeare wrote in Julius Caesar: 'Let me have men about me that are fat, sleek headed men and such as sleep o'nights. Yon Cassius has a lean and hungry look, he thinks too much, such men are dangerous!' Perhaps the same goes for women!"

"Lean and hungry?" Aurelia repeated in alarm. "You don't think I look 'lean and hungry' do you, Diana?"

The Englishwoman patted her own hips. "You are not as well nourished as I am – but no, you are not 'lean and hungry'. You don't look the kind who are dangerous! But don't think too much; accept things as they come!"

They stood back off the track as two more carts came thundering down the hill, the buccaneers pulling back on the shafts to slow them.

The first cart was under the command of a Dutchman who spoke enough English to understand Diana's question and imitate a man holding a pistol; the second cart was loaded with large wooden cylinders which were, the men told Aurelia, pipes of muskets, ten muskets in every cylinder.

The two women turned up a side-street and began walking uphill through the small town. Several houses had balconies running completely round the upper floor, the roof sloping well out to shade them. But the paint on the planking was peeling and on several houses the planks were dropping at one end or another, showing where termites were eating away round the nails and leaving the houses looking scarred and wounded.

Wooden shutters over the lower windows were obviously the favourite of termites and several, slewed on their hinges, gave houses the appearance of bespectacled old men winking lewdly at passers-by. On walls and under the eaves of most of the houses were stuck small balls of mud, looking like miniature nests of swifts. Diana pointed them out and Aurelia explained that they were made by wasps, and inside were small tubes in which they laid their eggs. The newly-hatched wasps broke their way out, but the nests remained.

Both women were startled when a frightened hen squawked away from under a bush. It was, Aurelia commented, the first living thing they had seen on the island, apart from buccaneers.

The two of them were trying to avoid breathing deeply, as though it would lessen the stench. Most houses had their own piles of garbage near the back door, and the only island noise was a persistent buzzing of swarms of flies which hovered over the heaps like clouds of smoke from smouldering bonfires.

Finally Diana said: "I think my curiosity is being stifled: this stench is appalling. Do they never pile up the rubbish and burn it? The women must toss everything out of the kitchen window. Look at that house – either the husband loves cabbages or they grow well in his garden: the old leaves and stumps outside the kitchen window must be five inches thick."

Aurelia agreed and they walked round several more houses before finding another street running back down to the water's edge. By chance they emerged where the buccaneers were unloading the booty from Santa Catalina. The wooden cylinders were being broken open and the muskets stacked; tubs full of pistols were ready to be hoisted into the boats, barrels of powder and shot were being checked and the quantities called out to a buccaneer who, seated at a table taken from one of the houses, was making an inventory.

"Lets go across to Santa Catalina," Aurelia suggested. "We'll let the Spanish garrison see the cruel and ruthless women buccaneers."

At that moment there was a muffled explosion and a black tube belching smoke left one of the batteries like a rocket and then began slowly cartwheeling as it dropped into the sea between the islands. One of the buccaneers, realizing that the two women thought the Spanish were somehow launching an attack, called out in English: "It's all right, ladies: the admiral's getting rid of some old guns he don't want."

"What's wrong with nailing them?" Diana asked.

"He ordered them to ream out the vent so it can never be repaired, which is better than nailing. (Drive in a nail and pein it over, ma'am, and a good armourer can drill it out. But this way...) Then they turn 'em round so that when they're fired the recoil drives them off the battery into the sea. Saves a lot of pushing and hauling, as you've just seen!"

"We'd better watch where we're going," Aurelia said warily. "We might walk in through the castle gate just as they are blowing it up."

At that moment a second explosion heralded another cannon flying through the air, spouting smoke and slowly turning as it splashed into the sea, sending up one last great bubble of smoke as though expressing exasperation.

"Iron guns," the buccaneer said. "The admiral reckons they date from before the Armada! They're just rust held together with blacking. Wonder they never fell to pieces in a high wind! It's the bronze guns we're after. We can use them."

When he saw Aurelia and Diana turning to go up the hill he said: "A crowd of us are just going back to Santa Teresa. We'll escort you ladies."

Late that evening Ned and Thomas, worn out from the day's work, almost deafened by the explosions which sent old cannon recoiling over the cliffs, and feet throbbing from so much unaccustomed walking, most of it up or down hill, looked at the pages of the inventory of materials taken from Santa Catalina and still being ferried out to the ships.

"One thing is certain," Ned said, "either Hernández didn't really know what there was in the castle and forts, or he was deliberately telling us there was a lot less."

"Why do that?" Thomas asked. "He knew we were going to take it."

"I know, but I can't credit a garrison commander being so wrong – unless, I suppose, you look at the governor."

"You saw Vásquez's house?" Thomas asked, and when Ned nodded, added: "You didn't come right inside with me. I don't think his wife, or mistress, that big, fat, sulky-looking woman, gives him a moment's peace in bed or out of it. But his main interests, I think are eating and playing cards. It was the house of a spoiled man, not a soldier. He's just living out the rest of his life on a pension, glad to be forgotten by his superiors."

Ned grinned at the thought of Vásquez, full of food and wine after an unlucky evening at cards, being harried in bed by an importunate wife. He started reading through the inventories, and referring to a list of his own.

"We have fourteen bronze falcons, all with land carriages. They fire a 2- or 3-pound ball and we have one hundred for each of them. They're useful guns and are light enough to be hauled by hand – half a dozen men, I should think.

"Then come eight iron falcons (I believe you can also call them half-sakers) and fortress carriages, firing a 4-pound ball. A hundred shot for each of them. Five bronze sakers and carriages firing a 6-pound ball, seven sakers (also called quarter culverins, aren't they?) with a 9-pound shot, and three mortars.

"We blew up nine culverins and eight whole culverins. They fired a 40-pound shot. Seeing the crown and rose on top of the barrel, and 'Pour défendre', one could almost imagine Drake watching us and shaking his head."

He put two pages to one side. "So much for the great guns. Oh yes, I forgot to mention – the falcons can be carried on horses, according to Secco. He showed me how you take the carriages apart. The wheels unbolt from the axles and you sling a barrel on each side on one horse, and another carries two wheels, trail and axle..."

Thomas grunted unenthusiastically. "We're turning ourselves into soldiers," he grumbled.

Ned's brow wrinkled with impatience as he said: "We've been into all that before... We stay soldiers until the Spaniards get more ships and put to sea. Anyway, let's read on. Muskets – seventy-three pipes. They've opened them up and shared them out among our ships, 730 matchlocks."

Again Thomas growled his disapproval. "Muskets in the Tropics. If your men are well trained and well disciplined, you'll be lucky to have 'em fire once in two or three minutes. A longbowman can loose off six aimed arrows in a minute and be a good deal more accurate over the same range. Man for man, it's twelve arrows against one bullet in two minutes."

Ned groaned and put down the inventory. The longbow versus matchlock was one of Thomas' favourite arguments. "Well, your longbowman can have a pistol as well – we have two hundred wheel-lock and four hundred matchlock."

"Matchlock for me," Thomas said. "I'd sooner trust my life – or someone else's death – to a good piece of slow-match that I can see and smell burning than an unreliable spring or faulty pyrites."

"Yes, quite, so you said before. You'll have the choice. Now, the armour. One hundred breast plates, one hundred back, and fifty helmets, one with a plume. Some repairs needed on the leather straps of the armour. Halberds – fifty, all with new ash staves; pikes – seventy-five, also with new staves."

"And powder and shot enough for all the great guns and handguns," Thomas said. "And two islands and nine forts... Not a bad haul, I suppose. Am I invited for supper?"

"You weren't, but Aurelia's already sent a canoe for Diana, so you'd better stay."

CHAPTER ELEVEN

Inspecting his ships through the perspective glass, Ned could see that on board the twelve that had a carriage gun secured on deck, the buccaneers were exercising at loading, training and elevating. Other men were taking advantage of the light northwesterly breeze, which gave them a quartering wind and a calm sea, to move about wearing armour and helmets as they exercised with swords, pikes and halberds. Ned did not envy them: the sun was hot enough to make metal uncomfortable to touch, but the buccaneers were experienced enough to know that in a few day's time that same armour might save them from a fatal wound.

Amidships in the *Griffin* two bronze falcons had been lashed down, with wedges under the wheels, and Lobb was patiently explaining that point-blank range did *not* mean with the muzzle stuck in the target's stomach, but the distance a shot travelled in an absolutely straight line before gravity made it droop – often as much as two or three hundred yards.

Aurelia and Diana were listening carefully while Thomas, who had taken advantage of the quieter sea to pay a visit, came up to talk with Ned. They had been at sea three days: with light winds it had taken more than a night and a day to drop the three peaks of Providence below the horizon, and they had sailed due east all the time they were in sight of the Spaniards. Due east was a course that gave nothing away to Hernández or Vásquez: the buccaneers were obviously intending to alter course at nightfall – and that could be north to Hispaniola and Jamaica, south to the Isthmus and Portobelo or Chagres, southeast to Cartagena, or east to turn away to Riohacha, Santa Marta, Maracaibo... Or on to any of the islands to windward.

Thomas took a folded paper from inside his jerkin and smoothed it out. "This is the best that Secco could do by way of a map of Portobelo. He has one or two old maps on board but they didn't help much."

"And Bahia las Minas?"

"He doesn't know it as well as I do, but he agrees it's the best anchorage."

"Have you drawn that chart yet?"

"Yes," Thomas said, diving a hand into his jerkin again and bringing out a roll of parchment. "At least, Diana did. She has a more delicate touch with the pen – and a better memory, too: it's a couple of years since we visited it with the *Peleus*. The *Pearl,*" he corrected himself. "I forget we changed the name. I prefer *Peleus* anyway; we've decided to keep it." He thought for a minute, trying to make up his mind whether to mention something. Finally he said: "I think Secco expected to be told more, Ned."

"Everyone wants to be told more. But if they walk into a trap set by the enemy they'll never admit it was because they gossiped."

"There's not much chance with us all at sea." Thomas protested.

"No, but one ship could stray and get captured. That hurricane scattered us and could have put a few ships ashore on the Main. Supposing something like that happens again before we get to Portobelo, and the Dons get hold of them and strap them to the rack?"

"But they would never talk!"

"Why not?" Ned asked quietly. "You remember the rack we saw in the cathedral at Santiago. Those leather straps were dark, stained with the sweat and blood of victims; the wheels and ratchets turned easily with the coating of tallow."

"That doesn't mean a man would talk!"

"What's there to stop him? Do you think they all have a burning loyalty to the Brethren, a sort of religious fervour? I don't! They are Brethren to get purchase. I wouldn't blame them for talking. But by not giving them information they won't need until much later we make it easier for them if they are caught and put on the rack; they can tell all they know – but they don't endanger anyone because they don't know anything that matters."

"But they all know we're going to attack Portobelo!"

"Yes, because people have gossiped. But have they any idea *how*? Are we going to sail straight into the harbour and engage the forts? Or climb the mountains and besiege them? If the Spaniards knew we're going to attack the place, the news wouldn't help much: they need to know *how*, and so far only you and I know that. Without us there'll be no attack, so if we're captured we could reveal everything without risking the lives of the Brethren!"

"They'd lose the bullion, though."

"Not necessarily: eventually someone might think of a good way of attacking..."

"Four forts to be captured by a few hundred men!" Thomas said sourly.

Ned grinned to cheer up a man he rarely saw depressed or nervous. "Why don't you start worrying about how to stow the silver bars – they're heavy to carry you know."

"I could bear it," Thomas said. "Now, is Diana's chart of the Bahia las Minas sufficient?"

Instead of inking in the outlines as in a normal chart, she had produced an excellent perspective drawing of a high-flying frigate bird's view as it flew in from seaward.

Although the bird would not know it was looking south, it would see to its left mountains and high hills which gradually flattened as they came to the right across its view to become a flat and uninteresting coastline fringed with mangrove swamps, rocky reefs and banks of coral and visited only by Indians in canoes scooped from solid tree trunks; people who lived on fish and never planted.

The two highest peaks in the drawing were close to the shore and the highest was called the Pan de Azúcar. It did not need a knowledge of Spanish to know that its name meant "sugar loaf" in English. Further inland three higher peaks beyond formed a distant triangle and warned of a rugged countryside where only goats and mountain sheep would feel at home.

Ned concentrated on the left-hand side of the drawing, trying to impress on his memory what he would see as he sailed eastward towards Portobelo. Then he looked at the centre of Diana's drawing, where her excellent use of perspective showed with remarkable realism three rivers running into the sea.

To the right of them and still moving westward, where the coast was shown as solid mangroves growing to the water's edge, like the slime lining a stagnant pond, there was another peak, Cerro Merced, with two islands in a large bay just in front of it.

Very cleverly she had emphasized Cerro Merced without exaggerating it but obviously meaning that it was a good marker for the particular two islands (among many others) which were small, low and lined with mangrove and would, from seaward, be hard to distinguish against the shore.

The two islands were together called Cayos Naranjos, which he recognized as meaning the Orange Cays. The left-hand one was named Naranjo Arriba and the other Naranjo Abajo, though he could not follow why one should be called "Upper" and the other "Lower". The two cays formed the eastern side of a deep bay strewn with islands, cays and reefs and which swept round to where the large island of Galeta formed its western side.

The bay was the Bahia las Minas while the largest islands inside it, scattered like fallen fruit, were Payardi, Samba Bonita, Pina Guapa, Drogue and Largo Remo. The names were written in Diana's neat calligraphy and Ned noticed that steering direct for the mountain Cerro Merced, while keeping the peaks of the Pan de Azúcar and Las Palmas (which were nearer the coast and close to Portobelo) to the east, would bring them right up to the Bahia las Minas. After that, Thomas would have to pilot them in: the entrance was four miles wide, but the bay was crowded with so many islands, cays and reefs that it seemed impossible that twenty-eight buccaneer ships could hide there, although Thomas assured him there was room for fifty.

Would it all work? Ned looked at Diana's drawing yet again, admiring her skill and picturing the approach to the bay, which was about twenty-five miles west of Portobelo. The plan for the attack was simple, and simplicity was the most important part of any enterprise involving a large number of men. Of course, simplicity alone could not guarantee success, but it was a *good* plan; Thomas admitted that, even though he did not like it. He could not explain why, and Ned began to suspect that Thomas was simply uncomfortable with such a large force. It was not large in the number of men (on the contrary, considering what they had to do) but it was in terms of ships.

Twenty-eight ships sounded a large fleet, and looking astern at the number of sails following the *Griffin* it looked it, until one realized that they were all small vessels, most of them carrying four or six guns, and some eight. Only a few had more than a hundred men on board.

Thomas, whose opinion he had to consider since it was the only one he heard, was particularly concerned that they might be seen by a *guardacosta* or, anchored in the Bahia las Minas, by fishermen. When Ned pointed out that fishermen and fishing boats could be captured, and certainly no one could get overland in time to warn Portobelo, Thomas had grunted his agreement; not entirely convinced, but not so uncertain that he wanted to make an issue of it.

It was the nearest to an argument they had reached so far in their relationship. Not disagreeing, though, because each trusted the other's judgement well enough to listen, to accept a criticism in the spirit in which it was meant, and modify ideas when necessary.

Diana (she and Aurelia knew the details; it was impossible to keep it from them and Ned never intended to) liked the plan and thought it stood a good chance of succeeding, but (like Aurelia) understood Thomas' reservations. Like Aurelia, she had said flatly to Thomas: "We have to use Ned's plan unless you can think of something better."

Lobb came up, his hair soaking and clothes sodden from perspiration. "They've got the hang of loading and aiming the carriage guns," he reported. "They prefer 'em to ship guns – barrel at a more comfortable height for ramming, so they say."

"Aye, and they're that much more exposed to enemy fire," Thomas commented. "Tell 'em that. Better an aching back with a ship gun than getting your head knocked off because a land gun has big wheels!"

Diana had walked up in time to hear Thomas and said impatiently: "Cheer up, Thomas; you are going round like a black cloud."

"Sir," Lobb said, "I was wondering if we could unlash the wheels of one of the falcons so the men could get used to moving it about and taking the carriage to pieces. Apart from running the falcons down the hill from the Santa Catalina bridge, the only ones they've ever moved are ship guns using train tackles."

Ned glanced round the horizon as he felt the slight roll of the ship beneath his feet. The sky was almost cloudless and an unbelievable blue; the sky had the deep purple tinge of the ocean. A few terns jinked and wheeled in the *Griffin*'s wake and the big black frigate birds soared as effortlessly as children's kites and dived after the flying fish. What the men would learn while hauling and pushing a falcon round the *Griffin*'s deck that would help them later he did not know, but taking the carriages apart would be useful, and it showed that at least they were keen. "All right," he said, "but secure it the moment we start rolling."

Diana stayed with them and Ned beckoned to Aurelia. This sort of gunnery exercise, he decided was not for women: the gun running away with the men could cause a great deal of damage with those iron-hooped wheels, even with guys secured to the eyebolts at each end of the axle to restrain them.

Early on Sunday morning, with a good northerly breeze driving the squadron towards the Isthmus, a look-out in the *Griffin* sighted the three peaks forming a triangle behind the Pan de Azúcar and two hours later the perspective glass revealed the lower mountains nearer the coast, including the Pan de Azúcar itself. Soon they were close enough to distinguish the land sloping downwards to the west like a wedge until it reached Cerro Merced, which it seemed to be trying to drive under and lift.

The sun still hung low, and the mountains were a dull grey, with one side in shadow and the peaks seeming to hang above the horizon, not connected to the land, looking like thunderclouds forming in the distance. As the sun rose and lit their lower slopes they grew down to the land, and then slowly the peaks turned a bluish grey and formed more regular shapes as the sun lifted away the shadows on the western slopes.

Finally they could see, well over on the larboard side, the high land that surrounded Portobelo and made the port little more than an alley cut into the mountains. According to Thomas and Secco, Portobelo was nearly always airless – the high hills, mountains really, cut of the winds, and the inner part of the harbour ended in a swamp right beside what passed for a town. Four forts, four hundred people living in the town and normally a garrison of a thousand… Secco said that yellow fever was as common as ague in England and killed as many in Portobelo each year as were born, so that year after year the population remained the same.

Ned looked astern at his little fleet and once again was reminded of ducklings following their mother across a pond.

Not that the *Griffin* was so much bigger, but the ships were spread out in a wide vee, as though they were the *Griffin's* wake. Each ship, it seemed, wanted to be a little more to one side or the other than her next ahead, presumably to have a good view.

Saxby in the *Phoenix* stayed precisely on the *Griffin*'s larboard quarter, with Thomas in the *Peleus* on the starboard quarter, so that with the *Griffin* ahead the three of them led the rest like a wedge. Ned was pleased to see that the buccaneers were making an effort to keep in some sort of station; if one of them began to forge ahead, she reduced sail or eased a sheet to slow down. Thomas had previously warned that most buccaneer voyages comprised a farewell wave at the beginning and then a ragged rendezvous at the town to be attacked, and this had been the reason for many failures, because the irregular arrivals gave the Spaniards time to escape to safety with their valuables or prepare a defence.

Ned had been emphatic when he talked to the buccaneer captains. They could surprise the enemy by arriving off a Spanish town all together and deliver a real punch; arriving singly over two or three days meant they were merely giving the sort of gentle slaps that would startle but not kill a mosquito.

Aurelia came up on deck and stood with Ned. The sun had bleached her hair even more. In Barbados it had been the colour of an ash branch stripped of its bark; now it was silvery-blonde, emphasizing the deep golden tan of her face, shoulders and arms. Ned, excited at the enemy coast ahead and his ships astern, thought he had never seen such an attractive woman: she stirred him so that with his ships astern he felt he could conquer the world, but for the moment would be contented with taking her down to the cabin.

"That's the Pan de Azúcar?" she asked, pointing over the larboard bow.

"Yes. Portobelo is just to the left of it. That line of lower hills form the western side."

"Don't you feel nervous? You slept well enough!"

"Excited, but not really nervous. Anyway, we won't be attacking it for another two or three days."

"I know, but I'm excited. Not over the prospect of fighting," she said frankly, "but the idea of all that silver... Ned, supposing they've taken it all back to Panama?"

"Don't," he pleaded in mock dismay. "I've been trying to avoid thinking of that possibility since I first heard about it!"

"Is that armour as hot as it looks?" she said, pointing to some men on the foredeck who were wearing it and fencing with wooden swords, obviously trying to accustom themselves to the change of balance with so much extra weight above their waists and the movement of their heads and necks restricted by the helmets.

"I haven't tried it, but I presume so," Ned said. "The sun is so hot that touching a metal fitting on deck almost scorches you. It's the helmet I'd hate."

"Spanish armour has such a distinctive shape – like the Romans wore. I've seen them on coins, I think. Or paintings."

"The distinctive shape is what gave me the idea," Ned said.

Aurelia watched for several minutes. "You know, *chéri,* those men move as easily as if they had been wearing armour for years."

"I hope Thomas and Secco have been training their men as well as Lobb has."

"Do you trust this man Secco?" she asked suddenly.

"Yes, completely."

"Why?"

Ned gave a dry laugh. "It's quite simple. He has been a buccaneer for some years; he has raided many towns on the Main – I checked that."

"But what makes you trust him?"

"Because if the Spanish ever caught him they would – if he was lucky – garrotte him slowly as a traitor. If he was unlucky they might make it last a month. Any man who takes such risks obviously has an enormous hatred of his own country. He's not going to betray us to them. The Brethren can make him rich; the Spanish can only kill him."

Aurelia nodded her head. "Yes, of course, you are right. Of all the captains, we can trust Secco. What about the others – the French and the Dutch, and the English, too, I suppose?"

"We have to trust them all," he said, turning to glare at the two men at the tiller as the *Griffin* luffed up slightly because of their inattention. "When you think about it, every one of the Brethren is hand-picked. The captains have nothing to gain by treachery, nor the men. Imagine a buccaneer who went to the Spaniards. Unless he spoke Spanish they'd garrotte him before he could tell them his news. But even if he managed to tell them, I'm sure most buccaneers would know what would happen once they'd sung their song. Instead of applause and a fat reward, they'd still be killed: the Dons feel very strongly about buccaneers and buccaneering, and the idea of getting information from a traitorous one and then executing him by way of reward would appeal to them."

Aurelia shivered, despite the sun's heat. "The cruelty of it all," she said.

Ned turned on her. "Cruelty, yes. But remember there'd be practically none if the Spanish let people trade freely with the Main. They stick to 'The Line'. Why the devil should they draw a line – or get a Pope to draw it for them – north and south just three hundred miles west of the Azores, and say only Spanish ships can cross it? And warn that any foreigner crossing it faces execution? 'No peace beyond the Line' – well, it hasn't stopped foreign trade with the Main, because the Dons living there need goods and have to allow smugglers, as you know well enough."

"I know, I know, I'm not making excuses for the Spaniards. It is just that my Huguenot blood makes me angry when I see religion mixed up with trade."

"It's a priest-ridden country," Ned said, "though until a few weeks ago England, at the other extreme, was as bad."

"Oh, Ned," she protested. "Cromwell was never as bad as that!"

"No laughing on Sunday, no ornaments in churches, wrecking the inside of Ely cathedral, for example, no Catholic daring to raise his voice and most forced to flee along with Royalists... Whether Protestant or Catholic, the extremes always anger me. Why are most of us buccaneers? Because we wanted to be left in peace, but Cromwell's Puritans and the Spanish king's Catholics would interfere."

"Think of the poor Spaniards," Aurelia said. "Their king and government interfere with them out here, from what I hear."

"Oh, yes. By law they have to live in communities; a man can't just build himself a house in the hills. They can only buy goods from Spain – and the problem is that Spain can't supply, so they have to go without. And one Spanish colony cannot trade with another: it has to go through Spain, which means crossing the Atlantic twice. And even if goods do arrive from Spain, they pay taxes on the value in the colony – which can be very high if no ships have come in for a year or so. That's why most Spaniards welcome smugglers!"

"Amen," Aurelia said. "Let's change the subject. We both agree we don't want to be subjects of His Most Catholic Majesty."

"I love you," he said.

Eight hours later the *Griffin*, led by a boat from the *Peleus* carrying Thomas as pilot, sailed into the lee of the island called Largo Remo, with Samba Bonita on her quarter and Galeta Island astern, and dropped an anchor in three fathoms of murky water.

Ned was not sure if it was the mangroves lining the bay and putting a fringe round each of the islands and cays, but compared with the clear water of Old Providence, Jamaica and Tortuga, the Bahia las Minas, big as it was, had the greenish brown of a village pond in England on a winter's day.

Ned walked over to Lobb, who was standing on the foredeck, satisfied that the anchor was holding. "Very well," he said, "now we must start getting the boats and canoes loaded."

As soon as it was dark Lobb supervised the lighting of a carefully trimmed lantern and then hung it out on an oar over the *Griffin*'s transom, where it made a small pond of weak light.

Ned and Aurelia stood by the taffrail, and Aurelia held a large pin and a sheet of paper on which was written a list. Fish attracted by light came to the surface, jinking like silver swallows and never stopping for a moment, occasionally leaping clear of the water as a large predator attacked from below a prey outlined against the light above. A school of mullet cruised near the top of the water large-eyed, keeping formation like well trained cavalry executing a caracole. Tiny silversides, the minnows of the ocean, jumped like spray blown by a sharp gust, desperately trying to avoid capture. While mosquitoes whined in the inevitable descant of the Tropics, tree frogs kept up a monotonous metallic scraping from the island. An occasional swooping white object showed a seabird, roused by the lantern, which could see all the fish swimming in its light but was too confused by the shadows to risk a dive.

Ned heard the creaking of oars in rowlocks and then the bow of a boat nosed into the circle of light. There were perhaps a dozen men in it, the light reflecting from gleaming eyes and shiny teeth, but incongruously two wheels were lying flat on the thwarts forward with an axle and the trail on the floorboards, and some sacks stowed aft.

"Name – *nom de vaisseau*?"

Ned thought he could just distinguish the stocky, black-bearded French captain, Jean-Pierre Rideau, and a moment later the man stood up to call: "*La Méduse*!"

"I've pricked her," Aurelia said, "She should be carrying a complete carriage and two hundred shot for a falcon."

"How many shot?" Ned called, now able to see clearly the parts of the carriage.

"Two hundred for the falcon and five hundred musket balls."

"Good – *bon voyage*: you can lead the way. Who's that coming up now?"

"Leclerc," Rideau said. "I will get out of his way!"

He growled an order to his men, who bent their backs to the oars.

One of the *Perdrix*'s boats then rowed under the *Griffin*'s stern. Leclerc had painted them yellow, but in the yellow candlelight from the lantern the boat now seemed almost grey and shapeless.

Leclerc stood up. "*Perdrix*'s first boat: two falcon barrels, five hundred roundshot, twenty-five muskets, two hundred musket balls, fifteen halberds, one barrel of powder."

Aurelia had been pricking at her list. "He has more roundshot than we expected," she commented.

"The more the better: the number I gave each captain was the minimum."

"*Bon voyage,* Leclerc: follow Rideau. I'll meet you at the rendezvous about dawn."

Boat after boat came under the *Griffin*'s stern, reported its ship's name and cargo, and rowed off eastward into to the darkness. As Aurelia pricked them on her list, Ned realized that all the boats were carrying more powder and shot than he had expected. The captains had taken to heart his warning that capturing four defended forts was not going to be child's play.

Lobb, who had earlier hoisted out the *Griffin*'s two boats and three canoes, came up to report formally that they were loaded, reading from a list Ned had given him. One boat carried a complete falcon in pieces – barrel, wheels, trail and axle lashed out of the way of the oarsmen – plus roundshot and musket balls, in sacks and barrels. One canoe carried only powder, another only shot, the third drinking water, boucaned meat, a half cask of nails and several hammers, while axes and half a dozen saws, well greased and sharpened that afternoon, were stowed ready for constructing scaling ladders from whatever saplings, bamboo and timber could be found near the port.

Finally the last buccaneer boat, one from the *Peleus* and with Thomas on board, came out of the ring of darkness in which it had been waiting. Thomas sang out the contents and Aurelia checked them against her list. Like several of the other boats, this one carried drinking water and boucaned meat. Ned sent him after the previous boat, told Lobb to dispatch the *Griffin*'s canoes, and turned to Aurelia.

"Until noon on Wednesday," he said. "Are you sure you can manage? Enough seamen? Shall I tell Lobb to stay on board?"

She sighed, an exasperated I-knew-you-were-going-to-say-that-sigh. "We've discussed all that a dozen times, *mon cher*. Go on, go now or I shall weep and embarrass everyone." She kissed him fiercely and then hurried below, as if wanting to avoid watching him go down the rope ladder into the boat.

From time to time when rowing through pale-green patches of phosphorescence they could see the oar blades of boats ahead dipping into the water like blurred fireflies. Southwards on the starboard hand the coast was like a sleeping serpent, here curving out to within a few hundred yards, there swinging in to a mile, and always distinguishable as an uneven black band ending where the stars began.

A windless night... Ned had prayed but never expected it. If the north wind had continued blowing on shore and strengthened, it would have made this an uncomfortable, perhaps impossible row, probably bringing heavy swells across the width of the Caribbee which would slide under the wind waves, driving up breakers to line this coast and make it impossible to land. Northers...luckily it was still early for them, but December and January would bring the cold north winds and the rough seas riding on the swells.

He mentally ticked off each part of the coast as he identified it: both of the Cayos Naranjos had slid past, low in the water; he had picked out the peak of Cerro Merced against a background of stars. The next six miles comprised a low shore, mangrove swamps blurring where the sea met the flat land, but gradually hills now appeared as the boat moved steadily eastward.

Then, stark against a part of the sky full of stars, Ned could make out the Pan de Azúcar and Las Palmas close to the shore, with the other three peaks, including La Machina, beyond them, well inland to the south.

The slop of the oar entering the water and the gurgle of it coming out again, the creak of the oar against the rowlocks, the grunt of the oarsman and the groan made by his weight on the thwart, the chuckling of the boat's stem as the oars thrust it through the water, the occasional skittering of a fish, probably a gar or needlefish, startled and escaping by skating along the top of the water like a flat stone skimmed across a pond... The noises were monotonous and he felt dazed; a sort of sleep without being asleep.

That was the mouth of the Rio Piedras, a scoop in the land. They had covered about six miles from the last river, the Rio Grande, which in turn was three or four miles east of the Cayos Naranjos...which made it another two miles to Punta Gorda, cliffs sticking out into the sea like a semicircular balcony... Then four miles on to their destination, the Rio Guanche. He only hoped that Thomas' memory was good, and the river entrance wide and the banks irregular enough to hide the boats without being so swampy that they could not get ashore.

The mosquitoes had attacked his wrists so that they were hot, itchy tubes of flesh a third thicker than usual. His face too, was so bitten and puffy that his eyes were swelling up; he must look like a battered prizefighter. Mosquitoes reinforced by the almost invisible sandflies that bit like sharp needles and could hardly be seen in daylight: the West Indies, he reflected ruefully, provided man with few if any really deadly natural enemies apart from disease but made up for it with many persistent irritations.

It took an enormous effort to concentrate as the *Griffin*'s boat worked its way to the head of the straggling column. No, he told himself, he was not so much sleepy as dazed. Too much sun during the day, he supposed and the monotony of the noises in the darkness. Ah, here at last was the leading boat, from *La Méduse* and with the bearded Rideau calling a greeting.

"We're nearly there!" Rideau called. "I can just distinguish Punta Gorda. We might arrive before the mosquitoes eat me completely. No lard or smoke now," he added ruefully.

No lard when moving about; no tobacco leaves which they burned on land to keep the insects away. The buccaneers, Ned realized, were changing. They had started, so many years ago, as refugees and were called "The Cow Killers": Dutchmen escaping the Spaniards occupying the Netherlands; Frenchmen, many of them Huguenots like Aurelia, escaping from the Catholics; Englishmen (and Scots, Welshmen and Irishmen) escaping the Puritans. Yes, and the scoundrels of all nations, too, apprentices breaking their articles, debtors, murderers.

Yet the majority were men who wanted to be free, and over the years they had gathered in small groups along the coasts of Puerto Rico, Hispaniola and Cuba, killing the beeves and hogs that ran wild after being left by the Spaniards working their way westward, leaving island after island in their fruitless search for gold, and finally finding it waiting in unbelievable quantities in Mexico.

Curing the hides and selling them to passing ships, or exchanging them for powder and shot to kill more beeves, or hot liquors to swamp melancholy and drown their memories, the buccaneers had smoked meat in boucans to preserve it (getting the new name of *boucaniers*), and used some of the hides to make rudimentary boots, breeches, jerkins and hats: dried sinews became laces for boots or jerkins; small bones were sawn crosswise into discs and drilled as buttons. They saw how the Arawaks made canoes by burning out the inside of a log. As Rideau's remark recalled, they smeared lard over the exposed parts of their bodies to ward off the dawn and dust attacks of mosquitoes and sandflies. On a plantation, of course, the wealthy planter always burned tobacco leaves so the smoke drifted across his hammaco or bed, noxious fumes which drove away the insects.

By now the buccaneers had, for the most part, their own ships – captured from the Dons or belonging to bold captains who had sailed out from Europe intending to trade with the Main by smuggling or to rob the Spaniards by raiding. Eventually, when this did not yield a reasonable living, these captains had recruited the buccaneers because they were men who had little or more to learn about life – or death – in the West Indies and who seemed to have some immunity to diseases like yellow fever (known to the Spanish as the black vomit, *vomito negro*).

By leaving their little groups on the coast and joining the ships, the original cattle killers had lost much of their original simple life and left a peaceful existence for a fighting one. The tubs of lard, for instance. Certainly when they slaughtered beeves and hogs to boucan enough meat to go on a raid, they could stock up lard and the hides to make clothing, but mosquitoes rarely reached out across the water to where buccaneer ships normally anchored. Still, at least half the men now in the buccaneer ships had never lived the life of the earlier cow killers. Yet, Ned reflected, they were still desperate men; they hated the Spanish and they sought purchase, and he was glad he did not have to say which they put first.

Aurelia. She was alone with the *Griffin*. Alone, except for enough seamen to work the ship. Diana, too, on board the *Peleus*. Each could be the lady of a great house in England; out here they were only women buccaneers. But now, he told himself hurriedly, was not the time to start worrying about their safety or their ability to bring the ships round – to lead the buccaneers. He was thankful that all the seamen seemed proud of the two women. They could have been resentful, even refused to obey their orders or sail with them. Instead the Griffins and the

Peleuses boasted about them to the other buccaneers, and both Ned and Thomas suspected that several of the other captains (Rideau and Brace, for example, who had taken to trimming their beards more carefully) hoped to find mistresses in Port Royal and persuade them to share life at sea.

Before seeing the benign influence of Mrs Judd, Ned would have been nervous about the consequences of captains taking trollops from on shore and turning them into the queens of individual ships, but Mrs Judd (far from being a trollop, of course) kept the *Phoenix*'s captain and crew smart and lively with masts oiled, sails always well patched and recently the hull repainted. She knew little about ships but, from Kingsnorth days, she knew how a trim kitchen should look and how a house needed care and attention.

And over there was Punta Gorda: one and a three quarters of a mile to go. The rest of the boats were still astern but bunching up, with Rideau and Thomas now only a few yards away, one on each quarter.

Slowly Ned steered closer inshore. He did it cautiously to avoid the risk of leading them all on to a particular reef which ran straight out to sea from near the headland. First he had to find it, then work round the seaward end, but at the same time he dare not risk missing the entrance to the river, the Rio Guanche, because they would then blunder into a shallow bay and two islands which were only a mile or so beyond and came immediately before Punta Cocal, the western entrance to Portobelo.

The oarsmen were tired, cursing blistered hands and aching backs, but they were lucky, because by some quirk of Nature the current along this part of the coast ran eastward. In most places the constant flow of the Trade winds pushed the water westward in a strong current, but along this stretch of the Main it ran the other way, a counter-current that was quite strong when the wind – as it sometimes did – blew from the southwest and reinforced it.

And there it was. The mouth of the Rio Guanche was a good deal wider than he had expected. The river seemed to flow from the distant foothills of La Machina, highest of the peaks, as though catching all the rain falling from the clouds which hid the top of the mountain most of the time.

A couple of minutes later a hail from Thomas showed he too had seen it, and a moment afterwards a yell from Rideau, aimed at the boats astern, made sure that no one would miss making the turn inshore.

Even half a mile up the river the banks were still high, and on the east side in several places an old track dropped down into clearings.

"Fishermen used to come here until fairly recently," Thomas noted. "Brought in their boats and catches and gutted the fish. They'd put 'em on racks of green wood to sun-dry or smoke, or more probably they'd salt them down in barrels and take them by boat round to Portobelo. Conches, too: just look at those piles of shells. You can see where they chop the slot with the machete to cut the muscle."

"Why not take the fresh fish direct to Portobelo? Why smoke or salt it here?"

"Probably some local tax. The Dons used to have a salt tax – probably still do. Anything a Spaniard does which seems odd or eccentric is usually to dodge a tax."

Each boat was finding its own section of river bank in the darkness and the men, cursing, encouraging, now joking and groaning as they straightened backs and stretched legs, began unloading. Ned clambered on to dry land and began walking along the track. In the faint starlight he saw that one carriage wheel was already lying flat on the ground. He paused and watched as the axle was inserted vertically, and then men pulled over the axle and wheel so that the second wheel could be fitted. The limber was then bolted on to the axle. Several men lifted the barrel while the newly assembled carriage was pushed underneath and the barrel gently lowered into position, one of the men crouching to guide it on to the carriage. As soon as the trunnions, the stubby arms on which the gun rested, were in place, semicircular metal plates, the cap squares, were flipped over and fastened down, preventing the trunnions from jumping out again when the carriage was hauled over rough country or the gun recoiled when fired.

Beside another boat he saw a barrel of gunpowder hoisted out and rolled on to a smooth stretch of land. That was followed by a two-handed saw, a tub of nails and a barrel of musket balls. A pipe of muskets and tub of pistols came next, and Brace, watching the men at work, commented to Ned: "We had the boat nearly gunwales under: lucky the sea wasn't rough!"

"In my boat the worst part was trying to find somewhere to put my feet," Ned said, watching the assembled falcon being hauled to the edge of the clearing where it would be almost completely hidden by bushes. Noticing Lobb, he said: "Keep an eye on the falcons; I want to see how the rest of the boats are getting on."

Thomas had his falcon already hidden and the shot, powder, muskets, cutlasses, halberds and pikes spread out on the ground, as though opening a martial bazaar, and the starlight was reflecting from the sharpened blades. To one side were a barrel of drinking water and a stack of leather satchels packed with chunks of boucan, the smell of great pieces of smoked beef making the men slap their stomachs in anticipation of breakfast.

Slowly Ned checked them off. Coles with the *Argonauta*'s boats, Gottlieb with the *Dolphyn*'s, Leclerc with his men from the *Perdrix*, Edward Brace with his two boats and two canoes from the *Mercury*...as they were unloaded the east bank of the Rio Guanche gradually began to look like an army camp.

Ned found Secco and his men half-way along the line of fifty-six boats and sixty-four canoes, and as he arrived he saw the Spaniard carefully inspecting a pike while two men beside him were slipping cutlass belts over their shoulders.

"Ah, *almirante*!" Secco exclaimed cheerfully, "you are just in time to bid us *buena fortuna*!"

"*Hasta la vista*!" Ned said. "But don't forget, as soon as you find the track, come straight back, marking the trail."

"Indeed we shall not pause even to seek out a *taberna*!"

"The sooner you get back," Ned said, "the sooner we shall take possession of all the *tabernas* – and every *bodega*, too."

"We go, then, *almirante*."

"Don't forget," Ned cautioned. "Not just the track but an easy way to it."

"Old ladies on Sunday evening," Secco said. "They will be able to make their promenade along it. They'll be so grateful they'll call it the *avenida* of the *filibustero*. I shall become a *cicisbeo* and make assignations there."

"By all means," Ned said, "but *after* we've finished with it!"

CHAPTER TWELVE

As the sun rose next morning over the mangroves which covered Isla Largo Remo like a thick carpet, Aurelia had tried to make up her mind whether or not to have herself rowed over to see Diana in the *Peleus*. She had stood in the early light at the taffrail of the *Griffin* – where last night she and Ned had checked the boats and their contents – and watched the pelicans glide down on their angular wings and suddenly dive vertically into the water with a crash that should break their necks. Instead, each surfaced with what could only be a grin on his face and seeming to wink conspiratorially as he squeezed the water from the sac of flesh hanging under the long beak. From the way the sac sometimes convulsed, she saw a bird often caught quite a large fish, but a toss of the head disposed of it, like an impatient toper draining the dregs in his tankard.

Occasionally a small white gull with a black head would fly down and alight on a pelican's back with a cackling laugh, but more often, with wings outstretched to steady itself, it would land right on the domed head of the pelican, which looked like an elderly grandfather patiently suffering the attention of a scrambling grandchild.

When the pelican decided to go off on another fishing expedition the gull, tiny by comparison, flew round until the pelican dived; then, the moment he surfaced, the gull would land on the head again and patiently wait for the squeeze that drained the sac. At once the gull would drop into the water under the pelican's beak, its head bobbing away in the water like a hen pecking up seed.

When she had first seen it, Aurelia had been puzzled; then she saw that several tiny fish, usually silversides, washed out when the pelican squeezed the sac, were sufficiently stunned or startled to be snapped up at high speed by the waiting gull.

Then, after the pelican had swallowed the contents of its pouch with another convulsive movement, like an old man with a thin neck and drooping jowls swallowing a raw egg, and the gull had finished the silversides, the gull in one elegant movement would return to balance on the pelican's head.

Aurelia never tired of watching this duet between a bird that at first glance was a clumsy and ugly distant cousin of a goose and the little gull, among the most elegant of seabirds.

Now the last of the pelicans had flown off to the next island, Samba Bonita, on the *Griffin*'s quarter, where presumably the fish would be less wary, less alarmed.

She went down to the cabin and combed her hair carefully and put ribbons in the lowest ringlets. She envied Diana's dark mass of curly hair: it had personality, a springy life of its own, and made a frame for Diana's beautiful face. She could imagine Thomas holding Diana's head, his hands and fingers deep in the hair, the two of them laughing or loving. But her own hair, this blonde, what Ned called ash, was colourless and lifeless: it did not make a frame for her face – more like a wrapping, in fact. And her complexion! Both she and Diana were tanned golden by the sun, but her own tan was more yellowish: Diana's skin had life and was the mellow brown of polished wood, but hers was greasy by comparison.

Her breasts were well tanned, thanks to the canvas screen Ned had put up aft, but it had taken so long! Especially the lower parts. Ned would come and inspect them – and she would retaliate by teasing him about his white buttocks which, try as he might, refused to brown like the rest of his body.

Everyone else, except of course Diana and Thomas, who were doing the same thing, thought they had gone mad: it was common knowledge that the sun dried out the essential oils and left the body open to the noxious night vapours, to which everyone knew they were more vulnerable to anyway because frequently they slept on deck at night. However, Aurelia reflected as she looked at the tan on her belly, which was still as flat as when she was a young girl, everyone did not know, or believe, that the mosquitoes did not bite tanned skin as much as white, and it was mosquito bites, not the heat and humidity of the tropical showers that could make life a misery in the West Indies. At least, for an hour around dawn and from an hour before sunset until the late evening. Apart from itching and almost driving you into a frenzy, the bites sometimes turned septic. Why did the mosquitoes and sandflies concentrate round wrists and ankles, where the flesh was thin on the bone?

Suddenly, sitting naked in the cabin, she burst into tears, a hairbrush in one hand, a tortoiseshell comb in the other. It was hopeless; she could fill her mind with all this nonsense, this comparison of Diana's hair and her own, the merits of a tanned skin, even speculate (yet again) how passionate Diana was and if the depth of her passion was indicated by her black hair, but none of it drove away this dreadful fear for Ned, a fear which soaked into her like fog drifting in along the harsh Atlantic coast of Brittany.

In Tortuga days ago it had seemed quite natural for Ned to accept the leadership of the Brethren; quite natural for him to agree to lead the attack on Old Providence and Portobelo. But now the ships were anchored and Ned and Thomas, with all the boats, were rowing along an enemy coast with little more than toy guns and swords to attack the third strongest port this side of the Atlantic. Havana and Cartagena were – so people said – enormous; but *nom de Dieu*, Portobelo had four castles to defend it. If anything happened to Ned – yes, she would be alone, but not for long: if anything happened to Ned she did not want to live. But how to die?

She realized that Diana, in the cabin of the *Peleus*, might be just as worried, unhappy and uncertain. She stood up, pulled on the divided skirt that had become famous among all the buccaneers as the wear of women on board the original three English ships, selected a jerkin and pulled it over her head and secured the lacing, and then ran the comb through her hair again. The tears had subsided into sobs; now the sobs were occasional hiccoughs which jerked her breasts uncomfortably.

The canoe took her across to the *Peleus*. It meant leaving the *Griffin* with not a man on board, because she needed them at the paddles, but there was little risk with the *Peleus* anchored less than five hundred yards away. A seaman took the painter and helped Aurelia on board. Her ladyship, he said, was in the cabin: a warning to Aurelia of Diana's mood, because the approach of a canoe would have been reported and normally she would be on deck to meet a visitor.

Aurelia hurried down the companion ladder, tapped lightly on the door and went in without waiting for a reply. Diana's eyes were red, her face puffy – and, naked, she too had been brushing and combing her hair.

"I won't kiss you, I'm all sniffy and horrible," she said. "I've been trying to pull myself together to come over and visit you."

Aurelia hiccoughed and then laughed. "I was sitting just like you, combing my hair, when suddenly I began crying. I thought of you, managed – " she hiccoughed again " – to dress and here I am. With hiccoughs!"

"Those damned men," Diana said, trying to smile, "there's only one thing worse than having them around under your feet and that's having them away."

"They'll be at the river mouth now," Aurelia said brightly.

"They should have arrived there before dawn. The boats should be unloaded and everything hidden from prying eyes, with sentries out."

"And that Spaniard should be going up the mountains looking for the track."

Diana sniffed and then blew her nose vigorously. "Yes, but if he doesn't find the track..."

"It *must* be there: Ned's whole plan depends on it."

"I know, and it is there, I'm sure, but will they be able to get to it from the river, I wonder? Those mountains..."

"Where there are mountains there are passes," Aurelia said, with more assurance than she felt.

"I suppose so. I like looking at mountains but I don't trust 'em. I come from one of the flat counties of England. A few rolling hills, but that's all. These mountains of the Main – particularly around La Guaira – make me nervous. Well, not nervous, exactly, but they make me feel so insignificant. Once upon a time I used to get the feeling only when I looked up at the stars and the moon; now mountains have the same effect on me, as though I've shrunk."

Aurelia nodded, although they did not have the same effect on her, nor did the stars; in fact mountains always gave her more confidence – the feeling that she could range over them without the restraints of priests, governors and petty officials of any government, that she and Ned could just walk hand in hand. It was the freedom a ship had to sail towards the setting sun, where the stars dipped down...

Diana had stopped sobbing now. "Thomas and Ned would be ashamed of us."

"I doubt it. They'd be flattered that we thought them worth a tear! Still, perhaps they don't picture tearful women taking the ships round!"

"Aurelia," Diana said quietly, "both men know what they they are doing and we're lucky. A few years ago Thomas found a naïve girl whose most exciting experience up to then had been riding a steady horse in the company of a groom. Slowly he gave me confidence – why, at first I could not meet strangers without blushing. To begin with he gave me confidence in myself, and then he gradually showed me what I could do. That I could make decisions without staying awake all night worrying. He taught me how to sail a ship and proved to me that my decisions were as likely to be as right as his."

"There aren't many such men," Aurelia admitted. "He's saying in effect you're as clever as he is, even though he's a man."

"Yes, although Thomas doesn't need to worry about his manhood. At first I thought he was really trying to show people that he was clever enough to choose a clever woman; then I realized it was nothing of the sort: he didn't give a damn what other people thought; he loved me and wanted to share everything with me – bed, buccaneering, voyaging, seeing new and strange places...

"And Aurelia," Diana added, "I think Ned is the same with you."

"Yes – it has taken longer, of course, because he is a different kind of man. Ned was shy and uncertain at first when we escaped from Barbados: he had lost his father and brother – they had fled to France – which meant the estates and houses where he spent his childhood had been taken by Cromwell. Then he heard they were going to confiscate the Kingsnorth plantation.

"It's almost unbelievable now, but when Ned and I escaped from Barbados in the *Griffin* with our people and a few tons of sugar, we thought we'd be able to trade. Or, rather, Ned did. I wasn't so hopeful.

"I knew we had more enemies than Ned realized. Anyway, Saxby was wonderful. Ned was lucky when he hired Saxby as the plantation foreman who could also be the master of the *Griffin*."

"Still, Ned saw what he had to do and did it – he took you with him! Kidnapped you!"

Aurelia laughed at the memory, but Diana was wrong, because Ned had not been like Thomas. He had been uncertain – both as a lover and as the leader of the group of people from Kingsnorth. She had been able to give him confidence as a lover, and she had been able – without him realizing it – to change his mind from planting in another island to smuggling to the Main. Meeting Thomas had done the rest: like a plant suddenly getting the sun and water it needed, he grew fast and sturdily.

Diana looked puzzled when Aurelia told her this, and after a minute or two of thought said: "I didn't realize! When we first met you, he seemed so decisive, so confident. Certainly it was obvious he knew nothing about dealing with the Dons, but he admitted that right away. Why, the way he captured the grain ship at Riohacha and dealt with General Heffer! Thomas was very impressed!"

"Oh, yes," Aurelia said. "When finally he realized that he had left the old life behind him, he knew what to do. The raid on Santiago," she said proudly, "I don't think anyone could have led that better than Ned."

"The whole thing – idea, plan, execution – was brilliant," Diana agreed. "That's why the buccaneers chose him as their leader. Thomas could never have done it. He's popular but he hasn't – one doesn't feel... I can't describe it. Ned is quiet but definite, like a pointing finger. By comparison, Thomas is a waving hand."

Aurelia wished that Ned could have heard Diana's comment. She had seen the pacing in the cabin, the hesitations, changes of mind, changes of plan – yes, and the black despair. She never knew whether he needed comfort, criticism or peace and quiet: she did not like to leave him alone in case he thought she was (briefly) deserting him, but there was never anything she could do by staying with him unless, as sometimes happened, he needed her for release and an hour's oblivion. Yet, strangely enough, to Diana and Thomas, who knew him better than anyone else apart from herself, he seemed so certain and calm...

Perhaps that was leadership. The ability to lead, not necessarily the ability to plan. Certainly it was curious how others followed one man willingly while a second would have to depend on authority (the backing of enforced discipline, like an army general) to make anyone follow. Thomas, one of the most charming, thoughtful, kindly, intelligent and amusing men she had ever met, a man who inspired confidence and could soothe two people having a bitter argument so that both thought him their friend, was not a leader: the buccaneers had never thought of that when they offered him the job – which Thomas had refused.

Yet they had certainly wanted Ned. Just because of his success at Santiago? No, although obviously that had a good deal to do with it – these men were only interested in purchase: they had no country to which they owed loyalty. Yet they had wanted first to meet Ned, although men like Leclerc, Gottlieb, Coles and Brace already knew him and had become rich because of Santiago. Then, after meeting him, the rest of the buccaneers had agreed that Ned was to be their new admiral.

Leadership… It was a strange thing. Compared with Thomas, Ned was remote from these men: Thomas slapped them on the back, tossed back rumbullion like water, laughed and joked earthily with them. Ned could not slap a man on the back to save his life, had a ready sense of humour but laughed at different things than these men, and preferred wine to rumbullion. Standing in a group of buccaneer captains he looked – well, like an aristocrat among poachers. Yet the captains talked freely with him, although always with a polite "mister". There was a slight remoteness which happened quite naturally. Was this one of the signs that indicated leadership? Not leadership itself, of course, because she wondered if anyone could really explain what that was. Easy enough, God knows, to point to a man that has it and dismiss another man who lacks it; but what was that curious "it"?

"Ned said six o'clock Wednesday morning. The day after tomorrow," Diana commented. "It gets light about five-thirty."

"Yes, he is giving us half an hour's daylight to weigh our anchors and then get under way. He didn't want me to run into the Isla Largo Remo!"

"You'll be leading the fleet, so be careful!" Diana said. "I wish we had an artist with us so that he could paint it. No," she said as Aurelia blushed, uncertain how the Englishwoman meant the remark. "I'm serious. Not so many months ago you were living with that drunken husband of yours on the plantation at Barbados, and the most exciting event of the week was if Ned paid you a visit. Did Wilson really beat you badly?"

"Yes, but he was usually so drunk I don't think he realized his own strength."

"Don't defend the devil!" Diana exclaimed. "He's dead now and he was a scoundrel. Any man who beats his wife so that she is a mass of bruises is a villain. Even once. But I understand he did it two or three times a week."

"He was a very unhappy man. He had many disappointments." Aurelia was half annoyed to find herself feeling she had to defend him. Did she do it because she felt any criticism of him was in fact criticism of her for having married him?

"Most men have disappointments without it making them beat their wives," Diana said sharply. "Stop defending him. He only wanted your money. You never loved him, did you?"

Aurelia shook her head and Diana went on relentlessly: "I suspect he was regularly unfaithful to you. Didn't he have a black mistress?"

"All that was my fault," she said. "I did not attract him. It drove him – to do strange things. He would never have done them if I had been able to rouse him."

"Rubbish," Diana said firmly, "he had no manhood. The fact you were his wife was a coincidence. It would have happened with any woman."

"Let's talk of happier things," Aurelia said. "All that's over now: a bad dream I can barely remember. I can't remember it at all without a lot of effort."

Diana nodded. "That's good. Barely remembered bad memories are useful sometimes just to measure present happiness."

"Do you think they're all right?" Aurelia said suddenly, her mind switching back to the expedition. "I have a feeling now and again that things are going wrong."

"They probably are," Diana said cheerfully, "but don't worry. Santiago was unusual – everything went according to plan. Thomas was getting quite gloomy near the end: things were going so well he thought a ship was bound to blow up accidentally, or something equally dreadful!"

CHAPTER THIRTEEN

Secco cursed softly, trying to get the most satisfaction from the fewest words and the minimum outlay of breath, because his lungs were straining. Lungs, he thought: if it was only the lungs, but it is the muscles along the front and back of the shins, and the great muscles of the thighs. And the kneecaps felt loose. His head, too, had a nasty dizziness and the warning behind his eyes that a headache was coming. His neck ached where it joined his shoulders. His heart was pumping; he was sure he had strained it.

He looked at the other two men. One was unusually pallid and the other redder in the face than usual. Well, climbing mountains took people in different ways, and for several weeks the three of them had had little more exercise than pacing the deck.

One of the men, Sanchez, slowed down for a moment and at once Secco snarled: "Don't say it! There's nothing beyond this next ridge except more ridges, each higher than the last. We're going to Heaven and we're having to climb all the way!"

"I wasn't going to say that!" Sanchez said sulkily, and was clearly not going to speak any more.

Secco paused to look down from the ridge, noting that in two or three minutes the red disc of the sun would be coming up clear of the distant mountains, though there would be no real warmth in it for another half an hour.

They had climbed up from the river bank after the long row from the ships, and as he looked westward, across the harbour entrance, there was just sea stretching for twenty, two hundred or perhaps even two thousand miles.

Below him, Portobelo harbour was a long rectangle cut into the rock. As he turned northwards towards the opposite shore, the entrance was on his left, a mile wide from one headland to another. The little town of Portobelo was huddled down there on his right, nestling – no, it looked as though it had been dumped there – at the inland end of the anchorage.

Only the anchorage itself had anything of a regular shape. Built into the high cliffs on the far side of the entrance was one fort, San Felipe de Todo Fierro, the one the English called the Iron Fort and which covered the approach like a sentry standing in his box.

Then gradually the far side of the anchorage sloped down as it came inland: rough rocks, bare hills, the kind of land that everyone left to the goats. At the inner end and on the same side as Todo Fierro was a castle. That must be the Castillo de San Fernando, which was opposite the town.

From San Fernando to the town, the narrow side of the box, and opposite the entrance, the land was flat, and although it was hard to tell in this light and from this height, it looked swampy. Mosquitoes could swarm up from there and fly to the town for victims…

Halfway between Fernando and Portobelo town, with its gates opening on to the swamp, was yet another fortification, by far the biggest. That must be the Castillo de San Gerónimo. Certainly its guns covered the whole length of the anchorage and the town, but what a terrible place to have to serve in: the hills nearby and the distant mountains shut off the cooling Trade winds from the east and the swamp must stink, apart from the insects.

San Gerónimo… That's the one. As he looked down on the harsh grey outline of its walls he could not suppress a shiver. A stone box at the water's edge. A wide jetty stuck out into the sea from the castle walls, and he could distinguish a doorway.

Perhaps boats from the plate fleet loaded there, covered by the great guns and the muskets up on the battlements.

There was a *galita* – he did not know the English name, he realized – built on every corner of San Gerónimo. Standing in one of those stone cylinders built into each corner, a sentry could look each way through the slits of the gun loops and see outside the castle walls which he overhung by the diameter of the *galita*. Secco sniffed and dismissed them as ornaments: sentries would squat on the floor and sleep, out of sight of the sergeant of the guard.

Between San Gerónimo and Portobelo town there was a smaller fort, which must be Triana, probably built long before the others. In fact, he guessed that it was originally Portobelo's only defence, the others being added much later.

Town! He could see that Portobelo was really just a large village – it was reckoned that only four hundred people lived there now, with a garrison of a thousand or more for the forts, although most of the troops were supposed to have been shipped off to Jamaica.

Looking down on the port he did not envy the Spanish plate ships: the whole of the southern shore was pocked with coral reefs, right up to the town. The main jetty seemed to be the one in front of San Gerónimo. The hills on which he was standing swept down in rolling terraces of rock like the soft folds in a woman's skirt to meet the southern side of the town, which was in a valley merging into the swamps to the east, while the opposite side (deserted apart from San Fernando at the inland end and the Iron Fort to seaward) was steep too, the whole side being, as far as he could make out, a peninsula or island sticking out of the swamps as if to make a temporary side to the port.

Uninviting, ugly, swampy, humid...and even from up here he could smell the mud, liberally perfumed with the town's sewage. What it must have been like fifty or a hundred years ago... Secco let his mind wander. Forty or fifty ships would be anchored down in the harbour. Not the great galleons – it was too shallow for them and they stayed in Cartagena. But the smaller ships would be plying back and forth, bringing in cargo taken from the galleons at Cartagena. Then they would start ferrying the plate to Cartagena, taking it on board here at Portobelo, probably from that jetty, straight from the mules and donkeys of the plate trains arriving from Panama.

That jetty over there in front of San Gerónimo would be piled high. All round the town, wherever there was flat space, the Panama merchants would have set up tents. It was said they came to Portobelo over the mountains (along the very track they were rying to find) by the score. Tall or short, fat or thin, they would sit astride donkeys or mules, sore and perspiring, hurrying from Panama to Portobelo the moment they heard the fleet was due, all ready to buy or sell.

They would be selling bales of leather and leather goods, tobacco, and probably some illicit gold, silver and gems, and they would be buying – well, everything! The merchants had customers stretching from Panama to the most southerly Spanish settlement along the Pacific coast… Almost down to Tierra del Fuego, in fact, and that was the end of the world, although why it was called the land of fire he did not know. Clothes by the bale – ranging from boots and hats for men to drawers and lace for the women by way of pots and pans for the kitchens, needles and thread for the sewing rooms, saws, hammers, and nails for the carpenters' workshops. Everything, in fact, that men and women needed for living, except leather goods. Oh yes, sporting guns, muskets, powder and shot for sportsmen and soldiers. And ink, pen and paper for bureaucrats and dutiful folk to write to their relations in Spain. And decorated floor and wall tiles from Andalusia and Granada for my lady's rooms…pretty materials for curtains…hinges and catches for the shutters…hoes, rakes, forks and spades for the gardeners…buckets, bottles, jugs. Wine and oil, because olive trees did not grow over here, nor grapes.

Being a merchant in Panama, Secco thought, must be like being a licensed buccaneer: once you had bought your stock from the ships in Portobelo, or taken delivery of goods ordered last year, you carried it over the mountains to Panama, where you put it in your warehouse. If you were a clever man (and could afford to) you left it there for a few months or even a year, until the other merchants had sold all their stock. Then, with mounting demand from every town south of Panama, you could name your own prices. For Guayaquil? A fifty per cent surcharge! For Lima? Why, at least eighty-five! Arica? Goodness me, a hundred! Antofagasta – ah, so far: two hundred per cent. Coquimbo and Valparaiso? Add yet another fifty, my dear sir, and if you talk of shipping goods to such remote places as Valdivia then three hundred per cent, and all of you pay an extra fifty if you argue!

Secco felt better for the rest and glanced at Sanchez and Ramirez, the third man, who mercifully was a cheerful fellow. "Come on, then, let's go."

"You didn't ask me what I *was* going to say," Sanchez said, still sulking.

Secco sighed with assumed patience and held out both hands invitingly. "Very well, Sanchez, what *were* you going to say?"

"I was going to say that I can see the track."

Secco took a deep breath and then managed a patient smile for Sanchez, cursing all Galicians under his breath. "You spawn of a goat's lechery, you leavings of an incontinent ox – *where*?"

Sanchez, a smug grin creasing his face, pointed below them. "That rectangular peak – you see it?"

"Yes, yes!" Secco said impatiently.

"Well, that's beyond it. Come back this way to the sugar loaf. You see it?"

"You mule," Secco murmured.

"From the sugar loaf," Sanchez said, basking in the full attention of the other two men, "you walk out as though along the hand of a clock pointing to five o'clock – the sugar loaf being the centre, of course. What do you find now?"

"A tall rock, like a church spire." Secco said, "What did you expect – a flock of sheep, a dozen dancing maidens, or the Bishop of Toledo and his acolytes?"

"The tall rock will do," Sanchez said complacently. "Using that in the same way, come towards us at eight o'clock and – "

"Be quiet, you bladder of Galician wind!" Secco snarled, "or I'll pitch you over this cliff!"

"Very well," Sanchez said, pursing his lips, "I shan't tell you!"

"I can see it myself," Secco said, turning to the other man. "Just below and to the left of that steeple, it twists like a path."

"Yes, I can see it now," Ramirez said. "We've climbed twice as far as we need. Three times."

"Thanks to this Galician owl," Secco said viciously. "Oh yes, he knows all about mountains; he's a mountain man from mountain country and his eye – do you remember him telling us before we started off? – is trained to spot where the passes would naturally go. Galicia," he hissed, "is really a flat plain covered a foot deep in the manure of mules."

"We can't go down directly: we'll have to descend at an angle and pick up the track," Ramirez said.

"Yes," Secco said, still angry with Sanchez, "at least we didn't cross the track as we climbed – it's still beyond us. Come on," he said, "I can see a way down, even though I come from the marshes of Las Marismas..."

As they clambered down, dropping several hundred feet, Portobelo drew nearer and they could see the details of the forts and castles. While they were high up the mountains in the early morning, the air had been fresh, sharp and cold, stimulating and unlike anything they had breathed for months. Now, as they scrambled lower and the sun rose, it became hotter and more humid; the very air seemed thicker and the stench from the harbour and the town reached up towards them like an invisible fog.

Suddenly, when they seemed only a couple of hundred feet above the level of the town and perhaps a mile from it and had just then climbed down a few feet of cliff, they came round a huge boulder and found themselves on the track.

Secco immediately pulled the other two men behind the boulder while he looked carefully both ways.

"No one uses this track," Sanchez announced. "Just look at the dust. Heavy rain washes the soil off the hills and on to the road; it dries and turns into dust. Then the wind smooths the dust. Look – the hoof marks of goats, many of them and some weeks old. But only an occasional ass and mule print, and no horses. Few people come and go to Panama."

"Or they use another road," Ramirez suggested.

Reluctantly Secco shook his head. "No, this is the only road." At that moment he hated to agree with the Galician clod Sanchez, and wondered now why he had chosen him, but there was no question of there being another track. This one wound its way from Panama by way of Venta de Cruz, first crossing the flat plain just this side of Panama and then rising up into the Cordilleras which divided the Isthmus along its spine like a dragon's back and then crowded the eastern side as far as Portobelo with ridges of mountains as though a baker was folding strips of dough on to trays ready for the ovens.

Secco went to the edge of the track and looked down at Portobelo once again. It seemed quite different: all the angles had changed of course, and it was difficult to realize now that the anchorage was rectangular. The forts and castles were larger than he expected and close enough now for him to see the weed and slime growing on the shaped stone of the walls of San Fernando, where the castle was built into the water, and the same for San Gerónimo. The stone blocks were enormous, cut to shape by prisoners and slaves. Portobelo itself was small indeed and the houses crowded together – it was said that when the ships arrived the Panama merchants slept five to a room and were glad to pay fantastic rents for the couple of weeks they spent here trading. Secco had also heard descriptions of the plate trains arriving from Panama to meet the fleet.

Apparently there were several trains, each comprising a hundred or more donkeys and mules laden with a canvas pannier each side packed with ingots of silver, a certain amount of gold, and leather bags of gems. The guards were soldiers, a company with a couple of officers, at the front, middle and end of the train which could stretch half a mile.

When the animals arrived in Portobelo they were simply halted near the jetty in front of the ships, or where the tallymen were standing on the quays with the royal assay master and all the rest of the king's officials, filling in lists, attaching royal seals, hammering in numbers and symbols. The mules and donkeys were fed and watered and the ingots in their canvas panniers were apparently left unguarded in piles on the ground until just before nightfall, when they were carried out to the ships. No one thought of an enemy attack: at sea it would be different, but here with these forts, the guns and the garrisons, who would dare to try to rob the king of his bullion...? Who, indeed? Secco thought to himself, and grinned.

Then two years ago the plate trains had arrived and the merchants waited, but the ships never came: storm and fear of the French fleet had sent them back to Spain and, since then, it was said last year that there was not the money in the Spanish treasury to provision and re-equip either the galleons for Cartagena or a *flota* for Vera Cruz. But according to Leclerc – and there was no doubting it – that plate remained here in Portobelo, waiting for the day when the galleons *did* come.

Secco pictured all the people who were waiting month after month. On the other side of the Atlantic there was the king and all those powerful Italian and Austrian bankers and moneylenders who financed him and his policies: they (like the king) relied on the plate fleets. Although no ships meant no money for the bankers, it must be disastrous for the king – he had several armies and the navy to pay, quite apart from all the functionaries of government. Presumably the Spanish army in the Netherlands, for example, was not paid or provisioned. Did the soldiers spend a freezing winter in Flanders munching raw potatoes and parsnips, confiscated from the local people? Ships' sails, rigging and planking rotted; the seamen would have been paid off and probably now starved.

Secco looked down on the Castillo de San Gerónimo. He could see the sun reflecting from the metal helmets of the two guards, one at the big gate on the southern side, facing Triana and looking towards the town, the other walking round the battlements. And "walking" was the word, not "marching". The man was carrying his halberd (it might even be a pike; it was hard to distinguish at this distance) almost horizontally over his shoulder, as a peasant might carry a stick with his noon meal wrapped in an old cloth and tied to the end.

Inside there – well, they were almost sure it was San Gerónimo and not San Fernando: it certainly would not be San Felipe, the Iron Fort – was a year's plate... A king's ransom: the year's cargo of the king's silver and gems, brought along the track from Panama to Portobelo to load in ships which had never arrived, and which was at this very moment locked in one of the castles to save taking it back to Panama.

The track was so little used that Secco decided to risk walking down towards the town to make a final check over the whole length that they would want to use. A sudden rainstorm might have sent floods down the sides of the mountains to wash away a section of the track; a rock fall could have blocked it. Because few people ever used the track, no one would be in a hurry to repair it, and he wanted to make sure that when he reported to Mr Yorke, he could assure him it was open from the point where the buccaneers would join it all the way to the gates of Portobelo.

He looked critically at Sanchez and Ramirez. Ragged hair, faces unshaven for many days, unwashed for as long, with perspiration making lines in the coating of dust, hides stitched round their feet as boots...they could be buccaneers or they could be herdsmen or even itinerant tinkers in sore need of work. Their safety lay in the fact that they were Spanish; they could (and would) roundly abuse and probably draw a knife on any persistent questioner.

Secco needed to know not only if the track was clear but roughly the size of the garrisons of the four forts and castles; he also needed to confirm roughly how many people lived in Portobelo. Was there a night watch? (He thought not: the place had not been attacked for so many years that they probably relied on its name to protect it – its reputation and the castles.) Did many fishing boats go out at night? Mr Yorke would be glad of scraps of information. A report on the lackadaisical guard on the buttress of San Gerónimo would be important because it showed discipline was slack.

The three men walked down the track into Portobelo's large and dusty *plaza* and Secco had the feeling of entering a small town abandoned by most of its inhabitants. A dozen pigs of varying sizes grunted and snuffled, barging each other and rooting through piles of garbage for the fiftieth time, obviously hoping against hope that someone had just added a fresh piece of rubbish. Several goats on the far side of the *plaza* wrenched and twisted blades of tired, brown grass and one, standing on its hind legs, tore at some leaves remaining on a high bush.

Once through the town gates, which were pushed open and held back by wooden props, they saw first a woman, a mestizo, sitting in the shade of a tamarind tree which was growing like a giant mushroom and speckled with pale yellow flowers. She had her back against the trunk, holding her baby with one hand and suckling it while the other flapped ineffectually at the flies.

Three old men sitting on a seat in the shade of a giant kapok tree, its roots like buttresses, a veiled woman in black walking slowly, followed by three servants, a drunkard slumped beside a low wall, a dozen or so lean hens pecking and scratching with a cockerel strutting… One lantern slung on a rope between the sides of the gate, lit every night judging from the fresh soot, two young boys with a barrow collecting the droppings of donkeys and quarrelling whose turn it was to use the shovel, a soldier opening the door of a house and calling as if telling his family he was back from guard duty... Secco and his two men walked through the town without anyone showing the slightest interest in them, although they were strangers, and it was clear that the town was not deserted: every house was inhabited, but with the rising sun increasing the heat, and humidity that drifted off the swampy land in waves, the men and women of Portobelo did only enough work to survive. For years they must have lived well on the profit from the arrival of the galleons and the traders, but now without either, they had to watch every hen to see where it laid its egg, milk every goat, slaughter pigs as soon as they were plump enough.

The three men walked back out of the town and ambled slowly past the Triana fort, counting the cannons, inspecting the great door, counting the number of gun loops – shaped like keyholes and through which the defenders could fire muskets or arrows – and from the number of soldiers on duty, trying to estimate the size of the garrison.

Secco decided that most of Triana's men had been sent to Jamaica, but as they walked slowly up to San Gerónimo it was clear that this one was still properly manned. Only two men might have been visible from up the mountain, but through the open doors they could see a score or more drilling lethargically on the parade ground forming the centre of the castle. Secco looked at the cannons as they circled the building. There were four guns on each of the narrow sides and eight on each of the long sides, overlooking the harbour to the west and the swamp to the east.

The jetty was strongly built of stone, as he had seen from up the mountain, and seemed to have deep water all round it. There was no coral growing, nor the usual wreck which obstructed so many Spanish jetties.

"They load the plate from there," Ramirez murmured.

Secco had been looking across at San Fernando, opposite Portobelo town, and decided that the plate definitely would not be stored there because when the ships arrived it would have to be carried back across the swampy land to the San Gerónimo jetty. If it was in the Iron Fort at the harbour entrance it must be carried a mile back to the jetty, and Secco knew the characteristics of his own people. San Gerónimo had the jetty, so San Gerónimo had the plate. Their information was probably accurate...

He was just estimating the height of the walls, after seeing the thickness at the entrance gate, when a soldier marched out, unstrapping the breast and back plates of his armour and obviously just coming off duty.

Secco assumed the stance and vacant grin of a near idiot and said in a heavy Murcian accent (copied from memories of his mother's father, who used to tell lurid tales of when the Moors owned the kingdom of Granada: they had been driven out only fifty years before the old man was born): "It must be hot work being a soldier!"

"It is," the man said. "Here, hold my helmet, this buckle has stuck!"

Secco giggled, as befitted an idiot delighted by such an important man's attention, and took the helmet, holding it as though it was a smoking grenade. "Why do you wear armour in such hot weather, sir?"

"Orders. Guards wear breast plate, back plate and helmet."

"What if you are not a guard, sir?"

"You're a lucky man: no armour. Not enough suits to go round, anyway."

"Ah, the king did not send enough!"

"No," the soldier said, wrestling with a leather strap, "more than three quarters of our men are away and they had to be fully equipped."

"To Cartagena on leave, I suppose. Lucky men!" Secco commented with another inane giggle.

"Leave! No, they're away fighting: chasing those English out of Jamaica. They'll have done it by now, I expect, and be back soon. I hope so, four hours on guard and only eight off duty, seven days and nights a week – it's wearing me out. There!" He finally wrenched out the last strap and grabbed the breast plate before it slid off. The back plate fell with a thump and Ramirez picked it up and handed it to him.

Secco, still holding the helmet, nodded enthusiastically as he said: "This must be an important castle if all you soldiers guard it! And that one too," he pointed to San Fernando and, indicating the Iron Fort, added in an awed voice: "That must be the most important of all, guarding the entrance."

As Secco hoped, the soldier took the bait and sniffed contemptuously. "This is the only one that matters! San Fernando, Todo Fierra, Triana – *they* just guard the harbour. But in here – " he lowered his voice and jerked his thumb towards the great door " – is all the king's silver. Locked up safely and waiting for the galleons to come!"

By now Secco had made himself look slack-jawed and wide-eyed with wonder. "The king's silver? Do *you* guard *that*? No wonder you wear armour and a special helmet! Supposing the buccaneers came, or the English or French fleets!"

The soldier spat contemptuously. "None of them would ever dare think of it, let alone get within a cannon shot of Todo Fierro. Why, we could sleep on duty – to tell you the truth, some of them do. Not me, of course, but some I could mention, including a sergeant or two."

He strapped the breast and back plates together to make them easier to carry, retrieved his helmet from Secco, and said: "Well I have a wife waiting for me, so good day to you."

The three buccaneers watched him march past Triana along the track as it curved round to the town, and Secco murmured: "He could just as easily have arrested us as vagrants!"

"Oh, no," Sanchez said sourly, "he could see clearly enough that you are the village idiot!"

He then bent double laughing at his own joke and suddenly disappeared.

Ramirez and Secco, several feet away, ran to where Sanchez had been standing and saw he had stepped back into an open cesspool and was now floundering up to his waist, speechless as he held his breath against the stench. Secco sniffed and eyed the walls of the cesspool. "You can climb up without our help. We're starting back along the track."

Two hours later the men arrived at the boats, Sanchez being forced to walk several paces behind Secco and Ramirez. His attempts to wash his breeches and himself in the water of the harbour had not been entirely successful: Secco swore that the harbour smelled only slightly less than the cesspool.

Secco reported at once to Ned, who was talking to Thomas. The three of them, Secco said, had marked the easiest path up to the track: it was about a mile long and met the track low down. The path was fairly smooth. They would have to cut away some low bushes with machetes and roll aside a few rocks to get the falcons through, but nowhere was it too steep to pull up the guns.

He then described their walk through the town and ended up with a report on the conversation with the soldier, which confirmed that the bullion was stored inside San Gerónimo, although not necessarily in the dungeon. He apologised for failing to discover the exact size of the present garrison, explaining that "acting as an idiot stopped the soldier being suspicious of me, but limited the questions I could ask…"

Ned grinned and patted Secco's shoulder. "Once we've captured the castle we'll have plenty of time to find the bullion! It'll be in the dungeon: you can be sure of that. Old ladies hide their valuables under the bed; soldiers always choose dungeons."

Secco spent the next hour with Ned, Thomas and Leclerc working out as precise a timetable as possible. The main task was hauling fourteen falcons over the mountains to Portobelo, along with five hundred roundshot, some langrage which the men had been making up while they waited, and a barrel of powder.

The armour, helmets, swords, pikes and halberds were no problem: they would be issued before the march started, and each recipient would be responsible for transport.

Because the hundred breast and back plates and fifty helmets were being issued to the Spanish-speaking buccaneers, Secco joked: "So there's a tax on being Spanish: you have to carry your armour over the mountains!"

"Tax? A bonus more likely!" Ned said. "Anyone with any sense would prefer wearing or carrying armour to hauling on the ropes of a falcon."

Ten men were chosen to carry satchels of boucan and five more would have water breakers. If they needed more food, Ned explained, they could always raid the Spaniards in Portobelo.

"That langrage," Thomas said. "Pity we couldn't have made up more." Langrage was a wickedly effective weapon: it comprised shot made up of scraps of iron, rusted bolts, old nails and any piece of metal that could be fired from a gun. The long pieces were tied together like bunches of kindling the diameter of the bore of the guns, three inches; smaller and jagged pieces were put in roughly stitched canvas bags.

"Those roundshot won't make any impression on the walls of the forts, but if we can get the Dons to rush us, a whiff of langrage will cut them down like hay under a scythe," Ned said.

"They won't rush us if they have any sense," Thomas said, "but firing langrage at the gun loops will knock the heads off anyone trying to see what we're doing."

"Timing," Ned said yet again. "We've so few watches I want to avoid having to time anything. But we've got to give the boats a time."

Thomas waved his hand airily. "If a dozen boats can't row a couple of miles round to Portobelo carrying only a few roundshot and barrels of powder and time their arrival within half an hour, I'd flog every third man!"

Ned thought again. "Come to think of it, the timing of the boats is not so important. The vital part of this plan is having a file of men marching in those Spanish helmets!"

CHAPTER **FOURTEEN**

Hauling the guns over the mountains was a nightmare the men thought would never end. Ned and Secco had estimated it would take at most five hours, so to ensure arriving at Portobelo at dawn, the buccaneers left the Rio Guanche just before midnight. Four men were left behind with each of the dozen boats which were later to go on to Portobelo; the rest hauled guns, carried powder, staggered under panniers of shot, or looked after gear ranging from halberds to pistols. The rest of the boats, now empty, would have to take their chance; oars and paddles were hidden some distance away.

Ropes secured to the loops, the eyebolts on the outer ends of the axles of the guns, made them easier to haul and the first part of the journey, up the rough path Secco had marked to the track, was not difficult. Half a dozen men were out ahead, slashing at bushes with machetes and rolling rocks out of the way. The buccaneers heaved at each gun and, at a warning shout from a gun captain, two men would jam rocks under the wheels to stop the gun running backwards, allowing those at the ropes and limbers to rest.

During the first half an hour Ned thought sourly that the mosquitoes would suck them dry of blood before they reached the track: face, neck, wrists were viciously attacked by the whining insects, which were invisible in the darkness and quite impervious to slaps and the perspiration streaming off every man's body. But as they hauled the guns higher, the attacks eased.

"We must be getting above the mosquito line," Thomas grunted. "Makes all the heaving worth while."

Finally they reached the track, and the men sighed with relief as the wheels of the gun carriages began to turn more easily over a comparatively smooth surface which for nearly two centuries had been worn by the hooves of the donkeys and mules walking back and forth. The men who had been cutting down the bushes and rolling aside rocks tailed on to the ropes and Ned found his party moving steadily up the track at a good pace yet slowly enough for Ned and Thomas to walk back and forth along the column, encouraging the men, checking that no axles were running hot, and ensuring that those carrying the canvas panniers of roundshot were not surreptitiously lightening their loads.

Although the moon had not yet risen, the stars were bright and the sky clear; for once the mountains were not capped with cloud spreading to leeward as though each peak trailed a white cloak.

Secco came up to Ned to report: "We are within a hundred feet of our highest point on the track. From then on it's all downhill to Portobelo."

"We'll stop there for a quarter of an hour," Ned said. "I want to make sure the men on the ropes know they have to pull back just as hard to stop the guns running away downhill! Issue boucan and a mug of water to each man."

As he walked along the track with Thomas he looked down at Portobelo. The harbour below was a rectangular dish filled with black water, the castles and forts crouched like toads, and he was startled to see how big was San Gerónimo. The town – as Secco had said – was little more than a large village. Everyone was sleeping – except the guards.

Dawn? Ned looked over to the eastward. There was no sign of it yet, showing they were well ahead of the schedule. The selected boats from the Rio Guanche would soon be rounding the western headland of Portobelo.

If his plan failed, the buccaneer ships led by Aurelia in the *Griffin*, and the buccaneer boats, would be sailing into a dreadful trap that would destroy them. Instead of capturing Portobelo – or the most important part of it – he would have warned the Spaniards of an imminent attack: an attack they never expected in half a century or more. From the day that *El Draco* died, the Dons had regarded Portobelo as impregnable. Come to think of it, Drake had died within sight of Portobelo: his leaden coffin had been buried only a few miles to seaward. That was in 1596, more than half a century ago, yet Spanish mothers still used *El Draco* to frighten their children. But across the Isthmus, in Panama, the Viceroy had obviously grown complacent: *El Draco* was long dead, and Portobelo with all its forts and castles was impregnable. Except, Ned reflected, that now the new admiral of the Brethren of the Coast had decided it was not, and had committed every life for which he was responsible to a crazy plan that rested not on cannons but on shiny breast plates and distinctive helmets.

As the *Griffin*'s mainsail slatted for a few minutes and then finally filled with the puffs of an offshore breeze that had just enough strength to make dancing shadows on the sea, Aurelia glanced astern, looking from one ship to another. All had their sails hoisted; most had weighed their anchors. The three – no, four – still at anchor had taken in most of their cable (Ned called it being "at short stay", she seemed to remember) but obviously were getting under way in succession to avoid colliding in the light wind which was across the current, so that a ship could be carried some distance before her sails were drawing and she answered her helm.

The *Peleus* was clear and following in the *Griffin*'s wake, so Diana and her men had met no problems; the *Phoenix* was there too. Aurelia wondered who was commanding temporarily in Saxby's place. Probably Mrs Judd! That vast woman had a cheerfulness, quickness of wit, and strength of mind that could conjure a wind from a flat calm, apart from an appetite for men that kept Saxby in an almost perpetual daze.

Ned would be at Portobelo by now. She felt a cold fear, having at last lost the struggle to avoid thinking about him. Four forts. The mayor was a man called Jose Arias Ximenez, and from what the Spaniards at Old Providence had said, he was evil: cruel and corrupt, he was a man almost ruined now because the absence of the plate fleet had cut the bribes and commissions he could extort from ship masters and traders from Panama.

Ned had fewer than a thousand men. Many fewer – there were five sailors in each of these ships, so at least 140 men were not with their admiral at Portobelo. So Ned had fewer than a thousand against four forts and castles with their garrisons, and a mountain range... He had a few of those little cannon on wheels, armour, muskets, pistols, and pikes captured at Old Providence... But those cannon fired a ball weighing only two or three pounds, although they were noisy and made much smoke. Such a gun would not knock down the front door of a house, let alone the walls of a castle. Still, Ned had a plan for them, although as far as she could see it must depend on magic.

The *Peleus* picked up a puff of wind which missed the rest of the ships and she surged ahead, closing with the *Griffin*. She saw Diana walk to the side and wave, obviously enjoying herself and perhaps remembering how they had led the way into Santiago... She had to admit that the twenty-eight ships looked impressive. They were all different sizes, different shapes – built in different countries, a fact which was reflected in their sheers, bows and sterns. Some were beamy, with a bow as round as a pendulous breast; others were lean, with sharp bows. Several had been built as coasting carriers of cargo, three or four had the fast lines of small vessels intended for smuggling or privateering. "The Motleys" was Ned's nickname for all of them, and she was thankful that the last one was now getting her anchor on board and steering clear of the land.

The sky to the east was getting lighter, although the wavelets were still that ominous grey, almost frightening, that was part of the dawn, but looking over the starboard bow towards the mountains, she could see that the peaks were clear of cloud. Ned had worried in case low cloud over the mountains round Portobelo would mean trying to find the track in thick mist. She remembered her terror as a young girl when her father's carriage, driving into the Pyrenees on an expedition from St Jean-de-Luz, had been trapped in low clouds that surrounded them. Neither coachman nor horses could see the road and they all sat for hours, cold and damp, shivering as the water dripped from the ceiling of the carriage and ran down the leather sides. It seemed a miracle at the time that they could breathe – she had been young and frightened enough to confuse cloud with smoke.

By the time all the ships were under way, she could detect to the east a light pink, a delicate oyster tint that was yet only a faint wash low in the sky. This was what Ned wanted: settled weather and a smooth sea. Now she prayed that the wind would not die. A calm was the only thing that would stop them getting to Portobelo.

Oh Ned, she murmured to herself... Had he found the track? Were they all going down it to Portobelo? Were they already there and attacking the Castillo de San Gerónimo? She clasped her breasts, which were almost bursting with longing for him.

Søren Jensen came from a small village called Gilleleje, a few miles westward round the coast from Helsingør. A Dane whose first childhood memory was of being hoisted on board his father's fishing boat in a fish bucket lined with a smelly old sack, he had long ago given up explaining to foreigners that Denmark comprised (except for the Jutland peninsula) a group of islands, and that his home village, pronounced 'Gilly-lie' was close to the port which the English insisted on calling 'Elsinore', although nothing seemed easier to pronounce than 'Helsingør'.

Apparently the English had even written a play concerning the big castle, a story about a Danish prince. They had that name wrong too; it certainly was not Danish. Englishmen called him Amlet, though he had heard Captain Leclerc referring to Omelette. Captain Coles, the Englishman who owned the ship in which Jensen had been serving as mate for the past two years, said he had heard of the play but thought it all happened in Verona, which was near Venice, and concerned two Italian gentlemen, not one Danish prince.

The flat, green countryside which made up the island on which stood Gilleleje and Helsingør (and, further round the coast to the south, København, which these strange English insisted on calling 'Copenhagen') seemed a lifetime away as Jensen walked from boat to boat along the south bank of the Rio Guanche, checking in the darkness that the men at the oars were ready.

Mr Yorke had suddenly said to him: "Jensen, you will be in charge of twelve boats carrying arms or food, and you will take them round to Portobelo tomorrow morning." Just like that. In the dust he had sketched Portobelo, showing him where the forts and castles were, and the cays and reefs. "Meet us on the jetty in front of the Castillo de San Gerónimo about an hour after dawn," he had said, as though Portobelo was deserted and all the buccaneers had to do was climb over the mountains and walk down the track to it.

He liked both Mr Yorke and Sir Thomas, but these English *were* eccentric: they never seemed to take anything seriously. "Meet us on the jetty" indeed! Still, to be fair, there was nothing eccentric about the way Mr Yorke blew up that castle at Santiago, nor how he captured Old Providence without losing a man's life.

Jensen paused for a moment as he made his way back to his own boat and wondered if they really *were* eccentric. If Mr Yorke had been Dutch, or a Scandinavian, or a Prussian, he would have given detailed orders with definite times and distances... All quite unnecessary instructions, Jensen suddenly realized, if you had a man you could trust: a man to whom you could say "meet me at the jetty an hour after dawn" and leave the details to him, so that if anything unexpected happened, the man could deal with it without being tied down.

Jensen looked up at the sky to the eastward. Still black. The ships would soon be leaving the Bahia las Minas. Suddenly it did not seem so eccentric that Mr Yorke had left his lady in command of the *Griffin* and Lady Diana had the *Peleus*.

The admiral, he now understood, was not risking ships and men by favouring mistresses: he knew they could do it, and that freed experienced buccaneers, masters and mates of ships, fighting men, for the attack on Portobelo. And, Jensen suddenly realized with pride, that was why Mr Yorke had picked him to bring the boats round: the admiral knew that few if any of the buccaneers had his experience with open boats.

He scrambled down in to the stern of his own boat, reached for the tiller in the darkness and gave orders to the oarsmen. Once the boat was clear of the river bank he turned and called into the darkness astern, "Kingsnorth". He knew his voice would just reach the next boat, and once it was clear of the bank and rowing after the leader, the man at the helm would call to the third boat, and all the way to the last one.

"Kingsnorth" – that was a strange password Mr Yorke had chosen and he was not sure what the whole word meant. "King's" he understood because it was very similar to the Danish word, and "north", but not the two run together... Perhaps it meant several kings from the north. Anyway, the English were very proud of their new king now this man Cromsen was dead.

The boat was beginning to butt into small waves and he could see the river bank on the starboard side beginning to trend away. He eased over the tiller a few inches and looked astern, where he could just see the stem of the next boat as it cut a tiny bow wave. A man would need to have sharp ears to hear the boats tonight. Supple leather and cloth were wrapped round the oars where they pressed against the rowlocks.

Jensen prided himself on not being what he called a "dreamer", a word he had taken from the English. No, he was a practical seaman who preferred to name his destination after his ship had arrived. But now, as the boat moved eastward in the darkness, seeming with its muffled oars to be gliding through the water like a great fish, he allowed his imagination to wander.

At the moment the boat carried some baskets of roundshot for the falcons, two or three baskets of ball for the muskets and pistols, a barrel of powder carefully protected from spray by an old piece of canvas, a cask of water and several satchels of boucan. All were to be landed on the jetty of the Castillo de San Gerónimo. What would the boat *then* load to carry out to the *Argonauta* when she had arrived from Bahia las Minas and anchored in Portobelo? Ingots of silver stamped with the arms of the king of Spain and canvas bags of coin and gems, pieces of eight, emeralds, doubloons...all the things that they dreamed about? The purchase that could then be changed so easily into rumbullion, tobacco and wine, and women who never tired while there were coins to clink one against the other. Or would the boat be carrying out wounded buccaneers to the nearest ship that could treat them?

In the darkness, death seemed very close and he tried to drive it away by thinking of women. He was glad that they had left Tortuga – which was simply that damned French fort, an anchorage and a rumbullion shop – and were going to make their base at Port Royal. Tortuga was a fine little island if you wanted to shoot pigeon (he had never seen so many before), if you enjoyed looking at the *bois de chandelle* and liked to use it as a torch at night to catch fish, or wanted to shoot wild boar, but for Jensen being in an anchorage meant drinking and wenching, and the devil take where you woke up in the morning.

Port Royal had the women, and many more were expected. And the liquor, too. Port Royal had promise; give it six months to get used to the new king, and it should be able to cater for every pleasure and vice devised by pliant women and imaginative buccaneers with their pockets full of gold. Even during their recent brief stay he had heard stories that some of the richest folk in Jamaica were the whores, who demanded payment in advance and locked the money away before starting business.

There was the headland half a mile ahead. Cocal Point was a black shape in the darkness and visible only because it outlined itself against the stars. He knew where to look for the three islets about three cables off the end of the point. Six hundred yards...yes, there they were, the largest one being the furthest out and called San Buenaventura.

So that was the southern side of the entrance to Portobelo! He felt a mild excitement as he slowly put the tiller over to pass a hundred yards to seaward of Buenaventura. Mr Yorke had impressed on him that there were many coral reefs between and round the three islets, and Jensen glanced astern to make sure the next boat was following him. He was startled to see it only four or five yards away – a tribute to the muffling of the oars.

Although they were meeting only wavelets, there was an occasional underlying swell, and he could hear the hollow boom as it buried itself among the rocks round Buenaventura – a useful sound because he would be able to locate the islet long after it had passed out of sight.

He steered to starboard in a slow curve which should bring him round Cocal Point and into the anchorage of Portobelo, giving them about a mile to row down to the castle of San Gerónimo, keeping close in to the southern shore but not running on to the straggling reefs of staghorn coral extending half a mile into the harbour. Harbour? It was a big anchorage really, with a village down at the end: Jensen, remembering the orderly villages at home, thought that calling the whole place by a single name gave the wrong idea of what it was like. The English did not make that mistake: in Jamaica, Port Royal was only a tiny town built on a spit which almost closed off the great bay. No one made the mistake of confusing it with the anchorage.

Suddenly Jensen realized that dawn was turning the blackness of night into grey and he was actually looking eastward into Portobelo through the wide entrance. As he instinctively moved the tiller he hurriedly tried to identify everything. Yes, there was the headland forming the other side of the entrance – Portobelo Point, and just inside a blacker smudge which must be the first castle, San Felipe de Todo Fierro, and which everyone called the Iron Fort.

Ah, this course should take them all safely down the south side, as far as the village of Portobelo, when they would turn to larboard to pass Triana, which they said was a little fort, before reaching the jetty of San Gerónimo.

How were Mr Yorke and his party doing? They should be coming down the track to the village by now. There were no flashes of musket or cannon, so they had probably been delayed.

Dawn took so long! He wanted some light to come faster so he could see where the devil he was leading the boats, yet he wanted to hold on to the darkness to give them all something to hide in. He reached down under the thwart and brought out his cutlass, calling quietly to the oarsmen to do the same, but without breaking their stroke. They might meet Spanish fishermen along here rowing out early to their fish pots, and there was only one way of preventing them from raising the alarm: cut them down with cutlasses while their jaws were still dropping in surprise.

Rowing down the anchorage towards the castle was like entering a cavern. Outlined against the stars on his right, to the south, were high mountains – the ones across which Mr Yorke was coming; on the left, northwards, steep cliffs formed the other side of the anchorage. It was flatter at the far end, according to Mr Yorke: down there, round San Gerónimo, it was marshy. And for now it was quiet: just the distant metallic grating of tree frogs, the occasional splash of a fish leaping to escape, the gurgle round the boat's stem sounding like a fast rocky stream.

Not like Gilleleje... Here it was so hot and humid that perspiration was streaming down his face and tickling as it ran down his back under his jerkin – and he was not even rowing. In a month or two they would be breaking ice off Gilleleje...

Secco had the men lined up along the side of the track in what passed for a military formation. They were still exchanging helmets with each other, men cursing blistered brows and trying for a better fit, and against the first hint of dawn in the sky behind them the shadows made them look like goblins. As soon as he saw Ned waiting to inspect them, he called the men to attention.

Secco himself looked exactly like a Spanish army officer: he had trimmed his beard to a sharp point, his moustaches now curved up and out like bull's horns. Ned was delighted to see that Secco had relieved a Spanish officer at Old Providence of his army breeches. They were of a distinctive cut, bulging as though each leg between knee and thigh was inserted in a pumpkin. His hose were clean and his high leather boots, the tops folding over at the knee, were polished. The original owner, Ned reflected, would be proud of them.

As Ned complimented Secco, he proudly put on his helmet and showed that he had selected the one helmet that had the plume.

Thomas inspected him too. "You look like a Roman centurion," he commented. "That helmet – I must say it's well designed. A sword slash might lose you the tip of your nose, but that's about the only part of your head that shows! And this sash!" He pointed to the red sash that Secco was wearing across his left shoulder. "What's that mean – you're a general?"

"No, a captain," Secco grinned happily, wriggling slightly in his armour, and calling one of his seamen to slacken a strap on one side holding the breast plate.

Ned then noticed that Secco's armour had shoulder pieces: like the overlapping pieces of shell forming a lobster's tail, the armour covered the shoulder and half-way down to the elbow. Secco had more cunning then the rest of the captains: at Old Providence, although he did not have the slightest idea that Ned's plan would involve him disguising himself as an army officer, he had appropriated everything he needed.

Ned continued to walk round Secco, impressed in the first light of dawn with the care the man had taken: like an actor with the most important part in the play (which he had), Secco had gone to a great deal of trouble, yet there was no sign that the breeches, hose, polished boots and flowing plume had been carried by open boat and then in a bag to this point in the mountain track to Portobelo which served as the Spaniard's dressing-room.

"Well, captain," Ned said, "let us inspect your men!"

Over to the east there was more than a hint that dawn was pulling back the black of night like someone stripping a blanket from a bed, but because they were still high above Portobelo the anchorage and town was still heavily shadowed.

The first man, standing to attention with a halberd by his side, looked as Spanish as Secco, except that his beard was trimmed square. His armour fitted him well, the helmet sat on his head as though he always wore one. He had a long sword hanging at his left side, and in a scabbard slung diagonally across his back was a short, broad-bladed stabbing sword, not more than eighteen inches long. The hilt was high on the man's left shoulder.

"A *main-gauche,*" Ned commented. It was the first time he had seen one worn, and he noted that the man need only reach his left hand over his left shoulder to grip the hilt.

Secco nodded. "You have your long sword in your right hand and this sturdy little chap in your left. You swing your opponent's sword to one side leaving his whole body open and step forward and jab with your *main-gauche*..."

The next man had a musket in his left hand and the rest for it in his right. Hanging diagonally across his chest was a strap from which hung a dozen wooden tubes, looking like whistles with wooden plugs in the ends.

Usually known irreverently as the Twelve Apostles and each holding the exact measure of powder for the musket, they were well-carved. The musketeer would take one and pull out the wooden plug, pour the measure of powder down the barrel, ram home a wad and follow it with a ball and another wad.

The musketeer would then take the flask which was slung over his shoulder by a thin strap. The flask, usually triangular, the top forming a spout and with a lever on one side, contained the priming powder, which was finer than the gunpowder in the Apostles. He would fill the pan of the gun and then, with the musket barrel placed in its rest, which was about four and half feet high, he would be ready to fire – once he had blown on the slow-match a few times to make sure that the burning end was glowing and hooked it on to the serpentine. By now, Ned reflected, two or three minutes would have passed, more if the man was clumsy.

The next man also had a musket and a rest but no Apostles: instead he had two brass flasks, one larger than the other but of the same shape as the first musketeer. He would load his musket by using powder from the larger flask to pour down the bore of the gun and from the smaller flask for priming.

No wonder impatient but wary men like buccaneers – who better than most knew about damp, rain and high winds – preferred pikes and cutlasses. Slow-match, which had to be lit and looped into the serpentine so that squeezing the trigger swung it over and pressed the burning tip of the match into the priming pan, needed only a light drizzle – a proverbial Scotch mist – to douse it, while a high wind could blow away the priming powder.

As if reading his thoughts, Thomas grumbled: "Only good for frightening horses, these things, and then it has to be a fine day. Pity the Dons at Old Providence didn't have wheel-lock muskets – thank goodness that at least they had those few pistols."

"At Old Providence you were praising matchlocks," Ned reminded him. "I remember you were scathing about wheel-locks."

"Who would trust a spring and those pyrites?" Thomas said gloomily. "Who would trust anything out in the open that relied on sparks or slow-match? Oh no, a cutlass and pike for me." He looked at the musketeer's waist and saw he was wearing a Spanish sword. "A good blade?"

"Toledo steel," the man said confidently. "This 'ere musket's just 'n norniment!"

Ned had expected the man to be Spanish and was startled by the London accent. The man grinned and, guessing the question Ned was about to ask, explained: "Cap'n Secco reckoned I look more Spanish than some of his own men."

"You do, too," Ned admitted.

The rest of the men in armour and helmets were armed with muskets, halberds or pikes. Seven or eight feet high, the pike was a weapon with which they were familiar, although several of the men commented that because the Spanish model had so much ornamentation on the head, it was not as well balanced as their own. Few liked the halberd, cursing the weight and asking who needed a combination of axe, pike and tomahawk all fitted on one pikestaff. "The axe gets in the way of the pike if you want to jab, the pike unbalances the tomahawk if you want to cut, and the axe won't even slice boucan," one of the men complained to Thomas.

Thomas was sympathetic. "Yes, it's very Spanish," he said. "While you're trying to decide whether to chop, hack or stab, the enemy runs you through with a sword!"

With Secco's soldiers inspected, Ned went on to look at the guns. The men hauling them – or, for this part of the journey, hauling back on the ropes to stop the guns running away down the hill – wore only breeches and were barefooted. Secco had explained that Spanish soldiers hauling guns across tropical mountains would not be expected to wear jerkins and hose, and those who had been in the Main for a year or more would certainly prefer to be barefooted: Spanish army boots were heavy and hot, and a long march like the one from Panama to Portobelo would cause huge blisters, quite apart from keeping the bootmaker busy repairing soles.

By now it was light enough to recognize a man's face at four paces, and Ned turned to Secco. "Very well, it's time your men were marching and the wheels of those gun carriages were turning!"

A couple of orders hissed in Spanish had the hundred men in armour forming up in four files on the track, Secco at their head and the fifty without helmets at the rear. Those at the guns – the first of the falcons, only ten yards behind – stood ready, a man crouching at each wheel to remove the rock that acted as a brake.

Saxby was in charge of the guns and was dressed in the nearest Mrs Judd and her women could get to a Spanish officer's uniform, presumably copying the real one owned by Secco. "These breeches," Saxby grumbled. "Don't know how the Dons can abide wearing 'em, all puffed out like a flouncy skirt."

"You look very handsome," Ned said soothingly, "and more to the point, none of the guns has run away with you, yet."

"Yes, sir," Saxby said heavily. "Downhill is the hard part."

The second half of the buccaneer party was two hundred yards behind. There was no doubt that they were buccaneers: most wore boots which were simply strips of hide secured by thongs, while their jerkins had more holes than material. Breeches were of a style unknown to tailors and which originated on board the ships, depending on the skill of the boldest man with scissors and needle. Hats with brims and without were made of felt or wild animal skins. Most men were armed with cutlasses, although some had curving cavalry sabres, and the majority had pistols stuck in the top of their breeches. All had powder flasks and water bottles, and a few wore small satchels on their back filled with boucan. Yet, Ned noticed, for all their ragged clothes and assorted weapons, they had a purposeful look about them;

they knew where they were going: there was no hint of a rabble of camp followers, eager to snatch any booty left behind by the soldiers.

"Keep at least five hundred yards behind," Ned told Leclerc, who was in command. "When the Spaniards see Secco's force, your men must still be out of sight."

The men in the armour of a Spanish company of infantry had begun to march down the track, stirring a cloud of dust, and a couple of moments later the wheels of the first falcon began their rumbling.

Thomas tapped Ned's shoulder and gestured towards the eastern sky, now lightening quickly as a hint of cherry washed some distant clouds. "This is really the beginning," he said happily as the two men walked down the hill. "The fleet will be leaving the Bahia las Minas and Jensen's boats should be coming into the harbour now."

Suddenly Ned could smell wood smoke. At the foot of the mountains Portobelo was at last stirring: just below them the women were lighting their cooking fires to start the day, and a couple of minutes later he could smell onions frying. Onions! He sneezed, and realized that Secco's men were raising the dust on the track. It was ironic that he was sneezing: he had expected rain to turn the dust of the track into sticky red mud which would bog down the guns. Portobelo, lying beside this range of high mountains, was notorious for its heavy rainfall. But instead of heavy, rolling clouds there had been (so far, anyway) star-studded skies with every promise of a fine cloudless but scorching day as soon as the sun lifted over the horizon.

Very quickly it was light enough for him to see Secco's men some distance away. They looked smart, the occasional glint from armour warning how fast the sun was rising. The guns were rolling smoothly down the hill, the men leaning back on the ropes. Seamen knew how to take the strain…

The *Griffin* should be under way now, leading the little fleet out of the Bahia las Minas as Thomas had commented. He pictured the ships, their sails barely filling in a light breeze. Then, in spite of himself, he imagined Aurelia and for the first time felt fear. If anything happened to her... He should never have left her with the ships. But where else? She was far safer in the *Griffin* than here, and he would worry about her just as much – probably a good deal more if she and Diana were waiting in one of the boats now left hidden along the banks of the Rio Guanche.

"Not far now," Thomas said as the two of them walked along the edge of the track where the hill began to drop away sharply to the town. The rooftops of Portobelo were now so close that Ned felt he could hurl stones down on to those chimneys from which wisps of smoke curled like kettles beginning to boil in a cold climate. In the heat of the Tropics, he thought irrelevantly, the sign of boiling water was a juddering lid, not clouds of steam.

Then he forced himself to look beyond Portobelo. The track ran along behind the town and then, finally having reached sea level, turned left to pass the landward side of Fort Triana and beyond to the Castillo de San Gerónimo. From Secco's description, a turning off the track actually led into the town, but from where he stood the houses themselves hid it.

It would never work. He realized that the first moment he caught sight of San Gerónimo from this level: in the shadow of dawn it seemed huge and carved from solid stone, impregnable to the battering of siege guns, its own guns and gun loops able to blast away scaling ladders. Yet here he was with these puny falcons, guns more suited to firing salutes than fighting, and for all his brave talk, they were an armed rabble that needed only a Falstaff. Indeed, *he* was their Falstaff; all he lacked was a pot belly and a raucous voice.

He told himself that all the way from Port Royal to Old Providence he had not had a real plan for capturing Portobelo (or at least San Gerónimo), but his good luck at Old Providence had helped persuade him that he was a military genius: capturing a castle, most of whose garrison were believed to be several hundred miles away, was simple.

He had had the idea – not a plan, he jeered at himself, just an idea – at Old Providence; the capture of the two islands and its munitions had given him the basis for The Great Plan. It remained The Great Plan the whole time it took to sail to the Bahia las Minas, and was still a plan when the boats rowed on to the Rio Guanche. His confidence in it began to fade during the tedious climb up the hills towards the track. Not vanish suddenly, just slowly fade. Then they reached the track, and at the highest point he was too busy watching the men tightening the straps of their armour, checking that Apostles had powder, making sure that powder flasks were also full and that the measuring springs worked freely to worry about The Great Plan.

Then Secco had stepped out down the track at the head of the men, and still The Great Plan seemed – well, at least a good idea. Now, looking at San Gerónimo, it seemed childish, the feverish wanderings of a simple mind. It would vanish in a shouted challenge, the castle door slamming shut. A brace of cannon would wipe out Jensen's boats as they approached and the echo of the shots would alert the Iron Fort, whose guns would be ready for the leading ships after Aurelia tacked towards the anchorage.

The Spanish gunners, seeing all the ships approaching, obviously would not be stupid enough to open fire too soon and raise the alarm; they would wait until there were plenty of ships in the anchorage – after all, once they were inside, the Iron Fort could stop them sailing out again, and the guns of the Castillo de San Fernando, San Gerónimo and Triana could pound them all day, and all night, if need be. The guns in the ships? Mere squibs compared with those in the forts; little more than blunderbusses loaded with nails and bits of scrap metal.

The track, now only a thin layer of dust on cracked rock, jarred on his heels as he walked down the slope. Everyone – well, Secco, anyway – said Triana was a small fort, but even that one seemed damn'd big from here, only a few hundred yards away, while San

Gerónimo looked a good deal larger than the fort he'd blown up at Santiago.

That singing was Secco and his men: he identified it from the words and rhythm as an old Spanish marching song, much of it bawdy, with several words he did not understand.

"Secco's brighter than we gave him credit for," Thomas murmured. "Or did you tell him?"

"No, I didn't think of it. But what a wonderful way to put everyone off their guard! Singing soldiers heading for the castle after their long march from Panama!"

By now the dogs had started barking, dozens of them; then the goats, startled by the dogs, began adding their sharp bleating protest, and in turn some donkeys started braying, sounding like oxen having their throats cut. Suddenly a bugle or trumpet began sounding from the ramparts of Triana. An alarm? No, the notes were too strident but not urgent. It might even be reveille and simply a coincidence. Or, hearing the approaching troops and expecting a senior officer to be leading them, perhaps a wakeful trumpeter had used his own initiative. Secco would recognize it and know what to do.

At that moment Ned and Thomas passed the end of a row of houses just in time to see Secco's men marching past the huge gates of Triana, and it was light enough to see that the little side door was open.

No, the trumpeter was not sounding an alarm: he had stopped at what was the end of a tune and was not blowing again. Obviously an alarm would be repeated and picked up and passed on by the other forts.

Now Secco had disappeared from sight round the eastern side of Triana and Ned remembered the Spaniard saying that the path was narrow there and the men hauling the guns would have to be careful not to get wheels mired in the swamp which began on the landward side. Now he saw the last of the men in armour...now the first team was hauling the leading falcon...now the second... That was Saxby on the swamp side of the track making sure that the guns were being hauled along as fast as the men.

Ned waited, knowing that the rest of the buccaneers were crouching behind him on the side of the track away from Portobelo, out of sight of anyone just below. Thomas whispered: "Secco will soon have the ladies rushing out with mugs of wine for him!"

And, Ned prayed, as the idea came to him, no one will notice me walking behind the troops and in front of the guns. Aurelia and Diana must be only a few miles short of the entrance to Portobelo; Jensen and his boats will be hiding just down there.

He had to be ready, in fact, to take command the moment everything went dreadfully wrong and San Gerónimo's garrison discovered that the newly arrived "Spanish" troops who they must assume were a partial replacement for the men sent to Jamaica were in fact buccaneers in search of the bullion they guarded.

"Take command here!" he told Thomas and before the startled man had time to protest, Ned was striding along the track, his throat rasping from the dust. Soon he was looking up at the great walls of Triana, black against the sky which was now merging from grey into a very pale blue.

It was difficult not to break into a run. If anything was going to go wrong, he wanted the great guns on the battlements of Triana and San Gerónimo and the Iron Fort firing as soon as possible to warn Aurelia, giving the ships a chance to get out.

Once again he could see the last of the men in armour. Their back plates, smooth and shiny, moving in unison, made them look in the distance like an iguana as Secco led them in a curve towards the enormous square black cavern that was San Gerónimo's gate. No, the gates were not open, but there was a small door on one side. Just what one would expect, in fact.

Secco had reached it – and stopped. Now he took a step backward and something metallic flared in the poor light. Now another man was standing in front of him, a man who had come through the door. A sentry? Yes, and the man's stance was of someone being servile: Secco, plume waving in his helmet, would be acting the arrogant *hidalgo*, stamping a booted foot and demanding to know why the castle gate was shut against him.

CHAPTER FIFTEEN

"Orders?" Secco snapped at the sleepy sentry. "Whose orders? You are expecting us, so – what are you mumbling? Murcia – you come from there? What an atrocious accent it is."

"Orders, sir?" the sentry stammered. "I've had no orders to open the gate. In fact, my orders are to keep them locked and barred!"

"Fetch your commanding officer!" Secco said coldly. "This is an insult. An important reinforcement for the garrison and we are kept waiting outside the castle like...like beggars seeking a crust!"

Again the man mumbled. "He's not here?" Secco repeated, pretending disbelief. "Where is he? Oh, he went to Jamaica too, did he? Well, who is in command? How many men are there here?"

While the sentry paused, obviously trying to sort the questions out, Ned ambled along the column of men as though he was an idle onlooker, and stopped within earshot of Secco.

"The sergeant is in command of the guard, sir," the sentry said carefully, and Ned appreciated Secco's comment about the man's accent.

"Well, who is in command of the castle?"

"There's no one superior to the sergeant, sir, more is the pity: he is a Madrileno and behaves like a general. Like the Viceroy," he amended.

"How many men are you, then, under this miserable sergeant?"

"Twenty-five sir. The sergeant, two corporals and twenty-two men sir. The captain is in Triana; he's got his quarters and his office there and refused to move over here when the rest sailed for Jamaica."

Secco swore violently, as though at last his patience was exhausted. "Come on now, get these gates open and turn out the guard: you know the respect due to an officer!"

Secco knew he had just taken a big gamble. Would this fool of a sentry obey the two orders in the sequence they were given, to open the gates and *then* turn out the guard, or would he first run for the sergeant, who – well, there was no point in speculating!

The man, bewildered, paused just long enough for Secco to exclaim impatiently: "The gates, man, the gates!"

The soldier ran back through the small door and a moment later there was a thudding as heavy wooden beams were removed, then the metallic clank of bars. Finally, groaning as though it was in agony, one of the great gates began to swing outwards, the condition of the hinges revealing that it was opened perhaps thrice a year. Then, with Secco thumping the scabbard of his sword impatiently against his left boot, the other gate swung back.

Secco noted that the guardroom was on the right-hand side of the gateway, and immediately gave the order for his men to march, effectively cutting off the sentry from the guardroom until all the troops and the guns had passed into the large courtyard round which the high walls of San Gerónimo were built.

The puzzled sentry, barred from his sergeant, who must be sleeping soundly, helped no doubt by a mug of rumbullion, stood to attention and saluted. Secco returned the salute and six minutes later the men in armour and the guns were all inside the castle. By then a dozen men led by Secco were forcing the sentry to lead the way into the guardroom.

Then suddenly Thomas was leading the buccaneers into the castle, the flamboyant chief of a band of beggars.

"Shut and bar the gates!" Ned ordered, and the two massive structures creaked closed again. San Gerónimo was enormous, and Ned realized that as far as the buccaneers were concerned the only way in was indeed the one they had just taken: through the gates. The walls must be fifteen or twenty feet thick, carefully carved interlocking stone, the work of masons, not a crude affair flung up by slaves.

A bellow in Spanish from a door beside the guardroom had Ned and Thomas wheeling round and drawing their swords. A moment later a large plump man with enormously long, curving moustaches, a sword in one hand and a *main-gauche* in the other, wearing only breeches, his chest bare and curiously hairless in contrast to his moustaches, barefooted and without hose, rushed out and came to an abrupt stop as he stared first at the muzzle of a pistol being levelled at him from a yard away by a buccaneer then at the column of cannon standing in the courtyard with men in Spanish armour moving round them. Then he saw the group of buccaneers.

Guessing that this must be the sergeant, who had probably been occupying an officer's room during its owner's absence in Jamaica, and knowing that Secco and his heavily-armed men would be securing the rest of the guard, Ned watched him. The buccaneer with the pistol was grinning, enjoying the near stalemate and baiting the sergeant with French obscenities.

The sergeant seemed to be growing smaller, deflating like a bladder with a tiny hole. His moustaches looked as though they were wilting. Then Ned realized they were protected by moustache cups fitting over the bristles like horns slipped over thinner horns, and secured by a line from the tip of each going round the back of the neck. The sergeant's wrath and then fear had somehow made the line slip, so that the unsupported cups now gave the moustaches – normally waxed when on parade – a defeated droop. The sergeant's behaviour reminded Ned of a large dog that began barking fiercely and growling but ended up wagging its tail and seeking a pat on the head.

There was yelling from the guardhouse: several voices were shouting in agitated Spanish. Suddenly there was silence and Secco strolled out, saw Ned and Thomas watching the buccaneer and the sergeant, and said: "All the guard are secured except this one, the sergeant."

"Send half a dozen men aloft to the top of the walls to keep a look-out – your men, in armour. Let them be *seen*. Keep the rest here as a reserve. Saxby!"

He had bellowed the name, but the *Phoenix*'s captain and the former foreman of the Kingsnorth estate was standing just behind him, obviously waiting for orders.

"Ah, round up your men and be ready to follow us. Secco, persuade that sergeant that we need the key to the cells, or dungeon, whatever he calls it. *Calabozo*, isn't it? In fact make him collect the key and show us the way down."

Thomas chuckled happily. "I can hear those ingots dropping with a nice thud on to our decks and the coins, pieces of eight in canvas bags, will make a satisfying clink..."

"We haven't found them yet!"

"We will, though. Most of the men have already spent their share of the purchase – in their imaginations, anyway!"

Secco was prodding the sergeant with a *main-gauche* and speaking to him with a quietness that contradicted the movement. It was almost completely light now and Ned could see the absurd line holding the moustache cups. One cup had just slipped off, leaving the other still in place so that one side of the sergeant looked startled and the other sad. He now lurched rather than walked to the door of his quarters, with Secco following him. A minute later both came out again, the sergeant holding a large key.

"This way," Secco told Ned, gesturing to a door across the courtyard.

The trumpet blaring out high above them on the battlements again took them by surprise but there was no mistaking the call: it was an alarm, a call to arms, which would reach Triana and San

Fernando and, on a morning like this, probably the Iron Fort at the harbour entrance.

The *Griffin*! Aurelia, and the *Peleus* and Diana!

For a few seconds Ned froze. As soon as the garrison in the Iron Fort heard San Gerónimo's trumpeter sound the alarm, they would look seaward: a minute or two later even the most stupid or panic-stricken of them, seeing twenty-eight ships sailing up to the entrance, would start loading the cannon.

Two of Secco's Spaniards with drawn swords were already running up the stone stairs leading from the courtyard to the battlements, while to Ned the trumpet became louder, its urgent notes seeming to bounce back from the mountains, race round the rooftops of Portobelo and echo the length of the anchorage so that the very walls of the forts trembled: how could a trumpet be so loud? Then it died away in mid-note, the last air in the trumpeter's lungs turning into a scream of pain. A man shouted down from the battlements, waving a bloodstained sword, and Secco translated. The trumpeter had apparently just sighted the buccaneers down in the courtyard and sounded the alarm without waiting for orders – a piece of initiative, Secco commented, that had ended his life on a sour note.

Jensen would hear and recognize the warning, and he and his boats would stay hidden. But the ships... The thought of Aurelia was paralysing: if she was early and leading the squadron into the anchorage this very minute, too far off to have heard the trumpet...

Now, damnation, there was a thundering at the side door which was set in the gates. "Saxby, take twenty men and that sergeant and search the dungeons for the bullion! Secco, I need your Spanish – who is that hammering at the door? Thomas – up on the battlements. If you see any of our ships coming round the headland, start firing cannon: the women will know what that means. Take some powder from the falcons. And no damned slow-match lit – oh," he exclaimed, noticing the thin wisp of smoke rising in the almost windless air beside Thomas. "When did you light that?"

"While you were marching after Secco. Remember, the three golden rules, Ned: keep your powder dry, a slow-match lit and your women well fed and ill clothed. I'm off!"

With that Thomas ran for the stairway, calling to a dozen of his men to follow and sending others for powder.

Now Secco was standing there. "The captain, a sergeant and three men from Triana are at the side door asking what the alarm is."

Ned thought carefully. At the moment he controlled San Gerónimo. Three more forts to go. The idea had worked so far. Now for a new one. If Thomas could keep the ships out of the anchorage, it might succeed. Quickly he gave his orders to Secco, who grinned and nodded and hurried back to the door, beckoning to half a dozen of his men.

He flung the door open with an extravagant gesture, invited the men outside to come in. They stepped through, the captain carefully, so that the tip of his ornate sword scabbard did not clang on the sill of the doorway, the others lowering their halberds.

Once they were all inside the courtyard, looking round and obviously bewildered, Secco spoke rapidly and the captain looked behind him to find that four wheel-lock pistols were indeed aimed at them from a range of about six feet, held by soldiers – Spanish soldiers, apparently – who had been hidden behind the door when it was open.

While the new prisoners were being disarmed, Secco spoke quickly to Ramirez, who nodded a couple of times, asked a single question and as soon as it was answered pulled open the door and vanished outside. Secco looked round again and waved to Sanchez, who hurried over, was given more orders, and followed Ramirez out of the door.

Secco came over to Ned. "That's a start, sir," he said, and the Spaniard realized that it was the first time he had called a man "sir", or its equivalent in any language, for many years.

"Find out from that captain how many men there are in each of the forts."

"I have. Fifteen in Triana, twenty in San Fernando, and thirty-five in the Iron Fort, counting everyone except the whores."

"Thirty-five in the Iron Fort, eh. Allowing five to a gun, they could have seven guns turned on our ships..."

Ned admitted to himself that the thought was disloyal to the Brethren of the Coast, who had so recently elected him their admiral, but at this moment he would trade all the treasure of the Indies for the safety of Aurelia and Diana, and Mrs Judd in the *Phoenix*.

The Iron Fort: how did one capture a powerful fort at the other end of the harbour? One and a quarter miles away... Only one thing would travel that distance, he thought bitterly, and that's bluff. And it might work, too! "Yes?"

It was Saxby, pale-faced and perspiring, his hands trembling. Ned had never seen him in this condition. Was Thomas dead, killed by that trumpeter? No, that could not be.

Thomas was up on the battlements while Saxby had been down to the dungeons.

"Pull yourself together man! What's the matter?"

"It's all down there, sir," Saxby said shakily. "Great blocks of silver, bags and bags of pieces of eight, sacks of doubloons... It's what we're looking for, sir. Oh my Gawd, it's the riches of El Dorado!"

Ned ignored the man's excitement and asked crisply: "Have you left a guard on it? Those men have locked the dungeons again?"

"There's just one lock, large. Yes, locked it and nineteen of them are down there guarding the key!"

"Five should be enough for that: tell them to stay down there with the key. I need the others up here as guards."

With the colour coming back into his cheeks, Saxby hurried down to the dungeon again. Ned signalled to Secco and talked with him for three or four minutes, but even before they had finished there was a banging at the door and muffled shouts. As Secco signalled to his men to open the door, he explained quickly: "The rest of the Triana men!"

The door flung open and more than a dozen men rushed in, paused as they looked round, and then stood rigid as Secco snapped an order. They turned their heads slowly as the door closed to confirm they were indeed covered by pistols, and quickly dropped pikes and pulled swords from scabbards and threw them to one side.

Two of the buccaneers collected up the weapons and Secco said: "We need somewhere to lock up the prisoners: there's hardly any more room in the guardhouse, and..."

"Quite. Well, let's lock them in the dungeon along with the bullion: they can't destroy it!"

Secco started laughing. "No better place!"

"Very well, have some men march them down, but keep the guards at the door because – "

He broke off as shouting outside and bangings on the side door announced new arrivals. Once again Secco gave the signal and waited while the San Fernando garrison rushed in, responding to an urgent call said to be from the garrison commander of San Gerónimo and relayed by Ramirez, who had explained that he was part of the reinforcements just arrived from Panama during the night. The garrison were wildly excited over the trumpet call and disappointed that Ramirez had not known exactly what the emergency was.

The door shut quickly behind them as they looked round, finally fixing their gaze on the black-bearded captain in armour who was standing in front of them. The captain said something and then repeated it, and like the others they looked over their shoulders into the muzzles of pistols, dropped their pikes, threw aside their swords and stood very still.

"I'll have these taken to the dungeon first," Secco said.

"Saxby's down there bringing all but five of his men up. You'd better tell him to leave all his men down there as guards. Twenty – that should be enough."

"I'll look at the lock, sir," Secco said, giving a string of orders to the men who had been opening and closing the door and covering the prisoners with pistols.

Just then Ned saw Thomas coming down the steps and he told Secco to wait.

"No sign of the ships, and no sign of life at the Iron Fort," Thomas reported. "I saw a couple of our men going to visit our nearest neighbours, and then the neighbours came to call." He waved at the prisoners. "We're getting quite a collection!"

"Listen, Thomas, all the plate is down in the dungeon: Saxby found it and his men are guarding it. We have so many prisoners we'll have to put them in the dungeon as well – they can't harm the bullion. Will you take over from Secco and secure the prisoners? The rest of them are in the guardhouse."

Thomas gave a happy bellow which brought over the buccaneers who had been guarding the powder beside the falcons, and using one of the Spanish buccaneers as a translator he soon had the Triana and San Fernando men marching towards the dungeon.

In the meantime Ned was deep in conversation with Secco. Once again the Spaniard had a delighted grin on his face.

"Sir, if I may suggest something… Yes, I can give this ultimatum, but it might help if I had some other captains with me, who could speak their own languages. They won't be understood, of course, but to these people buccaneers *are* foreigners! They'd be much more impressed by Englishmen, say, or Dutchmen, than someone they regard as a renegade Spaniard."

Secco was quite right of course. Ned looked round to where the buccaneers were standing in various groups, as they had been ordered, with their captains nearby. A Dutchman – Gottlieb really looked a foreigner, blond with widely spaced eyes and high cheekbones. Coles and Brace – a calm pair who, if things went wrong, would act as a steadying influence. And Rideau. Black-bearded, short, he was unmistakably French. He named them to Secco, who nodded in agreement.

"Now we want a white flag!"

"The officers' quarters," Ned said promptly. "They won't have taken all their table and bed linen to Jamaica!"

CHAPTER SIXTEEN

Charles Coles slapped at the swarming mosquitoes whining out of the shrubs and attacking the five men. The path skirting the anchorage from the Castillo de San Fernando round to the Castillo de San Felipe de Todo Fierro was narrow, often twisting to avoid big rocks, and – all too frequently for Coles, who had no head for heights – running almost to the edge of the cliff. Not exactly a cliff, Coles admitted, but a very steep drop to the sea. Still, he thought with a grin, it was in a good cause – a king's ransom, according to Mr Yorke, because the bullion was there, in the dungeon.

Would they get to the Iron Fort in time, or would the ships arrive and – to all intents and purposes – sail into a trap? Mr Yorke's lady, and Lady Diana, would not know that a damned trumpeter whom happened to be on sentry duty on the battlements and whom everyone had forgotten in the rush had been able to sound the alarm.

Coles cursed as he slipped, grabbed a bush and knew without looking that it was prickly pear: now he had a dozen fine spines, looking as innocent as the blow-away seeds on a dandelion, stuck in his hand, each as painful as a needle and broken off level with the skin.

Coles was unusual for a buccaneer: he had been at sea ever since he was nine years old, and he owned a ship only because, escaping after transportation to Barbados for a noisy affair in a Scarborough tavern leading to a man's death, he had joined a group of buccaneers on the north coast of Hispaniola and led them in a raid on a ship in La Plata. Ah, that had been an expedition! Through jungle and pampas, over mountains and across rivers to the port – but no one had expected them, least of all the ship's crew. Eight Spanish throats were quietly cut, and perhaps the rest of the Spaniards strolling along the quayside wondered why the *Argonauta* was suddenly sailing... Well, that was five years ago and he had kept the name. Now, with a king back on the throne in England, perhaps he'd fly English colours.

They were making good time: it was completely light now, although the sun was still below the top of the hill. The Iron Fort – well, it looked strong enough, built on top of the steep cliff so that it could not be attacked from seaward. Not by armed men, anyway. Bombarded from ships, yes, though the walls were probably as thick as San Gerónimo's, and it would take a month of Sundays to make any impression on them.

In a few minutes they would be far enough along the path to be able to see round the end of Cocal Point, which formed the other side of the entrance, and perhaps catch a glimpse of the ships.

Coles suddenly had an idea. "Wait a moment. Listen, if the ships come in sight we can set fire to this brushwood. It's dry enough to burn well, but there are enough leaves to make smoke. That'll warn 'em something is the matter and they won't try to sail in."

Gottlieb nodded and Brace said it was a good idea. Secco and Rideau thought for a moment and then agreed with enthusiasm.

"Flint and steel?" inquired Brace and both Gottlieb and Coles slapped the sides of their breeches.

"Come on, then," Secco said, "we'll be there in five minutes."

Now, in the clear sight of the Iron Fort, the men were hurrying in a crouch. Then, as the path straightened for the last hundred yards up to the big gates, Secco stopped them, motioning them to shelter behind the bushes. From there they carefully examined the Iron Fort. It seemed deserted. No sentry paced the battlements, watching to seaward, no sentry at the small door set into the gates guarded the entrance from the path. The barrels of cannon poked out through the embrasures, stubby black fingers streaked with rust. How many could be trained to fire at the ships entering the harbour? Coles and Brace guessed at six, the rest agreed on eight. "Six, eight, a lot," Coles commented wryly.

But all agreed that from here it must have been possible to hear the San Gerónimo's trumpeter sounding the alarm, so either the Iron Fort had no garrison – which seemed absurd to all except Secco – or they had prepared a trap.

"You don't understand the Spanish," Secco explained. "They probably garrison Triana, Gerónimo and Fernando because they have orders to protect the town of Portobelo. The Iron Fort's guns cannot reach the town, so…" He gave an expressive shrug. "The orders in writing from the Viceroy in Panama said Portobelo, so no commanding officer would interpret that as guarding the *harbour*. Portobelo is the town, the harbour is the harbour."

"Time we started," Brace said, holding out the pike he had been carrying. "Let's lash on the flag."

Secco unfolded a white tablecloth that had been torn in half to make it the right size, and a piece of line tied to each of two corners. Swiftly he secured it to the pike, using it as a flagstaff. "That's big enough," he commented.

"Right," Brace said, "off we go."

"I'll carry the flag," Secco said.

"No, leave it to me. The first one they'll shoot is the flag-bearer. We need you alive to protest about it in good Spanish."

The others laughed at Brace's dry humour, but all of them knew it was a possibility, and each was secretly thankful for Brace's offer.

Quite without being conscious of doing it, they spread out to make less of a target as they walked towards the fort. Then Coles saw that a door which seemed to be shut was in fact partly open: he could see a sliver of light down one side and a movement showed that someone was watching.

When they were twenty yards from the small door it swung open and revealed three men: one crouching with a pistol, the second kneeling and holding another and the third standing with a musket. From all three guns the breeze was not enough to disperse the smoke from the slow-match held in the serpentines: it curled up and reminded Coles of an old man's pipe.

As soon as the door was open the man standing with the musket shouted an order and Secco hurriedly translated: "Stop. Hold your hands out sideways so they can be sure you are unarmed."

A stream of Spanish followed and Secco waited patiently until it had stopped. The speaker could well be the brother of the sergeant at San Gerónimo: he was fat, he had flowing moustaches (the cups were missing: a sign, Coles wondered that they had heard the trumpet and were prepared?) and was short of breath.

This one, Secco thought to himself, is a stupid ox. Probably born out here – his accent has that slurring that those brought up on the Main seem to acquire: a laziness of the tongue.

"Listen," Secco said, "we are not armed and we come under a flag of truce, so put down those guns. Who is in command here?"

"I am," growled the man with the musket, "and that's a white flag!"

"Yes, it is the flag for an armistice. For a truce. For – " he broke off, realizing that this fat oaf had probably never served anywhere but Portobelo and that the words "truce"or "armistice" probably had no real meaning for him.

"Truce? You mean there's been fighting?" The man (Secco guessed he was a sergeant) was bewildered by Secco's Castilian accent. "Was that why the trumpet sounded?"

Warning the others in English to watch for the ships without giving anything away, Secco began a long but simple explanation of what had happened.

"So we have the garrisons of Triana, San Gerónimo and San Fernando locked in the dungeon," he said. "We come under a flag of truce to offer you terms. Either you surrender Todo Fierro and the garrison to us, or we will blow up San Gerónimo with all the prisoners in it. Your comrades," he added.

"I do not believe it. You tell lies. It is a trap!"

"Calm yourself, sergeant. You do not believe we have the garrison of Triana as our prisoners? Let me tell you the name of the commanding officer. Does the name Captain Peralta mean anything? You do not believe we hold San Gerónimo? But I am sure you have drunk many glasses of wine with Sergeant Bayona, as fat as yourself, and who is now locked in the dungeon with the rest of his men. And San Fernando, where normally there are one sergeant, two corporals and twelve men, all present and correct, sir. Sergeant Pardal and his corporals and all his men are in the dungeon too. Do you believe me *now*, sergeant?"

There was a pause. Coles heard the hissing of the two men with pistols talking to the sergeant. That was the silly thing about the Spanish language: it sometimes sounded like a boxful of angry snakes bargaining. Then the sergeant said: "I believe you, yes, but what is the reason for it? Why do our own people capture our forts and castles?"

The man sounded bewildered, so much so that Coles and Brace asked for a translation, and laughed heartily when Secco gave it.

"Sergeant," said Secco, "we are not 'your own people'; we are buccaneers. These two gentlemen are countrymen of *El Draco*." He turned to Brace and Coles. "Shout something about Drake in English!"

He waited until both men finished an impassioned impromptu eulogy about Drake, and then pointed to Gottlieb. "This gentleman is Dutch."

Gottlieb needed no explanation: with hands waving he described in Dutch the viciousness of the Spanish occupation of his country.

"Are you satisfied?" Secco asked politely. "There is a French captain here, too."

"No, I'm satisfied."

At that moment Secco realized that there was a musket barrel protruding from each of the dozen or so gun loops cut in the wall above the door: slots that allowed an archer or musketeer to fire at an enemy outside the walls.

He pointed up at them and said to the sergeant sharply: "Tell those men to put down those muskets; don't forget we come under a flag of truce."

The sergeant shouted into the courtyard and Secco saw the musket barrels being withdrawn and could picture the reluctant look on the men's faces.

"Well," Secco said briskly, "now you understand that we have seized Portobelo and the three castles." He felt the casual addition of the town was allowable. "We have come to give you your orders. You will march your men to San Gerónimo and leave this fort."

"March to San Gerónimo? Leave this fort – " the sergeant was incredulous. "But my orders are to command this garrison until my captain comes back from Jamaica!"

Secco sighed. At this point he was not sure whether to wheedle this ox or rage and shout. He glanced across at Cocal Point and there was no sign of the ships: the light wind was slowing them up, thank goodness.

Firmness, Secco decided. "Sergeant, either you form up your men and start marching to San Gerónimo, or we shall leave you and return to San Gerónimo ourselves. There we shall light the slow-match we have laid down to the magazines, and all your comrades will be blown to pieces along with the castle. You'll have a good view from here."

"But you can't do that! All the bullion – " he broke off suddenly, perhaps remembering old orders that its presence was never to be mentioned.

"All the bullion is now stacked well away from the castle," Secco said calmly. "What do you think nearly a thousand men have been doing all night?"

"A *thousand* men? Buccaneers? A *thousand*?"

"Oh, there were a thousand carrying the bullion," Secco said airily. "And a thousand more must be looting the town. When I left them the rest were talking of blowing up San Fernando and Triana..."

"But I don't understand... How did they get here? No ship has..."

Secco waved up at the line of mountains. "The road from Panama. We just walked in. Your comrades took one look and surrendered. Well, sergeant what are you going to do? Kill all your old comrades and destroy San Gerónimo or surrender like the rest of them? You can't fight, unless you have enough men to attack more than two thousand."

"We stay here!" the sergeant said firmly. Secco guessed the man was completely befuddled but in his own dogged fashion was refusing to leave the place he knew – and, although he did not know it, the place where he could do a great deal of harm.

"Very well, we'll tell your comrades in the dungeon as we light the slow-match. Your name, sergeant? I would like them to be grateful to the right man."

"Gonzales..." the man growled, "and I didn't kill them."

"You will," Secco said coldly. "You can save their lives by surrendering – or you can kill them, by being stupid."

"Stupid" was obviously a word with unhappy associations in the sergeant's past: he began jumping up and down, jowls quivering and waving the musket. "No one calls me stupid!" he roared. "Me, important enough to be left in command of Todo Fierro by the major, and you call me stupid! Run away with your silly white flag before we decide to turn you into real boucan! Farewell, *filibustero*!"

Secco shrugged his shoulders and turned away, followed by the four other men, and for fifty yards he reflected that it only needed the idiot or a zealot at one of the gun loops to put a musket ball between his shoulder-blades. Flags of truce, he realized, only worked when both sides understood the meaning of the word "truce".

Ned and Thomas watched from the battlements of San Gerónimo. "I can see the five of them coming back along the track," Ned said, watching with the glass. "They've taken the white cloth from the pike, and now the little door is shut at the castle. No, they haven't succeeded. The dam' garrison won't surrender..."

"That means they'll open fire at the ships," Thomas said.

"Look!" Ned exclaimed. "There's Jensen and his boats creeping along the side of those mangroves!"

He leapt on to the top of the battlements and waved his arms wildly and was relieved to see a man in the leading boat – he presumed it was Jensen – wave back. Thomas jumped up beside him. "My shape is more recognizable," he commented. "But Jensen seems reassured that we hold the castle – they look like ducklings, don't they, coming out of those mangroves."

Warning the ships: could one of Jensen's boats get down to the entrance in time – and avoid being blown out of the water as it passed the Iron Fort? Was there time? No, or rather he could not risk it. There was one other chance...

He turned to Thomas. "Send fifty men with pistols, pikes and cutlasses to get the prisoners up from the dungeon and into the courtyard. Bunch 'em in a corner and train all the falcons on them. Any nonsense, fire into the middle. You understand?"

"It'll be a pleasure; means we didn't haul those guns for nothing," Thomas said, and jumped down from the battlement and headed for the stairs down to the courtyard.

Ned took one last look round from the battlements and, catching sight of the Castillo de San Fernando out of the corner of his eye, realized that it would serve the purpose just as well. Except that Secco would have told the Iron Fort's garrison that all the prisoners were in San Gerónimo... Well, that settled that. He followed Thomas into the courtyard and then plunged down the steps into the dungeon, calling for Saxby.

The dungeon smelled like a sewer. It comprised six large cells along one side of a long corridor, and all the walls glistened in the light of lanterns from the water seeping through the stonework from the harbour. The floor was slippery, slimy with some sort of lichen or moss that grew everywhere. The doors of the cells were made of iron bars, giving the impression of cages for wild animals, and Ned remembered a description of the cells for animals and humans beneath the area of the Colosseum in Rome.

In the middle of the corridor was a rack and at the far end a thick post had been let into the stone floor. It took Ned a few moments to realize that it was the flogging post; a man had to put his arms round it and his wrists were tied on the far side, leaving his back exposed to the lash. And whether a man was being flogged at the post or stretched on the rack, all the other prisoners could see – in fact were probably made to watch – through the bars. Now the cells were crammed with Spaniards, two buccaneers standing at each door, a cutlass in one hand and a pistol in the other. Already Thomas, with more buccaneers, was getting the prisoners out of the first celll, having just explained to Saxby who, seeing Ned coming down the steps, hurried over.

"Change of plan, sir?"

"Yes, the Iron Fort won't surrender. Now, take all the men you need, apart from Sir Thomas' guards, and carry the bullion out of here. Pile it up outside at least five hundred yards away. Put sentries over it." He thought for a moment whether or not to use the Spanish prisoners as porters, then decided the extra buccaneers needed to guard them would be better used carrying bullion.

"Where is the bullion?"

"In the first two cells that Sir Thomas is emptying."

"Very well, get your men and start carrying! Don't forget the sentries. And a good five hundred yards away. Have you seen Burton?"

"He's there, sir," Saxby exclaimed, pointing at one of the guards. Ned called him.

"Have we plenty of slow-match, Burton?"

"Yes, with the falcons, sir."

"Good, get some. A quarter of an hour's burning time. Fuse the magazine of this castle so we can blow it up."

"Yes, sir," Burton said calmly, as though Ned had just told him to load a pistol. "Fifteen minutes. And shall I stand guard over it when it's done?"

"Yes. Take a couple of men – you may have to shift the barrels of powder round. But make haste!"

Thomas and his men already had the Spanish prisoners out of the first cell and Saxby was leading the first of the buccaneers up the stairs, wedges of silver under each arm, to show them where to stow it among the bushes and prickly pear on the edge of the swamp.

Up in the courtyard, Ned wondered when the place had last been so busy. A dozen buccaneers were ramming bags of langrage into the falcons and training them round to cover a corner already black with prisoners – all of whom, Ned was surprised to notice, were sitting on the ground with their backs to the guns. Thomas strolled over to him.

"They know the guns are there and being loaded, but they can't see what's going on. Must be very worrying!"

"It'd worry me," Ned admitted, "but as soon as we've got the bullion out of the castle, we'll transfer them all to Triana."

"Why not leave them here?" Thomas said, the surprise obvious in his voice.

"Because the moment we sight a sail approaching the other end of the harbour, I'm going to blow the place up."

"My goodness," Thomas said. "That'll warn Aurelia and Diana all right. Unless they think we're inside. Or they might try and rescue us."

"Perhaps, but it should put the fear of God into the Dons in the Iron Fort and keep them away from the guns. I want to discourage them from interfering when we row out with Jensen and his boats."

"Ah, that's an idea with merit," Thomas said. "Anything that means we don't have to climb back over those damnable mountains!"

"I'm going up to the battlements again: you're in charge of the courtyard. Saxby's getting out all the bullion, as you can see, and Burton's running a slow-match into the magazine. As soon as Saxby's got up the bullion, start transferring your prisoners to Triana. If any start making difficulties, shoot one or two to encourage the others to be more obliging. And Thomas, watch out for the good folk of Portobelo: they might suddenly take it into their silly heads to make a foray. It might be funny to have the butchers, bakers and candlestick makers set about us, but we might be laughing so much they'd succeed! When you have the prisoners in Triana, move our guns out of here."

Up on the battlements once again, Ned searched the sea horizon at the entrance with the perspective glass. No sails, no whitecaps, and judging from the near silence of the palm trees round San Gerónimo, next to no wind: the little fleet could be just drifting with the current, sails hanging like heavy curtains. Aurelia and Diana would be going mad with frustration, knowing they were due in Portobelo about ten o'clock – in an hour or so's time – and knowing equally well they would be very late. They would be terrified that they were letting him down, never guessing that for perhaps the only time in his life he was glad that the women were late.

The thudding of feet and a man gasping for breath made him swing round to find Søren Jensen standing there, a cheerful grin on a face red and stiff with sunburn.

"The boats are all alongside the jetty, sir. Where do you want the powder, shot and provisions?"

"Er...it's good to see you, Jensen. There's been a change of plan. That damned Iron Fort has not surrendered..."

"And those guns can..."

"Exactly."

"And we have to warn our ships!"

"Exactly!"

"Sir," Jensen said eagerly, "I'll unload three of the boats, double-bank the oars and we'll try to get past the Iron Fort to warn the fleet. One of the boats will, for certain."

If anyone could do it, Jensen was the man, but Ned realized that just warning the fleet solved nothing. With the fleet outside of Portobelo, the buccaneers and the bullion inside and the Iron Fort in between, there was stalemate, unless they were prepared to carry the bullion over the track back to the Rio Guanche, and meet the fleet there, using the boats that had remained. But what was Saxby's estimate? Five crates of silver, each weighing more than a hundredweight, twelve big canvas bags of silver coins, most of them pieces of eight, a hundred-pound crate packed with emeralds and another the same weight, containing a mixture of pearls and more emeralds. They could, of course, raid Portobelo for donkeys and carts – indeed the prisoners could be made to help – or they could break open the crates and make lighter loads. Still, a loaf of silver weighed seventy pounds.

But with Jensen's boats here, how much easier and safer it would be to load all the treasure into the ships anchored in front of the town! It boiled down to this, Ned decided. Would blowing up San Gerónimo with an almighty bang frighten the Iron Fort's garrison into surrendering? The Iron Fort had the key to everything. Well, he would have to wait for Secco and get his opinon.

He said to Jensen: "Take your boats to the next fort, Triana, and secure them there. Leave boatkeepers and then join Saxby with your men."

Ned finally stood alone on the battlements. So this is how it feels to capture a king's ransom, he told himself. Well, he felt flat; it was about as exciting as catching a cold, because at the moment he, like its rightful owner, His Most Catholic Majesty, could not spend even one piece of eight.

He walked along the top of the battlements, watching to seaward for the first glimpse of a sail. You have gone mad, he told himself. The amount of treasure you have captured would probably pay all the expenses of running England for a year – army, navy, the King and his court, and the great number of functionaries needed to do all the paperwork – and yet you are striding along with a face as long as a yard of pump water, feeling sorry for yourself. Why?

He stopped, startled by both the question and the obvious answer: he was in here and Aurelia was out there, the Iron Fort was in between, and no amount of treasure could bring them together.

He heard someone calling his name from the top of the stairs. It was Saxby, who reported: "The last boxes and bags coming up from the dungeon now, sir. The quantities are unbelievable. Some of these Spanish fellows have been translating what is painted on the boxes and bags. Millions of pieces of eight, sir: *millions*. Emeralds – thousands of 'em. Pearls, too, from Margarita Island I suppose."

"You've got it all well guarded? The Dons might suddenly sally out from the town."

"Every musket and pistol we have is loaded and has a man behind it in a circle round the treasure, sir. Sir Thomas is guarding his prisoners with the falcons."

So the Castillo de San Gerónimo now contained only Spanish prisoners. He walked down the steps with Saxby.

"You cleared that treasure very quickly!" Ned commented.

"Aye," said Saxby, "once the Spaniards had translated for us, I made sure all my lads knew what was there. Amazing how light a hundredweight box becomes when you know it's full of emeralds, some of which are yours!"

Ned laughed and told Saxby that Sir Thomas would now be transferring the prisoners to Triana, and Burton had run a fuse down into the magazine.

Saxby nodded and commented: "It might do the trick... There'll be a devil of an echo between these mountains, and plenty of smoke."

Ned saw Thomas and pointed to the gate. The bearded man understood at once and gave orders to his sentries before joining Ned.

"I was thinking that as soon as I've got the prisoners there, I might run a fuse down to Triana's magazine as well," Thomas said. "It'll be good insurance if the prisoners locked in the dungeon know that a few sparks from a flint and steel can send them to eternity..."

Ned thought of the people in the town of Portobelo. Many would still be having their breakfast. Apart from the trumpeter from San Gerónimo sounding a call which Ned thought few in the town would have recognized as an alarm, did anyone realize that Triana fort in their midst, and San Gerónimo, very close, were in the hands of buccaneers? And with a fuse running into Triana magazine, the buccaneers had the fort as a hostage: blowing it up would kill the garrisons and probably damage the town. Ned had no intention of doing it, but the threat would be useful.

He was turning to go back up the steps to the battlements when he saw a sweating, breathless and weary Secco come through the door, followed by Coles, Brace, Gottlieb and Rideau.

Secco came straight over, digging the pike into the ground to indicate his rage. "I failed, *almirante*," he said angrily. "The sergeant commanding that garrison is too stupid to breathe! He is a local man and did not even understand a flag of truce. Either he does not realize that blowing up San Gerónimo will kill all his comrades, or he is so *loco* that he will surrender only if ordered to do so by a senior officer!"

"You did your best. So the Iron Fort will fire at the ships as they try to come in."

"Yes, sir. I'm sorry. We did all we could..."

"Secco did all he could to persuade that sergeant," Brace said. "The man was too stupid."

Ned realized that the admiral of the Brethren was really doing little more than a seaman's job by standing on the battlements looking for ships, and something Secco had just said was stirring an idea.

"Gottlieb, would you go up to the battlements and keep a look-out for our ships?"

"Gladly!" The Dutchman set off up the steps.

"Secco," Ned said quietly. "You said that sergeant in the Iron Fort would only surrender 'if ordered to do so by a senior officer'? Are you sure of that?"

The Spaniard nodded vigorously. "Yes. He's born out here – no initiative, no brain, no ambition: being a soldier keeps him fed – and very well, judging from his belly – and that's all he's interested in."

"We have a senior officer here."

Secco looked puzzled and then exclaimed: "Yes, Triana had a captain, Peralta. He's probably in command of all four garrisons. He has the authority to deal with that crazy sergeant."

"Providing we can persuade him!" Coles said.

"We'll persuade him! He understands about fuses leading into magazines," Ned said grimly. "Let's find him and you can take him to Todo Fierro. Don't mention we have any ships coming in; let him think we're just completing the capture of all the forts."

Secco pointed to a group of prisoners still standing in front of the falcons while twenty or thirty more were being marched out of the castle on their way to Triana. "That's the captain, with the large hat and plume."

"Call him over: we don't want to stand in front of the guns!"

The Spaniard was stocky, with a plump face rather than fat, a thin beard and moustaches which obviously took up more of his virility and of his servant's time than their growth warranted, bulging eyes too close together, a surprisingly well shaped nose, and a narrow-lipped mouth. Ned watched him while Secco demanded his name, rank and position, and instinctively reached several conclusions.

Obviously he was a nephew of someone with influence. Not the son, or he would have a better position, but an unimportant nephew. It seemed unlikely that he had an ambition that could not be satisfied by a good cook: his complexion had that chubby pinkness reflecting too much rich food and good wine, not enough exercise and, Ned suspected, no interest in women.

He was the kind of man who, given the choice of being the uncrowned king of tiny Portobelo or a minor prince in a place like Panama, would choose Portobelo. He would not miss lively company: the knights of the dining table needed only a knife and a fork and a kitchen to turn the most provincial town or village into a gourmet's paradise.

The Spanish captain, assuming Secco was in command and thankful at finding someone who spoke Spanish, was outraged and needed to complain and excuse himself to someone. If the garrisons had not been stripped to send the men to Jamaica, he declared, the buccaneers would never have marched a hundred yards along the track: he had protested when the five transports took the rest of the garrison to Jamaica, particularly since every town had to yield levies – untrained men, he said contemptuously.

Secco interrupted to tell him that San Gerónimo would be blown up with all the prisoners in it unless the Iron Fort surrendered.

"The Iron Fort has its own commanding officer – and anyway, you would never dare!"

"The fuses are laid into the magazine of this fort and Triana," Secco said casually, adding: "The sergeant at Todo Fierro,

Gonzales, is superior to you, then? You cannot order him to surrender?"

Captain Peralta's eyes jerked from Secco to Ned. He was beginning to realize that the threat to blow up the castles was not an idle one, and he was obviously startled that Secco knew the name of the sergeant commanding at Todo Fierro.

"Well, no, obviously he is not superior, but the garrisons of Triana (myself included, San Gerónimo and San Fernando) were captured by a trick. Sergeant Gonzales obviously does not intend to fall into a trap. You can't take the fort by direct attack. He knows that and will not surrender."

"He will, or you go to Heaven propelled by a few tons of gunpowder," Secco said, translating from a comment by Ned, who found he could understand the Spaniard.

"But how can – "

"He will surrender if he gets orders from a superior officer. You are in command of all the garrisons – " Secco was not sure, but it seemed a reasonable guess " – so you will give him the orders. We go round there now. If you fail and the sergeant does not surrender, then this fort is blown up. Triana, too, if I know my admiral." Secco added with a cruel laugh which startled Ned until he saw an eye wink.

"But the Viceroy! I shall be accused of treason," Captain Peralta protested. "They are always looking for traitors, or scapegoats, when something goes wrong."

Secco shook his head sadly. "Who would ever have thought a quiet posting like Portobelo would land you in such trouble! You avoided being sent to Jamaica, but now it looks as thought the price you must pay is being hoisted on gunpowder. Unless, of course, you give the correct orders to the sergeant, when the certainty of gunpowder is replaced by the possibility of the Viceroy blaming you, although I don't see why he should."

Suddenly Gottlieb, standing at the top of the steps, shouted down: "Two sail in sight. They're three or four miles out and trying to make up over the current with a trifling breeze."

"Very well, keep reporting," Ned shouted, and saw that Thomas and several guards were returning for the rest of the prisoners and the guns.

If the ships picked up a sudden puff of wind they would be at the entrance long before Captain Peralta, Secco and an escort could reach the Iron Fort. Still, it was only chance and so had to be taken.

He said to Secco in English: "Take him to the fort and see if you can get him there before the ships arrive. The sergeant will surrender, I'm sure. Take enough men that you can nail all the guns. But make haste. As soon as you have control of the fort, haul down the Spanish colours – I see that the sergeant has hoisted them. But if the first ship looks as though she might come in before the Spanish flag's down, don't be surprised if you hear and see this place go up; I'm not risking anyone to those Spanish guns."

Aurelia was nearly in tears of frustration. The wind had not only turned light once they were abreast of the Rio Guanche, but it was puffing round in circles like a child blowing a dandelion. The fleet was now stretched across several miles of sea, each ship wary of accidentally drifting into another, sails hanging down like drying laundry.

The current – Ned had called it a counter-current here because it flowed eastward, in the opposite direction to the west-going current further out – was carrying them along the coast in the right direction but, with no wind to steer by, the ships most probably would soon be carried right past Portobelo.

What would Ned do? It was too deep to anchor – she had been delighted with herself for having that idea, but the seaman with the lead reported twelve fathoms. Certainly they (but probably not all the ships) had enough cable to anchor in seventy-two feet, but none of them had enough men to get the anchors up again from that depth when the wind set in.

Weighing at Bahia las Minas had been easy – shallow water and no wind.

More important, perhaps, what was Ned doing? By now he should have secured the forts and Søren Jensen should have led several of the boats round from the Rio Guanche. If everything had gone according to plan – she shrugged her shoulders: how often did that happen? – the boats should be waiting in Portobelo to bring the bullion out to the ships as soon as they anchored off the town.

She felt a slight breath on her cheek and glanced at the telltales, feathers strung on a line and attached to the shrouds where the helmsmen could see them. Yes, they were fluttering, and even before she could remember the right order to give, the seamen were trimming the sheets and the two men at the heavy tiller were leaning on it. The sails flapped three or four times and then slipped comfortably into curves.

Aurelia moved over to the compass, where a seaman was anxiously staring at the gap in the cliffs that was the entrance to Portobelo. "Bearin' sou'east ma'am," he reported. "If this breeze 'olds we'll be able to sail straight in, what with the current taking us down."

Looking round at the rest of the ships, she could see that all had their sails drawing now, but because the *Griffin* and the *Peleus* had been well ahead when the wind dropped they were a couple of miles or more farther to the east. She could imagine Diana's relief. And Mrs Judd's. It was absurd that three women in effect commanded three buccaneer ships. Of course, they did not really command them: Ned had left one of his best seamen with five others and so had Thomas and Saxby, but being polite they deferred to the women. At least, she laughed to herself, there was no doubt that Mrs Judd regarded herself as the master (or should it be mistress?) of the *Phoenix*.

Did she ever again want to go through the strain of an expedition? Supposing there was so much purchase that Ned's share was enough to start a decent plantation in Jamaica? They could sell Kingsnorth (by agreement with Ned's brother) and her own estate, and say goodbye to Barbados. It was a pleasant island but it held no happy memories for either of them, and Jamaica was more beautiful and according to Ned, with its huge anchorage would soon be the axle upon which the trade of the West Indies would revolve.

Yet could she and Ned, after the roaming life at sea of the past year or so, settle down in a plantation house, bait for mosquitoes and sandflies and the happy hunting ground of pompous planters, vainglorious soldiers and drunken sea captains, and their dreary wives for whom excitement comprised an hour's storm with lightning?

No, despite all this worrying about Ned, it was worth it. Well, she did not enjoy the worrying, but balancing one kind of life against another she preferred this. Tonight when they made love there would be a joyful screaming zest, a fantastic togetherness emphasized by their recent parting. Ned had once said that you had to risk dying occasionally to be able to put a value on living, and this was what he meant. But the waiting...and it always seemed to be the women who waited. Would you, madam, she asked herself ironically, prefer instead to give lemonade to the dreary wives (some would prefer sherry but none would ask) discussing the details of their last pregnancy, the merits of various midwives and, who knows what these women talked about as they embroidered, perhaps the sexual shortcomings of their husbands...

" 'Bout a mile ma'am." The seaman startled her, bringing her suddenly back to the quarterdeck of the *Griffin* from the imaginary drawing-room of a non-existent plantation house. The man had something more to say, though: he had that hangdog look of someone with bad news.

"That fort on the northern side as you go in, ma'am..."

"Yes, San Felipe de Todo Fierro – the Iron Fort."

"It's got colours flying, ma'am."

"Not a white flag?"

"No, red and gold, ma'am: the Spanish flag."

"Can you see flags on the castle at the far end?"

"No flags on the others, ma'am, not as far as we can see."

"And no sign of Jensen and his boats? One might be trying to reach us with orders."

"Nothing ma'am, we've been lookin'."

Now what? The seaman had quite reasonably left the decision to her. Had Ned's men forgotten to lower the flag and hoist a white flag in its place? If the Spanish still held the Iron Fort, there should be smoke from guns – the cannon of the Spanish, and the puffs (he had warned they would be little more) of Ned's falcons.

No smoke, no fighting: it seemed simple enough: some *sot* had forgotten to lower the flag.

"We'll sail straight in and anchor as Mr Yorke instructed. Don't forget the reefs along the southern side."

She looked round. The *Peleus* was now five hundred yards astern in the *Griffin*'s wake, and she wished she could talk to Diana. Having told the seaman to steer for the anchorage she was now having doubts. Her stomach seemed suddenly full of cold water, and the mountains round Portobelo were slashed with black and ominous shadows which she could have sworn were not there two minutes ago.

That flag. Think about it now. Carefully consider it on its flagpole. Ned would have made sure it was changed for a white one, because he knew it would be the first thing the ships would see as they came in. No white flag – stay out. That was obvious enough. But there was no smoke anywhere except, she could now see as the bearing changed, for wisps coming from a few chimneys in the town, cooking the first meal of the day and making a smoky haze in the light wind.

It *could* mean – she forced herself to consider it – that the whole attack had failed: that the buccaneers had been driven off somewhere in the mountains and that was why there was no gun smoke at any of the forts. Defeated, they could be making their way back over the mountains to the Rio Guanche, to rejoin the boats. In which case she should be leading the fleet to the mouth of the Guanche to pick them up.

The seaman seemed to sense her indecision and offered her the perspective glass. It was the second best one, and a section of the lens was blurred by what seemed to be mildew in the glass, but as she looked at the fort, Todo Fierro, it seemed to be enormous. There were the guns, some pointing across the entrance but the others aimed towards the ships, menacing, black eyes in the square embrasures of the battlements.

She moved the glass so she could see beyond the fort and into the harbour. Yes, on the same side as Todo Fierro was San Fernando. No flag. Swing right, and there at the far end was San Gerónimo, enormous – but no flag. And farther to the right, Triana, with no flag. And surrounding the base of the fort, like grass round a tree stump, and extending even more to the right, was Portobelo. What was that small brown patch below Triana? A dozen or so boats and canoes. She realized, much to her relief, that Jensen and his men had arrived safely.

CHAPTER SEVENTEEN

Gottlieb was calling urgently from the top of the steps, and without waiting to hear what he was saying Ned ran up them two at a time, fear making him weightless. He had not heard Gottlieb's words but guessed the message. From the battlements his eyes confirmed it: the two leading ships, the *Griffin* and the *Peleus*, had just picked up a good breeze, so they could lay the harbour entrance, and with the perspective glass which Gottlieb handed to him he thought he could make out the *Griffin*'s bow wave.

The Iron Fort's guns would be loaded, and even now the Spanish gunners under that mulish sergeant would be preparing to open fire. The ships would be in range in about five minutes, he calculated. Secco and the captain would not yet have passed San Fernando; they had a mile to go along a very rough and steep track, and then perhaps minutes of heated argument.

"Go down and join Saxby guarding the bullion," he told Gottlieb and ran down the steps after him. Thomas was getting the last of his prisoners out of the courtyard, and one falcon remained.

"Hurry up, Thomas!" Ned shouted. "Get that gun out – take it to Triana. I want every man out of the castle within two minutes!"

With that he flung open the door leading down to the magazine. "Burton? Burton, are you there?"

"Aye aye, sir," the seaman's voice came echoing up the stairway. "Mind the fuse sir, it's hitched round that heavy rock on the top step and then runs down the right side, to me down here with the powder."

"Where have you left the lighted slow-match?"

"Looped over the door handle of the guardroom, sir: there should be a seaman watching it."

"I'll get it. Meanwhile cut back your fuse here to give us ten minutes' burning time."

"Ten minutes, sir? That's cutting it close – very unreliable stuff, this fuse."

"Cut it, all the same. Leave the end across a step and then come up here. I'm going for the slow-match."

It all took so much time: it was like trying to swim in a butt of molasses. But unless he did everything himself, he had to explain and give orders, and there was neither the time nor the opportunity.

He nearly missed a step, and flung his arms out like wings to keep his balance. Now would be just the time to break a leg. There was the last falcon rumbling through the big gates, hauled by trotting buccaneers, and a quick glance round the courtyard showed that all the prisoners had now been marched out.

He saw the sentry at the guardroom, who confirmed that he was the last man left in the castle, apart from Ned and Burton, and immediately offered whatever help was needed when he saw Ned uncoiling the slow-match.

"No," Ned said, "go outside and make sure there's no one within five hundred yards. Shout to Saxby and Sir Thomas to expect a bang in a very few minutes. And then get under cover yourself!"

As the man ran out through the gates, Ned coiled the slow-match over his left shoulder, carefully holding the burning end in his right hand. For a moment he remembered the fortress at Santiago. Cuba seemed a lifetime away, and every extra moment he wasted now brought Aurelia and Diana nearer Todo Fierro's guns.

From the top of the magazine steps he called down to Burton: "All ready down there?"

"Yes sir: I'm holding the end for you."

"Put it down across the step and come up here."

"Why sir?" The man sounded puzzled, almost afraid that he had done something wrong.

"I have the burning match and there's no need for both of us to be down there. You come up – I want you to go off and warn Sir Thomas of what to expect."

"I'll do that afterwards, sir," Burton said stolidly. "In the meantime I'll hold this end of the fuse ready. It's easier to light it with two people and the less time we have your match spluttering sparks all over the powder down here the better..."

Ned realized that Burton was right and, jamming a stone under the door to prevent it blowing shut and leaving them in darkness on the stairs, he walked down carefully towards the man, holding his left hand under the sizzling end of the slow-match. Although it did indeed burn slowly, the narrow tunnel of the stairway seemed to emphasize the crackling.

"Here were are, sir," Burton said. "Once this fuse is alight, we should hurry..."

Ned held the spluttering end of his match against the piece of fuse being held out by Burton, who blew on it gently. "That's it!" he said suddenly as the fuse began sparking and sputtering. He put it down on the step where it looked like a thick piece of marline. "*Now* sir, let's step out!"

Ned pushed Burton up the steps, took one last look down at the short length of sputtering fuse, whose other end he knew was buried deep in a cask of powder, and then hurried up to the courtyard. Remembering Santiago, he shut the door of the magazine as he threw away the slow-match and grinned at a puzzled Burton. "Childhood habit, shutting doors of magazines," he said, and then stood back and bellowed in every direction, to make sure no men remained.

"Come *on*, sir!" Burton said urgently. "That fuse can burn in fits and starts, five minutes or fifteen, and we've already used up two."

"Let's make for Saxby and the bullion and watch from there. Not so far to come back if the fuse goes out!"

Burton shuddered at the thought of having to go back into the magazine. "Don't even joke about it, sir!"

The two men reached Saxby breathless, but Ned knew that the perspiration which soaked his jerkin and breeches was not caused only by running a few hundred yards. And Burton's jerkin, too, was stuck to his body. He undid the buttons and opened it. "Sweaty place, that magazine," he said to no one in particular.

"There'll be a lot of masonry flying about," Ned warned Saxby. "Tell your men to get behind what shelter they can."

It must be four minutes now. He looked across at Burton and then realized that from where he was standing he could see the length of the harbour and beyond. Out to sea were two ships. Presumably the rest were still round the headland to the south.

Santiago! He seemed to shrivel as a spasm of fear reminded him that the blowing up of El Morro had signalled the buccaneers' victory: had told Aurelia and Diana (and Mrs Judd for that matter) that Santiago was now in the possession of the buccaneers and they could sail into the harbour of Santiago to collect the purchase.

That was how they would interpret the explosion here: that everything was ready for them to sail in and load the bullion.

Should he run back to the magazine and douse that fuse? Four minutes to go.

The sun was scorching, and Saxby must have chosen the dustiest and smelliest place to put the bullion. Almost half a mile from here to Triana, and the fort grew out of the town like a huge cababage. There was no time to reach the magazine: it was due to go up in three minutes.

Three minutes, perhaps fewer. Burton was staring at San Gerónimo as though willing the fuse to continue burning.

The *Griffin* was sailing in fast. He could imagine only too clearly an excited Aurelia using that defective perspective glass to examine the forts and the anchorage. She would be puzzled by the Spanish flag still flying above Todo Fierro. Why there and not San Fernando, San Gerónimo and Triana? Would she be suspicious? There was no gun smoke, no sign of fighting: no, she would not be suspicious. And he was now certain that when this dam' place blew up, she would sail in joyfully, close in under Todo Fierro where she knew the water was deepest: at just the right range for the Spanish gunners to smash the *Griffin* with plunging fire.

Two minutes to go. As he looked at the *Griffin*'s sails against the horizon, trying to measure the distance to the entrance, he found himself watching with the right side of his eyes for the first puffs of smoke showing that the Iron Fort had opened fire: on the *Griffin*, Aurelia and five seamen.

Ten minutes had passed. The *Griffin* caught another strong puff which heeled her over, thrusting her towards the guns of Todo Fierro, a surge of power in the sails which must be exciting for Aurelia, who could not know it was carrying them all to their death. That benighted fuse snaking into the magazine had gone out. He looked across at Burton, who shrugged his shoulders.

It did not matter, Ned realized. If San Gerónimo blew up, Aurelia would misinterpret it and lead the fleet in, to be battered by the guns of Todo Fierro. If San Gerónimo did not blow up, she would still innocently sail under the Spanish guns. She was doomed whatever happened.

Yet...yet...an idea seemed to be fluttering round his head like a sparrow with a broken wing. He tried to grasp at it so that he could examine it. Yes! He saw it clearly now: there *was* a way of warning her, but he could not do it by himself. Nor was he sure it was fair to ask the others to help. "You're leaving it late, Ned," Thomas said, appearing apparently out of thin air. "I've got the prisoners stowed," he reported and added: "The *Griffin* must be almost in range of Todo Fierro."

"The fuse," Ned said. "It was cut for ten minutes. We think it has gone out." He did not mention his fear that Aurelia would misunderstand the explosion, if it had come: she was coming in anyway, explosion or no explosion; she was sailing into the very muzzles of the Iron Fort's guns.

"Ten minutes – that means it could be five or fifteen."

"I know." Ned considered a few more seconds. Thomas' fears for Diana must be a mirror of his own for Aurelia, except that Thomas had to trust him: Thomas had no choice but to leave Diana's safety in another man's hands. Could he leave Aurelia's life in Thomas'? He was far from sure but was thankful that it did not arise. It just made the question easier to ask. "Thomas – "

The note in his voice made Thomas jerk round, all attention.

" – there's one chance."

"Let's try it, then!"

"It means firing three or four of San Gerónimo's guns towards the entrance. Aurelia will think the Spanish still hold it and are firing at her."

"It could save them," Thomas said. "Can just the two of us manage it in time? I mean, carry up the powder, load the guns...we don't have to shot them."

"I'll help, sir," Burton said, and then added grimly: "May not be necessary to fire 'em; the fuse mayn't have gone out!"

"In that case we can wave to them as we go up through the clouds," Thomas said. "There won't be time for conversation!"

Ned turned, hurriedly explained to Saxby, and said to the other two: "Come on then, the *Griffin* must be less than a mile from Todo Fierro."

The earth gave a great rumbling belch which picked up the men like leaves in a sudden swirl of wind and hurled them several feet, as though the world, like a ship, had given a sudden lurch sliding them all into the lee scuppers.

The flash, brighter than the sun, momentarily blinded them, while the thundering explosion left them deafened, their ears ringing like gongs struck twice.

Then came the drumming on the earth of shattered stone thrown up in giant parabolas and now landing round them, and men screamed as pieces broke limbs.

As Ned blinked his sight back, realizing that an unnatural twilight had fallen over this end of the anchorage, he looked up to see smoke and debris billowing in great sulphurous yellow thunderclouds streaked with black and speckled with brown dust.

He staggered to his feet and looked towards the *Griffin*, but the light east wind was now carrying the seeming-solid mass of smoke and dust along the harbour towards the entrance like a sudden and blinding line squall. He saw Thomas crawling around on all fours like a bewildered bulldog, coughing as he breathed in smoke and dust. Between spasms he was cursing monotonously. Beyond him Ned could see, as though it was the root of the smoke, San Gerónimo. The outer walls still stood, but the tops were ragged as though chopped with a blunt axe.

Saxby was lying flat on his back, bleeding from a cut somewhere on his head which was soaking his hair. Ned then realized that his own left arm had no strength in it and a dull ache just above the wrist was now turning into a sharp pain.

At last the wind began thinning the great cloud of power, smoke and dust as it drifted towards the harbour entrance. Already he could just see the box-shaped shadow of Todo Fierro looming high on the cliffs as though he was approaching the coast through a thick fog; now a swirl of wind cleared the other side so he could make out Cocal Point.

Slowly, so very slowly, the entrance cleared: faintly he could distinguish the line of the horizon and the *Griffin*, sails drawing beautifully and followed closely by the *Peleus*, was steering for the gap between Cocal Point on the south side of the entrance and Todo Fierro on the north. Yes, Aurelia was favouring the northern side because of the line of reefs skirting the southern. Doing exactly what she had been told to do. She would have seen San Gerónimo blow up, just as El Morro had at Santiago… She had not seen it as a warning; she – oh God! She was well within range of the guns of Todo Fierro, they would be opening fire any moment, and he was so dizzy, so dizzy, everything was spiralling down, down, and his arm was agony now and he was whirling down and down.

He emerged as though swimming up from deep water, eyes blurred and head spinning, his whole being rapidly concentrated by an excruciating pain into his left arm. He was lying flat on his back, arm by his side, and Thomas – several Thomases – was suddenly coming into sharp focus and then almost disappearing in a blur, as though someone was playing with the adjusting tube of a perspective glass. And Secco, and Saxby, and Coles and Brace were staring down at him. But Secco and Coles and Brace had taken that Spanish garrison commander to Todo Fierro…

He felt himself slipping away again and made a great effort to hold on, trying to keep his eyes focused on the tip of Thomas' beard. "Secco…" he muttered, "…you didn't get to To' Fierro? Wha' happened?"

The dam'd man was grinning and the others were laughing. Why was Secco whispering?

"Speak up…can't hear…"

Now Thomas was speaking louder, crouched down so his mouth was close.

"The *Griffin* is anchored in front of the wreck of San Gerónimo and – " he stood up to look, and then crouched down again " – the *Peleus* is just anchoring. I can see Aurelia and Diana. They have no boats, so Jensen is going out to fetch them."

"Todo Fierro," Ned repeated, feeling the powerful pain in his arm again trying to pull him over the edge into unconsciousness.

Again all the faces looking down at him were distorted into puppet faces, mocking him and laughing because his arm was so painful, then suddenly they came into clearer focus and their voices became more distinct, and Secco was saying excitedly: "It surrendered, *almirante*, it surrendered!"

"Tell me abou' it."

"We saw the *Griffin* and the *Peleus* suddenly pick up a wind and approach very fast, so we made that captain hurry – "

"Tickled him once or twice with the tip of a cutlass," Coles said. "It moved him along wonderfully."

"So we reached the gate of Todo Fierro before the *Griffin* was in range, but madame was sailing the ship well: too well, we were saying."

"That gust of wind," Brace grumbled. "Both ships were stretching along straight for the entrance and making seven knots, I swear."

"Anyway," Secco continued, "the sergeant had the little door open: he recognized the captain, though the poor fellow was running in sweat, his hat had fallen off and his hair hung down like a mop, his breeches were torn and his hose shredded. His mother would not have recognized him, but fortunately the sergeant did."

"They were covering us with muskets though," Brace said. "They guessed the captain was our prisoner."

Secco said: "I told the captain what to say, and he ordered the sergeant to surrender, but the sergeant still refused. He said that we had tortured the captain. The captain said that if the sergeant refused to obey orders, all the rest of the garrison would be blown up in San Gerónimo."

"Aye, and by this time the sergeant was already shouting up orders to the men at the guns because the *Griffin* was very near," Coles said.

"The captain knew the danger he and his men were in – he thought that if he succeeded San Gerónimo and the prisoners would be saved, and if he failed they would be blown up: he never did realize the prisoners had been transferred to Triana. Anyway, he lost his temper with the sergeant, who was convinced we had put the captain on the rack but would not dare blow up San Gerónimo. In fact the captain's last words were that we would never dare, and he slammed the door shut and left us looking at each other wondering how we could warn the *Griffin* and *Peleus* that they would be coming under plunging fire in a few minutes. Moments, rather."

Ned waited for Secco to go on, but the man paused.

"Go on!"

"Well, just after he slammed the door, San Gerónimo suddenly blew up and the explosion blew the door open again and the sergeant came running out and then stopped and stared: it was a fantastic sight, like a great kettle boiling yellow, white, black and brown steam, with huge blocks of masonry shooting up out of it, and the boom echoing again and again and again between the mountains: I thought it would never end. The birds were going mad, the sea in the anchorage was rough from all the stones and beams and wreckage falling into it. Anyway, as soon as he could catch his breath, the sergeant surrendered and we sent him back inside to order his men to get away from the guns."

"We'd just got these men formed up outside, disarmed and taken prisoner, and lowered the Spanish flag, when the *Griffin* sailed in," Brace said. "You told madame to hug the Todo Fierro shore because of the coral reefs on the other side, and we all stood and cheered and waved and she waved back. Lady Diana came even closer, and we started the prisoners trotting back here!"

"Where are they now?"

"All locked in the dungeon of Triana."

"You made them hurry!"

"No, it was the sergeant. He was most anxioius to please us, and I think he's still nervous about some of the things he said to his captain."

"This arm," Ned said, "can we do something about it before Aurelia..."

"The surgeon will be here in a few moments," Thomas said. "Some of the men were badly hurt by falling masonry."

"If we blow up enough of these places, we'll learn what's a safe distance," Ned said and tried to laugh, but the movement gave him such a stab of pain that he fainted just as, unnoticed by any of the men, Aurelia and Diana ran across the dried grass.

Aurelia moaned as she saw what she thought was the bloodstained corpse of Ned lying on the ground, and Diana grabbed Thomas in a tight embrace and then started a shrill harangue, blaming him for Ned's death.

Ned regained consciousness yet again to hear, at a great distance, the plaintive voice of the surgeon asking to be let through to the admiral.

The office of the garrison commander in Fort Triana was cool: walls ten feet thick kept out the sun's heat; a large iron-barred window facing east and forty feet high caught the wind, even if it also scooped up some of the sickly-sweet swamp smells.

Ned rested his forearm on the table that served as a desk. It throbbed, it had shooting pains, it felt as though it was badly broken into five or six pieces instead of – as the surgeon had assured him – being neatly fractured once with no puncturing of the skin. Anyway, with four short lengths of bamboo splinting it, like a broken mast or yard fished with battens, and served round with a length of marline to keep it all rigid, the surgeon was satisfied and said Ned could move about providing he put the arm in the sling made out of an old piece of sacking which, from its smell, had been used by fishermen to carry the turban shells which they pulled off rocks and boiled.

Aurelia and Diana sat in chairs behind him: with all the ships of the buccaneer fleet now anchored safely in Portobelo (and only one grazing the coral shoal and escaping without damage thanks to the wind fluking round the moment she fired a gun for help), the two women had decided they would nurse the wounded.

The dead had been buried – in this heat the graves could hardly be dug quickly enough. Eleven buccaneers had been killed – crushed by stone flung up by San Gerónimo when it exploded. Thomas, reporting later on the condition of the six wounded, told Ned that he had been more than lucky: they had discovered that the actual piece of stone that dropped out of the sky to break his forearm weighed more than two hundredweight: it had landed right beside him and a jagged edge had just caught his arm. "If you'd been standing one pace to your left, we'd still be looking for you," Thomas said. "You'd be as flat as Diana's singing."

He then went on to report the results of the buccaneers' sally into Portobelo. Ned, still dizzy and dazed from his broken arm, had known that any delay gave the inhabitants of the town more time to hide their treasures, but the idea of all the silver, emeralds and pearls from San Gerónimo lying on the ground with only buccaneers armed with muskets guarding it made him order it to be carried to Triana and locked in the dungeon. The few buccaneers who grumbled at having to carry the treasure yet again were told by an unsympathetic Saxby that carrying cones and wedges of silver never tired a man that had his wits about him.

Ned had intended to lead two hundred buccaneers in a raid on the town but had not reckoned on Aurelia.

"What good will you be able to do?" she asked, pointing at his arm in the sling. "Thomas will command the men; you will stay here and rest for an hour or two."

Diana, seeing that Ned was going to argue with Aurelia, signalled to Thomas, who merely said: "I'll be back soon, Ned; I'll take Saxby with me." With that he was out of the door.

"Don't ever do that again," Ned told Aurelia angrily. "I'm in command of this expedition. Leave the decisions to me."

Aurelia smiled and said to Diana, as though Ned was not in the room: "He has so much to think about, and the pain of his arm makes his mind wander."

"I've seen it happen to Thomas," Diana said sympathetically. "He roars: 'I'm captain of this ship!' " she shrugged. "I usually leave him to it, and if he doesn't realize his mistake he finds he's sleeping alone."

"When the men complain they've only half the purchase they expected, I'll send them to ask you about it," Ned growled.

At that moment there was a hurried banging on the door and a voice cried urgently: "Mr Yorke... Mr Yorke!"

"Come in!"

Barnes, a seaman from Coles' ship, hurried in gasping painfully for breath and holding his side with a painful stitch. Slowly he managed to blurt out that he was one of the two look-outs left at Todo Fierro, keeping a watch to seaward, and they had just spotted five ships.

"At least, sir, five when I left. Hull-down on the horizon to the nor'ard they were, but there might be more in sight by now."

"Could you see enough from their rig to distinguish if they were ships of war?"

"No, sir, but they didn't seem really big enough, although they're all different sizes. If you'll excuse me, I'll be getting back. The other look-out was going to wait ten minutes and then follow me round to give you a later report. I'll look and be coming back while he is making his report."

With that Barnes was gone and Ned was left staring at the bamboo battens splinting his arm. Five ships? Not buccaneers, that much was certain, because all the known buccaneers were with him. Individual new ships might have arrived at Tortuga intending to join and gone on to Port Royal looking for the admiral and the rest of the Brethren, but they could not have gone on to Old Providence because the buccaneers themselves did not know where Ned was taking them when they left Port Royal.

Yet...wait a minute. Leclerc and a few buccaneers knew about the year's uncollected bullion waiting at Portobelo, but Leclerc and his men were here – at this very moment they were with

Thomas searching Portobelo town for purchase. Did anyone else know about the bullion who had not come on the expedition but might be trying to catch up now? No. Certainly not five ships.

Five ships...his head was spinning and it seemed as if a blacksmith's bellows was pumping blasts of roaring pain through his ears. Five ships, they had to be Spanish. But coming from the north? Yes, sailing here from Cartagena could mean a westerly run to leeward and then a stretch to the south. Five ships...why did the phrase "five ships" seem to have a deeper significance, to strike some chord in his memory?"

Again there was a banging at the door and a breathless shout for Mr Yorke.

He recognized the buccaneer coming into the room as a Norfolk man from Beccles who had worked on the plantation and was now in the *Phoenix* with Saxby. Woods, that was his name.

"The ships, sir!" he exclaimed. "Five of them, and they're Spanish, I'll stake my oath on that. Sheer, cut of the sails – aye, and the way they're being sailed too."

"Men of war?"

"Oh *no*, sir!" Woods said, as though reproaching Ned for using strong language in front of the ladies. "Transports, or more likely they're local ships being used as transports, and sailing together in convoy to avoid all those nasty buccaneers!"

Woods said he was returning to Todo Fierro and Barnes would be back in fifteen minutes with later news. Then Ned remembered. Five ships. Five transports. Five Spanish transports... Now he had it! General Heffer had the report of five Spanish ships intending to land troops in Runaway Bay and then the miserable captain left in command of the garrison here, who had tried to persuade the sergeant to surrender Todo Fierro, had bewailed the fact that each fort had been left only twenty or so men. *"When the five transports took all the rest of the garrison to Jamaica."*

Now they were coming back: the Portobelo garrison with perhaps the several hundred soldiers taken from Old Providence and as many more levies collected from all the nearby towns. Suddenly the bullion seemed to be receding into the distance.

Aurelia had been watching him closely. "Five ships?" she said casually. "Who are they?"

"The Portobelo garrison coming back from Jamaica."

"The garrison – or their ships?" she asked shrewdly.

Ned thought for a moment or two. "Both, I should think. If it's only the ships, that means they've left the troops there – abandoned them."

Diana said: "With General Heffer in command, I wouldn't be too sure. We knew he expected the Spanish to land on the north coast. Supposing they landed at Port Royal instead – could they capture it?"

"Two thousand properly led probably could," Ned said soberly. "Anyway, we've got to do something now on the assumption the ships *are* carrying troops"

"This is like some game," Diana commented. "While the first robber is out about his business his home is burgled and he returns and finds the second robber still at work…"

"I wonder Shakespeare never used the idea," Ned said. "He might have – " he stopped abruptly, realizing that the pain in his arm really was slowing down his thinking.

"Will one of you go up on the battlements and tell Burton, who is up there with half a dozen men, that I want him to fire five guns at half-minute intervals, starting as soon as he's ready? Use guns pointing across the swamp: I don't want sharp eyes in the Spanish ships to spot the smoke."

Diana ran out of the room with the orders and Aurelia said: "Why five?"

"Five, six, seven – it doesn't matter: it'll bring Thomas and all the rest of our men back here quicker than anything else."

"Unless any of them have gone into the *tabernas*."

"They'll have gone in all right, but to roll the barrels into the street to bring back to the ships. No one is going to spend much time looking for hot liquors to drink when he could be finding gold or silver, or jewellery."

Aurelia made a face. "I hate to think of a woman losing all her jewellery – wedding ring, necklaces that were betrothal presents, family heirlooms..."

"If the Spanish government let us trade, we'd be buying and selling. If the Portobelo garrison has managed to capture Jamaica, I doubt if the Spanish have left any woman with her chastity or even her life, let alone her jewels – and they are regular soldiers, not cut-throat *filibusteros*."

"I suppose you're right, but... Anyway, what are you going to do now?"

"Well, when you're trapped in a trap, I suppose the best thing to do is to try to trap the trapper."

"Ned," Aurelia said plaintively, "how do you expect your French mistress to understand such complicated sentences?"

"Don't worry," Ned said cheerfully, "I'm not sure I do, but now I have an idea."

It took more than a quarter of an hour for all the captains and buccaneers to get back to Triana fort, puzzled and alarmed, and by then a seaman messenger had found Jensen, so that his flotilla of boats was waiting at the San Gerónimo jetty.

By then both Barnes and Woods had each been back with later reports. The Spanish ships were running into calms where the buccaneers, led by Aurelia and Diana, had found fresh breezes. In answer to a direct request from Ned that they both look, they each reported that the damage to San Gerónimo was not very obvious from as far away as Todo Fierro: the dried and stony ground camouflaged the scattered masonry and the ragged edges of the grey battlements were not noticeable outlined against the distant rocky hills.

"I don't reckon," Woods said emphatically, "that the Dons will notice anything – except our ships, o'course – until they're actually in the harbour: the headsails make it hard to see dead ahead anyway."

"Except our ships" – Woods had put the problem into three words.

Before the captains arrived from Portobelo town, Ned had tried to see the anchorage through the eyes of the Spanish senior officer of the Spanish ships. Portobelo would look the same as when they sailed for Old Providence and Jamaica, except for two things: there were twenty-eight small ships now in the anchorage and, if he looked harder, he would see that the Castillo de San Gerónimo was badly damaged: not the walls, but as though someone had sliced the top crust from a square loaf.

Aurelia had once amused him by saying that the best place to hide something was by putting it where everyone could see it without effort, and now the phrase came back to him.

The moment he had a good look at them, the Spanish captain or admiral would guess that the anchored vessels were buccaneers and then, noticing San Gerónimo, conclude they had just attacked Portobelo – and attacked it successfully. He would also see at once that he had twenty-eight buccaneer ships trapped.

He would have to attack them at once. His ships would not have many guns because they were built as transports, but if he had all the garrison with him he had more than double the men needed to board and capture the ships and – as far as he knew – recapture the forts.

Very well: the admiral of the Brethren of the Coast needed to think of some way of making the Spanish admiral draw the wrong conclusion from what he saw, so that he would just sail his ships in and anchor.

Ned looked round the room. The buccaneer captains were all here, and most of them, wild-looking with bloodshot eyes after a sleepless night crossing the mountains, looked impatient, anxious to be back in Portobelo searching cisterns, wells and chimneys and poking behind lathe-and-plaster walls to see where the rich had hidden their wealth.

"I'm sorry I had to interrupt you all," he said. "But we haven't much time: the Spanish are coming back and we have to get ready for them." No actor playing the most dramatic scene in his life could have created such an atmosphere: suddenly more than a score of the toughest men at sea in the West Indies were tense and silent: having successfully captured Portobelo and a king's ransom in bullion, they suddenly heard from their leader that the job was not yet completed.

"Spaniards? Coming back, Ned? How? From where?" Thomas was so puzzled he was almost stammering.

"There are five transports on the horizon, heading for here. You can take your choice as to what they're doing: they're empty, having landed their troops in Jamaica; they're full because General Heffer beat them off; or they're bringing back the survivors having failed in their attempt."

"Which is it?" Leclerc asked bluntly. "What do you think?"

Ned shrugged his shoulders. "For the moment, it doesn't matter: we have to act as though they're carrying all the Portobelo and Providence garrisons."

"But we'll be outnumbered two or three to one!" Gottlieb exclaimed.

"At least," Ned agreed. "Now, you are going to have to work fast..."

CHAPTER EIGHTEEN

They stood under the hot sun amid the swamp stench drifting invisible across Triana, and Thomas wiped the perspiration from his face and said sourly: "Just imagine having to spend your whole life in this place... Always the stink of the swamp; mosquitoes and sandflies; the mountains making cloud, rain and humidity most of the time; always the same faces and the same conversation and the same gossip... The women complaining they can't get cloth, lace, thread or needles to make new dresses, the men cursing the lack of wine, or poor quality... The garrison steeped in the history of Francis Drake and guarding against the English who never come – until the one occasion when they're away...you know, I'm getting sorry for them!"

"Don't," Ned said, gesturing towards the five ships which were now past Todo Fierro and stretching into the anchorage, the leading one almost level with the last of the buccaneer vessels. "They might be cutting our throats very soon, or handing us over to the priests. Saxby, you said the church has a rack in the vault; perhaps you should have smashed it!"

The stone of Triana's battlements seemed to soak up the heat of the sun and almost immediately throw it out again twice as hot, and the only moving things unaffected by it all were the lizards, their skins shiny like chain mail, which watched with beady eyes for a few moments, reminding Thomas of politicians looking for votes, and then seemed to vanish, to reappear several feet away, eyes unwinking, apparently missing nothing.

Pelicans plunged into the water with reckless abandon down in the anchorage and then floated smugly, gulping fish like old men with heavy jowls emptying tankards of ale. Laughing gulls wheeled and shrieked overhead, demanding their share, while an osprey hovered motionless above San Fernando.

A sudden hoarse shrieking from the town made the three men and both women stiffen and then relax, grinning with relief. Some Spaniard was ignoring the buccaneers and slaughtering a pig.

"As long as they don't roast it now," Diana murmured. "I'm so hungry."

"There's a satchel of boucan at the top of the steps, in the shade," Thomas said.

"Please, my dear Thomas," Diana said, "don't mention that dried-up beef in the same breath as fresh roast pork!"

"We'll round up some hogs and roast them when we've finished this business," Thomas promised.

Ned looked carefully across the anchorage. To his eye it all *looked* genuine enough but how would it seem to a Spaniard? Was it *likely*? That, he was sure, must be the first question the leader of the Spanish ships would ask, whether a soldier or a naval officer. (One could never be sure which it would be with the dam'd Dons; the senior captain of the ships might in fact be taking orders from the garrison commander.)

Each of the twenty-eight buccaneer ships lying head to wind in the anchorage now had a large white flag streaming from the masthead. They were anchored so close together, lying with their sterns towards the entrance, that it would be difficult for the Spaniards to see exactly how many there were until they sailed past. And on the deck of each of them were a few men wearing the distinctive Spanish armour and helmets, obviously guards.

At this very moment the Spanish leader must be examining the ships with his perspective glass. Unless he was obtuse or stupid, Ned was convinced, the man could only conclude from the fact that each ship was properly anchored and flying a white flag and had Spanish troops pacing their decks, that *filibusteros* had attacked, failed and been wiped out.

So much for the ships. Supposing the Spanish leader then began examining the forts... Well, the flags were flying and a couple of "soldiers" in Spanish armour were obvious on the battlements of Todo Fierro, San Fernando and Triana. The only question mark (a large one, of course) was San Gerónimo.

"He might think it was an accident."

Thomas looked round startled, and Ned realized he had been thinking aloud. "The Spanish commander, when he sees San Gerónimo. When he sees the damage to San Gerónimo, I mean."

Thomas thought for a moment, brow furrowed and putting himself in the position of the Spanish commander. He held out one hand and ticked off the fingers with the other as he made the points.

"Buccaneer ships but obviously captured and guarded by Spaniards; all but one fort have Spanish soldiers on the battlements and Spanish colours flying; no damage to the other forts. With all the buccaneers captured why should only San Gerónimo be damaged? Yes, Ned," he said with a grin, "he'd conclude there had been an accident in the magazine..."

Aurelia laughed and said to Diana: "It would be ironic if the Spanish commander is feeling reassured by looking at buccaneers wearing Spanish armour!"

"Yes – unless some Spaniard in Portobelo town thinks of a way of raising the alarm."

"That's not likely," Thomas said. "We have the intendant and the other leading citizens locked up in the dungeon here."

"They're lively enough over there to slaughter a pig!"

"If they slaughter pigs while the garrison is sailing back home, they can't be very interested."

"No, I suppose not," Diana said. "One forgets the great gap between the Spanish people and the government."

"Remember they have to deal with the enemy – his smugglers anyway – to get new pots and pans and knives and forks," Aurelia said.

"They do it in England!"

"Yes, but for luxuries, brandy and lace, not for the things used every day, and the smugglers are English."

"Watch them!" Ned said sharply, wanting more pairs of eyes to supplement his own looking at the five ships. He glanced across and down at the buccaneer boats and canoes made fast at the remains of the jetty in front of the wrecked San Gerónimo. A dozen of them, secured casually by their painters just where men of the Spanish garrison would put them, having captured their parent ships.

There was no sign of the falcons or their crews. Thomas, Saxby and Burton had done a good job in siting them. Down there, the fourteen falcons were already in position, all aimed at a half-mile square a few hundred yards in front of San Gerónimo jetty. All were loaded with langrage, although beside each gun was a pile of roundshot.

Falcons! Compared with the guns in the forts, they were little more than fowling pieces, firing a roundshot three inches in diameter with a point-blank range of 130 paces and a random range of 1,500.

"You allow powder equal to half the weight of the ball... Be sure it is not pistol powder, which is finer and takes up less room and will split the gun... Select the balls to make sure you use only perfectly spherical ones..." Ned found himself recalling Burton's instructions to the buccaneers. The armourer was a patient and careful man with an enormous enthusiasm for his work. He had tried to place each falcon so that its target should be about 700 paces away, and this had led to some new trees suddenly appearing close to the water's edge, and small huts and beached boats being quickly moved to new positions where they would better camouflage the falcons and the men serving them.

Ned felt a quite irrational anger with the man, or men, who designed Triana and San Fernando. The embrasures were built so that the barrels of the guns could not be depressed enough to fire at a target close below. The minimum range was about half a mile from both forts, which meant that they could only fire at an enemy ship until it was half-way up the anchorage. For the last half mile the enemy would be quite safe, the roundshot going over his head. Ironically enough, this almost incredible shortcoming in the forts was saving the five Spanish ships from being destroyed by their own great guns…

"He's not going to make it," Saxby exclaimed suddenly, uttering the first words Ned had heard him speak for an hour or two.

A couple of minutes later the leading Spanish ship, which had been sagging across the anchorage to the northern side, unable to sail close enough to the wind to fetch the inshore end, suddenly swung round to starboard as she tacked, her flapping sails making her look like an impatient dowager bothered by a beggar. Her next astern, trying to follow in her wake but a good fifty yards more to leeward, tacked almost immediately and Ned could nearly hear her captain's sigh of relief.

"That one nearly hit the reef," Saxby growled. "Daren't tack before the leader even if it means going aground."

"Look at those jibs flogging," Diana said contemptuously. "We tacked faster than that, didn't we Aurelia?"

The French girl laughed but admitted: "Not at first!"

The leading Spanish ship's tack meant she was now heading for the *Griffin*, the buccaneer ship anchored nearest to San Gerónimo, while the second Spanish ship, now sailing towards the *Peleus*, made Thomas grunt: "I hope he's not as clumsy with his next tack!"

Now the third Spanish ship tacked, followed by the fourth and then the fifth.

Ned again trained the perspective glass on the leading ship.

"D'you see anything special, Ned?" Thomas asked.

"No, just three or four men in gaudy uniforms standing aft, big plumes in their hats. Must be soldiers... The leading ship has six guns a side, as you can see, but they're not run out and don't have crews standing by them... Looks as though they'll tack over to the north shore again and then back, rounding up in front of the jetty. They're preparing to anchor..."

"Sounds too good to be true," Thomas muttered as Ned handed him the glass.

Thomas looked from ship to ship and then lowered the perspective. "Our men in Jensen's boats must be almost barbecued by now!"

Most of the boats at the jetty had armed buccaneers crouching in the bottom, out of sight from the Spanish ships. But to keep themselves below the gunwales they had to crawl beneath thwarts or hide under oars which were stowed on one side to make a shelter, both from Spanish eyes and the sun. The Spanish were not likely to notice that the weight caused several of the boats to list slightly because they were secured to the jetty at random, the bow of one butting the stern of another, canoe next to a long boat, like a dozen dung beetles nestling beside a choice piece of carrion.

"If the Spanish ships are bringing back the Portobelo garrison from its Jamaica expedition," Thomas commented, "the soldiers must be below: there's no sign of 'em on deck."

"Wouldn't be, would there?" Saxby murmured. "Get in the way of the sailors while they're short tacking." He was obviously speaking from past experience, from a time he served in the King's ships.

"No, s'pose not," Thomas said. "Never been to sea with a few score landsmen. Batten the beggars below – yes, it makes sense, but I don't envy them in this heat. Means the Dons aren't suspicious, though!"

The leading Spanish ship was tacking again and Thomas stared with the perspective. "Ah," he said appreciatively, "everyone's waving to each other. The returning garrison must be impressed with the lads they left behind, capturing all these ships! Secco – goodness me, the hat with plumes that he took! He's standing aft in the *Peleus* and just swept it off in a salute to someone in that leading Spanish ship. Cunning fellow, he did it in such a way that his face was hidden!"

The remaining four ships were still on the other tack and now the second followed the leader.

"Lubberly scoundrel," Thomas grumbled. "I quite thought he was going to ram the *Peleus*, or get into stays and drift aboard her."

Ned sensed rather than saw that Aurelia, Diana and Saxby were watching him out of the corner of their eyes waiting for the signal. Well, they're going to have to wait: although the anchorage was narrower at this end of the harbour, the wind was lighter, partly shut out by the mountains and high hills. From the top of Triana the ships looked like five fat fish porters wheeling their barrows up a narrow lane: there was no grace in the curve of the sails and the vessels' sheer lines could not be seen: looking down on the decks from this height, the hulls resembled boxes, vaguely rounded at one end, and the masts seemed to be vertical poles from which laundry was hung out to dry.

No guns loaded and run out… "That Spanish commander has put down San Gerónimo as an accident in the magazine," Ned said to no one in particular.

"And he's getting ready to congratulate the young captain he left behind – the one whose hat Secco fancied."

Aurelia said: "I wonder if they captured Jamaica."

"If they have, we must look for another base," Diana commented. "That would be a pity. I was beginning to like Jamaica. Baiting General Heffer gave Ned and Thomas something to do."

"Not Tortuga though," Aurelia said. "That place depresses me, I don't know why. 'Opresses', I mean: I feel it is evil. Like Marigot Bay in St Lucia and Cumberland Bay in St Vincent; it has an aura of wickedness. *Triste,* too."

Ned sighed. "Can you two old ladies save your gossip for another time?"

"We're not gossiping," Aurelia said, speaking louder than normal because she was angry with herself for rambling on thoughtlessly while Ned was trying to concentrate.

The leading Spanish ship tacking back from the north shore would pass close across the end of the jetty. Or, Ned corrected himself, she would if she did not round up and anchor. Would the second ship anchor abreast of her or astern? The question was important, because almost certainly the rest of the ships would follow, and he pictured the imaginary box into which the falcons would fire.

The perspective, at this close range, showed up the group of men standing on the leading ship's afterdeck. He recognized three uniforms as army and two as navy. A group of seamen on the fo'c'sle were waiting for the order to anchor; another group were at the halyards, while more stood ready to furl the sails the moment they were lowered.

The men in armour on board the *Peleus* and *Griffin* waved cheerfully at the passing ships, and Ned was sure he heard some shouted Spanish. Trust Secco, who seemed to be taking a devilish delight in tricking his own countrymen.

A man without a country... Ned remembered that he and Thomas had been two such men until very recently, until Cromwell's death and the Restoration. But what about Secco? What had to happen in Spain to reconcile him? Perhaps his quarrel was with those who enforced the law, rather than those that enacted it. Ned suspected, though, that Secco's quarrel was with the church – which, in Spain, meant the king. His Most Catholic Majesty, Carlos the Second, had his descriptive title for a reason.

The headsails were flapping, the ship's bow was heading for the jetty, and she was slowing down as though grounding on soft mud. A splash and the anchor cable snaked out as the ship slowly gathered sternway and the cable straightened its curve. Nicely anchored, a stationary target like a tethered wild boar.

By now the second ship was luffing up on its leader's beam and a couple of minutes later her anchor plunged into the water. She was followed by the third, but the fourth and fifth, deciding that there was not room for them, came in and anchored astern of the first and second vessels.

Thomas nodded as the fifth anchor splashed into the water and glanced over at Ned. "That was what you predicted, wasn't it?"

"Guessed, not predicted. *Hoped*, to be honest."

Ned turned round and looked across the courtyard of Triana to the battlements on the southern side, where three cannon faced out across the swamp. There was only one buccaneer at each gun, and when they saw Ned looking across at them they waved their linstocks, reassuring him that they were ready.

How often, Ned wondered, could one see a cannon with only one man standing by it? Still, the three guns had earlier been loaded and run out, and those men had then gone off to help with the falcons, leaving only the trio behind. There was no aiming to be done; the Dons would never see the spurt of smoke when they fired because they were aimed over the swamp, nor would they be hit by a roundshot because the guns were loaded only with a powder charge. The Dons would only hear them firing – and for many of them it might be the last thing they did hear, because it was to be the signal for the falcons to fire.

Even now, Ned knew, the falcons were aimed, three at each of the first four ships and two at the fifth one. Each gun captain would be holding his linstock, occasionally blowing on the slow-match to ensure it was burning well, and waiting for the guns of Triana. As the ships swung slightly with a wind change, or because they settled back on their anchor cables, the aim of the falcons would be changed; just a degree or two one way or another would be enough.

Ned took one more look at the ships with the perspective. Each was anchored but sails were being furled. The army officers were walking away from the afterdecks as though there was nothing else happening that interested them. Surely the soldiers would be allowed up on deck soon?

Silver measured by the hundredweight, a year's income for Spain... The timing of this next move, Ned reflected, decides whether it goes into the pockets of His Most Catholic Majesty or the buccaneers.

The next move was *now*. He turned round, held up his right arm to point across at the three guns, and saw the men reach out with the linstocks. The sudden movement made his left arm feel as though it had been run through with a sword, and as his head swam from the pain there was a deep cough as the first cannon fired, the blam echoing back and forth among the hills and mountains, rising in pitch; the second crashed out and then the third, one echo overtaking another, bouncing among the mountains and valleys like invisible roundshot.

In the circle of the perspective glass he saw everyone on the leader's ship, officers and seamen, freeze and look up towards Triana, but seeing nothing and bewildered by the noise now echoing in from different directions, they were now staring at each other – and, he realized, the first of the soldiers had been allowed on deck and were running up the hatchways in alarm, betraying the landsman's fear of being trapped below in a ship.

He swept the perspective round the shore just in time to see the flash and puff of smoke as one after another the falcons gave their sharp bark, several of them shaking the bushes and knocking over the huts that concealed them as they rolled back in recoil. The buccaneers leapt out of hiding with spongers, rammers, powder and more bags of langrage.

He saw puffs of what seemed to be dust sweeping the decks of the ships and did not realize it was the langrage until he saw Spaniards falling, ropes parting and showers of sparks showing where metal ricocheted off metal.

There was a sudden silence as the last falcon fired but he could see the buccaneers were not rushing: each man moved decisively, never walking a step more than needed.

"Good shooting," Saxby said. "If they can hit with the first round, they should do better now…"

Ned watched the buccaneers sponging out the guns, loading powder, wad, bag of langrage and another wad, and aiming the gun again as the second captain carefully poured priming powder from a flask into the vent.

Then from one gun after another all the men jumped back out of the way and the gun captains, like magicians delicately waving wands, reached out with the linstocks and dabbed the spluttering slow-match on to the little pool of gunpowder piled over the vent. There was a sudden tiny spurt of flame from the vent as the burning match ignited the powder and a moment later each gun coughed a great spurt of yellow and black oily smoke and once again leapt back in recoil.

Ned saw a large group of soldiers standing beside a hatchway on the leader's ship fall as though the deck had collapsed beneath them, and he moved the perspective to the second ship just in time to see the langrage cutting down more soldiers as though an invisible scythe was at work. Yet more men were still coming up the hatchways, pushing aside the bodies in their panic-stricken rush to get out in the daylight.

By now the guns were again being sponged out with wet mops to extinguish any burning residue, then loaded again. After the third round of langrage had been fired they switched to solid shot, and after firing three of them the gun captains stood at the rear of each falcon and looked up towards Ned: they had carried out their orders: three of langrage, three of roundshot and stop.

Ned now watched Jensen's boats at the end of the jetty. Suddenly they were full of movement, seeming from this height and distance to be the brown seedpods of some exotic plant and crawling with maggots. Two or three at at a time, they jerked away from the jetty, sprouting oars or paddles like pond insects unfolding legs, and were rapidly rowed or paddled towards the five Spanish ships.

"Like water beetles," Thomas commented. "And they're keeping well spread out, too. Ah, look the Dons have woken up!"

Ned trained the perspective on the commander's ships and could see soldiers still rushing up from below, but these ran to the ship's side, clutching a musket in one arm and dragging a wooden rest with the other.

They lined up along the bulwark and Ned watched them go through the ritual of loading. Resting the musket on its butt, muzzle uppermost, each man took one of the wooden "Apostles" hanging from the bandolier across his chest, removed the cap, and poured the powder down the barrel. Then he took a wad from a pocket, pushed it into the muzzle and with the rammer drove it down, then took a shot from the bag also slung from the bandolier, wrapped it in a piece of cloth, and rammed that home.

More than two minutes had passed and none of the muskets was ready to fire, but Jensen's boats and canoes were approaching fast, surging forward under oars or paddles, each making a bow wave like a chevron in the water.

Ned saw Spanish officers in beplumed hats gesturing at the musketeers, obviously trying to hurry them (nothing, he noted with satisfaction, slowed men down more than having an hysterical officer shouting at them).

By now the first of Jensen's boats was making the turn to come alongside, and Ned realized that the coxswain had been very clever: the ships, lying head to wind, also had their bows pointing at the jetty, and the boats were approaching by steering straight at the bows, waiting until the last moment to choose which side to board.

The first boat's coxswain must have seen that the musketeers were lined up along the starboard side, and at the last moment he steered his boat to come alongside to larboard. Spanish seamen, obviously roused from various parts of the ship, paused to grab cutlasses or pikes before running to meet them.

Ned was puzzled by the way the Spanish musketeers, the heavy guns lodged in the rests, were obviously waiting for something. At least one more buccaneer boat was now almost alongside, making a good target at an easy range. Several of the Spanish musketeers were looking nervously over their shoulders, and suddenly he saw two men running towards them from forward, their arms outstretched, and looking as though they were carrying handfuls of long, thin snakes.

"Those two men running?" Thomas asked. "What's happening?"

"They're about to issue slow-match to the musketeers," Ned said, hardly able to believe his eyes. "Must have been lighting it at the galley fire. The ship came in without any match alight."

"Shows they believed everything they saw – white flags, our men dressed in their armour..."

"What about the lid of San Gerónimo?" Diana asked.

"Must have thought it blew up by accident." Thomas said. "It's probably the sort of thing they expect to happen."

"There they go," Ned said, watching the first buccaneer boat get alongside the commander's ship. In a moment men seemed to erupt from the boat and go up the ship's side like a cloud of smoke, cutlasses glinting in the sunlight.

He saw the Spanish seamen standing uncertainly at the bulwarks, and then suddenly they bolted. A moment later Ned saw why – the musketeers on the starboard side had turned right round, to face across the ship, and having completed looping the slow-match into the serpentines of their guns, were now rearranging the rests.

Whoever had given them that order, and shouted to the seamen on the larboard side to get out of the line of fire, must also be on the larboard side and have seen only the first boatload of buccaneers nearest him, because the musketeers in obeying orders had turned their backs on the boatload of buccaneers who would be alongside in a few moments.

The first few buccaneers reached the top of the bulwarks and were just starting to scramble over when all the muskets fired at once. Ned saw four or five tumble backwards. A moment later the rest of the buccaneers were swarming over the bulwarks and, with their cutlasses swinging, heading across the deck for the line of musketeers. Some of the Spaniards pushed away their muskets, which pivoted over on the rests and crashed to the deck, their owners tugging at swords. But as the majority of the musketeers retreated they were attacked by buccaneers just boarding from the next boat.

Ned swung the perspective to the next ship. Buccaneer boats were already alongside her, and the deck looked like a suddenly-disturbed termites' nest, with fifty or sixty buccaneers hacking away at a group of about the same number of Spaniards, half of whom wore the uniform of the Spanish army.

Why so few soldiers? Five ships with – he confirmed it by a quick look at the rest – between a fifty and a hundred soldiers on board each, a total of perhaps five hundred. Where were the rest of the Portobelo garrison and the levies who had set out to recapture Jamaica?

Perhaps they were still there. As prisoners? Or had they succeeded in recapturing the island, and these five ships were simply bringing back a few men because the Viceroy realized the Portobelo garrison was very much under strength?

The dozen boats, having ferried out buccaneers, were now going on to the buccaneer ships to pick up the men who had worn armour to fool the Spaniards. By now they would have taken off the breast and back plates and helmets and armed themselves with cutlasses ready to reinforce the men already fighting.

Ned kicked a tuft of grass growing between the two stones on which he was standing, then saw Aurelia watching him anxiously.

"You couldn't have done anything, with that arm broken," she said.

"The newly elected admiral was standing safely on top of a captured fort while his men stormed five enemy ships," he said bitterly. "That'll sound fine back in Jamaica – if we haven't lost it."

A booming laugh startled him. "Dear old Ned," Thomas said, "only you could have said that. We took all the forts in Portobelo – using your plans. We found all the bullion – just where you expected it to be. Then, following your orders, we blew up San Gerónimo and then captured – I don't think there's much doubt about that, they'll have done the job in the next fifteen minutes – five Spanish ships which could have trapped us all. Is Ned cheerful? Oh no, Ned's weeping in his pot of ale, feeling sorry for himself because he was hoisted by his own petard, or hit by one of his own bricks, if you prefer it. Ah," Thomas suddenly exclaimed, "I see what your little game is – you want compliments from us! And what about *me*: I'm only the admiral's second-in-command, but he wouldn't let me lead the attack on the Spanish ships. 'Oh, no,' he said, 'you're too valuable. You take command if anything happens to me.' He doesn't specify what is likely to happen to him standing on top of his fort, but what will the buccaneers think when they hear that the noble and brave Sir Thomas watched them cut, thrust and parry – but through a perspective?"

"Thomas is right," said Diana, "so stop feeing sorry for yourself. And I see the first Spanish ship has been captured: they're lowering the colours. If you want my opinion – and you shall have it anyway – the buccaneers see the whole thing quite differently."

"They don't want a husky great brute of a man with a voice like a bull leading them into battle waving a two-handed sword; they've all been in action a dozen, a score and some no doubt a gross of times. I suppose what I mean is, they know they don't have the brains and ability to plan a raid like this and, if things go wrong, produce new alternative plans that succeed.

"No, my dear Ned, I'll tell you what they'll do. They'll count up the purchase, which will be more than they ever dreamed of in their wildest moments of greed and venery, divide it by the number of buccaneers, and try to hurry you back to Port Royal, that being the nearest place offering wine, hot liquors and women. And they'll count up their casualties and marvel. And you, my dear Ned, will be their hero.

"Within a few hours of them getting to windward of a bottle or a tankard you'll be the greatest admiral that ever put to sea: by comparison, Drake will be a capon: the defeat of Medina Sidonia and the Spanish Armada a mere fracas. Quite apart from that, Ned, you and Aurelia are rich now – or you will be very soon. Thomas and me, too. Our new and noble King's fifth will make him a very nice Restoration present. Cheer up Ned, we love you."

Ned found it curious how Diana swayed and the horizon began moving like a seesaw. The anchorage was expanding and contracting, as though someone was turning a rectangle of blue wood so that one minute it was flat, the next on edge. It was so hot, yet he felt cold: his breathing seemed shallow, his knees trembled and his arm seemed to contain all the pain in the world, but he managed to hold the sling away from his body when the ground moved from under his feet and hit him in the face.

He recovered consciousness to find himself with his head cradled in Aurelia's arms. As soon as she was sure he knew what was happening round him, she said: "All the Spanish ships have surrendered, *cheri.*"

"Tell Saxby to arrange prize crews. Thomas had better finish in Portobelo town."

"That has all been arranged," Aurelia said, moving so that her breasts lightly touched his cheek, "and Saxby is sending the Spanish commander to see you."

Ned groaned and tried to organize his thoughts while Aurelia shaded his face from the sun. "I'm so proud of you," she whispered. "Will that arm prevent you… I mean, will we… The pain?"

CHAPTER NINETEEN

The commander was Don José Arias Ximenez, who was also the mayor of Portobelo, and he had been acting, he told Ned petulantly, under the orders of the Viceroy of the Province of Panama, Don Juan Perez de Guzman.

The commanding officer's quarters in Triana were cool and well furnished. Ned sat back comfortably in a reclining chair that was almost a hammock of interwoven soft leather straps. Aurelia sat on a stool by his head while Thomas, holding a cutlass, stood behind Arias, who was perched on the edge of an upright wooden chair. Secco, a wheel-lock pistol in his belt and holding a heavily jewelled ceremonial sword in his right hand (one which he had obviously just confiscated from its original owner, and the jewels of which he examined from time to time), sat between Arias and Ned and translated, although Ned found he could understand Arias without much effort.

"What happened in Jamaica?" Ned asked.

Arias gave an expressive shrug. "It was madness from the start."

"What happened?" Ned repeated.

"The Viceroy's orders. 'Liberate Jamaica', he said. Madness."

"Start at the beginning," Ned said patiently. "You say you are the mayor of Portobelo. Very well, one day you are here in Portobelo when a messenger arrives from Panama with orders from the Viceroy..."

Arias sighed, as if the memory wounded him deeply. He was, Ned considered, an improbable man to lead an expedition to recapture an island the size of Jamaica, but typical of the mayor of a town like Portobelo.

His black hair, sallow skin, thin and pointed face, protruding teeth and bulging eyes under a sloping forehead gave him the appearance of a startled piebald rabbit. The moustache was thin and sagged as though it was a weather-vane indicating the man's mood. The eyes were the man's most revealing characteristic: they were never still and apparently never looked above shoulder height. They jerked from one wall of the room to another; Arias inspected Ned from the waist down in a series of darting glances and then transferred his attention to Aurelia who, wearing her divided skirt, her skin a golden brown, was obviously a kind of woman he had never seen before.

Arias noticed that she and the other woman, the brown-haired one, spoke out just like men, commenting and suggesting, and the men listened. But this man with the splinted and bandaged arm was most persistent, and that renegade Spaniard doing the translating was getting impatient, so he had better answer fully.

"I am sitting here in my office in the town hall attending to important matters. I have to see the Intendant over some tax questions. Suddenly this lieutenant arrives, dusty and very insolent, saying he has just ridden from Panama with urgent orders from the Viceroy, and five hundred levies will be arriving in two days from Panama, Venta de Cruz and various other towns. With that he tosses a letter on to my desk and demands *comfortable* accommodation suitable for an aide to the Viceroy.

"I was very angry at his manner," Arias said, and added, a look of extreme craftiness settling on his face: "But I decided to say nothing until I had read the letter.

"It was from the Viceroy. It listed all my titles."

"What did it say?" Secco prompted because it seemed that Arias regarded the fact that the Viceroy listed all his titles as the climax of his narrative.

"Ah, the Viceroy was giving me the commission of a major, and this aide was a mere lieutenant, so I told him to get out of my office and find himself a bed in one of the brothels, or sleep under a table in a *taberna*."

"Where *did* he go?" Ned asked, curious about the way Arias was fiddling with his moustaches.

The man flashed, his face becoming an angry purple, his eyes looking as though they might pop from their sockets. "He knew my wife," he said. "I don't know where he went. I had too much responsibility now to be bothered with him."

"The Viceroy's orders?" Secco prompted.

"Ah yes. He put me in command of the whole garrison of Portobelo, one thousand men. *And* the five hundred levies when they arrived. *And* two thirds of the garrison of Old Providence."

"To do what?" Secco asked sarcastically.

"Why, to recapture Jamaica, of course."

"How were you to get there?" Ned asked.

"I was given authority to requisition as many ships as I needed. There were three in Portobelo, unloading grain, and two more came in from Cartagena next day to load hides. I requisitioned them all in the name of the Viceroy."

"And they're the five ships anchored down there now?"

Arias nodded, and to save time Ned said: "You embarked the Portobelo garrison and the levies, sailed for Old Providence to collect the rest of the men, and then went to Jamaica."

"No," said Arias triumphantly. "First I loaded the ships with provisions, and powder and shot."

"Good for you," said Ned ironically, "that was thoughtful planning."

"One must," Arias said seriously. "It took four days to unload the rest of the grain."

"Why did you not just dump it over the side?"

"Dump it?" Arias could hardly believe his ears. "But it was *my* grain. The shipments were consigned to me."

"I quite understand. There was no need for haste."

"None at all," Arias agreed, realizing that this Englishman with the bandaged arm was more understanding than he had seemed at first.

There was a pause, interrupted by Secco. "You've provisioned the ships, have the troops on board, and arrive at Jamaica. What then?"

"I order the troops to land."

"Where?"

"On the north coast."

"Then what happened?"

"Again I ordered the troops to land."

"Then?"

"Well, they were not enthusiastic. But the Portobelo garrison landed after I made certain suggestions."

"Such as?" Ned asked, intrigued by the tone of the man's voice.

"Well, I pointed out that their wives and families were still in Portobelo and that if the men did not carry out the duties of soldiers, then the families could not live in soldiers' families' quarters. I reminded them they had sworn loyalty to the king. Those kind of things." He dismissed the problem with a wave of the hand, as though such threats were routine.

"So you led your men ashore?"

Arias looked uncomfortable and his eyes moved from side to side like the flame of a candle flickering in a draught. "No, of course not. I remained at my headquarters in one of the ships with the reserves. One must always have reserves."

"What happened to your troops when they landed?"

Once again the evasive shrug. "Many were killed, many were captured, many were wounded, I suppose."

"Suppose?"

"How do I know? I was in the ship: I could not see what was going on up in the hills. The fighting went on for two days. We were betrayed, obviously: the English were waiting in ambush for us."

"And the men you have on board the ships now, who are they?"

"My reserve, because I could see there was no point in landing them. The enemy had five or ten thousand men waiting in the hills. My reserve of five hundred men – poof, they would not have crossed the beach before the enemy massacred them."

"So you brought them back?"

"Yes, I must have some protection for Portobelo."

Ned saw why the wily mayor-turned-major had kept a reserve – an insurance rather – never intending to land them on Jamaica unless his men met with complete success. He wanted to be sure that Portobelo would be safe, and one way of not losing all his men in Jamaica was to keep some in the ships: a course of action he could justify by calling them his "reserve".

"The Viceroy will not be pleased, if he ever hears the truth of what happened." Ned said quietly.

Arias understood immediately what Ned was hinting. The Englishman would have no difficulty in passing the story to Panama. That came of speaking honestly to foreign heretics.

"Can't I be ransomed?" he asked. "What would you gain by taking me to Jamaica as a prisoner? The Viceroy will punish me; surely that is enough?"

"Why will the Viceroy punish you? You say your men were ambushed by five or ten thousand English soldiers. How could you have succeeded?"

Arias held out his hands, palms uppermost. "One is not allowed to fail on the king's service. The king's men always say that failure must be due to treachery. Never," he added bitterly, "because one was asked to achieve too much with too few men, or the gunpowder is of poor quality, or the soldiers sullen and mutinous because they have not been paid for a year and their families are starving...the king and the king's servants, men like the Viceroy, can never be wrong, so people like me have to take the blame."

"You were talking of ransom. You may not have any possessions of any value left." Ned said pointedly, remembering Thomas leading the buccaneers through the town, and hurriedly deciding on the price.

"It depends on how much you demand."

"Well, the mayor of a big place like Portobelo is a very important man. Important enough for the Viceroy to entrust him with the task of recapturing a big island like Jamaica."

Sanchez's laugh was frank and bitter. "*Señor*, already you have a bad opinon of me. This man, Arias, you think, he is a coward: he does not lead his troops ashore when they land in Jamaica; instead he stays on board his ships and keeps back a reserve of five hundred men, presumably to defend himself. Yes, I can see from your face that I am correct. Those were your thoughts.

"And you are quite right. But you have not considered all the factors. For example, why should the Viceroy put the mayor of an insignificant place like Portobelo in command of an important military expedition to Jamaica? Everyone knows Arias has no military training. Everyone knows Portobelo has no connection with or interest in Jamaica. It is many miles away.

"Now this buffoon Arias, when he opens the Viceroy's letter, asks himself why the command was not given to one of the elegant and well trained military officers in Panama. The Viceroy does not lack for generals and colonels and majors who were trained in Europe and blooded in the campaigns in the Netherlands. Then they are sent out to Panama, which, unlike places like Portobelo, Santa Maria, Riohacha, and the smaller towns south of Panama, is regarded as a comfortable posting, very suitable for *hidalgos*, because the Viceroy has his own court in Panama, with his own favourites – and no doubt his own jester.

"Arias wonders why he is sent five hundred levies – the rubbish to be found in town jails, or begging in the *plaza* – and not a thousand men taken from the trained troops that the Viceroy has in Panama. Arias knows the Viceroy is aware that the

English have at least five thousand men in Jamaica, as well as many ships."

Ned noted that the Spaniards really had little idea how weakly Jamaica really was held: he thought of Heffer's men building batteries for the Spanish guns the buccaneers had captured at Santiago.

"And Arias tells himself," the Spaniard said, "that the Viceroy knows it is all useless, a forlorn hope made to show the king he is alert and doing his best. Losing five hundred from the jails and *plazas*, and the garrisons of Portobelo and Old Providence, is a small price to pay, and why put one of his favourite officers in command? The leader, like the levies and garrisons, is going to be sacrificed. What the Viceroy needs is a scapegoat, and who better than that man Arias, who has no influence anywhere?

"No one could have guessed that, while Arias is away, the English buccaneers would arrive in Portobelo," the mayor said with a wry grin. "Anyway, at least Arias cannot be blamed, because he was not here!"

Ned halved the man's ransom. The way he had told his story, with a kind of rueful honesty, showed that he did not yet know just how much trouble he would be in with the Viceroy. He did not realize that the buccaneers had found the bullion in San Gerónimo and removed it before blowing up the fortifications. Arias obviously thought that the bullion was still safe in the dungeons, although buried under tons of rubble. The king was going to need more than one scapegoat over the loss of an entire year's income.

It took two days to divide up and load the bullion in the five prize ships and to take some seamen from the twenty-eight buccaneer vessels to provide crews. The Spanish seamen and soldiers were marched on shore and locked in the dungeons of Todo Fierro and San Fernando, and, once the bullion was removed, Triana. Feeding the prisoners provided no difficulties: Secco found the deputy mayor – having been given his name by

Arias – and told him bluntly that the prisoners in the forts and castles were the responsibility of Portobelo, since their families lived there. The town would have to provide food for them, and it should be delivered each day at the appropriate fort.

On the third day Burton went round to the parapets of each of the forts with a party of buccaneers and, cutting the rope breechings and turning the guns so that their breeches pointed through the embrasures and their muzzles into the centre, loaded each of them with a double charge of powder and three roundshot and then fired them with slow-match, the linstocks secured to the guns with line. As each gun fired it recoiled violently and, without any breeching to hold it and aimed in the opposite direction, slammed back in recoil, hit the retaining wall at the bottom of each embrasure, and flipped through the slot, spinning in the air like a windmill blade come adrift and crashing to the ground, smoking and with the barrels split open like a flower.

The only exceptions were bronze guns, five in Triana, seven in San Fernando and seven at Todo Fierro. These were rolled down to the water's edge, slung one at a time between two boats, and rowed out to the prizes and hoisted on board. Other boats brought out shot for the bronze guns, and Ned and Thomas discussed their sighting in Port Royal. To strengthen the batteries Heffer was now building, or provide guns for a couple of new ones?

Thomas gave a chuckle. "You know, we behave as though we own the island: we tell Heffer what to do and he does it!"

"I should think he does! Right at the moment he doesn't know whether or not the next ship from England confirms his appointment, replaces him or arrests him. In the meantime we, the buccaneers, are his only defence because his own men are in a state of mutiny. Now we're bringing him nineteen more bronze guns, and we might as well take those falcons: they are handy enough in case he wants to fire a couple of pounds of langrage into the middle of a mutineers' meeting."

"Yes," said Thomas. "If he has any sense he'll parade a falcon round with him like a dog on a lead. As good as a lucky charm!"

"Thomas, you are wiser about money than I. Have you thought what happens when we arrive in Port Royal with all this money, gems and bars of silver?"

"One thing is certain – Heffer won't be able to change them into English money! The island has no currency, really. People seem to trade with sugar and beeves and hogs: just exchange. Sugar is the currency in Barbados, I know, but it all seems a bit crude."

"The island needs its own currency." Ned eased his broken arm in the sling, silently cursing the itching caused by the heat.

At that moment Burton, who had fallen naturally into the role of the armourer to the buccaneers, came up to report. "All the cannon and shot are loaded in the ships and stowed, sir. I've inspected the iron guns that blew off the parapets and all but one burst. That one I've nailed. I drove the nail into the vent so hard that when I cut off the extra length it looked as though it was part of the gun casing. Not enough sticking out to rivet over. They'll never drive it out, so the gun's finished."

"The falcons," Ned said, but as he paused to complete the sentence Burton thought it was a brief question.

"All stowed, sir, in the ships we brought them in from Old Providence. And the shot. I presume we don't want any of this Spanish powder, sir?"

"It's poor quality, isn't it?"

"About as fine as coarse gravel, sir: beats me how we get it to go 'pop' in the great guns, let alone 'bang'."

"So, apart from blowing up the other forts, we're ready to sail, as far as your department is concerned?"

"Quite ready, sir: I've had fuses run down into all three magazines. Just need lighting. Half an hour…"

"But we have to free the prisoners. Supposing they go back and put out the fuses?"

Burton looked crestfallen. "I had forgotten them," he said. "We could leave them there..."

"We could, but we won't. Don't give the Brethren the reputation of murdering their prisoners..."

"They've a worse reputation than that already, sir!"

"I know. Most Spanish mothers along the coast keep their children quiet at night with the warning that if they make a noise the *filibustero* will eat them up. Still, we might have to leave the prisoners here in Triana and not blow it up. Destroying three out of four forts and castles leaves the place defenceless."

Ned stood up and looked round the room that had been his headquarters for several days. The only thing of his remaining there was his sword, and Burton picked it up and carefully placed the leather shoulder belt, adjusting the sling holding the broken arm at the same time.

"Yes, Burton, take away the fuse here. It might get lit by accident. Then you can start lighting the other fuses."

Fifteen minutes later, as he was hoisted from a boat on board the *Griffin*, an anxious Aurelia making sure the rough and ready chair did not swing him into the ship's side, he called: "Todo Fierro and San Fernando will blow up in a few minutes..."

"What about Triana?" the mate asked.

"We're leaving them that. To keep the oxen in. Now, fire three guns to wake everybody up, and then weigh the anchor. Stay over to the southern shore in case Burton and his men were late with the fuse of Todo Fierro. Send a boat to pick him up; he'll be at the first landing spot he can find to seaward of Todo Fierro. We'll wait for him."

The three guns fired as seamen worked the *Griffin*'s windlass: the anchor was hoisted up and lashed in position as the ship's sails began to draw. As she passed the buccaneer ships still at anchor, Ned heard the men cheering, and with Aurelia standing beside him, he waved back. It took only a few minutes to get Burton and his boat on board. They were clear of the headlands when the two forts exploded.

At sunset the convoy was reaching northwards with a brisk easterly wind just strong enough to whip into spray the bow wave curling out from the *Griffin*'s stem. The *Peleus* was abeam to windward and the *Phoenix* to leeward, and following the three ships was the rest of the buccaneer fleet. In the *Griffin*'s wake came one of the prize ships, with a buccaneer ship on each side; astern of her, each flanked by a buccaneer vessel, came the rest of the prizes. The remaining buccaneers were sailing in an untidy squadron to windward, ready to race down to cover the prizes should any threat appear.

Ned and Aurelia stood at the taffrail, looking aft.

"Just think," Aurelia said, quietly, "what all that money would have meant for His Most Catholic Majesty..."

"It still does mean it," Ned said cheerfully. "He must owe much of it to the bankers in interest and repayment of principal; he probably needs as much again to pay, feed and supply his army in the Netherlands. And once again his navy received nothing."

"How do you know? Why do you say 'again'?"

"Well, obviously the navy hasn't had anything for years because they have no ships out here, yet they want to destroy us *filibusteros*. Can you imagine all the complaints the mayors of towns along the Main have been making to the Viceroy in Panama? And the complaints in turn he has been passing along to the Ministry of Marine in Madrid, and probably to the king. No, if the king had the money he would build more warships. But," and Ned gave a dry laugh, "you've seen the fix the king is in?"

Aurelia looked puzzled, and finally shook her head.

"Well, without money he can't build more ships. Without more ships he can't send the galleons to Cartagena and the *flota* to Vera Cruz for the bullion! In the meantime the *filibusteros* keep raiding the Main..."

"Well, hardly 'keep on'. This is only the second raid by *filibusteros*. I wonder what we'll find when we get back to Port Royal," Aurelia said.

"I'm looking forward to hearing Heffer's story of how he defeated those thousands of Spanish troops landed on the north coast. He will be as reproachful as he dare that we let the Spanish ships get there."

"Well, you'll have the satisfaction of pointing to the ships at anchor and telling him that although you missed them coming to Jamaica, you caught them on their way back."

"And then the satisfaction of telling him what they are using as ballast!"

CHAPTER TWENTY

The *Griffin* led the squadron into Port Royal and, as Ned commented to Aurelia, they could not have timed it better: the Blue Mountains had first come into sight the previous evening, a faint bruise on the northern horizon, and at dawn the island was stretched athwart their course, close enough that by ten o'clock the land was taking on colours.

As she tacked up towards the entrance of the great anchorage, followed by the *Peleus*, *Phoenix*, the five prizes and then the rest of the buccaneers, Ned examined the Palisades carefully with the perspective glass.

"He's almost finished the big battery on the seaward side: the guns are mounted, the sand is banked up and held by stone... Ah, the battery at the entrance: I can see men working on it now." They seemed in the distance like lethargic ants.

"The English flag is flying over Heffer's headquarters. The governor's house, perhaps I should say, in case he's been replaced, officially or unofficially!"

Thomas had been most emphatic, before they sailed from Portobelo, that they should arrive in Port Royal with as much of a bang as they left the Main, and each captain had been instructed to fire a salute as his ship passed the Palisades. Because no one knew how many guns should be fired as a salute to a governor, the buccaneers had been told to fire at least a dozen but, as Thomas had pointed out, they could fire as many as they felt inclined because the rumble of gunfire echoing back and forth across the Palisades would give Heffer and the rest of the army officers some idea of what a Spanish attack would be like.

"They'll better appreciate us," Thomas added. "It might cross the mind of some of them that the buccaneers are not all English – that seventeen out of twenty-eight are French, Dutch, Portuguese or Spanish. They don't seem to realize that only eight of them are English, not counting us."

Ned looked round and caught Burton's eye. The sand of the Palisades glistened in the sun, the sea was a pool of molten sapphire under a hot noon sun, and despite the scorching heat the island seemed green: there had been plenty of rain to freshen both trees and shrubs.

The view was becoming familiar: three cays ahead of them, tiny islands in the anchorage, showed up clearly: One Bush Cay was over on the larboard bow, Drunken Man's Cay and Broken Land Cay were almost dead ahead, and Smith's Cay close in with the end of the Palisades.

Now, as the *Griffin* rounded the Palisades, there was the long beat to windward up the harbour to anchor close to the jetty near Heffer's headquarters.

"I wonder if Heffer is still in command," he said to Aurelia.

She nodded her head, confidently. "You and Thomas dealt with those mutineers so swiftly, I'm sure that anyone else with similar ideas was frightened off."

"But we haven't been here since then. Once we disappeared over the horizon, it's a case of 'out of sight, out of mind'; any other group of officers could have made a move. Don't forget most of them still hanker for the days of Cromwell and the Commonwealth."

"They can't be so silly that they didn't realize everyone was glad to see the King restored!"

"Everyone? I would guess that half the garrison – that's fifteen hundred men, and most of the officers – would like to see Cromwell risen from the dead and back in power. The soldiers are owed a year's pay, or more, and I don't think they believe the King will give it to them."

"But surely Heffer is reassuring them?"

"I doubt it: he's probably not very sure himself."

"A year's pay for three thousand foot soldiers doesn't seem a very high price for an island like Jamaica," she said. "He should tell his men they'll get their money."

"It isn't a high price," Ned agreed, "but that's only the *purchase* price. It's like a plantation: once you've bought it it costs a lot to run."

"But the soldiers are already here."

"The position won't be explained properly to the King and the Privy Council because there's no one in London who understands it. And I can't see the King letting the island have the couple of frigates it needs."

"Why? You seem to be providing the navy!"

"Yes, but we're away much of the time. Like now, we were away when the Spanish attacked."

"Attacked?" Aurelia said contemptuously. "That was little more than a social visit! You knew it couldn't succeed or you wouldn't have left. You told Heffer where the attack would be and where to send his men. There was no risk!"

They both moved out of the way of running seamen as the mate gave the order to tack. Astern the first of the buccaneer ships, following in the wake of the prizes, began to fire a salute reminding Ned of a frightened squid squirting out a cloud of black ink and then swimming through it to safety. The smoke of the guns almost hid the buccaneer, who was firing a whole broadside, first one gun and then another, and while the guns were being reloaded the second buccaneer fired.

"Noise and colour," Aurelia said.

The buccaneers had painted their ships using bright colours with the careless ease and taste of gypsies: the leading buccaneer ship, now sailing through a cloud bank of greasy yellow and black smoke, was painted red, with a white strake picking out her sheer: the next astern was painted the dark green favoured by smugglers because it blended with the mangroves growing along the shores of bays and inlets. Following her was a vessel painted entirely in blue, but even from this distance Ned could see that the salt of the sea drying several times a day, and the sun itself, had already turned it into the faded mauve with purple tints which was the ultimate fate of blue paint in the Tropics, whether on the hull of a ship or the walls or shutters of a house.

Large flags streamead from the mastheads of all the ships –English, French and Dutch colours and even, Ned was amused to see, Spanish from Secco's ship. All the ships also had special flags, designed by owners or masters, flying from yard-arms. Long pendants streamed from mastheads, striped in as many colours as the sailmakers could find cloth.

All the paint and the bunting on the buccaneer ships only served to emphasize the prizes: the Spaniards did not spend money on paint, so the five vessels were weather-beaten grey with patches of bare wood. The only touches of colour were the English flags. The ships were so much larger than the buccaneers', and so drab, that even the soldiers must notice them.

Again the *Griffin* tacked, the ships astern following in her wake like ducklings following a mother as she paddled round clumps of reeds. The next tack would bring them far enough up the harbour to anchor.

No strange ships were anchored, showing that no news or orders had recently arrived from England. A few canoes moved over the anchorage like water beetles crossing a pond. After the last tack the *Griffin* came head to wind and dropped an anchor.

Ned inspected the jetty with the perspective and was startled to see that it was crowded with people. They stretched along the sandy beach towards Hangman's Point. The new battery – what he had thought was rocks was in fact people. And as the *Griffin* settled back on her anchor cable Ned caught sight of the flagpole in front of Heffer's house with the English flag flying.

The *Peleus* anchored and almost at once hoisted out a boat. The boat's crew scrambled down into it, followed by Thomas and Diana. The men started rowing while, from the direction of the Palisades, more buccaneer ships fired their broadsides. None of them, Ned noted, seemed content with using a single gun for saluting.

At that instant he heard the steady thumping of drums and the penetrating notes of trumpets. For a moment he looked towards the shore, thinking that the garrison was mustering a band, but then realized that the music, if one could be allowed to use the word, was coming from several of the buccaneer ships.

"It's exciting," Aurelia said. She eyed Ned and smiled. "Come on, it's no good you trying to look so serious. *You're* excited! And you just can't wait to find out just how big the purchase is!"

Thomas and Diana came on board, both deeply suntanned and excited. Thomas slapped Ned on the back and bellowed: "Two out of two, my lad! Two out of two!"

When Ned looked puzzled, Diana said: "Count Santiago as one and Portobelo as another. Two expeditions and two safe returns after successful raids!"

"Yes," Thomas continued, "and the sooner we start counting the purchase the better. These fellows elected you their leader and they'll follow you anywhere. But that doesn't mean to say they trust each other. The sooner that silver is weighed and the gems counted and valued, the better. As soon as everyone's anchored, it would be wise to send boats round to collect one man from each ship. He then represents his own ship and watches as everything is counted up in each of the prize ships."

"What are we going to do with the prizes?" Ned asked.

"Well, the share of the purchase for the owners, masters and mates is going to be so big that you should auction the ships because masters and mates will be able to bid, using their purchase money."

"Perhaps we could offer them to Heffer at a reasonable price."

Thomas shook his head. "No," he said firmly. "The sun has addled your brain. Or maybe your arm is hurting you. But firstly, Heffer – which means the government of Jamaica – has no money. Second, we don't want him to have ships of his own. One or two of the King's ships, if any are sent out from England, might be useful. But if Heffer suddenly has control of five goodly vessels, he will start becoming independent of us. While he has no ships, he does what we say."

Ned nodded in agreement, realizing that the pain of his arm was still slowing his reactions.

"You see," Thomas explained, "we are now in the underworld of politics, and if you'll excuse me for saying so, Ned, it's a world you don't understand."

"How could he?" Diana demanded. "He's an honest man!" She turned to Ned. "Thomas' family thought of nothing but politics and religion. Uncle Oliver mixed the two so that God always voted for him, and Satan led any opposition."

Ned grinned and admitted: "I get sorry for Heffer, he seems such a pathetic character."

Thomas swung round and said loudly: "Ned, make no mistake: if it was to Heffer's own advantage politically – even though you've saved his garrison from starvation and even saved his life when his men mutinied – he'd have you tried on trumped-up charges and hanged at sundown."

CHAPTER TWENTY-ONE

Ned and Thomas were announced by the sentry, a gloomy Devonian, who held the door open with seeming reluctance as they walked into General Heffer's office. Both men were surprised to see that a lieutenant and a half a dozen soldiers were standing to attention at one side of Heffer's desk.

Ned said a polite good afternoon, but an unsmiling Heffer, his face longer than Ned remembered it and the teeth yellower and drier and more pronounced, said in a monotone: "Edward Yorke and Sir Thomas Whetstone, you are both under arrest."

Turning to the lieutenant, he snapped: "Do your duty!"

Thomas suddenly kicked a chair across the room and by the time the lieutenant and his men recovered from their surprise, Ned had taken three paces round the desk and was holding a wheel-lock pistol with its muzzle a foot from Heffer's chest.

"In the King's name!" Heffer protested weakly, staring at the muzzle of the pistol like a rabbit paralysed by a stoat's eyes.

"Perhaps," Ned said calmly, "but unless you want this officer and his men to be pallbearers at your funeral, order them back to their barracks. Warn them against raising an alarm because Saxby – you remember him, he is master of the *Phoenix* – will be visiting us every ten minutes, and unless he returns each time and signals from the end of the jetty, several hundred heavily armed and enraged buccaneers will land and seize Port Royal and string you up at Gallows Point. You personally."

By now white-faced and frantically licking his protruding teeth, which were drying so quickly that his lips were frequently sticking along the line of his gums, Heffer waved the lieutenant and his men out of the room, managing at the last moment to gasp the single word, "Barracks".

As the door closed Ned walked over to pick up the chair and replace it in front of Heffer's desk. He sat down and put the pistol on the desk.

"There's one thing about it," he said evenly, "we never seem to come to your office without seeing some comedy or other. Better than the theatre. Now, what's curdled your milk this time?"

Before Heffer had time to answer there was a knock on the door and the sentry put his head in. "A Mr Saxby, sir," he reported to Heffer who, still suffering from dry teeth, signalled to send him in.

Saxby sensed the tension the moment he came into the room and looked questioningly at Ned. "Everything all right, sir?"

"We've just avoided being arrested – you probably saw a lieutenant and a section of soldiers, who were going to be our guards. So carry on with your occasional visits and send word to the ships that they should continue to be ready to land if necessary."

Saxby nodded, stared at Heffer for a few moments as if he was a performing bear with mange, and went out. Ned waved a hand casually at Heffer. "You see, we expected you'd play some boyish prank. Admittedly, we didn't know quite what it would be. Soon I shall begrudge all the gunpowder we've just used up firing salutes to you as we passed the Palisades. Now," he said, his voice becoming harsh and his anger showing, "tell us what all this is about."

"I have to arrest you," Heffer said lamely.

"Yes, yes," Ned said impatiently, "all in good time. But what brought all this on? The last time we saw you, if my memory serves me, we saved your life when some of your officers mutinied."

"I have no recollection of that," Heffer said, his eyes focused on the desk about a foot in front of his stomach.

"You mean you have not written a dispatch to London about it," Thomas said grimly.

"I have no recollection of any such episode," Heffer said doggedly. "My officers and men are quite loyal."

"To whom?" Ned asked.

"Why, to me, of course."

"They're supposed to be loyal to the King: they're not your own private army."

"I meant the King, of course. As governor I embody the Crown, you know," he said primly, like a parson explaining elementary church ritual to two very dense old ladies.

Ned took the spanning key of the pistol from his pocket and casually fitted the end on the axle. "I saw bodies slung in chains from gibbets on the cays. No one I recognized, of course." Holding the pistol so that the muzzle, apparently by chance, pointed at the general, he tightened the wheel-lock a fraction, and then put the key back in a pocket.

"Interesting pistol," he commented casually to Heffer. "Spanish, of course. They do beautiful inlay work. Just look at the pattern – that's gold wire round the barrel. Made in Toledo, I imagine. The sword, too – " he tapped the scabbard of the sword he was wearing " – it matches. A set, two pistols, sword and dagger."

"Most interesting," Heffer said politely.

"You're not curious about where they came from?"

"Oh – well, yes," he said, obviously deciding to humour Ned. "Where did they come from, Mr Yorke?"

"Portobelo. But Sir Thomas also has an interesting set which belonged to the governor of Old Providence. They have fine inlaid work, too. Toledo, like mine."

"You...you've been to Portobelo? And Old Providence? Why, I thought... Well, Portobelo has four forts – "

"One fort," Ned corrected.

"Oh, I thought there were four: my apologies."

"There were four, but we blew up three, so now there is only one. No guns though."

"No guns?" Heffer's brow wrinkled so much his hair joined the eyebrows. "Four forts – one, I mean, and *no* guns?"

"We brought the bronze ones away with us, and blew up the iron. No guns left in Old Providence either. It was interesting, though; some of those we blew up had Queen Elizabeth's arms on them. At least a hundred and fifty years old. Drake must have left them."

"How extraordinary," Heffer said in a strangled voice, "Sir Francis Drake!"

"Now tell us why you want to arrest us," Ned said casually.

"Ah…" Heffer licked his teeth, giving them a good wetting as if in anticipation of making a long speech. "Well, while you were away, a ship arrived from England. It carried orders. For me."

"Orders concerning and actually naming Sir Thomas and myself?"

"Well, not actually *naming* you."

"I think you had better tell us about these orders. Who were they from?"

"The Duke of Albemarle – "

"Who?"

"Well, General Monck that was. He has been created the first Duke of Albemarle."

"Were there orders from anyone else?"

"Yes. The Lord High Admiral. That's the King's brother, the Duke of York," he added hastily when he saw the expression on Ned's face.

"Very well, who gave what orders that gave you the strange idea of arresting us?"

Heffer began to look shifty, and Ned thought he guessed what had happened. Several days ago, when the ship called and delivered the packet of orders and instructions, Heffer had read them and in the wording had seen something which gave him an excuse for arresting one Edward Yorke and one Sir Thomas

Whetstone. And the muddle-headed Heffer had thought that with the buccaneers' leaders locked up, he would be able to give orders to the buccaneers. It was just the sort of – oh, well, Ned thought to himself, let us play out the present game until the last card is on the table.

Heffer took a deep breath, his tongue made a wild movement over his teeth, and he said: "The government's attitude towards Spain has changed. The King spent some of his exile in Spain. He has made certain promises to the king of Spain. New treaties, I suppose they are."

There was now a glint in Heffer's eye which warned Ned. "He is going to return Jamaica to Spain?"

Heffer nodded.

"He was not the king when he made the treaties," Ned murmured, "so they are probably not valid. Anyway, show me the letter that says that." Ned picked up the pistol. "You might wonder why I am holding a pistol, Heffer. If you knew as much as I do, you'd realize that here in Port Royal a good deal more than your pride or neck is at stake. Now, the letter."

Heffer pointed to a cupboard behind him. "The papers are in there. It is locked."

"Give Sir Thomas the key."

For the next fifteen minutes Thomas and Ned, interrupted twice by Saxby, read through the papers. There were several letters, all lengthy and all complex. The Duke of Albemarle confirmed Heffer as Governor of Jamaica, and gave him detailed instructions on how the island was to be governed "until the final decisions are taking concerning its future". All hostile acts against Spain were to cease forthwith, and Heffer was to take vigorous steps to prevent pirates and freebooters using Jamaica as a base "from which to make raids on Spanish ships". Money would be forthcoming to pay the army but, Albemarle said, it would not be possible to send any ships of war from England for the present. The rest of his letter concerned setting up a form of judiciary and a legislative council "which will advise the

Governor". The rest, as Thomas said contemptuously, concerned "milk and water matters", except that the Duke said the value of a Spanish piece of eight had now been fixed at five shillings. In another letter, the Duke of York, as Lord High Admiral, informed Heffer that the King was to receive a tenth and the Lord High Admiral a fifth of the value of all prizes brought into Jamaica.

Ned had tapped this part of the Duke's letter and read it out to Heffer. "If you are to stop all pirates and freebooters using Port Royal, how do you collect any royal prize money?"

Heffer shrugged his shoulders. "It does seem contradictory," he admitted.

Ned gathered the letters and put them down in a neat pile. "Where are the rest of them?"

"They are all I received," Heffer said.

"Come on," Ned said calmly, "you are hiding some, you naughty boy."

"No! Upon my honour," Heffer protested.

"Very well, answer some questions. First, what in those letters and orders leads you to think England intends to return Jamaica to Spain?"

"Well, the Duke refers to waiting 'until a final decision is taken concerning its future.' "

"Which you construe as meaning it goes back to Spain. You have not thought the Duke might be referring to the proposed type of government – an elected assembly like Barbados, for instance, instead of a military governor?"

"It could be, I suppose."

"Or, if returning it to Spain, do you think the King has enough ships to bring home all the garrison? Anyway, the Duke says there's no money at the moment to pay them. Do you expect the King to hand 'em over to the Dons, to be used as slaves?"

Heffer stared at the top of the desk.

"Very well, the second question. Under what sentence or paragraph do you propose arresting us?"

"The Duke's orders," Heffer said promptly, though careful not to look up. "Where he says I am to take 'vigorous steps' to prevent pirates and freebooters using the island to make raids on Spanish ships."

Ned sorted out the particular letter and nodded. "Yes, he says pirates and freebooters, and I notice he specifically mentions 'ships' not 'ports'. Quite right too; pirates and freebooters would give Jamaica a bad name."

"So you see," Heffer said triumphantly.

"So I see *what*?" Ned asked.

"I have to arrest you. You must submit."

"Heffer," Ned said sharply. "I, Sir Thomas and the masters of all the ships now in the anchorage, except five prizes, possess letters of marque signed *by you*. We are legally privateers, most certainly not pirates, and we sailed on this last expedition at your request, because you were afraid the Spanish would land."

"But they did, they did! You didn't stop them!" Heffer said excitedly. "Three or four thousand of them landed at Runaway Bay, on the north coast, but I was there to meet them, by the grace of God, and I drove them back to their ships. Killed hundreds, my men did, and without your help we drove off the ships!"

Ned nodded. "Thousands of Spaniards, eh?"

"Three or four thousand, at least. Perhaps five. All well trained and heavily armed, too."

"Before you make more of a fool of yourself than you have done already, Heffer, why don't you look across the anchorage and see if you recognize the five largest ships."

"Why should I recognize them?"

"They are the ones which carried the 'three or four thousand...perhaps five' Spaniards you drove off. There were in fact fewer than a thousand men landed, commanded by the mayor of Portobelo, made a major for the occasion. We captured him and released him after he paid a goodly ransom. We took his ships and left the rest of his soldiers, five hundred of them, locked up in one of their own dungeons. That was why we left one fort intact; we don't murder prisoners."

"I can't believe it," Heffer muttered.

"You sent a dispatch to the Earl of Albemarle describing your great victory at Runaway Bay?"

"Well, as the ship was leaving at once to return to England, I did mention the invasion attempt."

"Did you mention that when we returned you intended to arrest us?"

"When I assured the Duke that I would carry out his orders promptly, I may have mentioned your names."

"You didn't mention all those letters of marque you had signed?"

"I don't recall if I did or not."

Ned eyed him but Heffer kept his head down.

"I see the value of a piece of eight is fixed at five shillings." Ned said, in the same tone of voice one discussed the day's weather.

"Yes, but as I've told the Duke, there is no money in the treasury. Not a penny piece. I can't pay the soldiers or buy them provisions."

Equally casually, Ned said: "Have you ever looked at about half a million pieces of eight? Or seen 280 pounds of silver in loaves, wedges or cakes? Or sacks of cobs, or chests holding two hundredweight of rough emeralds? Or a hundred and fifty pounds of pearls? Or chests containing seven hundredweight of various gold and silver items: plate, candlesticks, ornaments, jewellery and the like?"

"Of course I haven't!"

"Would you like to?"

Heffer's head came up, like a wild ram startled by the bark of a hunting dog. "What do you mean?"

"All those things are out there, stowed in those five ships you drove out of Runaway Bay. Our purchase from Portobelo. And now the splendid Duke of Albemarle has helped us put a price on some of it by valuing a piece of eight at five shillings. A piece of eight is the same as a peso or a dollar and equals eight reals. So a real is worth an eighth of five shillings. The trouble is the men will have to share out the bullion and gems, and since you have no money they won't be able to spend anything here."

"But the pieces of eight – they can spend those!" Heffer said eagerly.

"What are you going to use for change – or is everything going to be priced in round numbers?"

"I shall of course claim the King's share, and the Lord High Admiral's," Heffer said sternly, trying to reassert his authority.

Ned laughed and was joined by Thomas, who slapped the top of Heffer's desk. The sudden thump made the general leap to his feet and then subside again sheepishly.

"General," Ned's voice dropped confidentially, "you have offended us. We have brought you a present of nineteen bronze guns and shot, fourteen falcons, more shot for the guns we took at Santiago, and a privateer squadron now comprising thirty-three ships. In return you wanted to arrest us, quoting orders which you did not have when we sailed – at your request – to deal with your enemies. Yours, not ours."

Ned stood up and tucked the pistol in his belt. "Well, I must bid you a final farewell, General."

"Final? Why, where are you going?"

Ned shrugged his shoulders. "Who knows – we'll have a meeting of captains and decide. When we came in here this morning we expected to stay. We hardly anticipated you'd behave like...well, like a pirate!"

"But where *can* you go?"

"With this much bullion and gems we'll be welcomed anywhere. We can even go back and sell it to the Dons. But Antigua, the Bermudas, Barbados, Curaçao, Dominica – we can make a progress through the alphabet. Just think of what tradesmen would say, all that money being spent in their shops, taverns and bordellos."

Heffer took a deep breath. "Won't you sit down again? I've just remembered another letter from the Duke which you should read. I forgot it because I was reading it earlier and just slipped it into a drawer." He glanced in alarm at Ned's pistol, not realizing that he had taken it out of his belt because when he sat down it stuck into his ribs.

"May I get the letter out?" Heffer asked warily.

Ned nodded and a few moments later was reading what was obviously the most recent and by far the most important of Albemarle's letters which, he remembered from the dates, had been written over a period of a month, obviously while waiting for a frigate to become available to carry them out to the West Indies.

The letter told Heffer in detail what he as a governor must do to establish Jamaica as a flourishing colony. There was no mention of handing the island back to Spain: on the contrary, he was instructed to appoint a legislative council of eight men who would advise him on day-to-day matters. He must at once establish a Jamaican currency, based on five shillings equalling one piece of eight. He was to encourage local tradesmen by allowing them to import goods from England (but nowhere else) free of customs and excise for a period of five years, the only exception being liquor, on which duty and excise was to be levied, whether it was imported or made in the island.

Settlers were to be encouraged, the Duke said, and Heffer was empowered to make grants of land; every settler was to have, free of payment, fifty acres for himself and fifty more for each member of his family with him on the island. Parcels of one thousand acres could be sold to settlers, and the price was to be set by Heffer, but was to be the same for everyone. A land registry office was to be set up to record the grants and sales, and a civil register of births, deaths and marriages should be started, in addition to regular parish records.

The Duke then outlined how the island was to start to pay its own way. Notwithstanding the new policy towards Spain, any prizes bought in to the island would be condemned in the usual way by an Admiralty court, which Heffer was to set up, appointing a suitable person to act as judge, and for the first year the King's tenth and the Lord High Admiral's fifth was to be paid into the island's exchequer.

Ned finished reading and handed the letter to Thomas. He then stared at Heffer, who promptly dropped his eyes. Finally Ned spoke. "You know, Heffer, your foolishness is beyond belief. Out there – " he gestured towards the anchorage " – are enough money, guns, powder and shot, settlers and ships to start Jamaica as a prosperous colony. Yet not twenty minutes ago you were going to arrest us; five minutes ago, hiding this letter, you were going to let us sail to another island. Heffer, if you are going to be typical of the governors of British colonies – and I fear you are – God help us all."

"You'll stay?"

"Sharpen your pen and get out the ink," Ned said. "Don't call for a clerk: I want an agreement written in your hand between you as governor and me as leader of the buccaneers in Port Royal to whom you have given letters of marque bearing your signature. We'll have a copy made for you. Date it, and write in your own words as I dictate the substance. The sentry can witness your signature.

"From today the official currency of Jamaica will be the piece of eight, valued at five shillings. You let all shops, warehouses, inns, taverns and brothels function without interference. We will pay you the King's share and the Duke of York's share on the Portobelo purchase. You supply us with liquors and tobacco free of duty. We supply more guns, but you levy a payment in gunpowder on all ships trading here. A simple declaration of name, age and country of birth is all that will be needed to establish citizenship. You agree so far? Very well, let's get on..."

Dudley Pope

Governor Ramage RN

Lieutenant Lord Ramage, expert seafarer and adventurer, undertakes to escort a convoy across the Caribbean. This seemingly routine task leads him into a series of dramatic and terrifying encounters. Lord Ramage is quick to learn that the enemy attacks from all angles and he must keep his wits about him in order to survive. Fast and thrilling, this is another highly-charged adventure from the masterly Dudley Pope.

'All the verve and expertise of Forester'
Observer

Ramage's Challenge

The Napoleonic Wars are raging and a group of eminent British citizens have been taken captive in the Mediterranean by French troops. The Admiralty traces their location and sends the valiant Lord Ramage to effect their release. As Ramage and his crew negotiate the hazardous waters off the Tuscan coast, they soon begin to doubt the accuracy of their instructions. Ramage comes to realise that in order for his mission to succeed he must embark upon a fearful and highly dangerous escapade where the stakes have never been higher.

Ramage's Challenge is another action-packed naval adventure from the masterful Dudley Pope.

DUDLEY POPE

RAMAGE AND THE GUILLOTINE

As France recovers from her bloody Revolution, Napoleon is amassing his armies for the Great Invasion. News in England is sketchy and the Navy must prepare to defend the land from foreign attack.

Lieutenant Ramage is chosen to travel to France and embark upon the perilous quest of spying on the great Napoleon. His mission is to determine the strength of the French troops – but his discovery will mean the guillotine!

'The first and still favourite rival to Hornblower'
Daily Mirror

RAMAGE'S PRIZE

Lord Ramage returns for another highly-charged and thrilling adventure at sea. Instructed with the task of discovering why His Majesty's dispatches keep unaccountably disappearing, Ramage finds himself involved in a situation far beyond his expectations. Based on true events, *Ramage's Prize* is another gripping story from Dudley Pope.

'An author who really knows Nelson's Navy'
Observer

DUDLEY POPE

THE RAMAGE TOUCH

The Ramage Touch finds the ever-popular Lord Ramage in the Mediterranean with another daring mission to undertake. He soon makes a shocking discovery which dramatically transforms the nature of the task at hand. With the nearest English vessel a thousand miles away, Ramage must embark upon a truly perilous and life-threatening course of action. With everything stacked against him, he has only one chance to succeed…

RAMAGE AT TRAFALGAR

Lord Ramage returns to fight in the most famous of Britain's sea battles. Summoned by Admiral Nelson himself, Ramage is sent to join the British fleet off Cadiz where the largest battle in naval history is about to take place. Finding himself in the front line of battle, Lord Ramage must fight to save his own life as well as for his country. The result is a thrilling, hair-raising adventure from one of our best-loved naval writers.

'Expert knowledge of naval history'
Guardian

OTHER TITLES BY DUDLEY POPE AVAILABLE DIRECT FROM HOUSE OF STRATUS

Quantity		£	$(US)	$(CAN)	€
	Fiction				
☐	Buccaneer	6.99	12.95	19.95	13.50
☐	Convoy	6.99	12.95	19.95	13.50
☐	Corsair	6.99	12.95	19.95	13.50
☐	Decoy	6.99	12.95	19.95	13.50
☐	Galleon	6.99	12.95	19.95	13.50
☐	Ramage	6.99	12.95	19.95	13.50
☐	Ramage and the Drumbeat	6.99	12.95	19.95	13.50
☐	Governor Ramage RN	6.99	12.95	19.95	13.50
☐	Ramage's Prize	6.99	12.95	19.95	13.50
☐	Ramage and the Guillotine	6.99	12.95	19.95	13.50
☐	Ramage's Mutiny	6.99	12.95	19.95	13.50
☐	The Ramage Touch	6.99	12.95	19.95	13.50
☐	Ramage's Signal	6.99	12.95	19.95	13.50
☐	Ramage's Trial	6.99	12.95	19.95	13.50
☐	Ramage's Challenge	6.99	12.95	19.95	13.50
☐	Ramage at Trafalgar	6.99	12.95	19.95	13.50
☐	Ramage and the Dido	6.99	12.95	19.95	13.50
	Non-Fiction				
☐	The Biography of Sir Henry Morgan 1635–1688	10.99	16.95	25.95	18.00

ALL HOUSE OF STRATUS BOOKS ARE AVAILABLE FROM GOOD BOOKSHOPS OR DIRECT FROM THE PUBLISHER:

Internet: **www.houseofstratus.com** including synopses and features.

Email: **sales@houseofstratus.com**
info@houseofstratus.com
(please quote author, title and credit card details.)

Tel: **Order Line**
0800 169 1780 (UK)
1 800 724 1100 (USA)
International
+44 (0) 1845 527700 (UK)
+01 845 463 1100 (USA)

Fax: **+44 (0) 1845 527711 (UK)**
+01 845 463 0018 (USA)
(please quote author, title and credit card details.)

Send to:

House of Stratus Sales Department
Thirsk Industrial Park
York Road, Thirsk
North Yorkshire, YO7 3BX
UK

House of Stratus Inc.
2 Neptune Road
Poughkeepsie
NY 12601
USA

PAYMENT

Please tick currency you wish to use:

☐ £ (Sterling) ☐ $ (US) ☐ $ (CAN) ☐ € (Euros)

Allow for shipping costs charged per order plus an amount per book as set out in the tables below:

CURRENCY/DESTINATION

	£(Sterling)	$(US)	$(CAN)	€(Euros)
Cost per order				
UK	1.50	2.25	3.50	2.50
Europe	3.00	4.50	6.75	5.00
North America	3.00	3.50	5.25	5.00
Rest of World	3.00	4.50	6.75	5.00
Additional cost per book				
UK	0.50	0.75	1.15	0.85
Europe	1.00	1.50	2.25	1.70
North America	1.00	1.00	1.50	1.70
Rest of World	1.50	2.25	3.50	3.00

PLEASE SEND CHEQUE OR INTERNATIONAL MONEY ORDER
payable to: HOUSE OF STRATUS LTD or HOUSE OF STRATUS INC. or card payment as indicated

STERLING EXAMPLE

Cost of book(s):........................ Example: 3 x books at £6.99 each: £20.97

Cost of order: .... Example: £1.50 (Delivery to UK address)

Additional cost per book:................ Example: 3 x £0.50: £1.50

Order total including shipping:........... Example: £23.97

VISA, MASTERCARD, SWITCH, AMEX:

☐☐☐☐☐☐☐☐☐☐☐☐☐☐☐☐☐☐☐☐

Issue number (Switch only):

☐☐☐

Start Date: ☐☐/☐☐

Expiry Date: ☐☐/☐☐

Signature: ____________________

NAME: ____________________

ADDRESS: ____________________

COUNTRY: ____________________

ZIP/POSTCODE: ____________________

Please allow 28 days for delivery. Despatch normally within 48 hours.

Prices subject to change without notice.
Please tick box if you do not wish to receive any additional information. ☐

House of Stratus publishes many other titles in this genre; please check our website (**www.houseofstratus.com**) for more details.